W9-ALW-532

SHATTERED SKY

ALSO BY NEAL SHUSTERMAN

Visit the author at storyman.com

THE STAR SHARDS CHRONICLES
BOOK 3

SHATTERED SKY

Neal Shusterman

JOHN C. HART MEMORIAL LIBRARY
1130 MAIN STREET
SHRUB OAK, NEW YORK 10588
PHONE: 914-245-5262

SIMON & SCHUSTER BFYR

NEW YORK LONDON TORONTO SYDNEY NEW DELHI

An imprint of Simon & Schuster Children's Publishing Division

1230 Avenue of the Americas, New York, New York 10020

This book is a work of fiction. Any references to historical events, real people, or real places are used fictitiously. Other names, characters, places, and events are products of the author's imagination, and any resemblance to actual events or places or persons, living or dead, is entirely coincidental.

Copyright © 2002 by Neal Shusterman

All rights reserved, including the right of reproduction in whole or in part in any form.

SIMON & SCHUSTER BFYR is a trademark of Simon & Schuster, Inc.

For information about special discounts for bulk purchases, please contact Simon & Schuster Special Sales at 1-866-506-1949 or business@simonandschuster.com.

The Simon & Schuster Speakers Bureau can bring authors to your live event. For more information or to book an event, contact the Simon & Schuster Speakers Bureau at 1-866-248-3049 or visit our website at www.simonspeakers.com.

Book design by Hilary Zarycky

The text for this book is set in Granjon.

Manufactured in the United States of America

2 4 6 8 10 9 7 5 3 1

Library of Congress Cataloging-in-Publication Data

Shusterman, Neal.

Shattered sky / Neal Shusterman.

(The star shards chronicles : book 3)

Originally published by Tor, 2002.

Summary: Inhabitants of a planet taken over by a terrifying power flee their world, planning to conquer a new one, and only five powerful teenagers, possessed by shards of a shattered star, stand between them and Earth.

ISBN 978-1-4424-5835-2 (hc)

ISBN 978-1-4424-5118-6 (eBook)

[1. Supernatural—Fiction. 2. Horror stories.] I. Title.

PZ7.S55987

[Fic]—dc23

2012046127

For Keith, Patricia, Terry,
Mark, Maureen, Eric, and Jan,
who have been there to remind me
that it's not the end of the world!

CONTENTS

Part I

Containment

"THERE WERE SIX OF US," HE BEGAN. HIS BODY SHOWED NONE OF the bruises from the ordeal he must have endured. Not a strand of his wavy red hair was out of place, his clothes were immaculate— not even the cuffs of his jeans showed wear. "Six when it all began. Now there are only three left. Winston, Lourdes, and me."

The man across the table took out a pad and began to take systematic notes. He wrote down his impressions, as well as the things the redheaded kid said. That's all he was, thought the man: a kid. Couldn't be any older than eighteen, if that. Then why am I so frightened? The man pushed the thought out of his mind, and concentrated on his subject, whose name had been seared into the world's collective consciousness over the past year. A young man by the name of Dillon Cole.

"What happened to the other three?"

Dillon didn't answer right away. He just sat there in the hard, heavy wooden chair. He didn't move his arms, but then he couldn't; they were both firmly bound to the arms of the chair with tempered steel handcuffs. The man noted Dillon's hesitation—that it was either the prelude to a lie . . . or perhaps brought on by the pain of memory. Then, something changed about the boy. He seemed to stop his introspection, and instead turned his gaze outward. The man could almost feel Dillon's eyes dragging across him as Dillon sized him up.

"You're a psychological profiler," Dillon said.

The profiler grinned. "Figured that one out, did you?"

Dillon frowned as if at an insult. There was the touch of Dillon's eyes again, like silk moving across the profiler's flesh.

"You graduated from Yale," Dillon told him. "You're married, no children. You live in a townhouse, and drive a Lexus—or maybe an Infiniti. Eggshell white."

Now it was the inquisitor's turn to falter. The boy could have picked up some of it from the profiler's gold band and class ring—but the rest? Just shots in the dark. Except for the fact that they were right.

"I see you're quite a profiler yourself," he told Dillon.

Dillon shrugged. "Not professionally. It's just a hobby." Dillon grinned, and the profiler looked away, then silently cursed himself that he hadn't kept eye contact with his subject. "I thought they saved you guys for serial killers, and stuff like that," Dillon said.

"If you're responsible for drowning four hundred people in the Colorado River, then you're a mass murderer. I would say that falls within my job description."

Dillon shifted in his seat, and looked down at the heavy cuffs on his hands. There was a moistness to his eyes. Was it remorse? Then, from Dillon: "Something has to be alive before you can kill it."

"An interesting philosophy."

Dillon tugged half-heartedly on his bonds, then looked at the profiler. "Yeah . . . I've done some unspeakable things in the past. But believe me, the punishment has fit the crime. There's nothing you can do to me that hasn't already been done."

The profiler tapped his pen on the table, the clicks echoing in the cold interrogation room. "Let's talk about your three dead friends," he said. Now that he had regained control of the conversation, he was going to keep a tight rein on it.

"Deanna was the first to die," Dillon said. "Her body lies trapped in the place between worlds."

"*A place between worlds,*" repeated the man, making a mental note of this delusional construct. "*Is this a place you created?*"

Dillon grinned. "*You seem to think I'm all-powerful.*"

The profiler found the grin far more unsettling than he expected. "*Didn't you claim to be a god?*"

"*I never made the claim—others called us gods. We just got tired of correcting them.*"

"*All right, then. What are you?*"

"*The six shards of the Scorpion Star.*"

"*The Scorpion Star? You're saying this has something to do with the supernova?*"

Dillon didn't move, didn't break eye contact. His eyebrows did not rise in the reflexive twitch of a lie. "*Our souls are the six fragments of the soul of that star, which went nova at the moment each of us were conceived.*"

"*How lucky for you.*" The profiler had to hand it to him; the kid's delusion was distinctively grandiose.

"*Lucky? For years each of us was plagued by parasites that leeched onto our bright souls . . . but we purged them. Then we were manipulated and used by a spirit predator . . . but we defeated it. There's nothing 'lucky' about what we suffered.*"

"*Soul parasites and spirit predators,*" said the profiler, with calculated condescension. "*Sounds like some nasty business.*"

"*It was,*" said Dillon, becoming annoyed. "*And why are you here anyway? I haven't quite figured out the purpose it serves. It's not like your report is going to make any difference. Those notes of yours will never see the light of day—you know that, don't you? They'll be locked up so tight there won't be anyone with high enough security clearance to read them.*"

"*Never mind that. Let's get back to the other two who died. The other two 'shards,' as you called them.*"

Dillon took a deep breath, attempting to regain his composure.

But it was more than that. The profiler sensed . . . something else. Something that had been there since he had arrived in the room, just on the threshold of perception. Now as he concentrated on it, he was certain it was there—a slow rhythmic pulse that he could feel resonating through his bones and aching joints. Impossible, the profiler thought, but the pulse seemed to emanate from across the table.

Am I feeling Dillon's heartbeat?

Dillon twitched his nose, and looked down at his shackled hands. "I have an itch on my nose. Could you scratch it for me?"

"There's a standing order that no one is to touch you under any circumstances."

"I see. Are they afraid you'll pick up whatever disease I've got?"

"Tell me about the others who died."

Dillon sighed, and tried to rub his nose unsuccessfully on his shoulder, then gave up. "Michael and Tory," *Dillon said.* "They were the other two. They died in the rubble of Hoover Dam . . . in the Backwash."

"Ah . . . your so-called miracle!"

"It wasn't supposed to be a miracle. I guess I just can't help myself."

Again that unsettling grin. It was even more troubling than the things Dillon said. That and the pulse of his heartbeat like an electric charge throbbing through the room. "A thousand years ago," *the profiler said,* "if a man prayed to the heavens, and it just happened to coincide with an eclipse, he was proclaimed a prophet. Does that make him one?"

"That depends. Was the moon anywhere near the sun at the time?"

"There's a logical explanation for what happened at Hoover Dam, and someday we'll find it. You just happened to be caught in the circumstance of coincidence."

"Then I suppose I have a talent for coincidence."

"And now you're having nightmares." The profiler sat back, his eyes steady, taking the tiniest sadistic pleasure in the discomfort his mention of it brought Dillon.

"Just one," Dillon corrected him. "It keeps coming back."

"Tell me about it."

Dillon grinned. "It's not in your files?"

"I'd like to hear it in your words."

Dillon slipped into himself for a moment, then he seemed to return, and his eyes became sharp and focused again. "Three figures, standing on the edge of some sort of platform. A man, a woman, and a child. The smell of perfume."

"Go on."

"There's someone else in the dream as well. A man. Balding. He's in a leather chair, but it's a strange color. Sort of pink, or purple. It's a recliner, and he's leaning back."

"Images from your past."

"No," he said, "from my future. They're bringing something horrible—something unimaginable, but of course you won't believe me. You won't believe anything until it's too late."

"I didn't say a thing."

"You don't have to. Everything you are—everything you think and feel is in the way you move, the way you breathe, the way you blink."

The balance had shifted, like a ship listing from starboard to port. Without moving an inch, without flexing a muscle, Dillon had seized control of the interrogation. It angered the profiler how easily he was able to do it.

Dillon's eyes probed him again, this time even deeper than before as if he were reading a biography in his clothes and body language, in the care lines of the profiler's face. "You took early retirement," Dillon divined, "but you were called back for this one last interrogation. You didn't want to come—but you did it as a favor."

The profiler lifted his arms from the armrests, just to assure himself that he wasn't the one shackled to the chair. "There are a dozen ways you could have known that. You could have heard someone talking—"

Dillon wasn't listening. "What I'm wondering is why you were called in, and not someone else?"

Again, the invasive look: a radar scan that left the profiler feeling naked and vulnerable. "We're here to talk about you," he said impotently.

Then all at once Dillon drew a breath, and beamed as if suddenly infused with a powerful new awareness. "You're not well!" he said, excitedly. "Worse than that—you're dying, aren't you?!"

The profiler threw a sudden gaze at the two-way mirror on the right wall. He regretted it instantly. It was on par with an actor looking at the camera. Entirely unprofessional, but his subject had chewed through his professionalism like a chainsaw. Dillon never took his eyes off of him—gray, unreadable eyes except that they seemed charged both with youth and weariness, as of an innocent who has seen too much evil in the world for his own good.

The profiler was determined not to break eye contact. A million ways he could have known. A million ways. "So now you're telling me you read minds."

Dillon scoffed. "I don't have to. It's written in the patterns of everything you do. It's a blood disease, isn't it? AIDS? No . . . No, leukemia. *How many months do they give you?*"

"I can't see how it's your business."

"How many?" Dillon demanded. Then when he didn't get an answer, Dillon sniffed the air, and cocked his head slightly, as if listening for some resonant frequency beyond that intolerable pulsing of his heart. "Six months," Dillon said. "You've been in remission before. Twice . . . maybe three times. This time you're refusing treatment. You plan to die with dignity."

The profiler pushed back from the table, infuriated by his own lack of restraint. "What is it you want?!"

Dillon was as composed as his counterpart was agitated, and calmly said, "I want someone to scratch my nose."

The room suddenly seemed too small, and the table too meager a barrier between them. "This session is over." The profiler tried to maintain a sense of professional control as he stood from the table, but his voice betrayed how shaken he was. "You will be locked away, and believe me, your friends will be caught!"

"Only if they want to be caught."

"We caught you."

"Exactly."

The interrogator reached for his notepad on the table—forcing temper to his trembling hands—and as he did, Dillon jiggled his hands. All he did was jiggle them, and the cuffs snapped open, and clattered off. "Your old boss didn't send you here to do a profile," Dillon said, "he sent you here for this." Then Dillon thrust an arm forward and grabbed him by the wrist, tightly. The profiler could feel his ulna pressing toward his radius—and the concussive power of that terrible heartbeat. But it wasn't the beat of the boy's heart at all, was it? It was something else. It was more like a blast of radiation, luminescence from some unknown reach of the electromagnetic spectrum. It resonated through the profiler's body now, and he could feel the change within his bones and joints. Something inside him was coming to order! He could actually feel genetic order returning to his mutated marrow!

Then the boy let go. And scratched his nose.

"There. Don't say I never did anything for you."

A bruising crunch of guards exploded into the room, grabbing Dillon, forcing him back down into the chair, Dillon offered no *resistance, but the guards still struggled as if he had. The profiler backed away. He had thought his training and experience had prepared him for any madness he might come in contact with. But what if the boy's touch coincided with a complete and total remission of his disease? Would that be madness? Would he still call that coincidence?*

"You're going to need more than handcuffs," he told the guards, and he ran out, hurrying home where he could cry in the arms of his wife.

1. TESSIC

THE NUCLEAR REACTOR NEVER WENT ONLINE.

The entire plant was beset by such incredible bad luck and untimely mishaps, it precipitated a storm of rolling heads from Michigan Power and Light, leaving a trail of blood all the way up to the Nuclear Regulatory Commission. Inferior bolts from questionable vendors, leaks in the coolant system, pipes that seemed to do nothing but terminate in solid concrete. No one with an ounce of sense was bringing uranium within a mile of the place.

For years, the stillborn power plant stood dormant and cold in the rural community of Hesperia.

Then, one day, the plant came to life.

The towers remained silent, but a flurry of clandestine activity gave that silence added sonority. Locals knew no power was being generated at the plant. The swarms of guards, and dark sedans that flowed in and out of the electrified gates, coupled with dismissive denial from all official sources, made the truth very clear; the Hesperia plant was now some sort of top-secret facility retrofitted by the government for a greater but undisclosed purpose.

Bobby's Eat-N-Greet Diner, which stood at the crossroads a half mile from the plant's outer gate, was the closest civilian establishment, and was where residents gathered over coffee to trade and distort unsubstantiated rumors. Though not a local, Elon Tessic was becoming something of a regular at the Eat-N-Greet, having popped in once a month since that spring. It was always his first stop whenever he visited the plant. He could have arrived at the plant directly by helicopter, but Tessic much preferred the feel of the road and had instructed that his Jaguar be waiting for him at the airport. Eccentric? Maybe. Besides, it afforded him the opportunity for unauthorized side trips.

On an overcast afternoon in late September, Tessic breezed into the diner, setting off the jingle-bells above the door, alerting the owner that he had a customer. The owner, an elderly man named Bobby, was leaning over, wiping down the counter with a damp rag. When he saw Tessic, he straightened and smiled.

"I'll be damned! Good to see you, Mr. Tessic."

Tessic opened his overcoat, revealing a white suit hopelessly out of season for fall. But then, when you were Elon Tessic, you could wear anything you pleased. "Hello, Bobby. My travels bring me your way again." Tessic looked around. It was three in the afternoon—an off hour. Only a couple of truckers sat in a corner, talking about wives and misery. Either they didn't know who he was, or they didn't care. Just as well. In these out-of-the-way places, Tessic often found himself the center of suspicious attention. It wasn't only his clothes, but the prominent way he held himself, and his Israeli accent, so rich and exotic to the ears of the American heartland. As he had no talent for being inconspicuous, he rarely tried. Still it was nice to go unnoticed from time to time.

Bobby, however, gave Tessic his full attention, fumbling with spotted hands to get together a place setting.

"My waitress took sick this morning, so it's just me and the cook today. I'll have a booth ready for ya' lickety-split."

Tessic noted yet another colloquialism he did not know; a reminder that his command of English was still less than perfect. "No need, Bobby," he said. "Do you mind if I just sit at the counter?"

Bobby looked at him as if it might be a trick question. Tessic laughed and clapped him warmly on the shoulder. "It's all right. Actually, I prefer it. I dine alone way too often."

Bobby shrugged. "Suit yourself," he said. Tessic slid onto a stool. The old man sounded apologetic. "I was sure you'd be used to more highfalutin black-tie kinds of establishments."

"Highfalutin bores me. That's why I come here."

Bobby smiled.

Tessic ran a hand through his salt-and-pepper hair, just a tad too long to be corporate. Like his clothes, it was genteelly defiant. He was a mote in the eye of the system, liked it that way, and as the twelfth richest man in the world, by the reckoning of *Fortune* magazine, he was one splinter that wouldn't easily be removed.

"So will it be the usual, then?" Bobby asked.

"Of course!"

Bobby went off to his pastry display case. "Lucky I even have it. If I woulda known you was comin' I coulda baked it up fresh. As it is, I only got a couple of pieces left." He took out a plate and a pie server, then gently lifted a piece of chess pie onto the plate. Even chilled, the thick filling oozed out over the plate, its chunky surface of nuts and chocolate slowly slipping on the rich nougat like a rock slide. Tessic dug in, took a mouthful, and savored the sweetness. Tessic considered himself a man who could appreciate the finer things in life—and knew they didn't *always* come with a hefty price tag. It was this appreciation that balanced him, and kept him at ease in most any situation.

As Tessic ate, Bobby leaned in closer and whispered. "I got myself a nice piece of Tessitech stock last month." He said it as if it were a classified secret. "Made me five hundred bucks already. Guess I oughta thank you for helpin' me get my granddaughter through college!"

"I didn't know you had a granddaughter that old."

Bobby nodded. "Got accepted to Princeton, and is hell bent on going. We're working out some financial aid. But if Tessitech stock keeps climbing the way it's been it might be the only financial aid she needs!"

"So much faith you have in my company!"

"Well, I figure the world's going to hell in a handcart. Weapons technology's got to be a growth industry."

Tessic grinned dreamily around a mouthful of pie, then said: "I have challenged a dozen chefs to make a pie this good. None have succeeded."

"No one will. Call it my little contribution to humanity."

"I would very much like the recipe."

"So would half the country."

"If half the country comes in here, business must be good!"

Bobby sighed. "Business comes and goes. Mostly goes. I thought I'd start seeing some military men come in once they took over that plant and all. But it's only been you. The others rarely come in or out of the plant. And when they do, they speed past this place like it don't exist." Bobby paused, and pretended to clean a glass, but his attention never left Tessic. "Y'ever gonna tell me what goes on in there?"

Tessic grinned. "Is that the price of your recipe?"

"I suppose we could swap national secrets, huh?"

"Secrets are secrets, eh? The government can buy my silence, but they can't buy your recipe. I, on the other hand, would like to do just that." He reached into the pocket of his overcoat, and produced a checkbook. Bobby waved it away.

"Hell, no! I was gonna give it to you anyway. You don't have to pay me."

"I insist." Tessic scribbled in the checkbook. "You can put it toward your granddaughter's tuition." He folded the check and slipped it into Bobby's apron pocket.

"Aw hell. Well, then that piece you just had is on the house." He took a napkin, writing down the recipe from memory. "It don't take a brain surgeon to make." When he finished he handed it to Tessic. "You ain't gonna sell it to Sara Lee, now, are you?"

"I give you my word."

Tessic stood, straightening his overcoat.

"I suppose you won't need to come here anymore, now that you got the recipe."

"And miss your company?" Tessic pulled open the door. "Rest assured, you'll see me again."

Tessic left and drove off in his silver Jag. In the diner, Bobby cleaned up Tessic's plate and then almost as an afterthought slipped the check from his pocket, suspecting that Tessic had given him a digit or two more than the recipe commanded. But the number that stared back at him was so laden with zeros it almost seemed to gain weight in his hand. It was enough to send all his grandchildren to Princeton. His wind stolen from him, he sucked a deep breath, and leaned on the counter to steady himself.

"Hey, Pops," called one of the truckers at the far booth, "you gonna fill up this coffee or what?"

"Yeah, yeah, be right there." He looked at Tessic's check again, blinking as if the number might disappear. *The man's crazy!* he thought. *I can't accept this.*

But as he went back to pour coffee for the griping truckers, he realized *yes, I most certainly can.*

HALF A MILE AWAY, Tessic's sound system blasted Vivaldi as he was waved through the guard gate of the plant. He was the only civilian granted unrestricted access. One of the perks of having friends in high places, and a vested interest in the facility. With the gate closing behind him and the winding, forested road to the plant up ahead, Tessic changed his personal audio soundtrack to the Rolling Stones, to remind him that, at fifty-six, he wasn't quite as old as he sometimes felt. He looked at the recipe-scribbled napkin that lay on the seat next to him and smiled. No recipe was worth what he had paid, but then, a *mitzvah* was not measured in dollars and cents. Besides, altruism was the best kind of business investment.

He shifted into a higher gear, singing along to "You Can't Always Get What You Want," feeling quite pleased with himself as he sped down his own particular path of enlightenment.

2. MADDY

Transcription excerpt, day 193. 13:45 hours

"They drug me when they take me out now. Problem is I metabolize the stuff so fast, they gotta give me elephant doses. Can't be healthy."

"Open wide. I can't see your mouth through the hole."

"I feel like a slot machine."

"If you were a slot machine, I might get something back."

"Naah. Suckers' game."

"Not with you around. Everyone knows how you shot down Las Vegas."

"To hell with Las Vegas. The slot machines all come up triple sevens, and a million people think it's something biblical."

"Is it?"

"How should I know? If the wheels had sixes instead of sevens, they would say I was the Antichrist."

"Haven't you heard? You are."

"Yeah, I've heard that one, too."

"Would you give your life for your country, Lieutenant Haas?" General Bussard had asked. "Would you give your soul?"

The second question caught her off guard. But as always, she had answered unhesitatingly. "Without pause, sir." Bussard had shown no reaction, but apparently she had shown the right level of commitment, because she had been chosen for posting to the elite staff of Project Lockdown. Now, however, months after the interview, she remained in the dark as to what exactly the project was. Even as a freshly minted Army Lieutenant she knew better than to ask too many questions. But even by Army standards the silence was deafening.

"It's Area 51 all over again," her sister Erica mused, as they sat saying good-byes at Chicago's O'Hare airport. "Why would you ask to be assigned to the Hesperia plant?" Her sister nursed a Starbucks decaf latte. The drink was so like Erica, Maddy thought: all style and no bite. Like the way she drove her Porsche—always on cruise control. Maddy, on the other hand, liked her coffee no-nonsense black, and hot enough to cauterize a tonsillectomy.

Maddy glanced around, brushing a hand through her dark hair, short enough to be military, but long enough to keep her as feminine as she cared to be. The airport coffee house had a full complement of harried travelers. Everyone was too absorbed in their own transit ennui to care about Maddy and Erica's conversation. Still Maddy was careful not to raise her voice.

"I didn't ask," she told Erica. "Assignments are handed out. We go where we're told."

Erika snorted. "Oh, please! Spare me the party line. You can't tell me a West Point *cum laude* doesn't get courted by half the military—even the ones who don't expect to get into your pants."

Maddy gulped her coffee, and relished its scalding sting. "It's still a boys' club." But, of course, Erica was right. Even in spite of the boys' club fraternity she did have quite a lot of options available to her. But rumors of an informational black hold in Hesperia, Michigan, had piqued her curiosity. Mystery was Maddy's nemesis, and she had become obsessed with knowing what they were hiding, or building, or dismantling in that dead power plant. Rumors had abounded in the halls of West Point—rumors that the Hesperia plant was housing some new Manhattan Project. After all, with the state of the world disintegrating at such an exponential rate over the past year, there was no telling where the next threat would come from. Some even believed the plant was the entryway into a series of subterranean tunnels built for an elite few to survive whatever dark age they were all spiraling toward.

Maddy went up to the counter for a second cup, but was brusquely reminded that, along a thousand other things in the crumbling world economy, there was a shortage of coffee, and even Starbucks was rationing. She settled for some hot water with lemon, then, disgusted, dumped the whole thing into the trash before returning to her sister, who was craning her neck to catch sight of the departure boards, looking for a flight that might or might not actually happen. Her sister was headed to New York to some ex-boyfriend, who had decided that pigs had, indeed, flown and he was deeply ready for commitment.

"All those freaks on street corners proclaiming the end of the world finally got to him," Erica had told her. "He probably just wants to get laid before it happens."

Maddy's flight was just a short hop to Grand Rapids, where she would finally be briefed on her assignment at the Hesperia facility.

"Maybe you get to babysit little green men," Erica suggested.

"More likely gray," Maddy informed her. "Haven't the Roswell lunatics taught you anything?"

Erica gave the obligatory chuckle, and gulped the dregs of her latte. "Roswell freaks, Backwash communes—maybe you've got the right idea. Lock yourself behind a fence. At least you won't get nabbed by some damn Colist cult."

Maddy had to admit she had been, for the most part, shielded at West Point from the aftermath of the Colorado River Backwash. But even so, she knew it was the defining event in people's lives. Like so many of those who had flocked to the spot where Hoover Dam once stood, she had wanted to witness it as well—to watch the waters of the Colorado River flow upward, in a rising backwash against the pull of gravity, into Lake Mead, if only to prove to her doubting spirit that it ever really happened. Then maybe she, too, might have joined so many others, searching the waters for the body of the martyred Dillon Cole.

Maddy knew it was more than Hoover Dam that had shattered that day. The very nature of creation was shaken to its foundations. If they had suddenly discovered that the world was flat, its consequences could not have been more far reaching than the physical impossibility of a mighty river crashing uphill at a thirty-percent grade. In a matter of days cults began to spontaneously generate on society's fringes and had quickly germinated into the mainstream. Maddy had found it both frightening and wondrous.

A United 747 came in for a landing and Maddy watched idly as its tires squealed to earth, setting off a tiny puff of smoke on the tarmac. In a moment the jet was a beast of the ground again, ponderous metal that seemed too impossibly heavy to fly. But here was a case of mind over matter—science over perception, mused Maddy. No matter how heavy a plane appeared, Bernouli's principle assured flight every time a mechanically sound jet sped toward the dead end of the runway. There had always been some comfort in the fact that some natural laws could never be repealed. Slim comfort now.

"Dare I ask what you think about all that business? The Backwash and all?" Erica asked.

"Three generals came to West Point just to tell us not to think about the Backwash."

"So why do you?"

"Contrary to popular opinion," Maddy said with a smirk, "cadets, and even we pissant fledgling officers, do have minds of our own. I just wish I could have seen the Backwash with my own eyes before it dried up."

"Not me," Erica said. "I have a problem with miracles."

There was no use pressing this with Erica—she had never been plagued by images of the Big Picture. Fact: Dillon Cole had shattered the law of entropy before he died in the Backwash. But how? Even now, in the places Dillon Cole had trodden, order still flowed from disorder, defying the most basic law of physics. With the law of entropy suddenly removed from the foundation, what, at the end of the day, would be left standing?

You think too much, Erica was fond of reminding Maddy. "You know what I did the day the dam broke?" said Erica. "I had a Backwash party. We poured vodka into Kahlua until we couldn't tell which way was up, so it didn't matter where the hell the water was going."

"That's what I love about you, Erica. The only proof you need is 180."

A team of junior executives hurried past. One of them caught Maddy's eye. He was no older than herself, twenty-two or so, tops. He noticed her gaze, and held eye contact just long enough to acknowledge it before vanishing into the crowd.

"Roll in that tongue, Madeline," Erica said with a smirk. "What would Mom say?"

"She'd say to bring one home for her."

Maddy thought back to her tally of distracting, if not quite fulfilling, relationships at the academy, and wondered what

opportunities her new assignment might provide. She shoul-
dered her carry-on. "I'd better go or I'll miss my flight."

"Hah—fat chance of that!" Erica nodded toward the
departure screens. In spite of good weather, most flights were
interminably delayed, several were canceled, and those flights
that actually did make it out did so on dubious jets in desperate need of maintenance. Even now, the aircraft pulling up
right outside their window looked weak and world-weary.

"Look at that thing," said Maddy. "It's like the poster child
for metal fatigue."

It was amazing to think that Americans—so smug in their
preeminence—had once scoffed at the shoddy state of air travel
in Third-World nations and—worst of all—Eastern Europe.
Maddy smile ruefully. Now every airline was Aeroflot.

If it were only air travel, the ailment could have been cured,
or at least treated—but it seemed every other world system
was infected as well. Pundits waxed rhetorical day in and day
out about a volatile global economy. Conservatives lamented
the loss of traditional values. Liberals attacked greedy corporate interests. Zealots and zanies predicted the coming of, or
the death of, God. There were a thousand other reasons why
the thin veneer of civilization was suddenly being stripped to
the grain. But the answer was clear to Maddy: If the power of
one person's thought could shatter the world's greatest dam
and turn back the massive flood that followed; if there were
someone in this world who could do that—then where was
the validity of science and reason? Who *wouldn't* lose interest
in their job and the petty ins-and-outs of their own life? And
since civilization depended upon seven billion docile and com-
pliant cogs keeping the Grand Clockwork running smoothly,
how could the system function with hundreds of thousands of
mutinies and desertions, as workers suddenly left their jobs,

abandoning their old lives? It didn't take an economic sage to figure out that everything from airlines to food lines would soon come grinding to a halt.

It was the great irony of civilization—that in the end it wasn't a bomb, or terrorism or some other global cataclysm that brought down the curtain on this modern world. It was lack of interest.

They both stood, taking deep breaths, preparing to launch into the frenetic stream of anxious travelers. "Once I get to Brooklyn," Erica said, "I'm swearing off the friendly skies for good and staying put. Because if I gotta live through the fall of the American Empire, I might as well do it somewhere trendy."

Maddy hugged her sister, perhaps for the last time in the foreseeable future, then turned away, forcing her feet in front of her, marching toward her overcrowded gate with disciplined military cadence. Refusing, as always, to look back.

THE MASSIVE VAULT SAT in the cold, seven-story dome of the power plant, a square peg in a round hole. This, reasoned Maddy, was where the plant's nuclear core would have been, but any machinery had long since been disassembled to make room for this cubic concrete egg in the cold womb of the containment dome. The cube was thirty feet on each side, and the only thing that gave away the fact that it was not solid was a silver titanium vault door on its face—a door which, by the way, was currently wide open. Looking around, Maddy could see no gateway into the dome large enough for this massive, incongruous object to fit through—which meant it must have been built right there.

General Bussard, a slab of a man in both appearance and personality, studied her reaction to the cube. "Not what you were expecting, Lieutenant?"

"Just observing, sir," Maddy answered truthfully. "I didn't know what to expect." The cavernous dome was lit dimly from above like the unpleasant half-light of a partial eclipse. The walls around them were filigreed with pipes, conduits and catwalks casting intersecting shadows. Maddy counted four sharpshooters posted on high catwalks, giving them a full view around the cube. Otherwise there was no one else present. She had anticipated that, whatever the purpose or nature of the installation, there would be swarms of personnel. Their absence did not bode well with her. Neither did the open vault door.

"This is *my* show," Bussard announced. In the cavernous space his voice rang with a hollow echo. Maddy assumed he had saved the reading of his riot act for this moment, when his voice would be most imposing. "You are not to discuss your work with anyone, either civilian or military. I am your sole confidant in all matters concerning this facility. Any comments or questions are to be directed to me, and me alone."

Somehow, Maddy couldn't imagine discussing anything with her superior, but she nodded and said, "Yes, sir. Could you please advise me on the nature of this facility?"

The general shot her a freezing glance. "Information is on a need-to-know basis."

Why was she not surprised? Bussard strode toward the open vault door with Maddy a pace behind. "You'll find this a very cushy assignment if you take to it with the proper enthusiasm," Bussard told her. "Plenty of downtime. But, like everyone else, you'll have to spend it within the gates of the plant. I'm sure you'll find yourself some recreational activities."

Maddy followed him up to the open vault door but couldn't quite make herself move across the threshold.

Bussard asked, "Is there a problem, Lieutenant?"

He stood in a door frame that was five feet deep, layered in lead and concrete. Beyond the extended threshold lay darkness. Maddy hesitated, and cursed herself for her failure of nerve. She took a deep breath to keep herself from stammering. "With your permission, sir, I request a verbal briefing to prepare me for whatever I am about to see."

The general chuckled, showing a set of perfect teeth. "'Verbal briefing?'" He stepped up to her. "Where did you spend the night after arriving in Michigan, Lieutenant Haas?"

The question caught her off guard. "I . . . uh . . . The Grand Rapids Marriott, sir."

"Good. Consider yourself briefed." Then he stepped deeper into the vault and flicked on a light switch.

If the cube was incongruous with its surroundings, the cube's interior was stranger still. It was, in fact, a hotel room. A queen-sized bed, a desk, a chair. The only difference was the absence of windows.

"We like to keep our guest comfortable," said Bussard. He walked around the room like a bellhop, pointing out the room's features. "TV with DVD library. Extra linens. Bathroom with shower." Then he got down to business. "Your assignment is very specific. It is your job to deliver three meals at seven hundred, thirteen hundred, and nineteen hundred hours precisely. You will have no contact with our guest, as he has therapy sessions at those times, and will not return until after you are gone. With each meal you bring, you will remove the tray from the previous meal. With the morning meal you will change the linens. With lunch you will clean the bathroom. With dinner . . ."

Bussard went on and on, but Maddy found herself unable to listen. Rage was rising in her. She had come through officer's training with commendations from everyone that mattered, and now the military saw fit to turn her into a chambermaid?

Bussard droned on as if reading her Miranda rights. "You will wear gloves at all times in this room, and dispose of them immediately after each use. You will find a detailed description of your duties in your quarters. Is there any part of your assignment you do not understand?"

"No, sir. Permission to speak freely, sir."

"Permission denied." He escorted her out of the chamber, and once they were back in the expansive void of the dead plant, he turned to her again. "There are only six people in the world with security clearance to be in that room—including the two of us. Consider yourself honored."

"I'll remember that, sir, while I'm cleaning the toilet."

"I've been here since the beginning, and Bussard hasn't seen fit to tell me anything," Lt. Gerritson told Maddy over a cafeteria pot roast filled with more salt than meat. The cafeteria, like the plant itself, was a dinosaur that never saw the light of day. It was designed to seat about 100 employees of Michigan Power, but now there were never more than ten military personnel at peak hours. By Maddy's second week, a meal with Lt. Vince Gerritson was a welcome relief to the oppressiveness of a large table and a solitary dinner. Maddy was quick to discover that Gerritson was the only person bold enough to discuss what little he knew about their shadowy purpose there.

"It's the lack of oversight that scares me," Gerritson said. "They let Bussard run this place any way he sees fit. Tessic's the only one Bussard doesn't control."

"They let civilians from Tessitech in this place?"

"No," Gerritson said. "I mean Tessic, himself."

"Really!"

"He had something to do with the design of the vault. But

now I think he pops in every once in a while just to piss off Bussard."

Tessic was a name well known in the military ever since Tessitech beat out every competitor for a dozen military contracts over the past five years. His name was synonymous with cutting-edge technology; a former wunderkind who, now in his fifties, was on his way to being the richest man in the world. Maddy judged that his presence here was an exception to protocol and not to be taken lightly.

"When did this whole operation start?" Maddy asked.

Before answering, Gerritson glanced around to scan their present company. A few tables away were three men in lab coats discussing sports scores. Maddy didn't know them, but had seen them at meals. The plant had a contingent of about ten Coats, as Gerritson had called them. Scientists, or technicians, or physicians—no one seemed to have a clue what their profession actually was. They didn't associate with military personnel, undoubtedly by Bussard's order.

"The plant was retrofitted for Project Lockdown about eight months ago," Gerritson told her. "I was about to get a disability discharge, but instead they assigned me here."

"Disability?"

"Long story." Gerritson shoved a piece of grizzly meat in his mouth, and worked his jaws like it was an oversized piece of chewing gum. Maddy hoped he might elaborate, but no dice. Whatever the story, he wasn't telling it.

"And exactly how do you fit into all of this? What's your job here?"

Gerritson smirked. "Now, come on, Lieutenant Haas. That kind of information is on a need-to-know basis."

Maddy volleyed back that smirk. "I need to know."

"Well, why didn't you say so?" Gerritson glanced around

again. It was almost a tick. A habit developed from being too long under Bussard's scrutiny. He leaned over his plate, confidingly. "Security detail," he whispered. "Right wing of team zero."

"Okay. Now in English."

"There are three of us who escort our 'guest' to his so-called 'therapy' sessions. Three times a day; before breakfast, lunch, and dinner. The rest of our time is spent on facility maintenance."

"And our guest is . . . ?"

Gerritson grinned. "Didn't quite hear that. You'll have to ask me some other time."

"You heard me perfectly," Maddy whispered, both irritated and appreciative of their little game of intrigue. Gerritson said nothing more, just grinned away. Maddy found herself taking a mental snapshot of that grin. His smile—his face—was worth remembering. Unfortunately her shutter speed was too slow. He knew he had just been scanned into her long-term memory, and he held the grin a moment too long, as if posing for her Kodak moment. There was, she knew, a danger couched in this sustained moment. Danger and opportunity.

"You hang around long enough," Gerritson said, "and you won't need me to give you ideas about our guest. You'll have plenty of your own."

"Well, can you tell me what he looks like?"

"Can't."

"Can't or won't?"

"Can't," he told her. "Ever read *The Man in the Iron Mask*?"

Maddy took a moment to let the casters click. "Oh." Maddy nodded. "I see."

"No, that's the point. Nobody sees. Bussard makes sure of that."

That was true enough. Maggie wasn't even allowed into the containment dome until their guest was removed, and, true to Bussard's word, he never returned until long after Maggie completed her room service detail. Whoever it was, he ate all his meals cold.

The cafeteria door banged open. Another member of "team zero," Gerritson told her. He grabbed a cellophane-wrapped sandwich from the counter, then left.

"So would Bussard rupture a sphincter if he knew we were talking like this?"

Gerritson laughed. "The man's been holding it in since his diaper days. I don't want to be there when he blows."

Maggie shrugged it off, feigning indifference. "I'm a military brat—I've been around men like him all my life. I suppose it wouldn't be so bad if he ran this place with more than just a skeleton crew. Then maybe he'd spread his good will a little thinner."

"Bussard's a minimalist," Gerritson explained. "He figures the fewer the bodies—"

"—the fewer the graves?"

"The smaller the staff, the easier it is to control. The fewer chances for leaks, and snafus." Gerritson looked down, and plowed a spoon around his mashed potatoes before giving up on them entirely. "Does it bother you that you're the only woman in this place?"

"No," she told him. "Why? Would you prefer it if I had a penis?"

Gerritson laughed. "Well, shut my mouth," he said, slipping into a stagey southern drawl. "Guess you don't got the plumbing, but I reckon you've got yourself a nice set of balls."

Maddy laughed. "You're wrong, you know—about me being the only woman. There are at least three Coats."

"The Coats don't count. They might be here with us, but they're not on the same deep dive."

Maddy looked Gerritson over, not quite catching his meaning. "Deep dive?"

Then Gerritson got serious. Too serious for Maddy's taste. "This place is a submarine, Lieutenant Haas. And whether you like it or not, your reputation precedes you."

MADDY SCRUBBED THE TOILET with a vengeance, and washed down the shower in the armored guest room that never even had a hint of soap scum. Still, she couldn't strip away the filthy feeling she had taken with her from the cafeteria. She had stormed away from Gerritson, without giving him the satisfaction of a second glance before she banged her way through the double doors. What had he meant? She had never thought of herself as having a "reputation" among her social circle at West Point. She was attractive, she liked men, and that left her in quite a power position. She could pick and choose her liaisons, always the one to decide the length of any lover's tenure. But a rep that followed her halfway across the country cast everything in a new light. It made her wonder if her sense of control had been nothing more than a convenient delusion.

She dined alone in her quarters, then sought Gerritson out. He, too, was alone—in the expansive complex it was hard not to be. He played pool against himself in the rec room.

"Want me to rack 'em up?" Gerritson asked. "Or did you bring your own?"

Maddy refused to take the bait. "From now on, Lieutenant Gerritson, I suggest we limit our conversations to topics that do not compromise the security of this installation. Any deviation from that mandate, and I'm afraid I'll have to report it immediately to General Bussard."

Gerritson racked up the balls. "Are you going to break, or shall I?"

Maddy pulled a cue from the wall, refusing to back down from the challenge. She broke, and sank the number one ball. "I graduated fourth in my class at West Point. Did you know that?"

"I do now."

"With honors, and high commendations. If that's the reputation you were referring to, I'm glad it preceded me."

"It's not."

She shot the cue ball, and sunk the number two ball, although she was aiming for the seven. "In that case, I have no idea what you were talking about." But her lie had neither conviction nor substance, and he knew it. She shot again, nicking the cue ball. It zigged wildly, but managed to find the number three ball, which dropped cleanly into a corner pocket.

"Nice shot."

It was, of course, luck—but she wasn't about to admit that to him. She made a play at scanning the table for the optimum shot.

"It doesn't matter where you aim," Gerritson sighed, hands in his pockets. "The pattern won't change. You'll sink the four ball next."

To spite him, she deliberately aimed at the pesky seven ball, only to have it ricochet away from the corner, sideswiping the fourteen, which careened into the nine, which tapped the four ball just hard enough for it to drop into a side pocket.

"See? No sense playing pool when our guest is still out of his cage," he said. "The game just doesn't work." And although Maddy didn't quite catch the meaning, it made her feel that the more balls she sank, the greater Gerritson's victory. So the next time, she tapped the cue ball just lightly enough to move it a few inches, clattering into a cluster of balls, but without enough momentum to send them anywhere. She stood back, and let him have the table.

"There are twenty-two men sequestered in this tomb," Gerritson said, taking his time about shooting. "No contact with the outside world, no phone calls or visitors allowed. Morale gets low under those conditions." He shot, and sank one of her balls. Number five. He sighed, and back away from the table.

"Are you suggesting that I was brought here just to provide you boys with a little recreation?"

"No. You were brought here because of your qualifications. But all it takes is one man who knew you at West Point to spread rumors about your social skills. For all I know Bussard planned it that way."

She gripped her cue, half believing she would bring it down across the top of his crew-cut head, but she restrained herself.

"And why would he do that?"

Gerritson shrugged. "Who knows. Maybe just to make things interesting around here, maybe to raise morale. Or maybe he's interested in you himself."

She dropped her cue to the table, decidedly disgusted. She was not a whore, but neither was she a saint. She had chain smoked her way through men like they were a carton of Camels—and apparently that was common knowledge. Had she been a man, her appetite and conquests would have been lauded. But she was a woman.

"If it *is* intentional, I think Bussard's way out of line," Gerritson said, sauntering close to her. "But the world's not the place it was a year ago. And when things go crazy, there's always men like Bussard who'll take advantage of that."

Although she was admittedly attracted to Gerritson, she

knew there was more danger in it than opportunity now. She laughed bitterly. "If Bussard plans to put me on poontang duty, he's in for a surprise. There are some parts of me the Army doesn't own."

"I hope that's true."

"Why wouldn't it be?"

Only now did she notice how close to her he stood. Had he moved into her space, or had she stepped into his? It troubled her that she didn't know.

She finally pushed away, gathered herself, and headed for the door, but she couldn't make herself leave. And if he stepped up to her again, what would she do? She knew what she would do. She would go to him. She would move into his arms, and if they weren't open, she would force them open to receive her.

Gerritson kept a respectful distance now, but there was an honesty to his voice that made him feel much closer. "I'll defend your honor here, Maddy. And anyone who wants a piece of you is going to have to get past me. Even Bussard."

She laughed out loud, not wanting or needing his protection.

"All of us were assigned here not just for our strengths, but because of our weaknesses as well," Gerritson said. "That's how Bussard controls us. But here, within these walls, there's a way to fix things that are broken."

He hesitated a moment, keeping a poker face. "I'm deaf," he said, with deadpan seriousness. "All the members of Zero Team are. Part of the requirement."

Her initial response was more laughter, believing that this was a joke at her expense. But Gerritson wasn't laughing.

"Last year I got too close to a land mine that wasn't even supposed to be armed. It was the concussive shock that did it.

But instead of a disability discharge, I got plucked up by Bussard for this assignment."

Maddy found herself reviewing their conversations in her mind. There was no sign in any of them that his hearing was gone, or even diminished.

"If you're deaf, then how did you know what I was saying when I turned my back?"

Gerritson grinned. "Careful," he said. "All information is on a need-to-know basis. And some things Bussard doesn't need to know."

THE EVENTS OF THE days that followed seared themselves into Maddy's mind no less powerfully than war itself. But this war was a small one, contained by the thick concrete walls of the dome.

It happened four days later, at lunchtime. Hers and Gerritson's paths had barely crossed over those four days, and when they had, Bussard was always within earshot, there was no conversation. Maddy had to admit she was in no hurry to speak with Gerritson again. In a couple of weeks maybe she'd force some perspective and take him on in another game of pool, but for now silence and solitude were her new best friends. If nothing else, there was the satisfaction of Bussard's dissatisfaction with her. Not with her job, but with her lack of contact and socialization with the rest of her submarine mates. To Bussard's chagrin, she became a source of tension, rather than its relief. It was a small victory, but a victory nonetheless.

Then came the day when the guard at Corridor A was not at his post. This was the path prescribed for Maddy when she entered the containment dome. She would wheel the tray from the cafeteria through the lower access way, then down Corridor A, where an armed guard would prevent her passage until their Honored Guest had been spirited from the dome through another corridor by Gerritson and the rest of Zero Team. But today the corridor guard had left his post, and gone into the containment dome, leaving the door ajar. Beyond that door, Maddy could hear shouting in the dome. Leaving her cart, she pushed the door wide to see what was going on. It was Gerritson. Apparently, he had gone mad.

He had taken the other two members of Zero Team by surprise. One was already sprawled on the floor, and the other he hurled over something that looked like an armored wheelchair which sat at the threshold of the open vault. The chair was occupied: their Honored Guest.

The Corridor A guard was next—Gerritson used the guard's own momentum to slam his head into the edge of the open vault door, and he collapsed in a heap at the threshold.

Up above, one of the sharpshooters took aim.

Maddy ran toward Gerritson, scrolling through all the possible ways she could disable a battle-trained, adrenaline-pumped officer before a bullet could do the job first.

Seeing the gunman above, Gerritson rolled, and the bullet ricocheted off the vault door. Then in a second Gerritson was moving again. This time he was behind the wheelchair, his legs sprinting as he pushed the wheelchair in an erratic serpentine path toward Corridor A.

A second shot cratered the concrete beside him, but the third shot caught him in the shoulder. Still it did not slow his momentum, or dampen his determination.

"Stop! They'll kill you!" Maddy yelled, standing in his path—but as he approached, she realized it wasn't madness or rage in his eyes. It was peace. A calm transcendence funneled into action.

"Out of my way, Maddy! I know what I'm doing!" He knocked her out of his path with the strange wheelchair.

"Stop him!" She couldn't see Bussard, but recognized his voice. His footsteps clattered down a metal staircase on a catwalk up above.

The Corridor A guard, his head still bleeding, got up, then raised his pistol with the practiced calm he had been trained for, and fired. The bullet whizzed past, inches from Maddy's ear, and entered the base of Gerritson's skull, detonating the right side of his head. A spray of blood left a red arc across the mouth of the corridor, and splattered across Maddy's face.

He was dead before he hit the ground, and the wheelchair careened forward, smashing into the food cart before skidding to a halt.

Maddy reacted with a directed wrath that arrived too late to make a difference. As the corridor guard ran past her, she grabbed his arm and snapped it at the elbow, then jabbed her fist into his epiglottis, so he couldn't even scream from the pain of the broken arm—only gasp for air as he collapsed to the ground. Now that Maddy's own adrenaline had shot into the red, she would have gone on decimating the guard for what he had done, had not Bussard's voice begun to boom in the space around her.

"Stand down, Lieutenant!" He crossed the floor toward her. "I said *stand down!*"

Maddy forced her arms to her sides. *Damage control*, she thought. While Bussard did his, she would effect her own. Gerritson was dead. Nothing could be done to change that. Now she had to divorce her mind from the context—belay the emotional imperative, and talk her way out of a court martial. Damage control now. Assess later.

"Yes, sir. Protecting the guest, sir. The guard's aim could have been off and—"

"Enough!" Bussard turned to one of the recovering members of Zero Team.

"McCall! Get Gerritson out of here. Take him to the loading dock for now. We'll deal with him after this situation is under control."

"Yes, sir." The officer turned briskly and ran off.

"Wait!" shouted Bussard. The officer halted, then turned hesitantly. "You *heard* my order, McCall?"

"Yes, sir."

"Then carry it out."

The exchange baffled Maddy, until she realized something. *He wasn't supposed to hear the order*. No one in Zero Team was. They had begun their jobs deaf.

"Haas, get the prisoner. Bring him back to his cell."

"Don't you mean, *guest*, sir?"

"Just do it!"

She followed McCall, realizing with a swell of horror that she would have to step over Gerritson's body to get to the wheelchair. The cement floor was slick with blood and brain tissue. A gurgling sounded bubbled in Gerritson's throat. Maddy felt herself getting sick, and silently scolded herself. She stepped over the body. All at once Gerritson's hand shot out and coiled itself around her ankle. She turned to find there was life in his eyes, that seemed to be growing stronger, rather than weaker.

"W-w-wonderful," bubbled Gerritson's voice through bloody lips.

"Jesus!" McCall turned to retch on the lunch cart.

Half of Gerritson's cranium was gone, and still he spoke. "Wonderful, Haas. Wonderful." But didn't that gaping fissure above his right eye seem smaller than it had just a moment ago? Maddy thought. Wasn't his cortex now showing a maze of convolutions where there had been nothing but pulp? And didn't the blood seem to be soaking back into him, instead of spilling out?

Bussard grabbed her and turned away from the sight. "Secure the prisoner! Now!"

Following orders was suddenly the easiest, most appealing thing to do. Her military training bypassed her conscious mind, and before she knew what she was doing, she was back in the dome, pushing the heavy wheelchair toward the open door of the vault. On her way, she passed the corridor guard, who was flexing his arm absently, as if she had done little more than tweak his funny bone. But she had broken it—she knew she had. Still there was no sign of the damage.

She crossed through the vault's threshold, into the cubic cell. Only once she was inside the claustrophobic chamber did she dare to look down at the mysterious guest.

The first thing she noticed was the true nature of his conveyance. It was less a wheelchair and more an Iron Maiden. Heavy steel bars came across his arms and legs. A plate molded to conform to his chest covered his whole upper body, and was welded to the chair. And yes, he did have a mask, but it was hardly iron. The alloy was a polished titanium composite, like the vault door. It covered his entire head, and the holes for his eyes, nose and mouth gave him the eerie semblance of a somber jack-o'-lantern. The entire apparatus had a fine seam right down the middle, as if it could be cranked open, but there was no sign of a release or keyhole anywhere. She thought she had never seen anyone quite so helpless.

And then he spoke.

"He was trying to free me," the voice said, much younger, much gentler than she expected it to sound. "I'm sorry. He meant something to you, didn't he?"

"I . . . I barely knew him."

Then she caught his eyes in the small sockets of the face plate. They were piercing gray, and seemed to float before his hidden face, rather than reside within it.

"Don't torture yourself," he whispered. *"This isn't your pain to bear."*

The words reached right through her, and her reeling mind came clear. It was as if he had reached into her soul, removed the shrapnel and sutured up the wound left by the day's nightmare. And then, in a quiet twinkling of revelation, it occurred to her who he was—who he *had* to be! It was there in his eyes, and in the flush of *presence* that steeped the room. It was the same atmospheric charged described by those who had stood on the rim of Black Canyon, and watched as Dillon Cole stood on the canyon floor, and shattered the great dam with the mere force of his will. More than four hundred perished in the canyon before the Backwash began, carrying their bodies back up into Lake Mead—but *his* body was never recovered. Now Maddy knew the reason why. And the reason for this fortress within a fortress.

"Is there anything I can do for you?" she asked.

Silence for a moment, and then a gentle response. "You could scratch my nose."

And so she reached in through the small breathing hole, and did.

ONCE HAAS WAS ESCORTED out and the vault sealed, General Benjamin Bussard cleared the area of all other personnel. Then, standing alone in Corridor A, he fired a full clip of hollow-tipped bullets into Gerritson's face until he had no eyes to see, nor mouth to speak; until his body held neither memory nor a glimmer of life. And when he was done, Bussard stood there watching and waiting, to make sure his death took.

3. WINSTON

TRANSCRIPTION EXCERPT, DAY 197. 19:25 HOURS

"I've been thinking about the way we fit together. The shards, I mean."

"I thought you hated each other."

"Sometimes we do, sometimes we don't. It's a complex relationship. There were things we learned at Hearst Castle, when we were doing all that healing. I could set broken bones, and break down tumors, but when there was someone suffering from a virus—nothing. And then Tory—she was better than antibiotics when it came to bacterial infections, but again, no luck on viruses. But when we were in a room together. When we touched someone at the same time, the virus washed clean."

"And you think that means something?"

"I don't know. When you mix the colors of the spectrum, you get pure white, right?"

"Or mud—it depends on whether you're mixing light, or pigment."

"So which are we?"

TWO TIME ZONES AWAY, Winston Pell dozed during an in-flight movie, into a dream that was no different at thirty-five thousand feet as it had been at sea level. He was sitting in a lavender lounge chair, floating in the air at a dizzying height, and gagging on the sickly sweet smell of some floral perfume. There was a building before him, and standing on the ledge were three figures. A man, woman, and child. They watched impassively as Winston's floating chair lost buoyancy and he plunged to the earth below.

Winston awoke with a start, and got his bearings. The flight attendants were collecting trash, and final credits were rolling on the in-flight movie. He blinked, trying to clear his eyes—the three figures in his dream had left an afterimage on his fovea. The dim spots in the center of his vision took a few moments to fade along with the residual sensation the dream left behind; the sensation that he needed to *do* something. The dream always brought with it a piercing call to action, and with no direction. He had no idea what he had to do, only that there was a burning need to do it. So he had hopped on a plane to pay his respects to Michael Lipranski's father—because if he had to do something, it was as good a thing as any.

Now he peered from his window to see nothing looming outside but unimpressive variations of normal as he descended into Orange County toward John Wayne Airport. The weather pattern in Southern California was back in control. Or out of control, depending on your point of view. There would be no hoarfrost at dawn on the sands of Newport Beach. No inexplicable downpours, or bubbles of sunshine defying the grim blanket of the marine layer. Outside Winston's plane, the clouds blew untethered, with no memory of Michael Lipranski, the boy who, for a time, had controlled them. His death had set the skies free.

Winston glanced at his watch, and adjusted it three hours back, to noon. Then he reached over and checked his carry-on—a black leather backpack that rested in the seat beside him.

"I'm sorry, but you'll have to put that back under the seat for landing," the flight attendant intoned in a practiced voice. It almost sounded recorded, like the White-Zone Nazi, whose voice resounded in every airport in the world.

"I know the drill," Winston said. He shifted it gently to the ground, as if to slide it under the seat, but when she was gone, he hoisted it back up. He needed the legroom, FAA regulations be damned. The nervous traveler across the aisle threw him an anemic miffed look, as if this baggage infraction could trigger a mid-air collision.

Winston returned his gaze. "You need a shave," Winston told him.

The man looked away, and mumbled under his breath. "I shaved this morning."

"Still need one."

Confused, the man absently passed his hand over his cheek and found stubble that could have been a week old.

Winston grinned. It was a guilty pleasure harassing the people within his sphere of influence. One of the few pleasures he allowed himself lately. Hair growth, nail growth—anything that could grow or regenerate did so when caught within Winston's field. Such was his unique talent; different, yet somehow connected to the various abilities and effects of the other shards. No doubt there would be several people on today's flight who would be making unexpected trips to Supercuts this afternoon.

After a bumpy descent, the plane pulled in five minutes late. "Santa Ana condition," the pilot had said; the periodic wind that brought hot, dry air from the desert, and forced planes to land from the west.

Once in the terminal, Winston suffered the ordeal of a 17-year-old black kid under an assumed name renting a car in a lily-white airport, trying to look as old as his fake ID claimed he was. Thaddeus Stone, 21, a combination of his brother's name, and his nickname. The clerk handed him the keys, then Winston waited for his luggage to come shuttling down the baggage claim carousel.

As he waited he caught sight of a security guard trying unsuccessfully to roust a clutch of Colists that had camped out like squatters.

"Incredible," grumbled one of the passengers. "It's the sixties all over again." Which was true to an extent—and yet in some ways this was markedly different. Back then it had been a generation that chose to tune in, turn on, and drop out in full view of a gawking silent majority. But this time, there were no generational boundaries. Nor were there racial or socioeconomic boundaries to the phenomenon. People of all walks of life had surrendered themselves to something too large to be called a cult, yet too disorganized to be called a religion. It could only be called a *movement*. In this case it was a movement that rivaled the motion of the tides in its scope and pervasiveness.

This particular group was a melting pot of various races and ages. There were at least thirty people engaged either in prayer or in accosting travelers as they passed. More security guards were called in. Although Winston usually avoided the many gatherings of self-proclaimed Colists, this time he ventured closer, drawn by the sight of a black man in a wrinkled Armani suit and bare feet. The man had clearly been a professional before walking this strange path. He reminded Winston of his own father, who had died much too young.

"Hello, friend," the gentleman said, as Winston approached. "Do you know Dillon Cole?"

Winston had to smile at the question. "Yes. Yes, as a matter of fact I do."

"He died for you."

"I thought that was Jesus."

The man grinned, knowingly. "History is a mirror, my friend."

Winston was sure the man had a pat response for any comment

thrown at him. Responses that were paradoxically as obtuse as they were wise. "Buzz off," Winston told him.

The man grinned like a leprechaun. "I saw the Backwash!" he told Winston. "It was real! I stepped in the flow of the river, and my dead pancreas was reborn. You're looking at a diabetic who hasn't needed insulin for a year!" He put an avuncular hand on Winston's shoulder. "Son," he said. "Say what you like, but I know I was touched by God."

"It's human nature to see divinity in anything greater than oneself," Winston said, recalling the prophetic words from his troubled past.

"In the coming days, there will be wonders."

And horrors, thought Winston. A world full of horrors, if Dillon's dire predictions were true. Winston wondered how much truth had filtered down the chain of rumor to these people. True, the Backwash, for as long as it had lasted, had been a quantifiable "miracle," but most everything else was subject to distorted word of mouth. How much did any of these people really know? And what would they do if they knew that he was *the* Winston Pell? Did they even acknowledge that there had been five others beside Dillon Cole, whose souls shimmered with the powerful light of the Scorpion Star?

"What about the others?" Winston dared to ask. "The other great souls, whose powers rivaled Dillon's?"

"Servants," said the man dismissively. "Servants only."

It was a slap in the face, but, thought Winston, a deserved slap. It had been their unbridled hubris that had created this mess to begin with. The brief time he and the others had walked the ways of Gods had set the world teetering off its balance. This man was prime evidence of that.

And now, in spite of how hard Dillon had tried to prevent it, he had become a religious icon of the highest order, with the speed of a satellite transmission—not like in the old days where it took generations to spread the word. There was a time when Winston had hated Dillon, until Winston finally came to realize that this destroyer/creator was neither god nor demon. Dillon was, in the end, just like Winston; a kid with no clue how to rein in his own powers, much less handle the affairs of a rapidly failing world. Dillon, who had once been a hated enemy, was now a friend. The only one he had left.

"Dillon brings life from death."

"So I've heard." Winston couldn't decide whether talking to this man was mental masturbation or more like picking at a sore. Either way, Winston had had enough. He reached into his pocket to hand the man a dollar, if only to shut him up. The man smiled indulgently, but he wouldn't take it.

"It's not your money we want," the man beamed. "It's your soul."

Winston shivered in the hot wind.

As WINSTON DROVE TOWARD Newport Beach, he could see that the Santa Ana winds had already done their damage this year. They had ripped over the mountains, tearing up over-watered trees in the Stepford-green neighborhoods of Orange County, and sending a barrage of plastic trash barrels rolling in and out of traffic, because the Santa Anas invariably blew in on trash day.

Michael's beach house was easy to find. It was the one with the big SOLD sign staring across the beach to the Pacific. He heard some noise from the rear of the home and made his way to the alley behind.

He'd expected he'd be paying his respects to Michael's father, but instead he saw Drew Camden laboring with some boxes toward a U-Haul truck.

Seeing Drew brought back too many memories he'd just as soon forget, so he took his time, and waited before stepping into view. Drew had been Michael's friend—Winston didn't know him well. Drew had been their biographer, deep under Michael's nature-changing influence in some unsettling way. Although Drew was not one of the shards, he was currently the closest thing to an ally.

Winston had seen Drew only once since the collapse of the dam. It was back in July. Drew had sought out Winston that time, finding him in the remains of his overgrown Alabama neighborhood, where few people lived anymore and the wrecks of homes stood overwhelmed by vines, like a Mayan ruin. Winston's effect in action.

"I want to put some closure on all of this," Drew had told him on the buckling boards of Winston's front porch. No longer under Michael's influence, Drew's nature seemed . . . well, much more natural. He had come all the way to Alabama to tell Winston how Michael and Tory had died, for he felt Winston deserved to know. According to Drew, they were caught in the dam the moment it gave way, most likely buried under thousands of tons of rubble. So it was a shock when Drew called weeks later to tell him that Michael had, indeed, been discovered—and in the desert, no less—a few miles from the fallen dam. How he got there was a mystery that Michael had taken to his grave. As for Tory, her remains were still unaccounted for.

The muffled sound of pounding waves resonated in the narrow Newport Beach alley. Winston stepped out into full view as Drew approached the U-Haul with a box. Drew saw him and set down the heavy box in the back of the open truck. If he was surprised to see Winston, he didn't show it.

"You missed the funeral," Drew said.

"I've got a problem with cemeteries."

Drew considered that. "They grow on you."

Winston dredged up a grin. "Yeah, that's the problem."

Winston found himself gazing off at some Bermuda grass poking through the cracks in the pavement. It was already growing fast and furious like the kudzu back home, new shoots sprouting before his eyes. Most of the time he chose not to look. He had long since dispensed with worrying about the things that were beyond his control.

Michael's father came out carrying a lamp in each hand. He was a man of forty-five, prematurely gray but in good physical condition, as Michael had been. He seemed to be bearing up well under his grief. He nodded a hello to Winston, and looked to Drew. "Friend from school?"

"Yeah, you could say that," Drew said.

Mr. Lipranski put the lamps in the back of the truck. "Take a break if you want, Drew. We've got all day." He went back inside.

"I'm helping him move," Drew said. "He could afford it back when Michael was selling his services, but not now." Drew leaned against the side of the rental truck, wiped some sweat from his brow, then reached into a cooler and handed Winston a Dr. Pepper. "Any word from Dillon or Lourdes?"

"Still AWOL."

"Both of them?"

Winston nodded.

"Do you think they're together?"

Winston popped his tab, feeling the fine spray graze his face. He shrugged. "I doubt it. I've got some hunches where Lourdes might be, but no clue about Dillon."

While Lourdes had strode into the sunset the day the dam broke, Winston had kept in close contact with Dillon . . . until the day Dillon just up and disappeared six months ago, leaving Winston alone to watch all of Dillon's prophetic predictions come true. Shifting alliances; breakdown of communication; a plague of apathy, the dissolution of reason. *And where are you now, Dillon? We've found Michael's body—where the hell are you?*

Since the old times were not worth catching up on, Winston got to the point. "I'd like you to show me where Michael is buried."

Drew put down his empty can. "Why? You gonna fill out his ivy?" Winston frowned, scalded by the remark. "I'm sorry," said Drew. "I didn't mean to say that. It's just—" He reached up and flicked a droplet from his eye that could have been sweat, but was most likely a tear. "It's not far from here. Let me finish up, and I'll take you."

CORONA DEL MAR MEMORIAL Park was a piece of land with a gorgeous ocean view.

"It's up here," Drew said as they trudged up the gentle slope. "There weren't many plots left for sale. It's a popular spot."

It struck Winston as odd that such a view would be wasted on residents with no windows to appreciate it. Best to be entombed like Snow White, in a casket of glass facing west to catch the rays of the setting sun.

They stopped by a rectangular patch of earth surrounded by other occupied graves—older ones with well-trimmed hedges and low granite headstones. Michael was buried among strangers. It was a modest grave. Still unmarked, with sorry plugs of ivy that had yet to take root.

"No gravestone yet?" questioned Winston.

"Not yet. And his father isn't even sure he wants one."

"Why not?"

"Ever been to Paris?" Drew asked. "Ever see Jim Morrison's grave?"

Winston had never seen it, but he knew enough to get Drew's point. It was a counterculture shrine, the area around it defaced by graffiti and spoiled with litter. The names of the shards were known now in just about every corner of the world, and whether or not they were considered mere servants of Dillon, fanatics were everywhere. For the same reason Winston had to travel under an assumed name, the marked grave of Michael Lipranski would never see any peace.

He noted the sad, forlorn way Drew looked at the grave. For a moment he wished he had Dillon's skill at divining a person's thoughts and feelings. "Were you and Michael lovers?" he asked.

Drew shook his head. Even without Dillon's power, Winston could read a whole canvas of emotions there. "More of an unrequited love thing," Drew said. "At least for me. He wasn't into it."

"I shouldn't stay too long," Winston said. "I've got to follow a lead that might bring me to Lourdes." Winston gave Drew his cell phone number. "If you find Dillon, let me know."

"I won't find him," Drew said. "I'm not looking."

Winston lingered a few moments more.

"Did you just want to pay your respects?" asked Drew, clearly uncomfortable to be at his friend's grave so soon after he was laid to rest. "Or is there another reason why you came?"

Winston knelt down to the grave. "I don't know." He reached his hand down to touch the earth, and for an instant the dream flashed through his mind again like a static shock.

A lavender lounge chair.

A ledge.

Three figures.

Why have I come here, Michael? I'm not Dillon, I can't give you back your life. What is it I'm supposed to do? But Michael's grave, like all graves, gave its answers in variations of silence. His only course now was south, following the solitary lead that might take him to Lourdes.

By the time they left a few minutes later, Michael's ivy was green and lush, and Winston's mind was still a dry heave, willing him to action against a painful absence of purpose.

4. LOST HORIZON

TRANSCRIPTION EXCERPT, DAY 202, 13:51 HOURS

"I'm worried about Lourdes. Winston's fine out there—but I don't think things are right with her. I think she got pushed off the brink, and never came back."

"How much damage could she do on her own?"

"Lots, if she chose to. When I last saw her, she could put a room of people to sleep, or turn them into a kick-line, hopping in time against their will. We called her the puppeteer, and she hated it. But now there's no telling how many she's got on the end of her strings."

"If she hasn't surfaced, maybe she won't. There's a good chance the government has her, like they have you, and are hiding her in some other secret installation."

"No. When I'm out there in the tower I can feel her somewhere out there. And it scares me."

THE CRUISE SHIP WAS never actually reported missing. Monarch cruise line simply listed the *S.S. Blue Horizon* as out of service, but rumors abounded. Rumors that it had vanished in the Bermuda Triangle; that it broke apart in a storm; that it was torpedoed by friendly fire. The truth, however, was much simpler, and slightly more embarrassing to Monarch Cruises. Simply put, the eighty-thousand-ton cruise ship had been seized by pirates.

Winston Pell had kept his ear to the ground for many months in search of such anomalous events, which was no easy task, because over the past year, daily life had evolved into one anomalous event after another. Riots springing up unprovoked, stocks fluctuating so violently that analysts were jumping out of windows. There was a surge in the number of militant religious zealots, as well as rampant hedonism popping up in the most straight-laced of bible-thumping towns.

And all because everyone could sense that the world had suddenly become a sinking ship. What began with the Backwash had taken on a momentum all its own, metastasizing to the far reaches of the globe. There was a prevailing, unnameable sense that something immense and terrible was about to occur. Winston suspected people had a kind of species instinct about it, the way dogs could sense a coming earthquake.

And so on the police bands, and in the media, and in the chat rooms, Winston searched for any anomalous event that was simply too anomalous to be anything but Dillon, or Lourdes.

Finally he narrowed his sights down to the *S.S. Blue Horizon*. As maritime industries were not immune to the decay of social structure that marked these days, the *Blue Horizon* was not the first large vessel to fall victim to latter-day pirates. Everything from freighters to river boats had gone missing. What made the *Blue Horizon* different, however, is that it was the only ship that defied being brought to justice. The ship would come into various ports, from Juneau to Jamaica, in the middle of the night for fuel and supplies, appearing like the flying Dutchman, only to be gone by morning—which was theoretically impossible, because every port was manned with a night crew. Yet every port gave the same story—no sooner had the ship arrived, than the night crew fell asleep at their posts. When they awoke, the ship was gone.

As Lourdes had a very special knack for rendering whole

groups of people unconscious, news of this particular ghost ship was of special interest to Winston.

It was on a Saturday in October that Winston drove a rented car across the Mexican border to Ensenada. The word was that the *Blue Horizon* had anchored off shore, staying put for the first time in many months.

As he drove along the coast, past a smattering of Ensenada resorts, he could see the great ship, half a mile off shore. He parked by the docks amidst a bazaar of trinkets and curios, where tourists from the other two ships in port bargained for deals. Most locals and tourists, fairly oblivious to the *Blue Horizon*'s presence, went about their business. It was when Winston tried to get a tender to take him out to the ship that he began to encounter resistance. The fishermen and boatmen would shake their heads when he asked, but offered no explanation, until he finally found one who would talk; the driver of a glass-bottom boat, docked too far from the ships in port to see any action.

"No, my friend," the boatman said. "I don't go out there. She is *La Llorona*—the wailing woman. A ghost ship."

"What makes you say that?"

"I know all the ships that come in: Carnival, Royal Caribbean, Celebrity. But this one. She not supposed to be here."

Winston pulled out his wallet and fanned out the corners of several bills. *"Dime lo que sabes,"* he said in perfect Spanish, *"y te pagaré por la informaçíon."* The boatman was caught off guard. Not necessarily by the money, but by the accent. Winston smiled knowingly. People were always surprised when he spoke their language, whichever language that happened to be.

The boatman then gazed forlornly at his glass-bottom boat. Business had obviously been slow. The man stared at the money in Winston's hand, then sighed. He shoved the bills in his pocket. "Yesterday, four men from the cruise line come in by helicopter," he explained. "Fancy suits, very important-looking. A friend of mine, he takes them out there, and as soon as they get near the ship, three of them pass out cold, like someone poisoned them or something. The one man left—he is the one they let on the ship. My friend waits and waits in his boat, but the man doesn't come back, and the other three, they don't wake up. Then he hears the man screaming on the ship, he doesn't wait anymore. He comes back, goes home."

"And the other three men?"

The old man shook his head. "The hospital. Still they don't wake up."

Winston pulled out a roll of bills, and handed the boatman a twenty, but kept his billfold out. "How much for you to take me out there?"

The boatman shook his head. "I told you—I don't go out there."

Winston slowly began flipping twenties. "You're telling me you're afraid?"

The boatman began to scratch his beard stubble, thoughtfully at first, and then nervously, as the number of bills increased. "It's drugs. Some drug lord took over that boat. You go out there, he cuts your throat—maybe mine, too."

"I thought you said it was haunted."

"That, too."

Winston had flipped four bills, he flipped a fifth to make it an even hundred. The boatman began to sweat. *"¿Estas loco, eh?"*

Winston flipped another bill. The boatman took one more glance at his passengerless boat, and sighed. He took the money, and let Winston on board.

They pulled away from the port, leaving behind the commotion of tourists. The sea was calm, and although the glass-bottom boat wasn't the fastest vessel, Winston was grateful for the time it gave him to prepare for what he might find. As they got closer and closer to the white behemoth, Winston could hear music growing louder as they drew nearer. Upbeat salsa. Cruise music. The kind of music that summoned images of streamers and balloons, and drunk couples sweating a hot lambada. He could see people on deck now, leaning on the guard rails. Bathing suits, sun hats, and everyone seemed to have a drink in their hand.

"If that's haunted, the ghosts must be having a hell of a time," said Winston. The boatman reserved judgment.

The ship loomed before them now, a massive thing that just kept growing as they got closer. The anchor was down, but the lower gangway doors were all closed. "No way on, my friend," said the boatman.

"Go around a few times."

Reluctantly the boatman turned the wheel, and began to circle the great ship.

Winston moved out to the center of the boat, where he could be seen from the *Horizon*'s deck. It also made him a target, but he was willing to take that chance. The boat circled twice, and by the time they came around to the starboard side for the second time, the aft lower gangway door was opening.

"Now they kill you," said the boatman. He set his engine to an idle, and they coasted to the gangway door. Just inside, two unusually corpulent crewmen greeted them with disapproving frowns.

"She says you're not welcome here," barked one of them.

Winston grinned in triumph. So he was right—it was Lourdes! "Tell her she owes me five minutes of her time."

"I suggest you turn your boat around, and go back where you came from."

The boatman looked first at the guards, then at Winston. His eyes were pleading.

The men wore earpieces. Winston guessed that they must have been getting their orders straight from the horse's mouth. He wondered if Lourdes could hear him as well.

"Tell her," said Winston, raising his voice, "that she's a stubborn bitch without a shred of sense."

The boatman took a deep breath and crossed himself. The crewmen hardened into a battle stance, and then a voice came down from heaven.

"Fine. Let him on."

Winston looked up in time to catch a glimpse of Lourdes looking down on him from the railing seven decks above, before she backed out of view.

The two-man welcome wagon wasn't thrilled about it, but they obeyed their orders, reached out and helped him aboard.

Winston turned to tell the boatman not to wait, but he was already pulling away.

The two overweight crewmen led him to a glass elevator in a six-story atrium of brass rails and polished marble. He passed several stewards on his way, noticing the air of despair that pervaded their eyes. They, too, were obese—so much so that they bulged painfully out of their uniforms. He looked at the ample gut of one of his escorts. "Cruise food?"

The escort said nothing.

As soon as they stepped out onto the pool deck, the weighty sense of oppression permeating the lower decks was blasted away by a party that stretched from stem to stern on the ship's open-air decks. It was a fiesta of slim, beautiful people. The pool deck was a contagion of indulgence. On a dance floor past the pool, at least a hundred people sated their senses to the beat of the brightly frilled band, which, in spite of a cool ocean breeze, kept insisting it was "hot-hot-hot." Gorgeous women in designer bathing suits that left nothing to the imagination sipped tall cocktails in every color of a neon spectrum. The beat of the music pulsed in the teak wood of the deck, and whoever wasn't dancing was luxuriating on lounge chairs, or partaking of a sumptuous buffet. The atmosphere was so intoxicating, Winston forgot for a moment why he had come. Until he saw her.

Lourdes sat on her own private verandah one deck up, with a grand view of the partying pool deck below.

Pushing past the gyrating bodies on the dance floor, he made his way toward her, noticing that among the perfect physiques on this pleasure cruise were reminders of that other class that inhabited this ship. A towel boy with an unpleasant bloat about him, lumbering like a troll on the perimeter of the deck. A worker polishing the brass railings with turgid limbs and fleshy folds, his body drenched in acidic, malodorous sweat. These were members of a bizarrely obese servant class that greased the machine, and kept Lourdes's movable feast afloat.

Winston climbed to Lourdes's private deck perch. She reclined on a plush lounge, and was attended to by two topless men with pectoral muscles the size of turkey breasts. Although she saw Winston approach, she made no attempt to acknowledge him. She simply waited for him to come to her. She had never looked better. Not exactly svelte—her frame would never allow that—but shapely, and well-contained within the smooth satin of her bathing suit. He now noticed that the two dark-haired, dark-eyed glamour boys who attended her were, in fact, twins. They threw him a disinterested gaze before returning to their duties. One rubbed Lourdes with tanning oil, the other dipped shrimp in cocktail sauce and held them to her lips.

"Cleopatra, I presume?" Winston said.

Lourdes bit the dangling shrimp off at the tail, and her shrimp boy dropped the tail into a silver bowl already brimming with them. "She was just Queen of the Nile," Lourdes said. "I've done a bit better."

A few feet away was a very large man in an expensive suit that was four sizes too small. Like the crew, he had that bloated look, but instead of being flushed, his face was a pallid shade of green.

Winston indicated her twin studs. "I see you're into matching luggage these days."

"Only way to travel." Lourdes ate another shrimp. The fat man in the fancy suit moaned.

"Lourdes, what the hell are you doing here?"

"I'm on vacation," she said, coldly. "Is that so hard to grasp?"

"And when does this 'vacation' end?"

"That's the best part, Winston; it doesn't." And then she gestured to the pained man in the bulging suit. "Meet Mr. Peter Marquez," she said. "Monarch Cruise Line's Vice-President of Operations. He just joined us yesterday."

The man seemed only able to move a pair of pleading eyeballs set deep within his porcine face.

"What did you do to him?"

"We're in the middle of negotiations," Lourdes said. "After test-driving the *Blue Horizon* these past few months, I've decided to buy it, and redeem my outlaw status."

"And how can you afford a cruise ship?"

"We're negotiating a steep markdown." Her shrimp boy hung another cocktail shrimp before her and she took it in her mouth, chewing slowly. "Very steep."

The cruise executive moaned. "Please," he said. "No more." His voice came from deep in his throat, sounding as Lourdes's voice had once sounded in the throes of her own obesity.

Lourdes licked her lips. "Recently, I've found a depth to my appetites I never knew I had."

"And yet it's the crew that gets fat," observed Winston. "Not you."

Lourdes shrugged. "I eat quite a lot; all that fat has to go somewhere."

Winston shuddered. There was no end to the way they could abuse their powers, when they chose to—here was the proof. First it was just Lourdes's ability to control metabolisms; put people to sleep, change the pace of their body functions. Then she found she could manipulate their muscles, as if they were puppets. And now this; she stayed slim by imposing her weight on others. A perverse conservation of matter. Winston wondered how many times her own body weight she consumed in food a day. Did she ever stop eating?

"What happened to you, Lourdes?"

She sat up, pushing away the hand of her shrimp boy. "I grew up, Winston. I finally realized that the only person I owe in this world is me."

"What about Dillon?"

"To hell with Dillon! He's the one who screwed things up. Whether he meant to or not, he set the world on auto-destruct, and if the world is falling apart, I intend to suck every last drop out of it."

Winston regarded her pretty-boy twins. The dark hair and wan expression on their faces was uneasily familiar. "Your matching luggage both look like Michael," he goaded. "Should I ask what that's about? Or do I already know?"

Her tanned cheeks began to flush at having been so easily

read. He could feel her anger, and perhaps a hint of shame, charging the air between them. Her feelings for Michael had been no secret—but enlisting these surrogates into her harem was a desecration of Michael's memory, and she knew it.

She stood suddenly, and like a petulant child grabbed the platter of shrimp and hurled it at Winston. It bounced off his chest and clattered to the ground, rolling down the steps to the pool deck.

"This is MY ship!" she screamed. *"MY life, and MY reward for the hell I've been through!"* On the dance floor, the music stopped and all eyes turned to Lourdes. "And if you had half the brains you claim to have, you'd stop taking your marching orders from Dillon, or it'll kill you like it killed the others!"

Then her eyes darted around to the spectators, and she realized she was, as always, the center of attention, but this time in an unflattering light. As if to add to her embarrassment, several gulls winging high over the ship cawed in the silence sounding like mocking laughter from above. Lourdes turned her eyes to the sky, the birds' wings went limp, and they plunged, dead, into the sea. Then she turned to her profligate partiers.

"Dance!" she ordered. Suddenly their arms began to jerk and their bodies to undulate, involuntarily pulled by their puppeteer's unseen strings. Flustered, the band quickly kicked into another number. Satisfied, she released the dancers with the slightest flick of her head, and although their steps missed a couple of beats, they quickly took over for themselves, regaining the rhythm, and not daring to leave the dance floor for fear of what Lourdes might do.

"Don't look at me like, like I'm a monster," she told him. "All of my guests are here by choice, because they appreciate me, and the pleasures I have to offer."

"What about the crew?"

She hesitated before answering. "They know their place." Then she turned and walked to an open-air bar farther back on her private deck, while her Michaelesque boys both hurried to clean the shellfish scattered on the ground. Even before she arrived at the counter, the bartender had mixed her a red and white "Miami Vice," heavy on the Bacardi.

"Aqui tiene, Señorita Lourdes," said the bartender, stuffing a paper parasol and a pineapple wedge into the drink. He took a quick glance at Winston. *"¿Uno para su compañero?"*

"No—he's underage," Lourdes said, irrespective of the fact that she, too, was underage. She sat on a stool, ignoring him as she sucked down her drink, its daiquiri head flowing like blood into the Piña Colada beneath.

What troubled Winston most was how easily Lourdes had seized control of her guests' bodies on the dance floor. Used to be it took incredible concentration for her to control such a large group of people, but, like himself and Dillon, her powers were still exponentiating toward an end he still didn't know. It frightened Winston to think what Lourdes might do if she ever really got angry.

Maybe it was best after all for her to be queen of her own little ship, her dominion limited to the souls on board, slaves and followers who were resigned to subjugating their will to hers. Let her have her ship, so that she might be satisfied, and extend her grasp no further.

Leaving her to vanish again to the horizon would certainly be the easiest thing to do, but for the shards, the path of least resistance always led to disaster. Winston knew that if Lourdes slipped off his radar again, it would be a dangerous step backward.

He came up behind her, waiting for her to turn around, but

she didn't, so he sat beside her at the bar. "There is something we need to do, Lourdes. You, me and Dillon. I'm not sure what it is, but it keeps me awake at night, and when I do sleep, I dream about it. You have to be feeling it as much as I am."

She slurped down the bottom of her drink. "I don't feel a thing."

"You're lying."

She turned to the bartender. "Gerardo, one more, please." Winston dimly recalled that she had a brother named Gerardo, and Winston found himself not wanting to know if she had put her whole family to work here. The bartender mixed her another drink, but by the time he slid it onto the counter, Lourdes had lost interest. She sauntered past Winston to the railing, looking out at the Ensenada shoreline.

"You've been dreaming, too, haven't you, Lourdes? About someone in a purple chair. And three figures on the ledge of a building."

Lourdes sighed. "It's not a ledge, it's a stage. Three performers taking bows at the edge of a stage, surrounded by the flowers thrown by the audience. I can smell them. And the chair's not purple, it's lavender."

"What do you think it all means?"

"I don't care." That was a lie, too, but this was one she was sticking to. She had almost softened, almost shown a hint of her old self, but now the expression on her face solidified to granite. She strolled back to her lounge, and, resuming her position of leisure, she called to her boy toys. "Paul, Eric, it's time for our visitor to leave. Throw him overboard."

The two brawny men advanced on Winston.

"What?!"

"No—wait!" said Lourdes. "After all this *is* a pirate ship. Make him walk the plank!"

Gerardo brought her the drink she had left at the bar, and she began to suck it down gleefully.

While the boy toys held him, two fat crewmen bounded off, returning with a long table from one of the decks below, and cantilevered it out over the side. By now the event had drawn the attention of Lourdes's guests and they crowded the rail, chattering and laughing as if this were just another bit of entertainment.

They prodded Winston onto the makeshift plank.

"Lourdes, don't do this!"

"Oh, please," she said. "We're barely half a mile from shore, and the water isn't that cold. Humor me."

Winston stood at the end of the plank, seven decks above the Pacific, being cheered on by Lourdes's hordes. No, thought Winston, the fall wouldn't kill him, and neither would the swim. But it was not his well being he was considering. It was Lourdes's. They had all been affected by the events in their lives, misshapen in many ways by what they had been through. Lourdes was broken, and he doubted even Dillon could fix her now.

"Good-bye, Lourdes."

With the cheering crowd behind him, and without looking back, he jumped into the sea.

The fall seemed to stretch on for a sickening eternity, and then the sting as he hit the water was quickly numbed by the chill. He surfaced beside the great ship, still hearing the cheers from above. The water was cold but not frigid, and although half a mile was a long way for an untrained swimmer to go, Winston stroked, finding his desire to put distance between himself and Lourdes enough motivation to propel him to shore.

5. CATCHING RAYS

Transcription excerpt, day 193. 13:45 hours.

"Pigeons pray. Did you know that, Maddy?"

"I never noticed."

"They did a study. Take a pigeon, put it in a cage, then feed it at random intervals regardless of its behavior, and pretty soon it starts to do some weird things—like hopping on one leg, or spinning in circles, or bowing its head over and over, as if that's what brings on the food. 'Religious behavior' they call it."

"The prayers of pigeons."

"Exactly."

"What makes you think their prayers aren't answered?"

"You know, Maddy, sometimes you remind me of someone."

"Do I remind you of Deanna?"

"She also would have championed the prayers of pigeons. And she'd make you believe they were answered."

"I'm a poor substitute for the goddess of faith."

Today Dillon was faced with a dead horse on a veterinary gurney.

Flies buzzed in a hazy cloud about its body and in and out of its nostrils. By the stench that filled the cylindrical expanse of the cooling tower, Dillon could tell the beast had been dead for quite some time.

Zero Team had been replaced by a single "zeroid," as Dillon called him. A few minutes earlier, the zeroid had assiduously wheeled Dillon from his cell, through the connecting corridors, and out to the now familiar spot on the center of the cooling tower. The only difference was that Bussard attended his transit now to make sure that Dillon did not speak to this man. Once positioned in the center of the cooling tower floor, the zeroid exited to his ready room, to wait in an informational void, never knowing what went on in his absence. Then Dillon would be alone with Bussard—an unpleasant circumstance, even if he hadn't been locked down in an exoskeleton of tempered titanium. Sometimes Bussard would take the time to brief him on the nature of the "therapy session." Other times he wouldn't bother, since it was Dillon's presence, and not his comprehension, that mattered. Then from his custom-built remote control, Bussard would open the door to the guest waiting area, and the circus would begin.

Usually it was the dignitaries and statesmen of any and every nationality. Some walked in under their own power, others were so weak from the ravages of disease that they needed to be wheeled in. Bussard would then show off Dillon like a trophy to those conscious enough to care. They would be allowed the honor of basking in Dillon's peculiar incandescence for up to an hour. Then, regardless of how they came in, they would walk out under their own power, their vitality restored. They would then go for blood tests and MRIs elsewhere in the plant, tests administered by military physicians who, like everyone else, were insulated from the purpose of their task, never seeing those test results, or knowing their significance.

"Funny that people come to a nuclear plant to get cured," Dillon had once commented during a well-attended session. Bussard didn't find it funny, however, and when the guests were gone, he had hit the red button on the side of his remote, sending a surge of raw electricity through him. Now Dillon didn't say anything during the sessions. He saved his comments for those times he was left alone with Bussard.

"What do you get from these people?" Dillon once asked him, for it was obvious that this kind of operation was not an altruistic endeavor—but Bussard merely invoked the "it's a matter for military intelligence" clause, and left it at that. But Dillon really didn't have to ask—he knew; he could read the pattern in the parade of visitors. Thanks to Dillon, life was now a bankable commodity. Every second spent in his presence was a quantum of health doled out with due diligence to those whose health best served the interest of American security. What diplomat or world leader would not mortgage their nation for a shot at eternal life?

And now there was a dead horse; a lump of flesh and bone not ten feet away from Dillon's exoskeletal chair. Not even Bussard could stand the stench, covering his mouth and nose with a handkerchief drenched in cologne. But the stench quickly faded, and a cold wind swooped down the wide throat of the cooling tower to clear its residue. It only took but five minutes, and the horse whinnied in terror. Bussard quickly called in a team of wranglers as the animal flipped itself off the gurney, sending it clattering against the concrete wall.

"Subdue it," Bussard instructed, "and bring it to the loading dock." No doubt there was a horse trailer waiting. The men set themselves to the task. By the unremarkable look on their faces, it was obvious that these men did not know the horse had been dead just minutes before; they were only given orders to remove a horse. And the zeroid never knew there was a horse at all.

Once the animal was removed, Dillon spoke.

"Why? Why *this*, of all things?"

He half expected Bussard to ignore him, but today Bussard

deigned to give him a response, perhaps more out of embarrassment than anything else. "It belonged to the daughter of the senior senator from Texas. We were asked to give it treatment, as a special favor."

"I didn't know you took requests."

Bussard considered the punishing red button on his remote control, but didn't depress it. Instead, he hit the button that unlocked the ready room, where the zeroid waited to wheel Dillon back to his plush little cell. His dinner would be waiting for him there, cold as always. But at least now he knew the face of the one who delivered it. She was young—only a few years older than he. Twenty-two, perhaps. But then Dillon didn't know if she was even on that detail anymore. After all—the entire zero team had been replaced; Bussard could have replaced her, too.

That Dillon was responsible for Gerritson's death weighed on him heavily. With all the death he had seen and had caused over the past two years, he thought he would have become more desensitized to it. The fact that he hadn't was some comfort. He had not been robbed of his compassion, nor would he let this imprisonment numb his spirit now. He would pick the lock of this fortress. He had to believe that he would. And once he was free—even being out there in a world he had set on auto-destruct was better than being Bussard's instrument.

As they traversed the access way toward the containment dome, Bussard sneezed, and the zeroid dutifully offered him a "God bless you, sir."

Dillon grinned behind his mask. This guard at least had not begun deaf as the first Zero Team had. Bussard had specifically brought in deaf guards, because it was already well known how Dillon's words could be the key to a man's soul. The right word whispered in the right ear would fix the most damaged mind. And the wrong word could take that same mind and shatter it in a psychotic detonation. All Dillon had to do was divine the right thing to say by studying the patterns of a person's behavior. Damage and repair, destruction and creation; all facets of Dillon's formidable gift. But it wasn't Dillon's *willful* acts Bussard was interested in. All Bussard cared about were the effects that Dillon could not control; the incandescence of his presence, which renewed life, and had once reversed the flow of a mighty flood.

And so Bussard assigned deaf men, his thinking too narrow to realize that they would not remain deaf for long in Dillon's presence. The fact that they had kept their audition a secret from Bussard was a victory Dillon wished he could share with them.

"There will not be a repeat of last week," Bussard had told him, and vowed to personally walk Dillon's little Via Dolorosa each day, to make sure Dillon didn't find the key to the new man's soul and win him over. This man was chosen for his absolute lack of physical ailments, so that he would have no evidence for guessing Dillon's identity. Dillon suspected Bussard would have caddied him himself, if his ego had allowed it.

Bussard got a few strides ahead of them and glanced back to look at him. For a moment, Dillon got a rare glimpse of Bussard's face. The shape of his care lines, the knit of his brow, some discolored skin on his neck. Enough for Dillon to divine something from his history, but not much.

"There was a fire when you were very young!" Dillon said. Bussard stopped in his tracks.

"What did you say?"

"A fire, and something awful about a younger child. A baby sister, I think." Dillon gloated. "One of these days, I'll read you down to the bone, Bussard. You can count on it."

Bussard didn't spare the rod this time, and zapped Dillon so suddenly the zeroid got a brief jolt of the shock as well before he could pull away. Dillon's jaw locked with the jolt, biting a gash in his tongue. By the time the painful current subsided, there was blood filling the inside of his mouth. He held his mouth closed, the pain sharp and severe. He then swallowed the blood, and pressed his tongue to the roof of his mouth, bearing the pain as it diminished, and the gash zipped itself closed, perfectly healed.

I'm a sadist's dream, thought Dillon. *Torture with no down time.*

His eyesight cleared, revealing a figure standing halfway to his cell. Dillon recognized him right away. He was a hard man to miss. Elon Tessic sauntered forward in his signature white suit and black T-shirt.

"Hello, General," Tessic said, with the hint of an Israeli accent.

Bussard stopped in mid-stride.

"Sir?" questioned the zeroid, decidedly confused as to why a civilian was strolling around the most secure installation since Alcatraz—and a foreigner, no less. Bussard summarily dismissed the zeroid, and Dillon heard the clip of his shoes exiting the way they had come.

Tessic casually strode forward. "I want you to know, Dillon, that shock treatment was not in my original design of the chair. This was a modification added by the general."

Bussard pushed Dillon anxiously toward his cell. "What's your business here, Tessic?" Dillon knew he should have hated Tessic—after all, Tessitech had conceived and built Dillon's state-of-the-art prison. But Tessic was a fly in Bussard's ointment, and for that reason alone Dillon couldn't help but appreciate the man.

"I was in the neighborhood," Tessic said, "so I thought I'd make a social call."

"Your unannounced visits are becoming a nuisance."

"Then ask me to leave."

"Leave," demanded Bussard.

"No!" Tessic burst out in hearty laughter at the sheer joy of being the only person in the entire installation who could tell Bussard no. Dillon snickered too, knowing that Bussard would not jolt him again while Tessic was here. Bussard had to suffer Tessic's insubordination because he was the crucial linchpin in the loop. And besides, Tessic had more friends on the highest rungs of the military ladder than Bussard did. Enough to get him a season ticket to the greatest show on Earth. Having designed the chair, the cell, and half the military's high-tech weaponry, Tessic's perk was the right to come and go here as he pleased.

Tessic surfaced every once in a while for a few days at a time, sitting in on Dillon's therapeutic sessions, even though he had no discernible ailments himself. And when there was no one scheduled for Dillon's time, Tessic became his only audience, engaging Dillon in conversations of politics, technology, baseball. Supervised small talk, really. Then he would leave, and Bussard would develop a heavy thumb, bearing down on the red button at the slightest provocation, punishing Dillon because he could not punish Tessic.

Now, as Bussard jostled Dillon over the heavy threshold of his cell, Tessic followed them, to Bussard's further irritation.

Inside, Tessic sat down in the chair. "Why don't you go?" he said to Bussard in a casual tone calculated to raise the general's blood pressure. "I'll lock up."

"I don't think so." Bussard set Dillon in the center of the room. "I might have to stomach you, but I don't take your orders. You stay, I stay."

"Suit yourself. Pull up a chair." But of course, there was no other chair.

Tessic leaned forward, peering into the eye slits in Dillon's mask. "You surely must despise us all," he said. "'But you must remember, you asked for this seclusion. You wanted your power contained."

"I've changed my mind."

"Too late for that," boomed Bussard from the threshold.

Tessic ignored him, and squinted his eyes to peer in the face mask, as if looking at Dillon through a fish tank. "The thin holes in the mask were designed to limit your perceptions of the people around you—and to prevent them from seeing your eyes. But still I see them. Perhaps nothing could close those eyes completely."

"The door is due to close," insisted Bussard, his impatience growing.

"Who are you trying to fool, general? It won't close until we have left." Tessic turned to Dillon again, peering in through the metallic shell his Research and Development department had designed. "I want to know you," Tessic said. "It is important to me that I do. I wish to know your hopes and your dreams. Your nightmares."

Nightmares? thought Dillon. How about his waking visions? There was only one now, snared within the white noise the world offered him whenever he was out of his cell. It would unexpectedly swoop down the throat of the cooling tower with the wind. Suddenly he would see himself in a ruined room, standing beside a man in a plush leather recliner, a light shade of purple. There was a TV before them, with a bright image. A diving competition. The Olympics, perhaps. Three figures on a high diving board. A man, a woman, and a child. The absurdity of the vision could only be matched by its intensity, and a certainty that he should not be trapped in the Hesperia plant. That he needed to escape at all costs.

But he didn't tell Tessic this, nor would he ever share it with Bussard.

"My nightmares?" Dillon said. "You're in them. Everyone is."

"Really. So we are all part of your nightmare?"

"No . . . but you're all subject to it."

"I see. That explains why you searched for sanctuary." There was neither judgment nor doubt in Tessic's voice—just a desire to understand. Perhaps, thought Dillon, so he could build an even more effective prison for him. But to be honest, Dillon had never read that in Tessic's intentions. "You cannot contain the breadth of your powers," Tessic said. "But here, we do it for you."

"I would rather learn to contain them myself."

"What if you cannot? What if, like radiation, you forever need concrete and lead to rein you in?"

Dillon was uneasy with the thought. "Radiation doesn't have a will. I do."

Tessic chuckled. "Very Zen of you to think the power of your will can control a field of energy. But I'm more of a Western thinker."

"It's more than just an energy field. I can focus my powers when I need to. There are things I do by choice."

"Yes, so the world has seen."

The world. One benefit—perhaps the only one—of being here was that he was cut off from the world. He didn't have to witness the ongoing effects of the choices he had made.

"What's it like out there?" Dillon asked. "How bad has it gotten?"

Tessic shrugged. "More than a depression, and less than

Armageddon. I still wonder why you set out to do this to the world."

Why? Should he tell him about the parasite that hungered for destruction? That the fall of the Hoover Dam was intended to stem the destruction, like dynamite at an oil-well fire? That the attempt failed, and only made things worse? He might have told Tessic, but Bussard was listening intently to the whole conversation, and Dillon didn't want to dish out any more information for him to broker.

"I didn't intend it . . . but it comes with the territory," Dillon said.

To Tessic's credit, he accepted Dillon's answer.

Dillon thought once more of the vision, and the uneasy feeling it gave him. He shifted his eyes, hoping to see how far away Bussard now stood, but all he could see when he moved his eyes was the dark blur of his own mask. He spoke quietly, hoping only Tessic would hear. "I can't be kept here. There's something I need to do."

"What?"

"I would know if I were set free."

Tessic sighed. "That's impossible. You know that."

Bussard moved into view. "Tessic, I'm losing my patience."

"You never had any, General." Tessic leaned closer to Dillon. "If there's anything I can do to make your confinement more bearable, you let me know."

A dozen things went through Dillon's mind, but it was no use. Anything Dillon asked for would be vetoed by Bussard—because although Tessic could walk freely through the compound, that was really all he could do. A fly in the ointment—and all the power of one.

Dillon looked past Tessic to his tray of food. "I'd like someone to eat with," Dillon said.

Bussard snorted at the suggestion, but Tessic nodded. "A dinner date, then."

Dillon smiled and wondered if Tessic could see it through the small mouth slit. "I'll see what I can do." He left, and Bussard lingered a moment longer to scowl, then exited as well.

As soon as the sensors registered their exit, the vault door began its closing sequence, electrostatic pistons pulling it sealed. Dillon waited until he heard the familiar sound of the triple lock mechanism, then counted to five, and his exoskeletal chair popped open at the seam, releasing him at last. Such was the failsafe Tessic had designed—only one lock could be opened at a time, and the vault door would not open again unless Dillon was seated and sealed in his chair.

Dillon stretched and shook his legs, forcing circulation to return. Tessic was a complicated man. A genius with far more going on inside than Bussard knew. Dillon longed to read him, and figure out what Tessic was about—it had to be more than money and power. But the mask muffled sounds and limited Dillon's view. He could barely read anyone now.

He thought back to his first encounter with Tessic six months ago, when he had first been interned here. Dillon had been cocky even within the shell Tessic had forged for him. "You know, I can get out of this place any time I want," he had told Tessic.

The man had just raised his eyebrows. "In that case I look forward to your escape."

At the time, Dillon was arrogant enough to believe there was no security in this world he could not breach, pulling order out of chaos until all locks flew open. Tessic had proved him wrong.

And yet the man didn't gloat over Dillon's imprisonment

the way Bussard did. He was neither proud nor ashamed of his accomplishment.

Dillon took a deep breath. There was one thing to be said for his confinement. Not only did it keep his powers contained like a genie in a bottle, but it kept the outside world from getting in. Once that vault door was closed, he could not *feel* the withering of the world around him. There was no white noise, and no visions. There was only himself, a singularity, separate and apart.

He pushed the shackling wheelchair to the far corner of the room, out of his sight, then sat in the armchair, and pulled the tray closer to him. Everything seemed in order there: something brown, something green, something else obscured by gravy. Then he noticed the curious pastry. A fortune cookie. His first thought was that it came from Tessic—but Bussard's eyes had never left the man—he couldn't have slipped it onto the tray. The cookie must have been left by the female officer who brought his meals. There was a fortune sticking out from the edge of the cookie, and Dillon slid it out without breaking the delicate shell. The fortune held two words, handwritten. It read:

"Favorite food?"

Smiling, Dillon found a pen in the scant supplies of his desk, and on the blank side of the fortune scribbled "Eggplant Parmesan." Then he slipped it back into the cookie.

6. 9906753

TRANSCRIPTION EXCERPT, DAY 199. 13:49 HOURS
"Do you think we have a purpose, Maddy? Or are we just like those praying pigeons, picking out patterns in something that's totally random?"

"You're the master of patterns, aren't you? If anyone would know, it would be you."

"Some patterns are too complex for even me to see."

"Or maybe it's just so simple, you keep looking past it."

MADDY FOUND GENERAL BUSSARD's office to be as Spartan and cold as the man himself. Only his own chair was plush and padded—the chairs on the other side of the desk were so rigid, they cut off circulation to one's legs.

"I'll make this brief, Lieutenant Haas."

Maddy had been expecting some sort of dressing-down. It was clear that Bussard was not happy with her performance and her integration—or lack thereof—into the team. After Gerritson's death, she had remained cold and aloof.

Bussard tapped a lead pencil on his blotter, not making eye contact, which was unlike him. It was the first clue that this meeting wasn't going in the direction she had assumed. "Apparently our efforts to see to our guest's comfort have not gone far enough," he told her. "Or at least that is the opinion of General Harwood, and the Joint Chiefs."

It was all Maddy could do to suppress her grin. So even the führer had a master. Now she realized that if Bussard was going to be brief, it was to minimize his own embarrassment at having to actually admit that he had superiors. She was, in effect, watching him squirm, and she had a front-row seat.

"General Harwood feels our guest might need some human contact—and that we might be able to use such contact to get information from him that he has been unwilling to share."

"They don't consider contact with you human enough, sir?"

He read her smirk, and chose to relent rather than retaliate, chuckling slightly. "I suppose my bedside manner is not my strongest point."

"I sincerely hope, sir, that you're not calling on me for my 'bedside manner.'"

This time Bussard held her eye contact. "He's restrained, Haas. And by my observations, so are you."

Maddy gave him the slightest nod.

"You will continue with your current duties, but now, when you bring your meals to him, you will bring your own as well, and wait there until he has been returned to his quarters. As his chair won't release him while you're there, you'll have to feed him. You will be wired with a video surveillance device, and in this way you will develop a supervised rapport with him. Then, once you've gained his trust, you will ask him the questions we provide you." Bussard took a breath, weighing how much information he should ration out, then finally he said: "Our guest is none other than Dillon Cole."

And although Maddy already knew this, she reacted with requisite shock. "My God!"

"God has nothing to do with this," snapped Bussard. "Remember that, Lieutenant Haas. And also remember that if you repeat his name or the details of your assignment to anyone else in this facility, you will be severely dealt with."

• • •

ON THE MORNING OF her new assignment, Maddy left her quarters just after dawn, wearing a sweatsuit. A daily run was one of the few liberties military personnel were allowed at the plant; it was one of the few activities not under intense scrutiny, and therefore Maddy's favorite time of the day. Maddy fell into stride by the time she rounded the north side of the reactor building, and followed the path into a patch of woods corralled within the facility's inner fence. Occasionally there were others on the path, but they always kept a respectable distance, like planes in a holding pattern. Today, however, she was joined by an unexpected companion. A golf cart pulled up alongside her from a connecting path, as if the driver had been waiting there for this ambush. Maddy moved to the side to let him pass, but he did not. He instead matched her speed.

She recognized him right away. Tessic. His overcoat was layered upon an expensive white suit that bespoke more pleasure than business.

"I've come to congratulate you, Lieutenant Haas."

The thought of *the* Elon Tessic pursuing her in a golf cart was ludicrous. Here was a man whose company built everything from surveillance satellites to fighter jets. What possible business could he have with her? "Congratulate me on what, Mr. Tessic?"

"On your new assignment."

Maddy slowed her pace down to a walk, taking a moment to size him up. His hair was only slightly graying, and his skin seasoned by the Mediterranean sun. Somehow she had thought he would look older. His smile seemed pleasant but unrevealing. "Why would you care about my assignment?"

"I not only care about it, I helped arrange it."

Maddy chuckled. "You? You convinced Bussard?"

"I don't bother with Bussard. His superior is far more reasonable."

"You met with General Harwood?"

He waved the thought away. "It wasn't a meeting, it was a luncheon. We both had the salmon special." He pulled his cart to the side and stepped out, abandoning it. "May I walk with you, Lieutenant?"

"From what I gather you can walk anywhere you want."

He chortled, but didn't deny it. "I called in many years' worth of favors to gain a high security access here. I assure you I don't take that for granted. Bussard, however, takes everything for granted." A fellow officer jogged up behind them. Tessic didn't speak again until the man had run past and the sound of his footfalls had faded. "The American military has in their possession the single most powerful person ever born to our humble little species. And what do they do? They bring him dead horses and aging politicians. Clearly his purpose is greater than this—but they squander him on petty, small-minded tasks. Just as they've squandered you."

He waited for a reaction from her, but she chose not to give one. Maddy didn't like this. No one—particularly a man like Tessic—spoke so candidly without expecting something from it. What did he want?

"Bussard is a very limited man," he continued. "With limited perspective. He can't see the big picture, like you or I."

"I see no picture, Mr. Tessic. I have a job to do, that's all."

"You say that now—but there may come a time when the picture you see and the orders you are given contradict one another. I wonder what you'll do then."

"Orders are orders."

The path was coming toward the end of the wood, and

the bare gray walls of the plant loomed between the thinning pines. Tessic stopped, and turned to her.

"Do you believe in God, Lieutenant Haas?"

She hadn't expected the question. "I can't see how my beliefs are your business."

"The way I see it, there are only two possibilities," Tessic said. "Either there is purpose and meaning to our lives, or there is not, and everything is random and meaningless."

"I'm not surprised you see everything in binary."

Again he laughed. "That's all everything comes down to, isn't it? Zeros and ones? The separation of light from dark on the first day of creation."

"And which do you believe in Mr. Tessic? The zero, or the one?" Oddly, she found herself actually caring about his response.

"I'm a practical man. The way I see it nothing can be gained by believing in a meaningless world. No accomplishments would be worth celebrating, no comfort in success. When you see life as meaningless, no amount of money in the world can buy the joy you desire. I've always found it practical to hold to the other alternative: that there is meaning and greater purpose to life." He casually brushed some pine needles from his vicuna overcoat. "And so my trappings of success do not trap me. For that same reason, I believe there must be a purpose for the existence of Dillon Cole—and I can assure you it is not to rejuvenate livestock and despots."

"I wouldn't have pegged you as a spiritual man."

He nodded. "9906753," he said, and at first offered no explanation. A phone number, she thought. Was this all just an elaborate come-on? His offhand demeanor darkened then, became a shade more solemn. "My mother was a survivor of the death camps. Did you know? The rest of her family died in the gas chambers."

"I'm sorry."

"Years ago, I arranged for her to undergo laser surgery to remove the number on her arm, but she refused. For her it was a battle scar. 9906753. A badge of courage and a reminder of those lost."

Another officer jogged past them, this one a bit more interested in their presence than the first. He caught their gazes, but offered nothing more than a quick "g'morning" as he passed. It got them both moving again toward the plant.

"You see, Lieutenant, I must have faith that there is justice," Tessic said before he left her. "Punishment for the wicked, and liberation for the innocent."

And as Maddy went to prepare for her new assignment, she couldn't help but wonder what Tessic was planning, the punishment or the liberation.

7. SLUGGER

"Do you think I'm evil, Maddy?"

"That depends—are you going to share that sundae?"

"No, I'm serious."

"Why should you care what I think?"

"People out there think I'm God or the devil, and they don't leave room for anything in between. I want to know there's someone who can see me as human."

"I wouldn't be here feeding you if I thought you weren't human."

"If the shards are agents of evil, here to end the world, I wouldn't be too pleased about that, but I'd understand it. If we were spat out here to be gods, I could understand that, too."

"From what I hear, you've been to both those places."

"And so I know it's wrong. There's some other purpose, I just can't figure it out."

"You've been in lockdown for six months, and you still haven't gotten over yourself?"

"What's that supposed to mean?"

"Just because you are what you are, it doesn't ordain some grand purpose. Maybe it's your purpose to sit here, and be fed by me. Have you ever thought of that?"

"You don't believe that, Maddy. Any more than you believe it's your purpose to feed me."

EIGHTEEN HUNDRED MILES AWAY, a dentist with no future was called to service in a war against Dillon, and the shards.

Martin Briscoe was, in fact, the perfect candidate, as his mind had been sharpened and focused into a weapon by a single image that plagued him. It was the image of his dead wife and son that obliterated most everything else in Martin Briscoe's mind. He was particularly focused on the day he was fired, and then saw the angels.

"How are things, Marty? Getting better?" His afternoon began in a conference. Banning, who sat at the head of the marble conference table, took the lead. He was a blowfish of a man with such bad breath that his patients preferred to be knocked out rather than endure his halitosis. They all must have heaved a collective sigh of relief when he gave up the drill for dental administration. He was the type of officious asshole who would add an "a" in front of a patient's name, as if their little dental factory wasn't impersonal enough.

"Fine, fine. Couldn't be better." It was a rote response, geared at curtailing any further interrogation. It wasn't anyone's goddammed business how he was. Martin sat down, grinning at the half-dozen faces seated around the table. None of the associates of Eureka Dental had much of a poker face; they telegraphed their intentions long before saying them aloud. "Actually," Martin added, "I'm having a marvelous day."

The clutch of dentists looked to one another with that troubled, self-important gaze, like members of a secret society. Yes, Martin knew why they were gathered, and he was going to force them to go through the exercise in slow, tortured strokes. Let them be the ones to suffer the pain of this particular extraction.

Judith the Compassionate was the next to speak. "We've had even more complaints, Marty—from quite a variety of your patients." She glanced down at a folder in front of her.

"I have them right here—would you care to look them over?"

Martin grinned, imagining that they were all bobbing heads in a shooting gallery, and he was firing away with the disgruntled joy of a postal worker. "No thanks."

Banning the Halitoxic snatched the folder away from Judith and flipped through the pages.

"A Mrs. Susan Bernstein claims that you injected her daughter's anesthetic right *through* her tongue."

What's the problem? The little bitch is pierced just about every-where else. Martin only grinned. Banning continued.

"And a Tommy Watkins claims that you carved your initials in his molar."

Just like he's been tagging his initials all over town. The spray paint was still on his fingertips. Martin only grinned. Banning angrily flipped a page.

"And now, a Mr. Fisher claims that this very morning, you urinated into his rinse sink during your examination! I couldn't believe it!"

"I could," mumbled one of Banning's minions.

Banning slapped the grievance folder on the table for emphasis. "Good God, what were you thinking?!"

That Fisher was a prick in a power tie who deserved a little piss on his life. "Listen, I've got a pulpotomy in ten, are we almost through here?"

The tribunal of dental pharisees gave each other hot-potato glances, wondering who would deliver the bad tidings. Banning, of course, took the initiative. "We know you've suffered great loss, Marty. No one should have to bear the death of a wife and child—God knows we all feel for you . . . but behavior like this . . . Well, whatever the reason, we just can't tolerate it any longer."

And then the potato went round.

"You've left us vulnerable to a dozen lawsuits."

"We could be closed down!"

"That's why we've got to take action."

"Quick action."

"In everyone's best interests."

"Including yours, Marty."

"You'll agree with us."

"In time."

"In time."

"And for God sakes, Marty, please get some help."

It was a mighty fine ice-cream sundae of a dismissal, with all the fixings. Then someone—Martin couldn't even remember who—came up with the cherry to top it off.

"We want you to know that we're all here for you, if you need us."

The building's seventy-year-old security guard supervised the cleaning out of his desk, and his departure from the building five minutes later.

MARTIN DIDN'T DRIVE STRAIGHT home. Eureka was a small town and nothing was more than fifteen minutes away from anything else, so finding a slow, meandering route was difficult. He took in a matinee, then stopped at Chick's Sporting Goods, picking out some baseball items his son would have liked, had he and his mother not drowned in four hundred million cubic yards of water. At the funeral, his pastor had lauded the mysterious ways of God. His golf buddies had shaken their heads, mumbling about life's curveballs, before returning to their families and rejoicing in their own domestic torpor. Well, there were curveballs, and there were wild, skull-crushing pitches. This particular pitch had been thrown by a redheaded teenager, who Martin had once believed was God himself.

Coast highway, more than a year ago now. It was a road trip to Disneyland, just the three of them. Eddie was in the back seat of their Taurus, complaining about how boring the radio stations were in central California. It was ten at night when they were driven off the road just north of San Simeon. Three men came out of the other car, and from the very first, Martin knew this would only get worse, because all three of them carried baseball bats. They smashed the windows and dragged the Briscoes out kicking and screaming. The men didn't take anything—they didn't want anything. They just swung their bats, and shattered his son's skull, and smashed his wife's spine. Then they pinned Martin down, as a fourth man approached. This one had a chainsaw.

After leaving Chick's Sporting Goods, Martin drove each street in his neighborhood, passing his house several times, then sat at the bar in T.G.I. Friday's, drinking tequila shooters, and stuffing his gut with tacos al carbon. It was eleven o'clock at night when the place closed, and he left, heading back to his former place of business.

Martin remembered very little once the chainsaw began to roar. He mercifully fell unconscious. When he awoke, he was in some sort of library . . . and he had no legs. There were just two stumps above where his knees would have been, crudely tied off with his own jumper cables. Around him were at least a dozen others in no better condition. His son lay sprawled, rasping an unconscious moan, his head a bruised, swollen mass of flesh the color of eggplant. His wife was there, too, slumped in a corner, most definitely dead. He wanted to panic—but there was something gripping his spirit, containing his emotions. At first he thought it was shock, but he quickly discovered it was something entirely different.

Eureka Dental's building only had one night guard, whose narcolepsy was well known. Still, Martin wasn't taking any chances. He came from behind and struck him with the Louisville Slugger he had gotten from Chick's—the same brand of bat that had shattered his wife's spine, and son's skull on the last day that the world made sense. Only the night light was on in Eureka Dental's waiting room, the sign-in sheet waiting for the morning patients. On the wall was a framed poster of a popular comedian touting the merits of flossing. The glass shattered as the poster became the next casualty of the Slugger.

The Library was filled with people clinging onto life, and there were only four standing. Teenagers. One boy was listening to an iPod in the corner, dancing to the beat, ignoring the pain around him. Then there was the blonde girl who pressed her hands on people's sores. Another girl moved around the room wearing a beatific grin that Martin could swear was numbing his pain. Then the red-headed kid went to his dying son. "Don't you touch him!" Martin screamed, but the kid ignored him. Just then the black teen named Winston came up to Martin, looking over his oozing stumps as if they were nothing out of the ordinary. "Welcome to Hearst Castle," he said, then removed the jumper cables. Blood gushed instantly, and as weak as Martin felt, he became weaker, darkness closing in his peripheral vision . . . but the moment Winston touched his hands to Martin's thighs, the blood stopped flowing. When he looked down, Martin saw flesh—his own flesh—folding out of the wound like the fabric of an inflating raft. He could feel the tingle of growing bone—actually felt his knee joint, then shin and ankle regenerate themselves. In less than five minutes toes sprouted from the end of his feet, and by the time Winston moved on to the next patient, Martin's toenails needed a trim. Then he turned to see his resurrected wife and healed son standing beside him, just as awed and bewildered as he. After that, the men with the bats and chainsaws didn't seem to matter.

Eureka Dental had fifteen dental stations, each room equipped with cutting-edge equipment. Indeed, they did not skimp when it came to technology. All that money gleaned from rich patients and fat insurance companies went right back into their facility. He was amazed at how quickly the overhead lights and chairs broke beneath the swing of his bat.

They called themselves shards, great spirits whose souls were born of a shattered star.

He had never been a religious man, but in the face of what he saw over those next few weeks, it was no longer a matter of faith but one of certainty. There was a divine power greater than himself. There was a greater purpose, and it had revealed itself through these youths. He would have followed Dillon, and Winston, and the others to the end of the world. And that's exactly what he did.

The porcelain sinks were harder to break than he expected. So were the X-ray machines, their mantis-heads predatory in the way they parried and pivoted, their long-jointed necks taking the impact and bouncing back for more. It took him four or five machines until he discovered the proper trajectory to decapitate them with a single blow. He kept waiting for the scream of sirens, anticipating being caught in the act. That would make him news! The Associates would then have cameras and microphones crammed down their throats, forced to explain all this in the midst of the wreckage. It would be worth it. But when no sirens came, he only became angrier.

A few weeks after his legs were shorn and regrown, Martin stood on the rim of Black Canyon with a thousand others. He watched as Dillon hand-picked four hundred followers to descend into the canyon with him—the four hundred to stand with him as he would rupture Hoover Dam, then hold back the water with the force of his mind. His wife and son were among them, but Martin was not selected. Instead, Martin had stood there at the rim among the unchosen, saw the dam fall, and watched Dillon's betrayal . . . for when the dam fell, he did not hold the waters back as he had promised. Instead Lake Mead spilled free, killing his wife and his son, and the rest of the four hundred. By the time the water reversed direction, and the undeniable miracle of the Backwash began, Martin was numb to it, wandering the desert until the police picked him up that night. His wife's and son's bodies were recovered days later, washed all the way back through the lake, and halfway through the Grand Canyon.

It took four swings to break the tempered glass window of the climate-controlled building, and that finally set off the pathetic alarm system. He hauled out the file drawers, dumping dental records out the window until the parking lot below was yellow with manila folders. Then he went into the conference room, smashing his bat against the marble table over and over again until the table won, and the bat splintered in half.

No matter how powerful Dillon's miracle was, he knew it could never offset the loss he had suffered. How did he think he could return home to Eureka and take up his old life? How could his associates ever expect him to devote his days to dentistry? Hell, in Dillon's order there had been no cavities—no crooked teeth. So what was the point of his own pitiful attempt to correct flaws when he had already seen flawlessness in the shadow of Dillon Cole? And how could Martin feel anything but virulent contempt for the families who came to him? There were times he wished his drill could reach straight through to their hearts, leaving his happy patients as lifeless as his wife and son.

Exhausted, he threw the broken bat handle down, and found a room where the dental chair was still intact—a room decorated for their younger patients, cartoons painted on the wall and a dental chair done in plush lavender leather. He threw himself on the lavender chair, and reclined in regal repose. This was station number eight. It had been his favorite in the old days. Ocean view and enough room to move around in. The ceiling was plastered with the disembodied smiles of celebrities—a regular grinfest, culled from popular magazines, and he could identify each and every mouth. There was a time that he had thought that was something to be proud of.

It was then, as he rested from his labors, that the reflector lamp above him began to glow. It should not have given off any light at all—the bulb was broken, but still it began to glow, its intensity increasing by the second. In a few moments it had become a spotlight. His eyes hurt from its brightness, but even when he closed his eyes, it didn't fade—it was as if he had no eyelids to shield himself from this light. He gripped the arms of the chair. If this was a hallucination brought on by cheap tequila, it was a good one.

When he heard a voice resounding within his thoughts, he knew it was a violation from outside himself. *"Martin Briscoe,"* the voice said, echoing over and over, resonating louder and louder until he had to stop it by screaming aloud.

His mind rang in a sudden silence. And then the voice again, filled with such depth and disharmony, he couldn't tell if it was one voice or a chorus. The voice, or voices, simply said:

"We require your services."

This made Martin laugh. To think that anyone who communicated in thought and blinding light could need a dentist was hilarious. But as his dance card was now open, he decided to entertain this delusion a bit longer.

"I'm a professional," he said. "I don't come cheap."

A pause, and the voice spoke again with mind-splitting intensity. *"Your task is one of retribution. Your reward will be forgiveness. Forgiveness and salvation."*

By now he was beginning to realize that this was neither hallucination nor dream—and that he could hear three distinct voices. Although spirituality had never been his strong suit, his brief service to the shards had left him fertile for any seed of possibility. Right now forgiveness and salvation sounded real good.

"Who are you?"

"The beloved of heaven," came the answer. *"Those who dance on high."*

Again. Martin laughed wildly at the thought that angels, if that's what they were, would actually suffer to speak in King James grandiloquence. "How do I know that you're real?" he asked through his laughter. "Will you make my palms bleed? Will you make my plastic Jesus weep?"

But the alleged heavenly hosts were not amused, and simply proceeded with their agenda.

"Who do you despise most on this earth?" they asked Martin. *"Who is the enemy of your soul?"*

There was no hesitation on that one. "Dillon Cole."

The hosts were pleased. *"Dillon Cole,"* they repeated. *"He has taken away your family, and brought your life to turmoil. And still he lives."*

The thought that Dillon could still be alive was a thought he never wanted to entertain—but now that it was put into his mind, it awakened a fury that couldn't be quelled by any amount of swings from the Slugger.

He thrust his hand forward, reaching into the light to get a hold on these beings that lingered there, but he could not reach them. It was as if some membrane stood between their world and his. "You want me to find him?" Martin asked.

"We want you to defeat him," they answered. *"Defeat him, and prepare our way."*

"What do I have to do?"

"You cannot kill him . . . but death will be your tool for his defeat."

"I don't understand."

And so the hosts explained. *"Michael Lipranski and Tory Smythe are dead . . ."* they began. Martin gave up any reservations now, and listened to their orders, letting them plant in him a mission and give a purpose to his ruined life.

FIVE MINUTES LATER, EUREKA police arrived to find a bruised, bewildered security officer and a dental office in shambles. There was no sign of the culprit, because Martin Briscoe was already speeding south on the freeway, his hate now focused toward a single goal. He played the final orders the hosts had given him over and over in his mind like a mantra. The words calmed him, giving peace and direction to his troubled soul.

"Michael Lipranski and Tory Smythe are dead," they had told him. *"Now you must seek out their bodies . . . and once you have found them, you will scatter their flesh to the ends of the Earth."*

Part II
Fall Back

8. ABYSS

Two thousand miles east of Eureka, and eight hours after the offices of Eureka Dental were vandalized, Dillon Cole awoke to the shrill chirp of a clock radio. The device was crippled by an inability to pick up any radio stations, the cell being so completely insulated. All it could do was chirp its alarm, and hum like a theremin whenever Dillon got too near it. He had time for little more than a shower before the chair began sounding its own alarm, far more caustic than the chirping of the clock. It would continue to blare until its sensors registered Dillon's body weight in the seat, and it clamped down around him like a fly trap.

Once he was secured in his chair, the outer door swung open, and his personal zeroid came in to wheel him out, with Bussard right behind.

It was as he crossed the threshold of his cell that the oppression began to fill him. He had been neither claustrophobic nor agoraphobic before arriving here, but each day of his imprisonment brought anxiety swimming up from some inaccessible trench in his mind. It was always the same, and it only hit him when he was outside of his cell, when he could pick up the hidden vibrations in the frequencies of life around him. He was prepared for another onslaught of the mental malaise that funneled down the open mouth of the cooling tower. But he was not prepared for this.

It hit all of his senses at once as he was wheeled into the open cylinder of the cooling tower, like a sound so loud it painted a flash of texture on the retina. His head jerked within his mask as if he had taken a deep whiff of smelling salts, and with no space to turn, his neck took the force of the action—straining against itself. He gasped in staccato, halting breaths, his chest muscles suddenly too tense to take in the air he needed. He was floating in space, and there was not enough oxygen in the world to fuel his brain to process the wave of sensation that flowed through him.

The sensation that something had been triggered. Whatever chain of dominoes he had set in motion, the last one had tipped and was beginning a long, lonely fall.

It was the man in the leather chair.

It was the three figures on the diving platform.

The sensation of falling was unbearable, throbbing in his nerve endings. Dillon couldn't be here anymore!

"I have to get out!" he wailed. "I'm *meant* to be out! OUT OUT OUT OUT!" But he knew his ranting sounded as deranged as the brimstone ravings of a street-corner prophet.

He could barely hear his own wails, but he could feel the pain as he convulsed within the unyielding bonds of his chair, his saliva bubbling into a rabid foam spewing through the mouth hole of his face plate, until one of the Coats mercifully jabbed a hypodermic into his arm, plunging his consciousness into a sea of white noise.

9. CURVED SPACE

NEWPORT HARBOR HIGH SCHOOL SAT ON PRIME REAL estate, and for years local developers had fought and lost many battles to relocate the school and build high-end tract homes in its place.

Even though the Colorado River Backwash was three hundred miles away, and had no connection to Newport Beach, security at the school still had to be beefed up. This was primarily because of all the in-depth news reports that had tracked down the roots of Michael Lipranski—as if the source of Michael's transformations of nature could somehow be found in the classrooms of Newport Harbor High. For months there had been waves of curiosity-seekers making pilgrimages to the school and other points of new-divinity interest, hoping perhaps to absorb some residue of the shards' passing. But it was Dillon whom most people were interested in, not Michael, so the tide of visitors to Michael's stomping grounds soon ebbed, leaving only the occasional zealot wandering onto the school grounds.

And then there was the man by the fence.

At 4:30 on a Thursday afternoon, Drew Camden did a few warm-down laps with the rest of the track team, setting the pace. He had noticed the man just on the other side of the north fence about ten minutes before. He walked a rankled Chihuahua back and forth, weaving through the eucalyptus breakwind. It was by no means an odd occurrence—this was a dog-happy neighborhood, and the residents had no reservations about letting their dogs crap in the eucalyptus grove by the school. This man, however, was different. Perhaps it was the way he tugged on the yapping dog with little care or sensitivity. Or perhaps it was the way he made brief eye contact with Drew each time he came around for another lap. His gaze made Drew pick up the pace.

"Hey, Drew, it's a warmdown," one of his teammates reminded him. "Ease up!" But Drew didn't slow down until the track curved away from the north fence.

There were several explanations for the man with the dog, and none of them were pleasant, but as team captain, he felt a responsibility to dispatch him. So when they reached the stands and the coach sent them off to the showers, Drew chose to take another lap alone.

Back in September, the Orange County Register had printed a nice-sized article on Drew, featuring a picture of him breaking through a finish line. When he had met the reporter for the interview, he was naive enough to think it was going to be an article highlighting his stand-out track performance. But the reporter was not from the sports desk. That should have been Drew's first clue. The article turned out to be a feature entitled "'Out' in Front," and was a coming-out manifesto likening Drew to Greg Louganis, as a local emblem of gay athletic pride. People were either appalled, or impressed. Some people would stare at him, their equilibrium thrown off by Drew's complete lack of effeminate affectations. Some of his friendships were lost, while others grew stronger, and now the fact that he was captain of the track team—which hadn't meant much to anyone before—was a political statement. Hell, if he went to take a piss now it was a political statement. But worse than any of that were the advances from strangers. Some were boys his own age, some were men much older—

teens and trolls who idolized him for what they thought he represented. Honesty . . . bravery—which was ridiculous to Drew, because his coming out wasn't about being brave at all. In the wake of the Backwash, and Michael's death, he simply found himself uninterested in maintaining his old facade.

And now there was this man with his yapping Chihuahua.

At about the time Drew began to smell the dog crap, the man called out to him from the other side of the fence. "Hey! You're Drew Camden, aren't you?"

Drew found himself particularly disgusted by this man's approach, and was actually looking forward to telling him where he could go. Drew slowed his pace to a walk, and stopped a few feet away from the fence. "You could be arrested for what you're doing," Drew said to him.

"Walking my dog?"

"Soliciting a minor."

For a moment the man appeared flustered. The dog just barked.

"That is why you're here, isn't it? Or are you just here to look?"

The man adjusted the Angels cap he wore, and glanced down at his dog, giving a sharp tug on the leash which did not quiet the animal. Then he recovered his composure. "I'm sorry if it looks that way. Actually I just wanted to talk to you. I'm an old friend of the Lipranskis'—I understand you knew Michael."

A breeze tore a flurry of eucalyptus leaves from the trees. Drew could feel his sweat chilling on his shirt, which clung uncomfortably to his back. He took a good look at the man, trying to see how much sincerity he could parse from the man's face. Neither Michael nor his father had ever mentioned any old family friends—but then they never spoke much about their lives before moving to California.

"So, you're a friend from when they lived in Vermont?" Drew asked.

"No—Long Island. I didn't know they lived in Vermont."

Drew grinned. "They didn't."

The man chuckled, acknowledging the test, and the fact that he had passed it. "The name's Martin," he said. "Martin Briscoe."

Drew took a step closer, then realized the fence negated any need for a handshake. The dog growled at Drew, then growled at Briscoe, then went back to its yapping fit.

"So if you wanted to talk to me, Mr. Briscoe, why didn't you just call?"

"Didn't know where to find you—but the people I'm staying with gave me this." He held up a copy of Drew's fifteen minutes of fame, the newspaper already turning yellow at the edges. "I figured the best place to look would be the Newport Harbor track."

"Why was it so important to find me?"

Briscoe didn't answer. Instead he studied Drew for a moment—and in that moment, Drew thought he recognized something in his face. A sensation that bordered on déjà vu.

"You were close to Michael, weren't you? Like brothers, I mean. I always felt Michael needed a brother. He was always such a loner."

"Not the Michael I knew."

"I always felt that Michael was profoundly special. I just never realized how special. I wish I could have been there to see him part the skies."

"So you believe all those stories?" said Drew.

"Why shouldn't I believe them? They're true, aren't they?"

Drew chose to neither confirm nor deny the things that Michael and the rest of the shards were capable of. The less he spoke of Michael, the less painful the memory of his last moments with him, and the more distant that image of Michael and Tory looking back at him from the dying dam. Even with all their power, they had been powerless to save themselves.

The wind blew again, drawing gooseflesh beneath Drew's sweaty shirt, and he longed for the relaxing release of a shower. Again a vague sense of this man's familiarity set him on edge. Perhaps he had been in one of the pictures in Michael's house. Regardless, it dragged him back to the reality that he was talking to a man he did not know through a chain link fence. Whether or not Briscoe found that awkward, Drew and the dog certainly did.

"Is there something I can do for you, Mr. Briscoe?"

"Jimmy moved," Martin answered. "I showed up at his door, and the place was empty."

"Jimmy?"

"Michael's father. No one seems to know where he went."

Drew had never heard anyone call James Lipranski "Jimmy." But then, two years in Newport Beach was just a small fraction of the man's life. "He's renting a townhouse in Costa Mesa," Drew told him. "215 Placentia. You need directions?"

"Thanks, but I think I can find it."

"I'm sure he'll be glad to see you. No one came to the funeral from back east. Not even Michael's mother."

"I doubt Jimmy even called her." Briscoe lifted his baseball cap to reveal a thinning head of hair on a scaly scalp that was irritated and red. Briscoe dug his nails in and scratched vigorously, dislodging flakes, and making the irritation worse. "Funny thing," he said. "I stopped by the cemetery to pay my respects, but I couldn't find Michael's grave."

"Ask his father," Drew suggested. "Maybe he'll take you there."

Martin nodded a polite thank-you, and Drew left to hit the showers.

He put Martin Briscoe out of his mind until much later that night, when the news chanced to report on a stolen Chihuahua found hanging by its leash in a eucalyptus grove.

THE BIBLE IN THE stolen Taurus said it was placed there by the Gideons. This was, of course, untrue. Not the fault of the bible, which had neither motive nor capacity to lie, but the fault of Martin Briscoe, whose scriptural void had been easily filled upon checking out of the Sheraton.

Somewhere in his Gideon bible, toward the middle of Exodus, it said, "Thou shalt not steal." But such moral ballast had no place in the ship he now sailed. He sailed higher waters now, and was, by divine appointment, above the law.

Still there was a vestige of ambivalence within him. A conflict that kept bringing his hand to his head to scratch his flaking scalp, giving himself over to the compulsion—as if his fingertips could reach right through his skull, and into the convolutions of his cortex, digging out all the brain-jam he imagined had collected in there; a gelatinous waste product of too much thinking, and feeling.

He wondered how the three Heavenly Hosts that had visited him felt about the mental bilge that clogged his brain, seeping into his every action. They certainly did have a window into his mind—he could feel that, too. There was a membrane in the midst of his thoughts, stretched thin as parchment and clear as glass, through which the hosts observed from a telescopic distance. He had spoken to them occasionally, after the grand satori of purpose they bestowed on him in the ruins of his dental office. He would call on them now and again, asking them for advice on how to proceed, but they never answered. They stayed at the other end of their tunnel. *"We must not deliver ourselves into your world,"* they had told him. *"Not until you have completed your task."* So for now they sat as silent voyeurs of his mind, and he could feel both their intimate presence, as well as their distance. It made him want to scratch his head all the more.

The oldies station he had tuned in played a queue of feelgood sixties standards. Marty sang along with the derivative voices of the Association, getting only about half the words of "Windy" right.

He continued unhurriedly down Pacific Coast Highway, relishing the clean-air innocence of the song. It was ten o'clock at night—still a bit too early to begin his evening's work, so he drove back and forth through Corona del Mar—a Laguna Beach wannabe at the heel of Newport. On either side of him, the storefronts showed a string of coffee houses close together, uniformly bohemian. The only dim spot on the street was the Port movie theater, a dinosaur with boarded doors that had given up the ghost. Its unlit marquee read "Rosebud," in mismatching letters.

After cruising back through Newport, and Corona one more time, he turned left, heading down narrow residential streets toward Corona Del Mar Memorial Park.

All considered, the day had gone well to this point. With the unwitting help of Drew Camden, he had located James Lipranski, and had gained access to his home with little difficulty. Long before actually finding him, Marty had decided it best to kill the man—and when he put the suggestion forth to the Heavenly Hosts, they predictably offered neither resistance, nor encouragement. Surely if "Thou shalt not kill" were a commandment they expected him to follow, they would have spoken up to prevent him from the act.

But when Lipranski opened the door, Marty found the man scarcely worthy of execution. The stench of bad scotch permeated the air around him, and he held a stance Marty himself had grown familiar with; a hand high on the door jam to keep one's feet in place, and stop the world from spinning. Not at all what Marty had expected from a man who spawned Michael Lipranski, Perverter of Nature.

"Yeah, what do you want?" he had said to Marty, who could only gawk. He had worked out an elaborate scheme for getting in—something involving the neighborhood newcomers club, and a new key to the association pool, but his words left him. So instead, he picked up a stone the good lord had provided in the flowerbed beside the door, and smashed Lipranski over the head with it. It was inelegant, and in full view of the neighborhood, but no one was watching, and Lipranski's reflexes were far too slow to fend off the unexpected blow. He fell backward into the house and ceased to be an inconvenience. Once the door was closed, Marty once more tried to impel himself to kill the man, but shied away at the last moment. He consoled himself by realizing that homicide was an acquired taste, and his palate was not quite ready for it.

Very few boxes had been unpacked in the house, although the man must have been living here for several weeks.

Marty found what he was looking for right there on the dining table, as if it had been set out as a buffet for him. Photo albums lay open amidst legal documents and other paperwork. Birth certificate, certificate of death, newspaper clippings . . . and those wonderful mortuary bills. It was as if Lipranski was putting together a lugubrious memory book of his son's life and death. Near the computer, the edge of a newspaper article stuck out from beneath a scanner that was turned on. This wasn't for a memory book, Marty realized, but for a website;

an online shrine to Lipranski's preternatural son. The thought so repulsed Marty that after collecting the mortuary papers, he gave the unconscious man a swift kick to the ribs. Then, as an afterthought, stole the computer and scanner, realizing that it would not only ruin Lipranski's plans, but would veil the real motive of Marty's visit beneath the robbery. By the time Lipranski came to, he would be too busy dealing with the theft of the computer to notice the missing mortuary documents.

But this next part—this was the meat of his task, and although his hallowed taskmasters most certainly had their noses pressed to the pane of his mind, they remained silent, offering him no encouragement to ease his way into this indelicate duty.

He picked up the Gideon Bible and randomly flipped it open, hoping to find some passage that might sandbag his will against the fear raging within him. Fear of what, he wondered? Dead was dead, and Michael Lipranski had been so long exposed to the elements that there would have been little left to bury. A shredded sack of bones. Nothing frightening there.

But what if he was more than a sack of bones? What if he was down there, lying in wait like a vampire? After all, he was a star shard—who knew what their flesh was capable of? What if, when he opened the casket, Michael's eyes were open and aware?

His finger fell in Proverbs, chapter ten, verse eight: *The wise in heart will receive commandments: but a prating fool shall fall.* Humility was not one of his stronger points, Marty was certain on which side of the line he fell, and the knowledge motivated him to step from the stolen Taurus, taking the shovel from the back seat.

When he found the plot, as shown on Lipranski's paperwork,

Marty felt certain something must be wrong, because the unmarked grave showed no sign of being new. He began digging. The roots of the ivy turned out to be soft, and had done much of the job for him, having broken up the loosely compacted soil so that the first few feet was like digging through an earthen meringue. If nothing else the silent seraphim in his mind were stacking the odds in his favor. And so he hummed some golden oldies to pass the time as he dipped deeper and deeper into the grave, each shovel stroke another moment closer to exhumation, and the irrevocable destruction of Michael Lipranski's remains.

EVEN FROM HIS GRAVE, Michael was curving space around himself, pulling Drew Camden into an orbit that spiraled inexorably toward its center. As Drew climbed the cemetery fence, he could hear the bang of a shovel, which had hit wood, doubled by its echo from the monolithic mausoleum wall at the top of the hill, glowing a black-light sapphire in the moonlight. Briscoe had already reached the casket—but the fact that Drew could hear the shovel at all meant that he wasn't too late.

Drew now knew where he had seen Briscoe before. It had come to him even before he found James Lipranski in his home, icing the blow to his head. Briscoe had been one of the thousand followers who had worshipped the shards, from the grounds of Hearst Castle all the way to the Black Canyon. He must have stood there at the rim as the dam burst, and the four hundred were taken under. Drew didn't even want to guess at what had brought him to this.

Drew ran up the hill, keeping to the grass at the edge of the narrow cemetery aisles to silence his footfalls, until he could clearly see the double mound of grave tailings, between which Martin Briscoe's head bobbed as he dug, grunting with each thrust of the shovel. Ten feet away, Drew pulled the gun from his jacket pocket, and didn't speak until it was trained on Briscoe's psoriatic head.

"Not exactly walking the dog, are you, Mr. Briscoe?"

Briscoe gasped and stumbled, his feet bo-jangling a soft shoe on the casket until he regained his balance. Out of breath from digging, he said nothing, he just wheezed as he stared down the barrel of the pistol.

"I'm not sure Michael would appreciate you dancing on his grave," Drew said.

"You'll get out of here, if you know what's good for you," Briscoe said, then returned to digging, as if the gun meant nothing to him.

Drew took a few steps closer, never dropping his guard. Although the grave was dark, his eyes had adjusted to the light of the gibbous moon. Briscoe had unearthed the dark oak dome of the casket, and was working his way down to the latch.

"There aren't many things that would get me to kill someone," Drew said, "but robbing my best friend's grave definitely makes the A list."

Briscoe rested again, sweat showering from his forehead, his breath coming in rapid gusts. *Good,* thought Drew. *Let the bastard have a heart attack and get this over with.*

"You can't kill me," Briscoe said with such dismissal in his voice, it made Drew grip his pistol even harder. "I'm here on higher business than you could ever imagine, so get your queer ass out of here now, before you become a permanent resident of this cemetery."

"You have to the count of three to drop the shovel, and climb out," Drew said, but Briscoe completely ignored him.

"One . . ."

The shovel threw a splatter of dirt on his running shoes.

"Two . . ."

This was a poker game, Drew knew, from which he could not fold—and he realized with great alarm that he would be forced to show his cards.

"Three."

He did not fire. Briscoe hesitated for a moment to see exactly how Drew's hand played out. And then Briscoe grinned.

"That's a starter pistol, isn't it?"

Drew screamed in rage. If it had been a real gun, he would have used it, then used the man's own shovel to bury him. Drew leapt into the grave, dropping the starter pistol, and prepared to tear the man apart with his bare hands if he had to. The grave was an uneven, constricting space, and there was little chance to dodge the punches Drew threw. Drew connected a powerful punch to Briscoe's gut, then to his chin, then to his gut again, until they both lost their balance and they fell to wrestling on top of Michael's coffin.

Drew slipped on the curved varnished dome of the coffin lid, giving Briscoe the upper hand, and Briscoe pressed Drew against the earthen wall of the grave. Drew reeled at the smell of his rancid breath.

"Twice the fun," said Briscoe. "I get to kill you, and destroy Michael's remains all in one day!" That motivated Drew to hurl him off, and swing a punch so strong it would have shattered Briscoe's jaw if it had connected, but Briscoe pulled back at the last instant, the punch only grazed his chin, and the momentum torqued Drew too far around. His feet flew out from under him, and he came down hard, jarring loose a mudslide that covered his legs.

Briscoe stood above him and grabbed the shovel.

"The news article said you broke a collarbone last year.

Fifty percent chance I break the same one." He plunged the shovel down, and Drew raised his arm to block the blow. The shovel cut a deep gash in his forearm. He screamed as Briscoe drew the spade out. "I wonder how many blows it would take to slice off your head."

As Briscoe raised the shovel, Drew freed one of his legs from the mud, and prayed that all of his running had left his muscles strong enough to do the job. He kicked out his leg, catching Briscoe's ankles, and it knocked Briscoe down to his knees—but he didn't let go of the shovel. Scrambling, Drew found the starter pistol in the dirt beside him. Briscoe pulled the shovel back, ready to swing it like a scythe, so Drew lunged up, jammed the starter pistol into Briscoe's right eye, and pulled the trigger.

The blast, muffled by the flesh of Briscoe's eye socket, sounded like little more than the crack of a child's cap gun.

Briscoe screamed, and the shovel fell from his hands. Although it was too dark to see whether his eye was covered with blood or dirt, Drew could smell the singed flesh. There was no telling how much damage the starter blank had caused, but it was enough to rob Briscoe of his "higher purpose," and send him scrambling out of the grave. He ran down the hill, wailing in agony, leaving behind his shovel and a backpack.

By the time Drew had pulled himself out from under the mud, Briscoe was scaling the cemetery fence. There was no chance of catching him, and even if he did, Drew's arm was hurting far too much to be able to apprehend Briscoe.

Drew heard a window slide open somewhere up above in the upscale neighborhood of Spyglass Hill, and a man poked his head out like a cuckoo clock, a minute too slow. "Get out of here, you hoodlums, before I call the cops!" Then the cuckoo popped back into his hole, and the window slid shut.

Sitting back down in the grave, Drew took off his jacket and pressed it against his bleeding arm, until the sharp pain resolved into a slow, throbbing ache. Then, with his good hand, he began to brush the dirt off the coffin lid. Whatever Briscoe's particular brand of lunacy, he would not be easily discouraged—and who knew how many more lunatics were out there with similar intent. Drew had to keep faith that Dillon, wherever he was, would show his face again, and call Michael back to the living. But that couldn't happen if Michael's body fell victim to one of the vandals. It had to be protected, so Drew dug out enough of the coffin to free the hinges, and took a good long moment to prepare himself.

"Man, Michael—the things I do for you . . ."

Then he closed his eyes and heaved open the lid.

10. TURNING TRICKS

SOME TIME AFTER MIDNIGHT, WINSTON STOOD IN A PLUSH Bel Air bedroom. The aging actress watched him from across the room apprehensively.

"Is there anything special I should do?" she asked.

"No," said Winston, flatly. "Just take off the leg."

The woman sat down on the edge of the bed, pulled up the hem of her dress, and unstrapped her prosthesis. She gave Winston a reticent glance, then placed the leg on the bed.

"Okay," said Winston. "Now close your eyes, and relax."

She closed her eyes, taking a few deep breaths. Winston approached and knelt before her, lifting her dress a bit higher, until he could get a full view of the stump of her left leg. His proximity to it was already bringing forth change, the scars beginning to stretch.

"It tingles," the actress said.

Winston traced the line of scars with his fingertip, then began to massage the leg with both hands.

Winston hated that he had to do this. Not only did it expose his identity, but it demeaned him as well. If he had to use his talent, it should have been administered for free, but with no money left, he had little choice than to treat it as a commodity. Michael had done it when he was alive, Winston figured, so why couldn't he?

For the past few weeks, Winston had been vamping. Every hour of every day since swimming from Lourdes's ship had been an anxious, directionless stall. It was too dangerous to go home, and if he stayed in any one place for long, the conspicuous growth around him brought too much suspicion. So he wandered, watching the money dwindle, knowing he'd have to start turning these little tricks to get by.

Winston's phone buzzed and he flinched, not expecting it.

"Your next customer?" the actress asked.

"Shh," he said. "Keep your eyes closed." It was, in fact, the first text he had received in a long time, since so few people had the number. He had bought it almost a year ago, so that one person could get in touch with him. Dillon.

He ran his hands down the women's new knee, deeply massaging her calf, and flexing her ankle. Her foot was still in the process of regenesis. He massaged the emergent tarsals, until the five nubs elongated into toes.

"All better now," he said, standing up.

The woman looked down, and gasped. In a moment she was up, testing her new leg, walking on it, bursting into tears.

Winston quickly reached into his pocket, pulled out his phone, and read the text.

Come ASAP 483 Mill Road, Lake Arrowhead.

And the message was signed *"D.C."*

Dillon! Winston's heart skipped a beat, and he began to calculate the fastest path from Bel Air to the mountain community of Lake Arrowhead, a two-hour journey, at least.

The woman was now absorbed in ballet moves, watching herself in a full-length mirror. "I don't know how to thank you," she said.

"I do." Winston approached her, and handed her a slip of paper that contained a bank account number.

"Whatever you feel it was worth, deposit in this account,"

he said. "And when people ask, don't tell them anything." Then Winston showed himself out.

AT DAWN, WINSTON DROVE past the Lake Arrowhead address three times before finding it. The deteriorating cabin just off the hillside road was hidden behind a gauntlet of overgrown pines, and appeared as unloved as a place could be, except for the fact that a shiny red SUV sat in the driveway.

It only took a moment for Winston to make the connection—something he should have considered from the moment he received the page—but he had so wanted it to be a message from Dillon, that he neglected to consider that the initials D.C. could belong to more than one person.

Winston knocked on a door painted a deep rustic blue, and peeling like eucalyptus bark. When he received no answer, he knocked again. This time a very tired voice beckoned from within. "Come in. The door's open."

Winston slowly pushed open the door to reveal a figure sitting in the gray shadows of the cabin. He couldn't see the face, but he knew who it was. Drew Camden sat lazily in a rocking chair, his feet up on a coffee table, gently pushing himself back and forth.

"Welcome to my humble commode," said Drew.

Winston stepped closer, his eyes beginning to adjust to the dawn yawning through the dusty windows. He tried a light switch, to no success.

"Don't bother," said Drew. "My parents haven't paid the electric bill on this place for years. I think they've forgotten they own it."

What Winston had first taken to be a coffee table in front of Drew was actually a foot-locker, strangely out of place in the faded country furnishing of the cottage.

"Three and a half hours," said Drew. "Wherever you were, you made good time."

The casual laziness to Drew's voice was markedly off, and there was a bloody dressing encircling his left forearm.

"Twenty-three stitches. I told my parents I ran into a gate while jogging. The simplest lies are the best."

On the edge of the foot locker sat an orange vial of pills. Winston reached for it, but it was too dark to read the label.

"Vicodin," volunteered Drew. "Takes away the pain and a whole lot more."

"How many of these did you take, Drew?"

"Oh . . . more than I should have, but not enough to kill me." He took a glance at the foot locker. "Can't numb everything, though."

Looking at Drew made his own arm hurt. Winston rolled his neck, and rubbed his eyes. The looming dawn was no friend to Winston today. Not when he hadn't slept for almost two days.

"You paged me, Drew, and I came. Would you mind telling me why I'm here?"

Drew looked away for a moment, then angled his eyes toward Winston again. "I want to talk about my mother."

Winston sighed. "I'm not your therapist."

"My mother began packing things away in our house last week," Drew said, ignoring him. "First it was just old clothes, but once she got started, it was like she couldn't stop. She boxed clothes we still wore, kitchen utensils, plates, crystal. I come home from school, and half the house is neatly packed away in boxes. 'What's the matter, Ma,' I said. 'Are we moving?' 'No' she says, sitting at the table, drinking coffee, 'just getting our affairs in order.' She doesn't know why she's getting her affairs in order. She just is. Like the way my father cleaned out a year's worth of crap in his downstairs office. Getting his affairs in order."

Winston sighed. This was nothing new. It was no more strange than the millions of other people sensing an end to the comfortable paved roads of their lives; a coming evil they dared not consider in their conscious life.

"What do you want me to tell you, Drew?"

"I want you to tell me what the hell is going on. Why is everyone suddenly acting like someone just canceled our lease on the planet? And what is Dillon doing about it? He's the one who holds things together isn't he? 'The King of Cohesion.' Isn't that why he's here? Isn't that why you're all here? Or are you just going to watch as everything falls apart?"

"Hey, I've got my own troubles, so if you called just to bitch at me, you can take your attitude and shove it."

Drew smiled a slow, sedated grin. "Looks like we've both earned bitching privileges these past few days." Drew took a deep breath, pumping enough oxygen to his brain to sober him. "Sit down. There's things we've got to talk about. Important things."

Winston crossed his arms. "I'm listening."

"Trust me," said Drew. "You're going to want to sit down."

Reluctantly Winston pulled up a musty high-backed chair, and took a seat across from Drew. The cushion stank of mildew.

"Ever hear of someone named Vicki Sanders?"

Winston shook his head. "Should I have?"

"I don't know. Maybe." Drew reached beside him, picked up a backpack, and tossed it to Winston. "Take a look."

Winston peered into the pack before reaching inside, as if whatever it held might bite. Inside he found some paperwork from a funeral home, a plot plan of a graveyard, and a red Bible with a gold Gideon stamp.

"Stealing a hotel Bible, Drew? That's low."

"It's not mine. Check the inside cover."

Winston opened it to find that someone had used the watermark as a note pad, filling it with various phone numbers, and doodles. The only name on the page was that of Vicki Sanders, but there was no phone number beside the name.

"The blueprints are of Corona Del Mar Memorial Park," Drew said. "The circled grave belongs to Michael. And this backpack belonged to the man who tried to rob his grave."

Winston snapped his eyes up from the backpack in surprise, but it quickly resolved into resignation.

"Reason enough for the bat signal?" asked Drew.

Winston flipped through the bible, but found no other marks beyond the ones on the inside cover. "Who was he?"

"His name is Martin Briscoe, and he's pretty damn self-important. Even more self-important than you. He said he was on some kind of mission. Now do you want to hear the creepy part?"

Winston wondered if there was any part of this story that wasn't creepy. "Sure, why not."

"He said he had to destroy Michael's remains."

The morning sun did nothing to carry away the chill of the news. Even in death could there be no rest for them?

"He jammed his shovel into my arm, and I shot him in the eye with a blank," Drew said. "I'll survive, but unfortunately so will he."

Winston stood and began to pace the dusty floor. "Do you know where he came from? Was he from some cult?" If one person found Michael's grave, Winston knew others would, too. There were cults and crazies out there, more now than ever before. He remembered stories of how people regularly pried open the crypts of every celebrity from Marilyn Monroe to Elvis until their bodies had to be moved to protect them from their own legend. And now there was a man out there hell bent on destroying Michael's remains. In a world where logic was diffracting out of focus, why should Winston expect this man's actions to make sense . . . except for the fact that they did. Because destroying Michael's remains was not the senseless act it seemed. It was a surgical strike against the shards; there had to be a body for a resurrection. "Destroying Michael's remains is the only way to make sure Dillon can never bring him back."

Drew nodded. "Somebody big doesn't like you guys a whole lot."

Winston shuddered at the thought. Somebody big? How big? "If there's someone who wants to make sure Dillon doesn't bring Michael back . . . maybe there's a reason why Dillon *should* bring him back."

"Whatever else you might have been," Drew said. "You guys were a truly fearsome fivesome."

It was true. Even with their formidable powers, the shards had always been stronger when they were together. Even with Deanna gone, Winston, Dillon, Tory, Michael, and Lourdes had been far greater together. "Whoever's doing this wants to make sure that we're never together again. Never whole— never complete."

And all at once it occurred to Winston that this grave robber could be the man in the lavender chair, who invaded his dreams. The man who prepared the way for the faceless three. The more he considered it, the more certain he was. "Michael can't be left there unprotected."

"I'm way ahead of you," Drew told him, as he rocked gently back and forth, his feet on the edge of the foot locker. "Michael's safe," Drew said. "He's among friends. . . ."

When it hit Winston just what Drew was saying, it hit him

hard. He hadn't eaten much over the past twenty-four hours, but now his late night burger and fries came surging toward daylight.

Drew had robbed Michael's grave to prevent someone else from doing it first, and now sat sentinel beside his friend's body. Michael was in the foot locker. God! No wonder Drew had tried to numb himself senseless with painkillers.

Winston fell to his knees, turned away, and retched onto the floor.

Damn you, Dillon, where are you? If ever there was a time Dillon needed to be here, now was that time.

"Don't worry about cleaning up," Drew said in that even, Vicodin-buffered voice. "The carpet's history anyway."

When Winston had recovered, he approached Drew, trying to keep the foot locker in his blind spot; then he gently touched Drew's wounded arm. "I can't heal it for you, but this should do something."

Drew nodded. "I had lost some sensation in my fingertips. I just found it again. Thanks."

"Nerve tissue regeneration," said Winston. "No biggie." Winston picked up the Bible, and looked at the notes scribbled across the watermark.

"I've tried the phone numbers in a dozen different area codes," Drew told him. "I got a dry-cleaner in San Diego, a nursing home in East LA, and that's about it. Nothing that seems related."

"And Vicki Sanders?"

"I've found about a dozen of them on the Internet."

"Then we'll track down every one, until we find the one who can tell us what's going on." Winston forced himself to look at the foot locker resting ominously inert in the center of the room. Someone was fighting a guerilla war against them, but it was time to fight back. And if anyone were going to touch Michael's body, they'd have to go through Winston to do it.

11. PARTY OF TWO

Sharks. Maddy Haas could not stop thinking about sharks. How the big ones would lose their stability, listing drunkenly in the largest of tanks, not knowing up from down, until they finally died. Hammerheads, Great Whites, Tiger sharks—none of them could survive in captivity.

"Shoop. Tomatoshoop."

Dillon's stupor was drug-induced, but like those sharks, it was an awful thing to behold. A being of such awe and majesty so suppressed as to choke on his own senses.

"Howstheshoop. Schloop. Sloop John B . . ."

An octopus in a tank, Maddie recalled, could squeeze itself through a hole in the glass an eighth of an inch wide, and die on the floor rather than be held in an aquarium.

" 'So hoisht up the John B's shails, shee how the blah blah blah. Call fr the cap'n ashore n'lemme go home . . .' "

She hated Bussard for doing this to Dillon, and hated the fact that she was also a party to it.

She tasted the soup, which was saltier than the Dead Sea. Apparently Dillon's blood pressure was not of concern to Bussard. Maddy dipped in the spoon and blew on it to cool it down for Dillon, who sat before her, immobilized in his chair.

Maddie looked around Dillon's cubical cell, as he continued to sing, his volume slipping in and out like a radio with a bad tuner. Bussard had told her there were only a handful of people with security clearance to be in there, and she wondered what on earth made Bussard trust her enough to be one of those people. Then it occurred to her, it wasn't how much he trusted her, it was how little he trusted everyone else.

In her three weeks of meals with Dillon—especially those days before they began to drug him, she had learned from Dillon firsthand what he had been through, and who he truly was. The man beneath the myth, more boy than man. He was not, as Bussard suggested, secretive about himself, or his motives. It was the fact that he was so forthcoming that made Bussard suspicious, and he continued to scrutinize the tapes of her meals with Dillon.

"Are you afraid of me, Maddy?" Dillon had asked her early on, when her hands still shook while feeding him. And since he could read the pattern of a lie, she had told him the truth. Yes, she was. When she had first arrived at the plant—and first came to know who they had trussed up in this place— she had been frightened of his eyes, invasive by nature. They seemed uncontained by the mask. His presence had been— still was—a tidal wave before her; a wall of looming force from which there was no hiding. No wonder he was worshipped. No wonder he was feared. Yet although the sensation of his power hadn't diminished, it was a feeling she had come to enjoy. If he asked her now whether or not she feared him, she'd have to tell him that she wasn't really sure.

" 'Let me go home . . . I wanna go home . . . I feel so broke up I wanna go home.' "

By the last line of the verse he was actually hitting some of the notes, and the slurred words were beginning to coalesce into English.

"My dad always sang that to me," Dillon said. "That was before I killed him."

He was fishing for a word of comfort. He wanted Maddy to remind him what he well knew—that his parents had been accidental victims of Dillon's emergent powers, before Dillon had understood the power he had. It was like this at the beginning of each meal now. In grand, sedated melodrama, he would make vague but sweeping claims of guilt, and she would assuage them. It was already an old dance, and this time she wasn't getting on the floor.

"Feeling sorry for yourself again?" Maddy raised the spoonful of soup to the small mouth slit in his mask. "Feel sorry for *me*—I have to listen to you." He slurped the soup in, and spat it right back out.

"MSG," he said. "Stuff'll kill ya."

Maddy calmly blotted the spots of soup from her uniform, feeling a new blossom of her anger toward Bussard. Dillon picked up on her anger, but was still too loopy to seize its direction.

"I'm sorry for being horrible, Maddy. It's those shots. They make me horrible."

Maddy wiped the orange spittle dripping from the mouth hole in the mask. "Nonsense. You're beautiful when you're sedated."

"You're beautiful when I'm sedated too."

Maddy smiled. "I may have to eat your dessert for that one."

Dillon snickered behind his mask, and took a few moments to take deep breaths. *Good,* thought Maddy, *he's working his way out of the fog.* She took the time to eat some of her own meal, then began to cut Dillon's meat for him. When he had eaten alone in his room, he had been free from his chair, and could eat with his own hands. Yet he didn't complain about this new arrangement.

"The shots keep getting bigger every time they take me out," he said. "Problem is I metabolize the stuff so fast, they gotta give me elephant doses. Can't be healthy."

Maddy speared a potato scallop, and lifted it toward his mask. "Open wide. I can't see your mouth through the hole."

She slipped it through the hole, and his tongue took it the rest of the way. "I feel like a slot machine."

Maddy laughed. "If you were a slot machine, I might get something back."

"Naah," Dillon said. "Suckers' game."

"Not with you around," Maddy noted. "Everyone knows how you shut down Las Vegas."

Although Dillon's arms were banded to the chair, there was some range of motion to his hands. Now he clenched them until his knuckles turned white. The influence of his presence in Vegas had altered the odds of every game—it had taken months for simple randomness to return. Even now there were pockets where the laws of probability were still in remission. "Stale house zones," the casinos called them, and moved their gaming tables far, far away.

"To hell with Las Vegas," Dillon said. "The slot machines all come up triple sevens, and a million people think it's something biblical."

"Is it?" Maddy found herself truly interested in his response.

"How should I know? If the wheels had sixes instead of sevens, they would say I was the Antichrist."

Maddie smiled. "Haven't you heard? You are."

Dillon sighed. "Yeah, I've heard that one, too. So how about some more red meat for Satan's spawn?"

She swabbed a piece of meat in some A-1 and fed it to him. Maddy knew this would be a line of conversation Bussard would be interested in. She could almost feel him slithering like a snake in the wire that ran through her uniform. She could feel his eye in the tip of her buttonhole video camera. At first there had been a strong sense of betrayal each time she stepped in to dine with Dillon, but she suspected that he was aware of the camera, and that he understood her unwilling complicity with Bussard. His knowledge would make it all right—because then it would be a game the two of them were playing against Bussard.

Their ice cream had melted by the time they got to it, but rather than forming a puddle in their bowls, it held the shape of the scoop. Just one more little reminder that Dillon's sphere of influence was ever present. Even molten ice cream stood at attention for Dillon, refusing to give in to entropy.

It was now, after Dillon had completely regained his faculties, that his hands began to tremble in a subtle full-body shiver. Maddy knew it wasn't from the ice cream.

"Something out there?" she asked.

"There's always something out there," he told her. He took a few deep breaths and kept his panic suppressed. "It's not so bad while I'm in here—but it doesn't go away completely until they seal that door."

Maddy didn't pretend to understand what Dillon was sensing. Whatever it was, it was bad enough to send him into convulsions every time they wheeled him out of the room. But rather than seeking the source of the seizures, Bussard had chosen to just shut them down, knocking Dillon out whenever they took him from his cell. Apparently consciousness was not a necessary factor in his "therapy sessions."

Dillon took a deep breath and moved his fingers, pumping his fists open and closed.

"Make Bussard understand, Maddy. Make him understand that he can't keep me here." Any sluggishness had completely drained from his voice, the last of the tranquilizers already gone from his system. "You don't know what will happen if I stay."

"Death and destruction," she said. "No one preaches doom better than you."

"But you don't know. I've seen hundreds of people whose bodies lived while their souls digested in the belly of a creature I'm still afraid to think about. Destruction doesn't begin to describe it . . . and now I know there are worse things than death."

Maddy suppressed her own shiver, and forced herself to look at the unexpressive mask that didn't quite hide his intensity. "If things are as bad as you say out there, why do you want to be in the middle of it?"

"Even a losing battle has to be fought."

"But you don't even know what you're fighting."

"I *will* know. I'll know once I'm out there."

A moment of silence, and Maddy found herself looking away, shifting her attention to the vanilla simplicity of her ice cream. There was no sense even considering the thought of his freedom. She certainly couldn't set him free, and suggesting as much to Bussard would be tantamount to suicide. And yet, as much as she wanted to see him free, she had to admit there was a side of her that wanted him trapped here. There was something incredibly heady about being Dillon Cole's sole link to the outside world. There was a sense of significance that nothing in her life could match. The best way to ensure her position was to do her job, and continue to solicit Dillon's trust. As long as her performance was exemplary, and Bussard had no reason to doubt her allegiance, her tenure was intact.

She wondered how much of this Dillon had figured out through the intonations of her voice, and her body language. The eye-slits in his mask had been made so narrow to keep him from perceiving anything in the people he had contact with. Although it slowed him down, he was still able to discern quite a lot through his little peep holes; a thousand things about her, that, in a moment, became a thousand and one.

"It's your birthday!" he said, pulling the fact right out of thin air. "Why didn't you tell me it was your birthday?"

She sighed. "And how did you know that?"

"Easy," Dillon said. "The way you moved your spoon through the ice cream—like you were the reluctant center of the room's attention. The way you noticed the wrinkles on your knuckles. The way your breath is just a few cubic centimeters deeper each time you cast your eyes down to the table, like some funky old body memory of blowing out candles when you were a kid."

Maddy shook her head. Of all of Dillon's gifts, she was most impressed by his ability to divine truths in the patterns of minutiae. "Birthdays don't mean much to me," she said.

"Still I'd like to give you a present."

Maddy grinned, nervously. "The slot machine's finally going to pay off?" She could see that hint of his eyes now; feel them rushing through the metallic squint of the mask, like an octopus willing itself through the breach of its tank. Maddy tried to resist that intrusive gaze, but found she could not. She had once commented to him that sitting before him was like playing a game of strip poker, where he held all the cards. But until now he had kept his hand to himself.

"I see a maze of mirrors when I look at you, Maddy. You've spent a lifetime raising the mirrors, confident that no one will get to the center. That no one will ever truly know you. You find lots of power in reflecting everyone away, don't you?"

She tried not to speak—to say anything to deflect his gaze, but he would not let her.

"Listen to me carefully, Maddy," he said. . . .

"I know you. I know you down to the thoughts you tell no one. I know you down to the dreams you can't remember. I know you."

She tried to speak, to make light of his words, but found she couldn't. She could only slowly exhale, feeling the last vestments shielding her soul fall free.

"There. Happy Birthday, Maddy."

She knew at once that he had begun some work in her, and she didn't know how to accept that. He was uninvited, and yet welcome.

A few minutes later she wheeled the tray out and left him, trying to shield as best she could how deeply his words had touched her. But even Bussard was able to pick up on it.

"He's getting to you, isn't he?" Bussard asked when he next saw her, later that day.

"He's a very powerful personality, sir." Then she added, "All the more reason to keep him here."

Appeased, Bussard congratulated her on what a fine job she was doing, and Maddy hoped to God he didn't have a window to her soul the way Dillon did.

That night she went for her evening run to clear her mind, only to find that it was already clear—uncongested enough for her to appreciate all the sights and sounds of the run. All of her senses had been tuned to a more resonant idle.

"I know you," Dillon had said. Three simple words—anyone else could have said them, and it would have meant absolutely nothing—but with no one else would it have been true. And until he spoke them, she had not realized how much she needed to be known.

ELON TESSIC, HOWEVER, WAS not yet prepared to be known. He was a complex man to be sure, but held no illusions about himself. Given enough time, he knew Dillon would decipher him as well. This is why Tessic made a point of making his visits to Dillon brief, and only moving into his line of sight when there was a specific point to it. In this way, Tessic held his own in Dillon's poker game.

Bussard did not allow Tessic a moment alone with Dillon. This was all right, because although he didn't have an ace to play against Dillon, he had several to play against Bussard.

A half mile from the plant's outer gate, the bells above the door of Bobby's Eat-N-Greet jangled their merry tune as Tessic entered. The waitress, who was jabbering with some locals in a far booth, didn't notice, but Bobby did. He stiffened as he always did when he saw Tessic, but this time, he came practically bounding over the counter like a man half his age to greet him.

"Such enthusiasm," Tessic said, "for the man who practically stole your prize recipe!"

"My granddaughter's with her mother at Princeton, already looking for an apartment," Bobby said. "I can't tell you how much your generosity—"

Tessic put up his hand, cutting him off. "I was hardly generous. I paid you half of what I felt that recipe was worth to me, so there! You can now call me a stingy bastard."

Bobby laughed. "If there's ever anything I can do for you— anything at all . . ."

Tessic nodded, and put a hand on Bobby's shoulder, leading him to the counter. "First a piece of pie," he said. "Then we'll talk about what you might do for me. . . ."

Half an hour later, Tessic returned to the plant, his private summit meeting with the grateful restaurateur unobserved. Although Bussard had the guards keep track of Tessic's comings and goings—his trips to the Eat-N-Greet never made the slightest blip on Bussard's radar.

· · ·

MADDY AND DILLON HAD been talking about Lourdes, the only surviving shard who was completely unaccounted for. "I don't think things are right with her," Dillon had told Maddy. "I can feel her out there, and it scares me."

It was just the kind of thing Maddy would want to listen to—to help her understand the strange relationship Dillon had with these other powerful spirits, but she found her thoughts elsewhere. It had only been one day since her so-called birthday present. That night, for the first time in years, she had found her sleep untroubled, and woke with the enthusiasm of a child on her way to camp. The acuity of her thinking the night before had not been her imagination. Now her idle thoughts that had always seemed filtered and astigmatic had a clarity so pronounced she could almost hear herself think—and could almost see the images those thoughts evoked. She found herself hyper-focused to distraction. If this lucidity was Dillon's gift to her, it would take some getting used to.

When Elon Tessic entered the room unannounced, it pulled her focus so completely the fork flew from her hand.

Although Dillon's chair was facing the other way, he said, "That's not Bussard."

"Good afternoon." Tessic sauntered in as if he owned the place, which wasn't far from the truth.

"I'd smile for the camera," Tessic said, "but unfortunately no one will see it. Some unforeseen glitch in the system has left the control room picking up a local broadcast of *I Love Lucy*. That gives us several minutes of quality time until Bussard finds out and makes his way down here."

Maddy looked down to the second button of her uniform, angling it up so she could see. It gave no indication that the camera hidden there was out, but then there was never any indication that it was on, either.

"I knew exactly where it was," Dillon said. "Why Bussard needs a camera is beyond me; I don't move."

"He'd put a stone under surveillance if he thought it might crack," she said. It occurred to Maddy that this was the first time—perhaps the only time—she'd be able to speak to Dillon out of Bussard's sight . . . and with all her lucidity of mind, she had no idea what to say. So she just fed him another piece of pot roast.

Tessic came up behind Dillon, keeping out of his sight line.

"I'd invite you to join us, Elon, but there are no extra chairs," Dillon said.

Maddy glanced at them both. "You're on a first-name basis with the man who locked you in this chair?"

"I just built it, Lieutenant Haas, I didn't apply it." Tessic moved closer, putting a hand on the head of the metal monstrosity. "And besides, we are kindred spirits, Dillon and I. Oh, perhaps my voltage is not as high—but, like Dillon, I once believed I had a spark within me that could save the world— and now I find myself making weapons of war. Just like Dillon, I don't know if my efforts will, in the end, destroy more than they will save."

Maddy stood and strode to the threshold, glancing out into the containment dome. No one was coming. Good. No doubt the sharpshooters were on their perches, but they had no authority to prevent Tessic from being here. The best they could do was report his presence to Bussard. "Do you plan to make something of this quality time, Mr. Tessic?" she asked. "Or is this just a social visit?"

Tessic only grinned, then ran his hand over the titanium ribs that curved along Dillon's chest. "I'm really proud of this entire restraint system," he said. "You see, given a minute or two Dillon can jiggle himself out of any lock, so I had to create a lock he could not break. It was quite a challenge—the first systems we developed proved useless. Then it came to me; it wasn't a stronger lock we needed, but a key that was never the same twice!"

Tessic became animated as he explained his device, looking more and more like the wunderkind he had once been. "The electromagnetic lock on the chair is linked to the lock on the vault door, which in turn is controlled by a subcutaneous chip we've implanted behind Dillon's ear. The chip changes the combination three times a second, based on randomized algorithms from Dillon's own brain waves." Tessic gave a broad smile. "It was the only way to create truly random numbers, because any normal randomizer would start spitting out chains of consecutive numbers in Dillon's presence."

Maddy glanced at Dillon, who said nothing. "Looks like you win the science fair," she said.

"I always do."

She wondered what Tessic could possibly gain by further demoralizing Dillon with the nuts and bolts of his cage. Then Tessic took a glance toward the open vault door, and sat down on the edge of the bed. "Of course the system's not without its bugs—after all we never had a chance to test it, and daylight saving time never occurred to us."

Now he had caught her interest, and although Dillon didn't as much as flick a finger, she knew he had zeroed in on this as well. "Daylight saving?" Maddy said.

Tessic shook his head, and sighed. "Sadly, the locking mechanism has no protocol for dealing with the extra hour next Sunday. When its internal clock falls sixty minutes back, the vault door just stays stuck on that same electronic combination for the entire hour." And then Tessic smiled. "You would think with all the money the government paid me, I wouldn't make mistakes like that."

Then came the sound of clattering on metal stairs, then the click of feet on concrete. "Bussard!" Maddy said, and took her seat across from Dillon.

Tessic leaned one arm on Dillon's chair, and stood. "Yes, I'd recognize that goose-step anywhere."

Through all of this, Dillon hadn't said a thing—but Maddy could see his eyes. They were full of hope, and focused on her.

Bussard hurried into the room, and double-took on Tessic. "What's this all about?"

Tessic was so smooth, it assuaged the tension. "We were just discussing television viewing habits."

Bussard looked from Tessic, to Dillon, and his gaze settled on Maddy for corroboration. "Lieutenant Haas?"

"It's true, sir," she told him, borrowing some of that semi-gloss that Tessic so smoothly painted on the situation. "Mr. Tessic wanted to know if there were any specific videos Dillon would like added to his library."

"I asked for some Bond flicks," Dillon added. "The Connery ones."

Bussard judged the response, and accepted it with the same reluctance with which he accepted any unverified information. "I see. Lieutenant Haas, I'll have to ask you to cut your meal short today. Elon, I need your help with a technical problem."

Tessic was more than happy to comply. "Your problem is my problem, Dr. No." He turned to Maddy. "Lieutenant, it's been a pleasure, and Dillon, I look forward to our next encounter."

As they made their way across the floor of the containment

dome, Maddy considered what Tessic had said. To keep the information to herself would be an offense worthy of a court martial, or worse.

The sound of the slamming vault door peeled around the dome with the finality of a tomb. Having become so accustomed to Dillon's presence, she could feel the absence of his powerful aura the moment the vault sealed. It was only a moment of void until her senses adjusted to a world without Dillon—but she found that void harder and harder to live with.

12. DREAM LIGHTNING

THE OPEN CLAMSHELL OF DILLON'S CHAIR SAT IN THE COR-ner of his room. He always pushed it there after the vault door had closed, and the chair released him. Sometimes he threw a blanket over the chair, so that he didn't have to look at it, but now he left it unveiled. He wanted to see it now, so that if his nerve began to fail him, he could look upon the chair's wait-ing clamps, and know that death was a better alternative than lingering in this purgatory for one more day.

The TV played an old Bond film, delivered a week after it was requested. Goldfinger was being sucked through the shattered window of his private jet. Not a bad way to go, all else considered. Dillon watched the TV but was only passing time. It was midnight. Hesperia, Michigan, had just rotated its way into Sunday, and in less than two hours, American time would hiccup itself back one hour. An end to daylight savings; the early tidings of winter.

Dillon lay on his bed, trying to focus his thoughts. He was no stranger to slim changes and narrow escapes, but now he had a sense that everything hinged on his actions over the next few hours. Not just his life, but the lives and futures of far more souls than he could ever hope to count. The many psy-chiatrists who had analyzed him would call him delusional, to think that his escape from this place was the fulcrum on which the world hinged. And he would agree with them; after all, a generic label of insanity made perfect logical sense. Except for the fact that it was wrong.

He tried to put his mind through a regimen of drills and contingencies for his escape. He was at a disadvantage, because he did not know the layout of the plant. All he knew was his cell, the cooling tower, and the corridors in between—none of which led to the outside. Even what he did know was limited by the tunnel vision imposed on him by his chair's unyielding face-plate.

He wondered if Elon Tessic truly believed he would escape, or was just curious. Perhaps the rich industrialist was taking wagers on Dillon's escape.

As his thoughts often did in moments of stress, Dillon's mind drifted to Deanna. She was the first of the other shards he had met. They had been a duo, before they became part of a sextet.

Time had not made her death easier, and his love for her had not diminished in the two years since she died. He could still see her expressive Asian eyes. He could still see the sheen of her long black hair. Moonlight on water. He could still feel her dying in his arms. He had no pictures of her beyond these images he held in his mind.

They were fifteen, then—both too young and too damned screwed up to do anything but cling to each other, Dillon thriving on her intense fear of the world, and Deanna thriving on his anger and need for absolution. In the end she had purged herself of her serpent of terror, and had discovered her gift, even before Dillon discovered his.

Her gift had been faith. Nothing so tangible as Dillon's gift of creation, or Lourdes's gift of control. Nothing so utilitarian as Winston's gift of growth, Tory's cleansing aura or Michael's control of nature. Deanna's gift of faith was a simple bridge over fear, but she had died before she could cross that bridge and explore the ramifications.

"Lend me an ounce of your faith, Deanna," Dillon would pray when fear and futility teamed to overwhelm him. *"Just one ounce to get me through this."* He would pray with the intensity with which he had once prayed to God, before his fall from grace. And he prayed now that somehow he would find the faith to bridge the gap between his cell and the outside world.

The film ended. The TV timed itself off, and he was left in the dark to knit the seconds into the minutes for more than an hour, until 2:00 a.m. was finally upon him.

When his digital clock hit the hour, nothing seemed to change. The clock, of course, wouldn't. Like most other clocks, it would need to be reset by hand. He reset the alarm clock back to 1:00, stalling. He listened, but there was nothing beyond the usual soundproofed silence of his cell, where any sound made was made by him. 1:02. He stood, flicked on the light by his bed, and stepped into the dead-end alcove, firmly plugged by the titanium vault door.

Hadn't he broken into a vault once? One of the many things he had done early on, when his powers of order and cohesion had first begun to emerge. It had been a game back then. But breaking into a vault was much different from breaking out of one—especially one as sophisticated as this.

Tessic had said the combination changed three times a second, and with all of Dillon's powers there was no hope of cracking a code that was in constant flux. But if Tessic was right, and the combination was now stuck in one place for a full hour, it leveled the playing field. Still, how could he access the locking mechanism from the inside?

He ran his fingers along the brushed metallic inside surface of the door. It was cold to the touch. He tapped on it with his fingers like a physician palpating a patient's lungs. There was no echo at all, no resonance. This door was too solid to give anything back to him. He pressed his fingertips against the line of the door jamb that was so well sealed, there was barely a line at all. 1:16.

Damn it! What was he expecting himself to do? This wasn't the physics of the Hoover Dam, where he could zero in on a resonant frequency, and use it to rattle the thing apart. This alloy was too well tempered for that. By design it had no resonant frequency that could destabilize it.

Will this door be foiled by virtue of what I am . . . or by what I do?

He had an understanding of his power now—as much as a human mind could understand such things. His power was a dance between *being* and *doing*. His mere presence had a profound effect on the world around him, but he could also use his power like a tool, actually molding it to his will. Opening a lock was a little bit of both. He could actively push his mind into the mechanism, and feel the pattern of movements that would open it, but more often than not, the lock would pop open even before he was finished, his presence greasing the mechanism into alignment. The military didn't care about the things Dillon actively willed. His will was a variable. But his passive presence was a constant.

Combinations. Codes. Random numbers. A series of symbols.

Who knew how many numbers were in the combination? Even if he could focus his mind and divine each number in its proper order, what good would it do him on the inside?

1:28. He kicked the door in frustration, and succeeded only in stubbing his toe. He rubbed his toe through his sock, feeling the minutes tick away. In another half hour the combination would start changing again. Then what? More unconscious trips to the tower. More stilted, scrutinized meals with Maddy. He had seen in Maddy's eyes that she wanted him to escape, even if she didn't dare speak it. He didn't want to see her eyes in the morning if he failed. He would be humiliated that he had not risen to Tessic's challenge.

Random numbers . . . a string of random numbers . . .

But they weren't really numbers at all, were they? Combination locks were mere mechanical devices; casters and bearings rolling within a preordained mechanical maze. The eye saw the numbers on the dial, but the lock saw only the movement of the maze as the dial turned. When Dillon picked such locks, he didn't look at the numbers. He reached his mind into the mechanical maze, solving it from the inside out, and when the bolts sprung, he never looked to see what the combination had been.

This lock was very much the same—but the mechanical casters had been replaced by electronic ones; binary charges layered upon one another, negative and positive creating a digital encryption matrix. That meant that the solution could not be mechanical. No pushing or pulling, or stroking or tapping would bring the casters into position.

The solution has to be electrical.

When the answer came to him, he laughed aloud at its simplicity . . . but then why should simplicity surprise him? He had once cast a stone that begat an avalanche on the slopes of Lake Tahoe. He had whispered into a single ear, and detonated the sanity of an entire town. He had touched a spot of flesh, and seen the wave of healing spread out from a single point of contact. Perfect simplicity of action had always been the hallmark of his power; it only followed that his escape from an electronic prison could only begin with the simplest of electronic phenomena.

Dillon paced the room faster, moving his sock-feet along the dry carpet. Like much of the room, the carpet was plush for his comfort—a gilded cage for their golden boy.

He recalled how, when he was a child, his father had once amused him by rubbing a balloon against his shirt, and sticking it to the wall. His mother had a trick, too. She would take Dillon to the laundry room, and turn off the light, then pull the sheets from the dryer. They clung to one another, and as they pulled them apart, lightning would flash in the ripples of the linens. "Dream lightning," his mother called it. "It fills the sheets and sparks your dreams."

1:39. He shuffled his feet like a boxer, building the charge, then approached the vault door, slowly extending his index finger toward the jamb.

Open sesame.

Even before his finger touched the door, static sparked from his fingertip—a healthy shock—but he could feel that this was not a random static blast. It was controlled, and prolonged, as if the gap between his finger and the door was just another synapse, and the lock was simply another appendage to flex.

In that protracted instant he could actually feel the mechanism as a part of himself, the gears, the deadbolts—but more than that, he could feel the pattern of the digital combination within the shock pulsing through his fingertip. The sensation was automatic, but what he did with that sensation was an act of will. In the instant it took for the static to discharge from his finger, he shaped it to match the series of charges of the digital combination, and by the time his hand flinched back from the shock, the job had been done. The most sophisticated security system in the world had just been undone by a carpet shock.

The mechanism engaged, and the triplet of huge deadbolts began to pull back. An alarm sounded immediately, no doubt reaching to the far corners of the plant. In any normal plant, it would be the panic signal of a meltdown.

But the blare of the alarm was nothing compared to the blast of perception that flooded Dillon as the door began to swing its long arc to the open position. It was the same wave of awareness that sent him into convulsions when he had been confined to his chair. But now, instead of clogging his mind, it activated it—galvanizing him beyond a mere adrenaline rush, filling him with determination. If he could not have Deanna's faith, he thought, at least he had the brute force of his will, and perhaps that would be enough. He peeled off his socks, and without even glancing back to say a final farewell to his cell, he squeezed through the widening slit of the opening door, and into the expanse of the containment dome.

With the alarm mounting into a ghastly echo in the great stone chamber, Dillon cut a jagged, serpentine path toward Corridor A—the only corridor he knew. His zigs and darts were perfectly choreographed to defeat the efforts of the sharpshooters stationed on the catwalks above. He heard the crack of one rifle, then another. Were they ordered to kill him, he wondered, or just to disable him? The bullets nicked the ground, setting off coughs of concrete dust just a few feet away. Then, as he lunged for the closed door of Corridor A, one of the shots hit the mark. It caught Dillon behind the right knee, and its exit blew his kneecap to shreds.

He collapsed in excruciating pain, and almost succumbed to it—but he told himself not to look, not to consider the damage, because the moment he did, it would be over. He could not give up—he would either escape, or die trying; there could be no in between. So he reached his hand up, and grabbed on to the knob of the locked door to Corridor A, hoping the sharpshooters would hesitate, seeing he was wounded. They would assess before firing again, and that moment of assessment would give Dillon the advantage.

The door to Corridor A had a simple mechanical lock. He focused his will, forcing it into the keyhole, jiggling the knob with his hand, with just the proper torque and rhythm to make the mechanism spring. Then his leg took a second shot; this one in his calf, just beneath his shattered knee. He screamed, but let the sound of his own pain fill him like a war cry. He turned the knob, and fell forward into the corridor, pulling himself along by his hands until he was out of the sharpshooters' sights.

"Face down! Now!" a voice screamed right beside him. It was the Corridor A guard, who held his pistol at point-blank range, aimed at Dillon's head. If the other guards were instructed to merely take Dillon down, this one was definitely planning on taking him out.

"I *am* face down," said Dillon, pushing himself up on his hands.

"You know what I mean."

He put his boot on Dillon's back, pushing him into a prone position, cheek against the concrete floor. Dillon took a deep breath. There was a trail of blood to the door behind him, but the blood had stopped flowing. The sharp pain of his wounds was already beginning to subside.

Dillon pushed himself up again, defying the guard's direct order, then turned to him, catching his gaze. There was not enough time to unlock the guard's mind and find the perfect thing to say that would make him lower the weapon, so Dillon played a dangerous angle.

"If you shoot me, the gun will backfire," he told the guard with calculated calmness, "and the blast will blind you."

"Don't move!" shouted the guard. "I'm warning you!"

"A piece of shrapnel will wedge in your temporal lobe," Dillon continued. "You'll lose the ability to speak. To read. To communicate."

The guard's finger was still firm on the trigger, but his hand was shaking the slightest bit.

"Your misery will be so great that in three years you will take your own life," Dillon told him. "If you pull that trigger—"

Dillon's leg still ached, but he knew his ruse would only sustain him another moment, so he bolted upright, and ran down the corridor. His healing power that had done so much for so many, had already pulled enough of his bone and cartilage back together so that he could limp away, his pain still intense, but bearable—but if this guard shot, there would be no mending. Dillon knew a blast to the heart or brain would kill him before he had the chance to heal.

He didn't look back to see what the guard would do, instead he just impelled himself forward. Only when he turned into a side corridor did he know his ploy had worked. It was a bluff, of course. Nothing he had said to the guard was true, but it had the semblance of a prophesy, and coming from Dillon Cole, even the most disciplined of soldiers would have paused for thought. For once, his celebrity had saved him.

The corridors he traveled through had no windows—no hint of any connection to a world beyond the plant, and the sound of the alarm kept him from hearing any approaching guards. His only advantage was the skeletal nature of Bussard's crew. It had served the general well while Dillon was imprisoned but had no contingency for the complete breakdown of the security system. It was a big plant, and as long as he kept out of the visual arc of the videocams mounted on the ceiling, they couldn't pinpoint his position.

He burst through a double door, hoping it led to the outside, but instead found himself in the empty cafeteria. It was an open space, and open spaces weren't good . . . but on the other hand, kitchens usually had service entrances. He leapt over the service counter, knocking several metal pans to the ground, and although he heard someone banging through the cafeteria doors behind him, he didn't wait to see who, or how many of them there were. A cold draft flowed past his ankles, and, following the direction of the draft, he located the kitchen's back door. He pushed his way through it, and found himself standing on a loading dock, in freezing rain.

He took an instant to get his bearings, and see the best route of escape. The entire plant was flooded in spotlights, and everything beyond those bright lights was darkness. He heard a crack of lightning, then realized it wasn't lightning at all—because he felt a sudden pain in his gut, and warm blood began to pulse from his abdomen. He turned as the second shot pierced him, higher this time. The right side of his chest. Unable to bear the pain, his legs gave out, and he crumbled to the wet ground. *It's Bussard*, thought Dillon. *It has to be Bussard.* But as he looked up, it was a far more familiar figure standing over him with a smoking weapon. Dillon felt betrayed. And for a moment his despair almost overwhelmed the pain.

Lieutenant Madeline Haas had spent a restless night, waiting for the alarms to go off. She knew they would. She didn't know what she would do, but she knew it would be something decisive: Either something that would mark her for a promotion, or mark her for disgrace, but she wasn't sure which it would be.

She left her room even before the alarms went off, not willing to wait, and stood by the entrance to the sleeping quarters, beneath an overhang that protected her from the downpour. When the alarms when off, she was the first one out, circling the plant, eyeing the exits. There were six exits from the main building of the plant. Three of them led to the underground utility accessways that didn't connect to the containment corridors at all, so Dillon would not come out of those doors. Two exits were in the main office wing, where Bussard's office and quarters were. It was one of the best patrolled areas of the plant, so if Dillon went in that direction, he would be brought down in an instant. That left the loading dock as the only true chance of escape that Dillon had.

She rounded the path to the dock, and stood behind a Dumpster, waiting, hearing others approaching. That's when Dillon burst through onto the dock, slipping on the wet ground. The loading dock was like a shooting gallery. Even in the blinding rain he was an easy target beneath the floodlights.

What Maddy did next was a split-second decision, that might never have come to her had Dillon not already cleared her mind and brought her thoughts into fine focus. With other officers approaching behind her she raised her gun and fired, then fired again. Her aim was precise, as she knew it would be, and Dillon collapsed to the ground.

She ran to him. Blood was everywhere, pulsing into the flooded pavement, mixing with the rain, and spilling over the edge of the loading dock. Dillon tried to speak, but Maddy leaned down to him, holding her weapon to his face.

"Quiet," she demanded.

He gasped his breaths, but Maddy ignored him. Her duty was clear, and her purpose justified. She could not be sidetracked.

"I've shot your right lung, and your left kidney," she told him. "Maybe your spleen and liver, too. Most people would die from it, but you're not most people. Do you understand?"

He moved his jaw, but no sound came out.

"How badly do you want to get out of here?"

Still no words, but this time Dillon nodded. *Do whatever is necessary*, it communicated. *Do what it takes*. And so she did. Before anyone else reached the loading dock, she put the gun against his cheek, pulled the trigger, and blew apart Dillon's face.

BUSSARD'S CAREER FLASHED BEFORE his eyes. The moment he was jarred awake by the alarm, and made aware of the nature of the emergency, he knew it was either him, or Dillon. If Dillon escaped, Bussard had enough enemies in the Pentagon to send his career down in flames. After thirty years of struggling to get where he was, he was not going to let himself get shot down. His superiors feared Dillon—and that was an asset in this situation. They saw Dillon as an armed warhead—too useful to destroy, but dangerous to maintain. Dillon's death would be unfortunate, but his escape would be catastrophic. The Pentagon would rather see him dead than on the loose, and there might even be a collective sigh of relief on word of Dillon's death.

With his own gun drawn he fired orders left and right, making it brutally clear that if they could not catch Dillon, then they must kill him. When word came that Dillon was in the cafeteria, Bussard led the way, and he followed the sound of gunfire through the kitchen to the loading dock.

Shielding his eyes from the spotlights and rain, he found Haas kneeling over a blood-drenched body. Dillon. She held her hand to Dillon's neck, feeling for a pulse.

"He's dead, sir," Haas said.

Bussard tried to hide his own sigh of relief at the news. "Are you sure?"

"He turned as I shot, sir. He took a blast in the face, leaving a pretty big exit wound in the back of his head. Would you like to see?"

Bussard looked down at the pulp of Dillon's face. His nose, and cheek had been shredded. Blood covered his chest and abdomen as well. Although Bussard was no stranger to gore, he had no burning desire to see Dillon Cole's splattered brains either. Besides, he was already contemplating the report he would file.

MADDY KEPT A CLOSE eye on Bussard through all of this. She watched his eyes linger on Dillon's inert form for a brief moment, but as soon as Bussard's men began to arrive on the scene, Bussard began to delegate duties, refusing to give even a moment of respect to the passing of Dillon Cole.

"Haslovich, get to the control room, and shut off that damn alarm. Haas and Burns, get the body to the infirmary. Johanson, clean this mess." And the rest he sent back to their quarters. "Show's over."

The contingent of officers began to break up, but Bussard didn't seem in a hurry to leave. "Shouldn't you get on the line to General Harwood, sir?" Maddy prodded.

Bussard sighed. He took one more glance toward Dillon, then nodded to Maddy. "You did the right thing, Haas. He couldn't be allowed to escape." And then he added, "You're twice the officer I expected you to be. When this fiasco is over, assuming we still have careers, I hope I'll have the privilege of having you under my command again."

"Thank you, sir."

He pushed his way past Burns and Johanson, who were still tending to the body, and into the plant.

Once he was gone, Burns turned to Maddy. "Who was this guy anyway?"

Well, thought Maddy, if nothing else, Bussard had been successful at keeping the majority of his officers in the dark.

"Nobody anymore," she told him. "Tell you what—why don't you two bring the gurney, and I'll wait with the stiff."

"Okay by me," Johanson said and left with Burns, both probably happier to be out of the rain than away from the body.

As soon as they were through the door and out of earshot, Maddy got to work.

"Dillon? Dillon, can you hear me?"

No response. She put her fingers to his neck. She had lied to Bussard, of course, about the pulse—she had felt a weak pulse a minute before, but she could not feel it now. Her own heart was pounding so furiously it defeated any attempt to feel Dillon's. The blood had stopped flowing from his wounds. That either meant he was dead, or that he had begun his miraculous healing process. She had to believe he was still alive—and that the bullet had cut cleanly through his jaw and nasal cavity without splintering any bone back toward his brain. She had to believe it because she could not live with the alternative.

An Army-issue delivery truck was parked twenty yards away. It was the only port in the storm, and the closest thing to a plan she had at the moment. She hauled Dillon onto her shoulders and climbed down from the loading dock, splashing her way toward the truck.

The passenger door was locked, so she put Dillon down, and rammed her fist through the window. It hurt more than she expected it to. She undid the lock, pulled open the door, and when she turned to Dillon she was surprised to see him struggling to his feet, climbing into the truck under his own power. Seeing him alive lifted a huge weight from her. She even thought she could make out some features of his ruined face. He was already bringing order out of the chaos, undoing his wounds.

"Hey, Haas—what the hell?"

It was Burns. He and Johanson were out on the loading dock with the gurney. She thanked God that these officers were not too quick on the uptake, and tried to play on their dim awareness. "Change of plans," she shouted back to them. "Bussard will explain it to you."

But no sooner had she said it than Bussard came out onto the dock behind them, his BS detector finally kicking in. It only took an instant for him to size up the situation.

"Haas!"

She jumped in the passenger door, forcing her way over Dillon to the driver's seat. How long would it take to hot-wire a truck? Too long—Bussard was already on his way, sprinting the distance from the loading dock, with Burns and Johanson close behind.

While she fiddled with wires beneath the steering column, it was Dillon who had the presence of mind to grab her weapon and fire, blowing off the ignition completely. With the ignition gone, all it would take was a screw driver to start it, but there was nothing in the glove box but maps and gum wrappers.

Bussard jumped up on the running board, grabbing Dillon through the window. "You son of a bitch!"

And then Dillon did something strange. He turned to Bussard, and spoke. His voice was a garbled mess, his lips barely able to form words, but from the instant he began to speak, Bussard was transfixed. It only took a moment for Dillon to say his piece, but for that moment even the raindrops seemed suspended in air.

"She was dead before the fire," Dillon hissed at Bussard. *"You suffocated her."* Then Dillon leaned closer to Bussard and delivered his final line with a guttural growl of enmity:

"You suffocated her . . . and they knew."

Something snapped. Something detonated with such force, Maddy could feel the shockwave pass through her in a single migraine pulse that made her hair stand on end. And suddenly Bussard didn't look right. His eyes were wrong—mismatched. One pupil was open and dilated, the other closed to a pin prick. He fell from the running board onto Burns and Johanson, screaming, flailing his arms, tearing at his own scalp. Dillon slumped down, completely spent. Maddy frantically searched the cab for anything flat that could fit into the open sore of the broken ignition, and, finding nothing, she tore the mirror down from the visor, broke it against the dashboard, and jammed the largest sliver into the ignition. She cut her thumb and forefinger as she turned the jagged shard of glass, but the engine started. With Bussard still wailing, she tugged the shift into gear, sideswiped Burns who was trying to block her, and took off toward the electrified gate, her wounded right hand already on the mend, tingling in its point-blank proximity to Dillon.

In the commotion only one guard had the wherewithal to find a jeep, and take off in pursuit of the truck that crashed its way through the electrified gate. He was able to keep the truck's taillights in his sights, but a half mile past the gate, a pickup came barreling through an intersection near Bobby's Eat-N-Greet, sending the jeep spinning off the road into a muddy ditch. An old man stepped from the ruined pickup, gripping what was most certainly a broken arm, angrily spouting about stop signs, and damned crazy-ass military driving. Meanwhile the vehicle the guard was pursuing had quickly sped out of sight.

So dazed was the security officer that he never stopped to

wonder what a seventy-year-old man was doing rolling across this particular intersection at this ungodly time of night.

It was almost too much for Dillon's system to take.

The massive loss of blood, the violent rending of his sinus cavity. Maddy's final bullet had entered through his left cheek, and exited through his right, shattering his teeth and jaw in between. The effect had been bloody, and destructive enough to make Bussard believe the bullet had entered his brain. But apparently Maddy knew her anatomy, and the only injury to Dillon's brain was the concussion from the blast. The bullet never came close. He understood now that there was no other course of action that would save him. No other place she could shoot would have fooled Bussard—but these awful wounds were not like any wounds he had ever suffered. His experience had been with gashes that zipped themselves closed in a matter of seconds and broken bones that set themselves in a matter of minutes. But the shock to his organs and nervous system was too great for even his reparative spirit to remedy. Healing would take hours, maybe days, if he could reconstruct his body at all.

Crumpled in the passenger seat of the delivery truck, he slipped in and out of consciousness, feeling every lane change, every bump in the road like a fresh wound. The rain pelted the windshield and he couldn't tell the beat of his heart from the beat of the wiper blades. Were they being closely pursued, or had they left so much confusion in their wake that they were able to get a sizeable head start? He had no idea. The outside world was still screaming at him, as it had from the moment he stepped out of his cell, but his own dopamine release drugged him into not caring.

"You'll be all right, won't you?" he heard Maddy ask.

"Your face is looking better already, isn't it?" She sounded so uncertain. She wanted some corroboration from him that she hadn't gone too far. It hurt too much to move his jaw, so he reached over and squeezed her hand. *She did what she had to do,* Dillon thought. Any more, he would have died on the spot, any less, and Bussard would not have been duped. A trapped animal would gnaw off its foot to escape from the jaws of a spring-trap. This is what Maddy had done for him, and sacrificed her career to do it.

Some time later, he was dimly aware of being moved through the rain from the truck to another car that Maddy must have hot-wired. Then, once they were moving again, Dillon allowed himself to let go of his shaky grip on consciousness, not knowing whether it was death or sleep that pulled him down.

WHAT DID HE DO TO ME what did he do to me what did he do to me what did he—

Bussard had heard the gate fall as Maddy crashed through it in the truck, and a moment later he had heard her break through the outer gate as well. But that didn't matter. Nothing mattered now, because of what Dillon had made him understand.

They knew.

He pushed his way past his men, hurling them off as they tried to calm him. It all seemed part of a different reality. A lost reality. Now everything moved in fractured frames. Out of sequence. Out of step.

He is four years old. He holds a pillow in his hands.

From the rain into the gray chambers of the power plant. The kitchen. The cafeteria.

While his parents are out, and the babysitter sleeps, he carries a pillow to his sister's room.

Stumbling through the halls of the plant, barely able to remember his way.

He carries a pillow to his sister's room. A white crib. Pastel rabbits on the wall. Sweet smell of baby lotion. He can't do it from the floor. He must climb into the crib with the baby.

Corridor A. Blood pooling at the end of Corridor A. The guard turning to him, looking at him with frightened concern. "Sir? Are you all right?"

A pillow in his hand. She is asleep. It's easier this way. The baby struggles weakly, like the goldfish did on the floor, until the pillow wins, and she goes away to the angels.

Raising his gun, silencing the guard with a single shot. More blood on the floor of Corridor A.

Gone to the angels, but his parents might know. They might smell it on his pillow. They might see it in the eyes of her stuffed animals. He must make it all go away. And he knows where Daddy keeps the matches.

Moving through the containment dome. His footsteps echoing in the huge space. Ahead of him the giant concrete cube, and a vault door. An open vault door.

He watches with the babysitter from the lawn as the house goes up in flames.

An empty vault, and an open vault door.

His parents tell him it's okay. That everything will be okay . . . except for the fact that Dillon is right. His parents know. Why should that matter? It should no longer matter. But it does. It's the only thing that matters. They know.

The vault door, and to the right, the door's control panel.

They know when they send me off to school.

Reaching for the control panel.

They know on Christmas morning.

Beginning the closing sequence.

They know when they tuck me in.

Gears grinding, the door moving.

They know from their graves, beside hers these many years, and they will always know.

Solid titanium cutting a slow arc behind him.

So I will kneel for forgiveness.

Kneeling in the path of the closing door.

I will bow my head.

Head hung low in the jamb, the door only inches away now.

I will press this memory out from me.

The door becomes a vise; his skull engages; the pressure builds. . . .

I will smash this guilt away leaving my flesh as fractured as my mind.

And the bone finally gives, Bussard's last thought crushed from him by the sealing door, his blood greasing the shafts of the deadbolts.

13. RESTORATION

DILLON WAS DREAMING.

He was dreaming the way he dreamt when they sedated him, for although the sedatives could control his body, they could not shut down his mind. Once again his mind was violated by images that had no business there. The bruise-colored recliner.

The man had long since left his recliner, and was out in the world, but his chair remained. The image wasn't a dream unto itself—but instead infected whatever dream he was having. The chair would be there, sitting on the divider of a freeway, or out in an empty field, or at the bottom of the sea. Wherever his dreams took him, that chair would follow, and the conspicuous absence of its occupant disturbed Dillon more than anything else. There were times Dillon could see him in the distance, at the edge of the horizon, or the other side of a chasm that Dillon could not cross.

And then there was the diving platform, infecting his thoughts and his dreams with the same alarming frequency. Unlike the man who had left his chair, the three divers were still there, waiting on the platform. But he knew that sometime soon they would be gone, just as the man had left his chair.

Today he dreamed that the platform was in the sky. Oily wooden piles encrusted with barnacles sprouted from its base, holding it above roiling cumulus, like a pier in a sea of clouds. There was something new today; the three figures held fishing rods. They speared worms on the tips of their barbed hooks, and cast their lines into the clouds. He tried to see their faces, but they kept their backs to him.

"Why am I here?" he asked them. "What am I supposed to do?"

"Pray," answered the smallest of the three. "Pray like a pigeon."

Then the small one's line went taut, and he jerked on it, pulling a bird from the clouds below. He ripped the pigeon from the hook, and dropped it, dead, to the floor. Only then did Dillon notice that the platform had turned a mottled gray. It was covered with the bodies of birds. Pigeons. Thousands of them, pressed flat beneath the march of thousands of feet. Suddenly the air was too thin, and Dillon had to gasp for breath. And as he fell to his knees he heard a new voice. An ominously familiar voice; neither male, nor female.

"You're so pathetically limited," the voice said. "You see everything, and yet you see nothing. You disgust me."

Dillon rolled over onto his back, still unable to breath. This was a voice he hoped he would never hear again. "Okoya! No! Not Okoya!"

He began to scream, over and over, until the scream broke free from the dream, and took root in his throat. He could hear it now, and the sound of his own scream dragged him out of sleep. Hands pressed on his shoulders, holding him down.

"Easy, easy!"

He opened his eyes to see Maddy looming over him. Above her head hung a gathering of lobsters.

"You were dreaming," Maddy told him.

He closed his eyes again. "I still am," but when he opened his eyes, the crustacean menaces were still there. Large red claws—hundreds of them hung from above. They were nailed to the posts, they were crawling on peeling wallpaper. They were almost as unpleasant as the pigeons. "Where are we?"

"Somewhere between nowhere and nowhere else," she said. "State Route 93. I forget which state. Arkansas, I think."

Dillon sat up.

They were in a restaurant, or what was left of one. The place had been deserted for years. Lakes of rainwater had formed on the warped linoleum floor, beneath holes in a termite-tattered ceiling. The smell of mildew saturated the air with such intensity, Dillon could taste it like aspirin in the back of his throat. Although the rainstorm had ended, droplets still trickled through holes in the roof, plinking an irregular rhythm in the puddles below.

"Welcome to 'The Crawfish Maw,'" Maddy said. "The sign said 'always open,' so here we are."

She was dressed in dark sweats—probably the same clothes she was wearing when she shot him and spirited him away from the Hesperia plant, but he had been too busy convalescing to notice what she wore. Having never seen her in anything but her uniform, it struck him how much younger she looked.

The humidity was thick enough to swim in, and his own clothes clung to him, pulling in the moisture from the air with the same voracity with which it had drunk the blood from his body. Now the blood had dried, and the holes in his shirt had woven themselves closed. There was no evidence on his body of the wounds. The pain in his knee and gut was gone, and the wound to his chest had closed, resolving into a faint ache when he breathed too deeply. But his face didn't feel right. It felt as if a spider had woven its web across his nose.

Maddy touched his shirt, where the wound had been. "I've never seen anything so amazing," she said. "The wounds closed themselves while you slept."

"How long was I out?"

"About twelve hours. I didn't know where you wanted to go, and until we got that straight, I thought it best to find a place to lay low, so Bussard won't find us."

Dillon stood up and looked out of a foggy window. Beyond some overgrown trees, he could see cars passing on the highway. "Bussard's not a problem anymore."

Maddy hesitated, but didn't ask how Dillon could be so sure. She just accepted it. "Still, they're not going to let you disappear."

"I'm no stranger to being a fugitive." Dillon threw her a grin, but found that one side of his mouth didn't quite rise to the occasion. He reached up to touch his face, and felt a jagged network of troughs and crags in his skin.

"The scars will go away soon, too, won't they?" Maddy asked.

Dillon didn't answer her. "This place have a bathroom?"

She pointed him to a cramped little washroom that had long since lost its door. "I promise I won't look."

"Your loss," he said, then immediately regretted it. He was not beyond blushing, and so he left before she could see.

The toilet was dry and ringed in filthy strata. He relieved himself in the dry bowl, then turned to view himself in the mirror above the sink. He wasn't quite ready for what he saw.

Deep canals cut across his face. The web of knotty scars that wove across his cheeks and nose was even worse than he had imagined. He hardly recognized himself, and had to take a few deep breaths to get over the shock of his new appearance. When he touched his face, there was no tenderness to the flesh, only stiffness, which meant there was no more healing going on there—whatever healing there would be had happened while he slept. He ran his tongue on the inside of his mouth and poked at his teeth. Several of his molars were missing. The raw holes had healed over, as if the teeth had been pulled long ago.

Maddy appeared behind him. "How long till they're gone?" she asked. "The scars, I mean."

He took a moment to consider how he should answer, then decided on the simple truth. "The scars won't go away," he told her.

She shook her head, not getting it. "But . . . you heal . . ."

"That's different from regenerating. If you give me a broken glass, I can put it back together again without a crack, but if a piece of that glass is missing, the glass will have a hole where that piece would have gone."

The color of her face took a turn toward green. "So you're telling me that I left . . . part of you . . . back on the loading dock?"

"Couldn't be helped, I guess."

Her eyes turned away, suddenly looking everywhere, except at Dillon. "Listen, I think there's some food in the store room," she said. "Old cans of beans, tuna—you know, stuff that'll survive the next ice age. I'll check it out." She couldn't move away from him fast enough.

Maddy had watched Dillon as he slept, marveling at the power he had to undo the damage to his flesh. The wounds on his face sewed themselves closed at a speed just below her ability to see it—like shadows beneath a slowly arcing sun—but if she looked away for a few moments, his face would be different when she looked back. Seeing his miraculous healing made her believe he could do anything, and deep inside her, in a place that knew no reason, she was beginning to believe that Dillon was, indeed, a new incarnation of God, as so many in the world now believed.

But he could not be, because by his own admission, his scars would not heal. It was a relief to know that he was less than perfect, because it made him human, and yet a profound disappointment as well. But far more disturbing to Maddy was the strained, crooked smile her bullet had left him. She had singlehandedly maimed the closest thing to God on earth.

So she turned from him, unable to face him in that

ridiculous, lobster-ridden wreck of a diner. When she reached the storeroom, she only wished the room had a door that would close behind her, but like most every other door, its hinge was broken, and the door sloped at a lazy angle to the floor. She tried to busy herself with the rusting cans of food. Jalapeños, tomato paste—whatever vagrants hadn't already scavenged. That was all right. She hadn't come here for the food anyway. She fought back an unwanted barrage of tears by getting angry at herself for such an emotional display, but this time the anger was no barrier. She had always been aware of that vague sense of inadequacy that had been subtly instilled in her long before she could build a defense against it. She liked to think she had triumphed, finding inadequacy to be one of the best motivators toward overachievement. Most of the time her bold accomplishments were more than enough to fill her cup.

Dillon sidled up cautiously on the other side of the door, peering in. She saw him through the corner of her eye, but wouldn't turn to face him.

"Guess I was wrong," she said, moving the cans purposelessly on the shelves in an aluminum shell game. "Nothing here but junk."

Dillon looked at the unbalanced door; he hefted it a bit, and the broken hinge rehooked itself to the frame. Abracadabra. Then, when Maddy looked once more to the cans on the shelf, they were no longer rusty. "Guess you're getting your strength back," she said. Her hand was shaking now, and when she reached for the cans, she knocked several of them over; they fell onto her toes.

Dillon swung the door open all the way. It didn't even squeak. "Maddy, don't worry about my face. You didn't know."

"I disfigured you. I tried to save you and I permanently disfigured you." She finally turned to him, knowing it was useless to hide the tears, because he saw through her anyway; it's what he did—and no matter how deeply he had reached into her to change her, he couldn't change how she felt in his shadow. Now she understood why men like Bussard had to chain him, lock him down, suppress him. They simply could not bear their own insignificance in his shadow.

"You did what you had to do," he told her. "I understand."

But it wasn't just the scars. "I'm in over my head here," she admitted.

"Weren't you trained to deal with extreme situations?"

"Not this extreme! Not with something like you!"

"Some*thing*?" She could feel his anger and frustration, and although her own frustration felt normal and justified, she was not expecting his. "I'm the same person I was when you spoon-fed me!"

"But *I'm* not. Back then I was taking orders—doing my job."

"And now you're a human being."

He stared her down, and it took all of her strength to pull away from that gaze. Yes, she was now more human than she had ever been and that made her more vulnerable. She wondered if she'd even be here now if Dillon hadn't violated her soul the way he had; seeing through her. Knowing her. "Damn you, Dillon, I didn't need your little 'birthday gift'! I enjoyed being clouded just fine."

Dillon gave her his new crooked grin. "Looks like you're still partly cloudy."

She stormed past him, but he grabbed her wrist. "Let go."

"Let me show you something." His voice was no longer angry. What frustration he felt had dissipated—brought back into order, like everything else. Still holding her wrist, he reached up his other hand, gently touching her cheek with his index finger. When he pulled his index finger away, one of her tear drops pooled on his nail.

"What about it?"

"Shh. Watch."

His hushed tone made her feel like a child watching a butterfly break from its cocoon. So she watched, as crystals formed in the tear droplet, settling into his cuticle. Then he tilted his finger. The drop coursed across to the other side, leaving the tiny crystals of salt behind. Then he brought his finger to her lips. Almost reflexively she took the very tip of his finger in her mouth, tasting her own tear. Sweet. Not the slightest hint of salt. "There," he said, smiling gently. "I've taken the bitterness from your tears." Now that they were this close, Maddy couldn't help but see that in spite of the scars, his eyes were unchanged. His was the soul of a star, and indeed, she could see a universe when she gazed inside. A person could get lost in there.

"Do you know what it's like for people around you, Dillon? Do you know what it's like to feel so powerless and insignificant?"

"No," he answered. "I wish that I could."

She couldn't turn away from him now, and didn't know whether this locked gaze was his doing, or her own. All that she knew was that in this single moment, the insignificance he engendered in her was now more a comfort than a threat.

Time seemed to skip a beat, and she found herself kissing him, not remembering the kiss beginning, and not knowing who had instigated it. If this was another attempt to clarify her thoughts, it did the opposite, fogging her in, leaving her thoughts in a holding pattern, waiting for a place to land.

Dillon seemed even more flustered than she. Clearly, this had not been part of his plan. Even if this was a moment he could foresee, it was obviously something he was unprepared for. And she found to her unexpected delight, that the great Dillon Cole, in spite of his luminous spirit, was blushing.

"I'm sorry," he said. "That was stupid. I'm sorry."

"Don't be," she told him gently. "Feel as stupid as you want." In spite of all the darkness he had lived through—all the destruction he had willingly, and unwillingly, been a party to, there was still an innocence about him that rose above any guilt. The fact that she could offer him anything made her feel elevated. Ennobled. She brought her hand up, her fingertips tracing the pattern of the pale scars in his reddening face.

For Dillon, who had experienced a great many things in his life, this was a first. He had to admit he had considered this moment, but in a distant, disconnected way. The rigors of his past travels were more than adequate to suppress any appetites, and Tessic's chair, well, it was quite a chastity belt to say the least.

Maddy ran her fingers along the new ridges in his face, and he found it curiously erotic—and now he found his own hands moving to places—touching places he had never been close to before.

"I have to warn you that I have no idea what I'm doing," he told her.

"I think I'd be disappointed if you did."

He was awkward as he guided her to an oversized booth, the table scraping on the floor as his shoulders bumped it aside. He chuckled nervously. Then moved his hand through her hair. Although her hair was short, it had a thick, rich texture. With the caress of his fingers, he hair renewed, taking on a smooth, dark sheen.

Just like Deanna's.

But that was a thought he banished to a distant corner.

Maddy sensed the moment his kisses crossed from respectful to passionate, and it struck her that Dillon *did* know her. It was the first time since her first time that she let a man be the aggressor—and here, this young man moved from awkwardness to grace in a single breath. With his touch, she could feel herself changed by his spirit of creation, of *rejuvenation*. He undid the most soiled knots of her life with his body, and with each wave of sensation she could feel those old bonds tear free.

The sweaty, drunken face of the neighbor man, who had defiled her at thirteen.

The high school teacher she had chosen to seduce.

The scores of boys, then men she had conquered, and dismissed, taking from them, so they could never take anything from her. All her patterns, all her painful connections were smoothed by Dillon's embrace.

They shared a sanctuary from all their troubles in each other's arms, then as their tension released, Maddy saw that the dilapidated restaurant around them had been restored to the spotless moment it had been built. And she realized that, within her heart, the place where it truly mattered, she was a virgin once again.

14. RETURN OF A THIEF

HUNDREDS OF MILES FROM THE CRAWFISH MAW DINER, AT a train station in Atlanta, a small-time pickpocket was having a truly lousy day.

His moves had always been stealthy, and even when caught in the act, he was usually able to slither away with finesse, dissolving into the rush-hour crowds of the Atlanta train station. Those crowds, despite Atlanta's southern belle reputation, were every bit as frenetic these days as crowds in any Yankee burg, and the molecular hustle of bodies always provided ample cover for a quick escape.

The train station was a fine locale for petty larceny. Better than New York, or PA, since there was less competition. He would usually slip past his marks just before they entered their respective trains, relieving them of their wallets and billfolds, and by the time they realized that they had been robbed, their train would already be barreling away from the city.

But today he had gotten greedy. His mark—a waddling, varicose-legged woman, clearly an old-money patrician, complained to the red-cap loading her luggage onto the train, as if the red-cap cared. And there it was: her Gucci clutch, protruding from an oversized coat pocket. It grabbed his focus and reeled him in. He simply had to have it.

Unfortunately this woman was no imbecile. She had learned the trick of wrapping her pocket accessories with a rubber band, and as he pulled on the edge of the clutch, it snagged on the pocket lining, instantly alerting the woman to his presence.

Some of his marks were gaspers, some were screamers. The waddling woman was definitely a screamer. She let loose with an ear-splitting camel call the moment she felt his hand in her pocket. He flinched, and hesitated, which he never normally did, then pushed her away, wrenching the clutch from her pocket.

He tried to slip into the crowd, but found his reflexes had slipped a beat behind the moment, and rather than cutting through the crowds, he crashed into them, each body becoming an obstacle impeding his progress toward the stairs that led to the platform.

"Stop him!" the woman screamed with such aristocratic command that he knew it would galvanize the crowd into that mad mob of outraged citizens that was known to beat and dismember poor innocent criminals like himself.

He kneed a businessman who tried to stop him, and used his crumbling body as a vault onto the steps, taking them three at a time until he was up in the station.

But the open space provided him with no cover either. Two police officers raced toward him, apparently more interested in apprehending him than they were in the Krispy Kreme donut concession.

The pickpocket quickly calculated his most likely vector of escape, and took off. Unfortunately the direction he ran took him deeper into the building, rather than toward an exit. He used the woman's clutch as a countermeasure, hurling it behind him, but the officers ignored it, continuing their pursuit, already pulling out their weapons, probably hoping he had one of his own, so they could plead self-defense when they blew him away.

No, this was not one of his better days.

There were two doors in front of him now. One was unmarked, except for a poster plastered across it advertising a local revival of *Cats*. The other was the ladies' room.

The lady or the tiger, he thought. He chose the lady.

Hurling himself through the restroom door, he pulled from his pocket a wooden doorstop that he kept for occasions such as this, and shoved it beneath the door as it closed, kicking it over and over, until it was wedged in deep. The officers were already on the other side of the door, pounding on it, trying to force their way in, so for good measure the pickpocket kicked the doorknob repeatedly until it tore free, and clattered on the ground like a Christmas ornament. He heard the knob fall on the other side of the door as well.

"Damnit!" he heard from beyond the door. The door bowed inward as the officers threw their weight against it, but it didn't give.

There was a strange taste in his mouth—the ferric tang of blood, and he realized that he had bitten his lip while running from the police. Small injury, all considered. The pickpocket sized up his surroundings. He was alone in the restroom, and although there were no other doors, there was a window above the furthest stall. It was a small, clouded-glass pane, its edges caked in the grime of thirty years of union cleaning. It would be a tight squeeze, but he could make it, hopefully before the boys in blue took down the door.

But as he made his way toward the window there was something in the bathroom mirror that caught his attention. His reflection wasn't right—but it wasn't his reflection, it was the mirror itself. Its surface rippled like a pool of mercury, turning his reflection into a shifting fun-house image.

Then all at once a hand thrust out of the mirror, reaching for him like a cheap gag in a 3-D matinee.

He was a gasper, not a screamer, so he gasped, throwing himself away from the hand, hitting the tile wall behind him.

The mirror had not broken, for it was no longer rigid—it was now more membrane than glass. There was a vertical tear in the surface, only about six inches wide, now stretching wide, creating fleshy folds of silver as a second hand pushed itself through, and a groan came from beyond the breach. He could see a mass of dark stringy hair forcing its way through, stretching this hole in the world even wider.

Now he screamed, instinctively knowing that it was more than his life lying in the balance now, and suddenly the police outside the door became the lesser of two evils. He returned to the door, only to find that he had successfully sealed himself in the room—he couldn't kick the doorstop free, and even if he could have, the doorknob was too damaged to fit back into place.

So he raced toward the window, once more passing the creature that was pushing its way through the mirror. Its head was out now, and one shoulder. Long black hair dangled over a tortured face. It made eye contact with him. It was human but its eyes were wild—almost mad, and those mad eyes held his gaze before returning to its task of birthing itself into this world.

He bolted into the stall, and pounded on the small window until it shattered, then pulled himself up into it, ignoring the cuts across his palms left by the jagged lip of glass. He could hear the thing grunting and groaning behind him. The pickpocket stuck his head out into the dim alley. He reached his hands through, pulled his shoulders through one at a time, praying he could be born into the alley before that thing was born into the restroom.

He had gotten to his hips and was almost free, when he felt the ghoul grab his ankles, and pull him back inside.

"No!"

As he fell, his head struck the pipe that fed the toilet, and although the pain was sharp, he barely noticed it, because his other senses were too overwhelmed to care. The thing grabbing at him was only marginally human. Most of its face was hidden beneath the caul of dark, sodden hair, and its body was covered with mottled, leopard-like bruises. It was naked, and reeked of a fetid, guttery stench, but worst of all was what he saw between its legs. Whatever this creature was, it was neither male, nor female, but both. The pickpocket wailed like a child.

"Give me your clothes," it hissed.

The creature was by no means strong—in fact it was spent from its ordeal coming through the breach. Still the pickpocket could not resist the force behind its deep-set eyes.

"Give me your clothes," it repeated, "and I'll spare your flesh."

He didn't pretend to know what the thing was talking about, but that didn't matter. If he had to give his own clothes to cover this abomination, it was a small price to pay. He tore his shirt off, sending buttons flying, and pulled off his pants over his shoes, leaving him only in his underwear. Quickly the creature slipped on the clothes, but as the pickpocket tried to scramble away from it, it reached for him again, flipping him around. Grabbing him painfully by his chest hairs, it pulled him face to face with it.

"Please . . ." he begged. "Please just let me go. . . ."

"In a moment," it said, staring at him.

There was something in the creature's eyes. A spot of light deep within the pitch of its dilated pupils. The spot of light grew, becoming red, and pushing forward from its eyes and mouth, like tongues stretching for the pickpocket, probing the pores of his face.

"No . . . please."

"Be still," it said.

The tongues of light reached through his flesh—he could feel them like surges of electricity—twangs of pain shooting through his joints and organs. Then deep inside himself, in his gut, in his heart, in his mind, he felt something vital disconnect, as if the marrow were being drained from his bones. But it wasn't marrow; it was something else. He felt himself tugged loose, his soul discorporating from his body. And although he could feel his body was still alive, he also knew that he was no longer in it. Instead he was in the grasp of those red tendrils of light that pulled him into the gaping maw of a creature hiding within the flesh of a hermaphrodite: a creature of living light, and living shadow. In a moment he was so far from his own thoughts that he could not recall his own name, he could not think, for his spirit no longer had access to a brain. All he could do now was feel. Feel himself pulled deeper by the tendrils; feel himself sliding down its gullet, and finally feel the lonely agony of his consciousness dissolving as his soul slowly digested within the belly of the beast.

THE TWO OFFICERS HURLED their bodies against the door until the door frame finally splintered, and the door crashed in. Regaining their balance, they raised their weapons, half expecting to be fired on. They were not prepared for what they saw. It was odd, even by public restroom standards.

The perpetrator was there, in a fetal position on the floor, in his underwear, weeping. Above him stood a woman, half dressed. Or was it a man? Whatever it was, it had an unsettling, undead look about it, like an addict one trip shy of the morgue.

"What the hell is this?" the younger officer asked.

"I don't want to know," said his older partner.

The perp looked up at them. "It did something to me," the perp wailed. "It *did* something."

"Whatever it was, you damn well deserved it."

They pulled him off the ground, and he offered no resistance. The older officer had seen his share of petty criminals, and few gave in with such ease. It was as if he had been sapped of his will to fight—but it was more than that. The older officer caught sight of the perp's eyes. There was a discomfiting vacancy there; a desolate void, as if this pickpocket wasn't a man, but just a shell; a walking, breathing shell of a man, with nothing living inside. Not even hard timers got the death-look that bad.

"What do we do about the other one?" asked the younger cop.

The abject, straggle-haired specimen looked at them like a vulture waiting for roadkill.

"One freak at a time."

But the younger cop was playing by the book. "You got a name?" he asked.

"Okoya," it said. "My name is Okoya."

"We'll want your statement."

"Give it a rest," said the older cop, wanting more than anything to be free of that restroom. "Let's read this one his rights, and get him out of here."

The doleful pickpocket was still whimpering, "He robbed me . . . he robbed me."

But the older officer was wise enough not to consider what might have been stolen, and as they pulled their suspect out of the restroom, he made sure to keep his gaze away from the vacant eyes of the pickpocket, and the charged eyes of the freak.

. . .

MEANWHILE, FAR AWAY, IN the rejuvenated ruins of an old diner, Dillon, dozing with his arm around Maddy, was startled awake by a strange sensation somewhere in his head, like an unexpected popping of his ears. But the sensation quickly passed, so he closed his eyes, and thought no more about it.

15. GAINER

"I'm beyond myself now."

Dillon gripped the steering wheel with both hands as he spoke to Maddy, worried that some unseen force might jerk the wheel out of his hands. Nothing was to be taken for granted anymore. It was his third day free from the oppression of his cage—but that cage had offered him containment. There was nothing to contain him out here on the back roads of the rural south, and Tessic had been right—his will was not powerful enough to do it. "My body is too small a vessel to hold me," he said.

"Maybe I should drive," suggested Maddy.

Dillon turned his attention to the lush oak forest on either side, arcing over the road around them. "You see how the trees move in the wind? I can *feel* them move. I can feel the currents of breezes in the forest. There must be a lake nearby, because I can feel rippling on its surface." He tried to shake the feeling away, but it persisted, tugging at his attention. This was the first time he had taken the wheel of one of their many cars since their escape. He found the simple task of driving kept his focus tethered, but it was still an exhausting battle to keep his concentration narrow in the face of such overstimulation. "I'm beyond myself," he said again. "I don't know where I end, and the world begins."

"Like a newborn," Maddy offered.

"What?"

"A newborn can't differentiate itself from the world around it. Maybe you're a newborn, too. The beginning of something we've never seen."

"There you go again, calling me a 'thing.' I'm human, Maddy. I can bleed. I can die."

Maddy didn't appear convinced. "Maybe, but Tessic was right about one thing. People like you don't just get spit out on a regular basis."

"Tessic." Dillon gripped the wheel white-knuckle tight. Yes, Tessic had believed in Dillon's "purpose," but Dillon had no such faith anymore. All he could feel was a blind drive to do something, but with no clear objective. If anything, he could sense futility and failure, and the laughter of the three faceless divers, reveling in his defeat.

"If I need to do something, wouldn't it help to know what it was?" All he knew for sure was that his own influence was swelling further beyond his control. "And if it was intentional for me to be this powerful, wouldn't I be able to control it? You can't imagine how far my reach goes now. Fifty miles away, there are grains of sand slowly gathering into pebbles, and shattered leaves piecing themselves together again, all because of me. The farther away, the slower the process gets— but I can still feel it happening, maybe a hundred miles away."

They passed a sign announcing their entrance into Alabama. The road lightened, and took on a rougher texture. Maddy gently touched his arm.

"Forget about what you feel a hundred miles away. Feel the wheel. Feel the road. Focus on finding Winston."

Her voice was both compelling and comforting enough to ease the maddening static hum in his mind. Find Winston. Finding him wouldn't be the solution, but it was a positive step toward something. "I wish my mind could be as clear as yours," he told her.

She smiled. "You forget that you made it that way."

• • •

MADDY KEPT HER HAND on his arm, gently stroking it. Since he had first touched her two nights ago in the derelict diner, she found herself taking every opportunity to touch him again. There were no words to express the way Dillon had changed her. Bitterness had always been the fuel propelling her. Her wounds had become comfortable friends, but Dillon had exposed them for what they were, took her into his arms and excised them. In one intimate moment, her entire past was healed. The clarity he had brought her weeks ago was just a prelude, for far beyond the clarity was a grand sense of connection. She understood what Dillon had meant when he talked about being beyond himself, for now she felt a shadow of his connection to the world around him, and in his moments of self-doubt Maddy took the initiative, moving them toward their goal of finding Winston.

"Nothing's ever easy for us," Dillon griped, and chastised himself once more for having a mind that could decipher every pattern and code in the world, but couldn't remember something simple like Winston's phone number.

"Now I have to rely on my senses, but I don't get much of a feeling from Winston, or Lourdes," Dillon told her, as they passed on a tangent to Birmingham. "There's too much interference, too much static out there. I mean there are moments that a sense of one of them comes to me, kind of like a scent on the wind, but it passes too quickly for me to get a fix on the direction."

Maddy felt the car accelerate, and wondered if Dillon even realized that his foot had become heavy. Although Maddy trusted Dillon's instincts implicitly, she did have her reservations about his choice of destination. Winston's hometown was an hour south of Birmingham. Dillon figured that if he wasn't there, his mother and brother would be. Perhaps they might know where he was.

"But, as you're public enemy number one, that's the first place they'll look for you," Maddy had been quick to remind him even before they left the old diner the day before.

"Maybe not," Dillon had said. "They'll think I'm too smart to head there."

She wondered if his naiveté would save him or destroy him. "The military has no illusions about human intelligence. It thrives on the assumption that the world is full of imbeciles, so everything the military does is filled with redundancies and contingencies. You can bet the entire town where Winston lived is under twenty-hour-hour surveillance by multiple teams, in case one or more screw up."

"What do you want me to do," Dillon had answered, his frustration building. "Sit around and wait for something to happen? I might as well be back in my cell at the plant."

And so, a day and a half later, just around noon, they barreled past Birmingham and into a fresh danger zone.

She reached over and touched his leg. "Slow down," she said. "We don't want to be pulled over."

She left her hand gently on his thigh, feeling that sense of connection again. She had grown used to the sensation of simply being beside him, her cells infused with his aura, neither aging nor decaying. It was a sense of being at the peak of her own existence. But touching him closed a circuit, making her not just a recipient, but a participant.

"We're not exactly Bonnie and Clyde," he told her. "You're not obligated to come with me."

"Three days ago, I made the choice to give up everything to set you free," she reminded him. "Do you really think I'd stay with you now just because I felt obligated?"

"Then why *are* you with me?"

She took her hand away, the question stinging. "Aren't you

the one who told me you knew me? If you can see into my soul, why do you have to ask?"

He turned to look at her, but his gaze wasn't penetrating as it so often was. Instead it was a gentle caress. For an instant she felt schoolgirl bashful. She was both irritated and appreciative of the feeling. "Shouldn't you be watching the road?"

He immediately turned his eyes forward, but she knew that his attentions still remained on her.

Twenty minutes later, they pulled into an old filling station with pumps decades shy of automation, that still clanged bells as gears spun up the price. That and the attached general store was all that survived of a crumbling hotel which, by the looks of its remains, must have been an old plantation home. Maddy figured they had better get out of there fast, before the building succumbed to Dillon's presence, and the South rose again.

"I don't like this place," Dillon said as they stepped from the car. "I feel . . . unsettled here."

While Dillon pumped, she went in to pay and pick up sandwiches and drinks. The woman at the register was obviously a fixture of the place. She had pallid, liver-spotted skin that almost camouflaged her against the faded, whitewashed wall behind her.

"Will that be all for ya'?" she drawled.

Maddy's attention had been snagged by the last newspaper on the counter, and the photo smack in the center. *Her own face stared up at her from beneath the headline.* Next to her picture was a photo of Bussard.

She snatched up the paper, angling it so the cashier couldn't see the front page. "This, too."

Maddy watched the woman's rheumy eyes, which already seemed far less rheumy than they had only moments ago. Their fog had faded with her liver spots in less time than it took Dillon to fill up. The woman studied the items and the register, giving no indication that she recognized Maddy from the newspaper photo. "Cash or charge?"

Maddy paid in cash, and left with all godspeed. She couldn't resist taking a closer look at the paper the moment she was out. The military's official story was that she had murdered Bussard after an affair gone bad. She didn't know whether she was more infuriated or disgusted. There was, of course, no mention of Dillon at all—which meant that she had gotten it wrong. *She* was public enemy number one, not Dillon. They could never admit they had Dillon, much less admit his escape, so instead the military spin-doctors had made *her* the enemy.

Dillon was not at the car. She quickly surveyed the area to find him slipping through a hole in the chain-link fence that surrounded the dilapidated hotel. Damn! If anything, he was consistent in his distractions, like a hound in search of a lost scent.

She ran to the fence and found that the hole had healed as soon as Dillon passed through, so she climbed it, following a path of flattened weeds until coming into a clearing behind the building. The tall grass behind the condemned hotel was filled with the rotting remnants of wooden lounge chairs surrounding the concrete shell of a pool built in a time they truly made them deep. Dry brown leaves clogged the drain.

Dillon was nowhere to be seen. She tried the back porch, and peered in the dark windows. It was as if he had vanished—but there was evidence that he was here, right on the peeling wood of the building. The spots of paint that hadn't peeled now had a freshly painted look. *I can't put back what's no longer there*, Dillon had told her. Where the paint was gone, it was gone, but the exposed wood looked brand-new, leaving an effect of strangely mottled rejuvenation.

The sound of footsteps on metal made her look up. Above

the deep end of the empty pool, there was a high-diving platform. Dillon stood at the edge of the platform, silhouetted against the sun. This was strange, even for him, and she had no idea what business he had in mind. It wasn't until she moved, and the sun was out of her eyes, that she saw a second figure standing behind him. She raced toward the ladder.

UNSETTLED.

There were so many things out there agitating Dillon, he hadn't known why this place should stand out. Maybe it was that they were only thirty miles from Winston's home, and he had absolutely no sense of his presence there. Then he had seen the diving platform through the trees, and it had given him a sudden flashback to the vague visions and dreams that had been plaguing him.

Now he stood on the end of the platform, the tips of his sneakers an inch over the edge. He could see the old hotel, the gas station, Birmingham in the distance. He grew more unsettled by the moment, but there was nothing here.

He held his hands out to balance himself on the edge, and closed his eyes, trying to recall details from the visions. He heard Maddy climb the ladder, and in a moment could hear her breathing behind him.

"I've seen a place like this, in my dreams," he said, hands still held out, eyes still closed. "There are three people. They're important. They're dangerous. I see them standing side by side on the edge and the pool below them is full of flowers. I can almost smell them."

Then a voice behind him spoke, but it wasn't Maddy.

"If you intend to dive, I must warn you there's no lifeguard on duty."

Dillon knew the voice instantly, and that moment between

hearing the voice, and turning to see that face was a moment as awful as it had been waiting for the flood waters of Lake Mead to sweep him under with the soulless four hundred. If there truly was an embodiment of evil in the universe it stood behind him now. He turned to see the leering, sexless face of Okoya, the manipulator of Gods, thief of souls, and would-be destroyer of worlds.

"Hello, Dillon."

Dillon gaped, paralyzed by fear.

"You're speechless!" said Okoya. "I knew you would be."

This was what Dillon had sensed in this place. He wondered how long Okoya had stalked him before getting this close. Dillon mustered his courage as quickly as he could and studied him from across the platform. Okoya was not the sleek, muscular specimen he had been before. His muscles had atrophied, and his rich Native American skin had taken on a muddy, ashen pallor. His long, luxuriant hair with the raven shine, so feminine the way it flowed over his shoulders, was now a straggly snarl. Okoya was a wraith; broken, beaten, but still alive.

"If you've come here looking for revenge," Dillon said, "you've made a mistake. I'm much stronger than I was a year ago, when I first defeated you."

Okoya's face clenched in a venomous expression of hatred. "Yes. I never got to thank you for that last trick you pulled."

Dillon recalled that final look of horror and desperation on Okoya's face, the moment Dillon had unleashed the two beasts on him. The parasite of destruction, and the parasite of fear. "So, did you take care of my pets?" Dillon asked. Those ravenous beasts had leeched onto Okoya, as Dillon knew they would—and Okoya, racked with an urge to destroy, and an insurmountable fear brought on by the parasites, had leaped out of this universe, and back into his own, taking the two beasts with him. It had been the perfect plan. But if it was so perfect, why was Okoya back?

"Your 'pets,'" said Okoya, controlling the rancor in his voice, "lingered within me only until they found better quarry."

"Better than you?" mocked Dillon.

Okoya didn't answer; instead he turned to see Maddy as she climbed up to the platform.

"Dillon, what's going on? Who is this?"

"My old 'spiritual advisor,'" said Dillon. "Back to devour more souls." He had told her everything about Okoya, and for the first time since he had known her, Maddy was truly terrified. "I thought you said he was dead."

"I said he was worse than dead."

Okoya looked Maddy over, sizing her up. "Well, Dillon, I see you've found yourself a bitch. Good for you!"

Apparently Maddy's terror was short lived. She advanced on him.

"Maddy, no!"

She high-kicked Okoya in the chin, and to Dillon's surprise he went down. In an instant she had her foot wedged tightly against his Adam's apple, pressing him down against the concrete platform. Okoya made no effort to fight back. Instead he laughed, and rasped with a larynx half closed. "And she's your personal assassin as well. You really have done well for yourself!"

In response Maddy turned her ankle, closing off more of his wind. "Give me the word, Dillon, and I'll snap his neck right now."

"Yes," Okoya said. "Give the word. And once this body dies, it will free me to inhabit another." Although he couldn't move his head, his eyes turned up to Maddy. "In fact, she'd make a tasty host for me."

Dillon almost involuntarily found his foot swinging at full force, connecting with Okoya's ribs. Okoya groaned, and Maddy turned to Dillon, surprised by his uncharacteristic brutality. But a creature as vile as this one didn't deserve the smallest measure of sympathy or dignity.

"I'm not your enemy!" Okoya gasped. "I thought you would have realized that by now!"

Dillon regarded him there on the ground. Okoya seemed so weak now. But that didn't mean anything. He was a master of deception.

"Let him up," Dillon told Maddy, then watched with caution as Okoya slowly rolled over, pushed himself up on all fours, and labored to his feet.

"I came here to make a deal with you."

"Not a chance."

"Then you'll never know the things I can tell you," Okoya said. "And that tragic end to this world you keep prophesying will come to pass just as you expected, and you'll have no idea how to stop it."

Dillon hesitated. Okoya was a liar through and through, serving no one's needs but his own. Dillon had to be careful.

"What kind of deal?"

Okoya took a step closer. "I can tell you what's coming, and what you need to know to stop it. I can even tell you where to find Winston. You won't find him without me—you're not even in the right time zone!"

"In return for what?"

Okoya smiled. "Your blessing," he said. "Permission to live freely in this world under your protection."

Dillon began to fume, thinking back to the hundreds of souls Okoya had consumed, leaving behind walking, breathing bodies of flesh with nothing living inside. Death that mimicked life—the very negation of life itself. How could he even think of making such a deal with this *thing*?

"How many souls have you gorged on since you've been back?"

"My doings here are insignificant!" he shouted. "Whether it's one, or a hundred, it means nothing."

Wrong answer. It meant quite a lot to Dillon. He lunged forward and grabbed Okoya by the shirt with both fists. "If you stay here among humans, I swear I will chain you up in a place where no one will ever find you, and you'll never be free to walk the Earth."

"I was told that once before. But mountains crumble, and shackles break."

Dillon gripped him tighter. "Not the shackles I'll give you."

MADDY WATCHED, KNOWING BETTER than to get caught in the battle zone between them, wishing she could help Dillon, but knowing she could not. Incapacitating Okoya was one thing, but truly battling him? From what Dillon had told her of Okoya, only another Star Shard could help Dillon now, and that was something she could never be.

A siren drew nearer and Maddy turned to see a police cruiser pulling up by the gas pumps where the cashier pointed the officer right toward them, as they stood there in clear view on the high platform. The woman had recognized Maddy after all.

"Dillon, they've found us."

Okoya took that as a cue, and suddenly burst free from Dillon, took two bounds to the end of the platform, and launched himself off in a clumsy gainer to the distant scream of the cashier.

A sickening thud, and they looked over the edge. Okoya lay flat on his back on the concrete pool bottom, skull crushed, blood running down toward the drain now clogged with bright green leaves.

Maddy grabbed Dillon, pulling him toward the ladder, leaping the last few feet to a patio where the cracks had healed, crushing out the weeds growing between them. But these weren't the only things that had repaired themselves in the short time Dillon was there. Something was moving in the shallow end of the pool. It was Okoya, who ran to the shallow end, and climbed out.

Dillon almost bolted after him, but Maddy stopped him. "No. There'll be another time." Together they raced off into the woods before the police got there, and just kept on running.

DILLON KNEW OKOYA HAD used him again. When he had dived off that platform, he had known that Dillon's own healing power would mend his broken body in seconds, before they could climb to the bottom of the ladder. He had used Dillon's restorative powers to escape, and it was one more weight on Dillon's head. Maddy said there would be another time, but there was no guarantee of that, and in the meantime, Okoya would be out there, feeding. Yet he had said he wasn't the enemy. How could that be true?

A half mile away, they came upon a dirt road and a small house in the woods. Now that the authorities knew their whereabouts, federal agents would be called in—it was only a matter of time until the entire area was secured. They had to get out now.

For once luck was with them: the battered jeep beside the house had a set of keys lying with the mail on the passenger seat. Maddy took the wheel.

If nothing else, Okoya had left them with one kernel of information. He had told them that Winston was in a different time zone. Assuming he had stayed in the country, that meant he was somewhere to the west. The dirt road opened to a rural highway that led them to the interstate, and they disappeared into the flow of nondescript vehicles headed west.

16. BLIND-SIDED

THE FLASHPOINT OF HUMAN FLESH, WINSTON RECALLED, WAS 451 degrees Fahrenheit, just like that of most other organic matter.

With both the front door and rear iron doors closed, the chamber was lightless, and Winston couldn't fight the urge to turn on his flashlight. The claustrophobic space in which he and Drew now crouched was the most uninviting place Winston had ever had the misfortune to visit. Oversized gas nozzles spaced at precise intervals on the side walls and on the low coffered ceiling were an ever-present reminder of the chamber's purpose. The soot charred bricks of the crematorium walls still retained residual warmth from earlier that day.

Commercial mortuary crematoria, Winston recalled, reached 1500 degrees Fahrenheit, reducing balsa wood caskets and their occupants to cinders in under three hours.

Winston turned off his flashlight, deciding that darkness was better than the view.

"Another fine mess you've gotten us into," delivered Drew, in an impressively accurate Oliver Hardy.

"Quiet—you'll give us away." Winston's nerves were frayed, and it annoyed him that Drew could keep calm. The room was dusty and dry, but quickly growing humid from their sweat. It was all he could do not to cough and give away their presence to the funeral director, who loitered just outside the closed furnace door. They had heard him on the phone, then flipping papers, opening and closing drawers, taking care of odds and ends in his lucrative business of morbidity.

Although they hadn't heard him for at least ten minutes, that didn't mean that he wasn't still lurking after hours.

The average funeral home, Winston recalled, *processed about four earthly departures a day. The ashes of a human body weighed approximately two pounds.*

Winston's mind, as always, was a traffic jam of salient facts, none of which helped matters. So he tried to reinitialize his mind, reminding himself of what had brought them here in the first place.

Their path to this hiding place had been a circuitous one, beginning with an investigation into the scant clues left behind by the would-be grave robber. Winston, with his vast supply of knowledge, was not a puzzler like Dillon, who could pull patterns and solutions out of chaos. And although Drew was insightful, he was no investigator either.

They had first submerged the footlocker in Lake Arrowhead, behind Drew's cabin. No grave site, no way for Briscoe or any other lunatic to find Michael's resting place. Then the two had returned from Lake Arrowhead to Drew's Newport Beach home to begin their search.

Drew's parents were awkward and stand-offish around Winston, not knowing his relationship with Drew and not wanting to ask. Aside from complaining to Drew that the lawn needed mowing (which unbeknownst to them, was twice daily, now that Winston was around), his parents left them alone.

Their investigative efforts led them to the hotel from which Briscoe had taken the Gideon Bible, and they tried unsuccessfully to ferret out the room from which it had been stolen before being evicted by security. Then, they spent the better part of two days sifting through the Internet in search of Vicki Sanders—the single name scribbled on the bible's inside cover. Vicki Sanders of Des Moines was a retired school teacher who enjoyed quilting and Harleys. Vicki Sanders of Liverpool was a frustrated factory worker who haunted sex chat rooms while her husband worked the night shift. Vicki Sanders of Minneapolis was actually Victor Sanders, and was damned pissed off at whatever half-assed computer had proliferated an electronic sex change. And Vicki Sanders of rural Tennessee was an SWF looking for a long-term relationship, and currently doing five-to-twenty for armed robbery.

"It's pointless," Winston had complained to Drew. "Even if we found the right one, how would we know? We don't even know what connection she has to Briscoe, if any."

Then, toward the end of the second day, Winston tripped a land mine within his own thoughts. Something that had been there, underfoot, all along, that he should have considered earlier.

He asked Drew for his initial notes on the phone numbers also scrawled on the bible's watermark. Drew had tested each phone number in more than a dozen different area codes, and the combinations that actually yielded connections had no obvious relevance.

The only number that was the slightest bit troubling was that of a funeral home in the California desert town of Barstow. Barstow, aside from being home to the world's largest McDonald's, had been in national news a year ago. With the morgues and mortuaries of Las Vegas as overbooked as the hotels in the grim aftermath of the Backwash, a good number of the dead had been diverted to Barstow.

The names of those who had died had filled news reports for weeks. The more famous names took the spotlight, of course. The former senator from Wisconsin; the prominent architect; the notorious celebrity attorney. But the names of the common people were washed into obscurity just as quickly as their bodies had been taken under the waters.

It didn't take much searching to discover one Vicki Sanders among the dead.

"I don't get it," Drew had said. "What would this guy want with some woman who died in the Backwash?"

The answer came to Winston in a slow and sickening revelation.

And so now they hunched in a Barstow crematorium chamber.

It had been hard enough to slip into the establishment unnoticed before closing, and although climbing into the chamber had seemed the only way to hide from an approaching staff member, the idea had quickly fallen out of favor, for the funeral director didn't leave the anteroom for more than forty-five minutes. Winston couldn't help but worry whether these devices were set to some cleaning cycle after hours.

Twenty-eight people, Winston recalled, *suffered accidental deaths each year in funeral homes.*

When all had been quiet for twenty minutes, Winston slowly pushed open the heavy furnace door, and they climbed into a dark room that seemed bright when compared to the chamber. There were no windows, but someone had left a light on in an adjacent closet, and a perimeter of light escaped around its closed door. The coolness of the antechamber was a welcome relief.

"I saw the main office when we came in," Drew said. "It should be this way."

They passed through a large medicinal-smelling room with a stainless steel table, and instruments that were mercifully obscured in the darkness; then they opened a door into the business office. Winston turned on his flashlight to reveal a room that could have been part of any business establishment. A secretary's desk decorated with family pictures around a computer; a copy and fax machine in the corner; and against the far wall, a row of black filing cabinets. Those cabinets suddenly were more ominous to Winston than the crematorium.

Please, let me be wrong . . . let me be completely wrong.

He had told Drew of his suspicions, but Drew reserved judgment, not wanting to extrapolate until all the facts were in. Now, neither would speak of it, as if speaking it aloud would baptize their hunch into reality.

I'm wrong, Winston told himself as they approached the filing cabinets. *I have to be wrong.*

Winston found the drawer labeled "SA-SN" and tugged it open. The files smelled of age—apparently these folders went back for many years, and since the dead rarely returned to audit their own records, no one had bothered to input them into computers.

"There it is," Drew said.

"I see it."

Vicki Sanders's file was a new manila folder, sandwiched between the aging ones. Winston pulled it out, but didn't look at it just yet. He took a deep breath, and then another, feeling lightheaded from the stench of embalming fluid that had followed them in from the mortician's station.

"You want me to read it?" Drew asked.

"I'll do it." Winston clenched his jaw. There was some knowledge that came easily, and other knowledge that came with great pain. Either way, he couldn't wait anymore. He flipped open the file, spread it across the open drawer, and shone his light at it. It was minimal—just a few pages. Information forms, medical examiner's report, death certificate, liability releases, and finally a signed order to cremate.

"Tell me," said Drew, who, despite the calm he had showed earlier, wouldn't bring himself to look at the pages.

"Vicki Sanders," began Winston. "Body found in the Nevada desert, last October 21st. Cause of death: acute physical trauma consistent with fall. Sixteen years old."

"Oh, Jesus . . ."

Winston blinked then blinked again, the information leaping off the page making his eyes sting. "Her mother came all the way from Florida to claim the remains." He took a deep breath before imparting the news. "Her mother's name was Sharon Smythe."

Drew pounded his fist on the filing cabinet, the sound tolling through the moribund silence of the funeral home.

"Vicki Sanders—*Victoria* Sanders—went by her mother's last name," said Winston. "It's Tory."

MARTIN BRISCOE COULDN'T BE bothered with the taxi's seat-belt. No matter how bad the Miami cabby drove, Martin knew there could be no accident. His mission put him above such things. He was protected against such inconsequential concerns.

"The law says I gotta take you where you want to go," the cabby told Martin. "But that don't mean I gotta like it."

The cabby shrugged his shoulder uncomfortably, revealing the edge of a nicotine patch on his neck. It was obviously not doing the job, because the cab reeked of stale smoke, and the open mouth of the ashtray bulged with twisted Marlboro butts.

The cabby glanced at Martin in the rearview mirror. "Detached retina?" he asked, taking notice of the bandage over his right eye. "My son had a detached retina—hit in the face with a goddamn hockey stick."

Martin took a deep breath. A thousand cabbies in Miami,

and he had to get the one who spoke English. He answered by not answering, hoping the cabby got the hint.

"Yeah, eye trouble is the worst," blathered the cabby. "Can't set it like a bone, can't lance it like a boil."

"How much farther?"

"Almost there."

Martin smoothed out a ruffle in his eye dressing. Although he had pared down the gauze and tape to a bare minimum, there was no way to hide the wound. The eye Drew Camden had blinded with a starter pistol still ached and oozed, having been untreated for more than a week, or at least untreated by anyone but him. Emergency rooms were out of the question—he was wanted in Eureka, and surely that damn kid had set the Newport Beach police on his tail as well. Self-treatment was the word of the day, but dentistry was a far cry from ocular triage. After six days, he suspected that his sight wasn't coming back, and infection had taken hold.

Pain is good, he told himself. It reminded him of his failure in the graveyard—which made him determined not to fail again.

Martin unzipped the travel bag beside him to check that the lid hadn't come off the urn he carried. Once he was satisfied it was secure, he glanced with his good eye at the address on a crumbled slip of paper and looked at the neighborhood around him. It was a neighborhood that decayed more with each block they drove, looking even worse painted in the half-tones and shadows of a failing twilight. "Exactly what part of Miami are we going to?" he asked.

The cabby spat out a rueful chuckle. "Haven't been here before, have you?"

Martin shook his head.

"You're going right to the middle of 'The Miami Miasma.'"

Martin sank back in the worn seat. "Sounds wonderful."

"It got voted 'Best place to drop the bomb,' three times in a row," the cabby told him.

They crossed an intersection, and the bottom seemed to drop out of whatever fabric held the neighborhood together. They had entered an overpopulated slum; a human sump that caught the dregs of every cultural group; the bitter bottom of the melting pot.

The cabby hit his lock button, even though all the locks were already down. "Keep your hands and arms inside the vehicle at all times," he said. "The animals bite."

The streets were infused with a sense of despair that permeated the souls around them: pushers and prostitutes competed for clients; angry youth with carnivorous glares. Bleak alley-shadows crouching in cardboard dwellings. Even the decaying, graffiti-tagged walls seemed to breathe hopelessness in the oppressive Floridian humidity.

Martin had known his mission would take him to the edge of hell, but he had assumed it would only be figurative. "How much farther?"

"Just a few more blocks."

They turned a corner where children played in and around an abandoned rust-bucket Buick straddling the sidewalk. A brick fragment was lobbed like a grenade across the hood of the taxi.

"Son of a bitch," grumbled the cabby, but just drove on.

Martin reached into his bag, nervously rubbing the side of the funeral urn he had brought as if it were a gene's lamp. When he looked at its polished surface, he could see a faint reflection of his own face, oblate and distorted by the curvature of the brass. Were the angels watching him now? he wondered. The sense of intangible paranoia told him that they were still there. Observing. Judging. Perhaps the loss of his eye was a judgment as well. Perhaps bliss could only be achieved through pain. Or maybe they were just screwing with him.

"A loved one?" the cabby asked.

"Excuse me?"

"That's an urn in your bag, isn't it?"

Martin toyed with the various indignant remarks he could respond with, and the various ways in which the cabby might be silenced both temporarily and permanently, but in the end decided none of it was worth the trouble. "I'm a funeral director," he said, trying the lie on for size.

The cabby raised an eyebrow. "I didn't know you guys made house calls."

"Would you like my card?"

The cabby shrugged his neck uncomfortably again, glanced at the ashtray, and scratched his nicotine patch. "No. No, that's okay."

Martin grinned smugly. Yes, he was sufficiently funereal to pull off his current charade. He cleared a smudge from the urn, then glanced out of the window again.

To his surprise, the neighborhood had changed.

Gone were the graffiti-burdened walls and boarded windows. The gutters that had been filled with debris were clean, and the stench of misery was replaced by the smell of wet paint.

Just up ahead a barrier blocked the sidewalk, and narrowed the road to a single lane. It had the semblance of a civilian barricade: chairs, tables—anything that could be piled upon, had been wedged into the blockade, and smaller household objects became the mortar in the gaps. Through the barricade, Martin caught the blue flickering of an arc welder.

"What's going on here?"

"Urban renewal," the cabby told him.

They pulled over near a clean black and white sign that said PARDON OUR DUST DURING BEAUTIFICATION.

"This is as far as I go," the cabby said. "They don't let taxis into the Miasma. Nowadays it's what you might call a 'gated community.'"

Martin turned to look out the back window, where several blocks away he could still see the crumbling streets. "I thought we just passed through the Miasma."

"Naah," the cabby said. "That was the funk around the pearl."

"I thought you said it was a horrible place."

"That was then," explained the cabby. "This is now. The Miasma cleaned up real good . . . if you call that clean."

Martin almost asked how such a thing could happen to such a localized area in such a short period of time . . . but he answered his own question. "Tory Smythe . . ." he mumbled under his breath, but this cabby missed nothing, and threw him a knowing grin.

"She used to live here. That's the rumor, anyway. Kind of makes you wonder."

Martin opened the door, but didn't pull out his wallet. "You'll wait for me," Martin instructed. "I won't be long— keep the meter running."

The cabby threw him a disgusted look. "Yeah, yeah." He threw the cab into park. "Why did I know you were going to say that." He rolled down his window and lit a cigarette.

As Martin approached the gap in the barricade, a guard with a clipboard came out to greet him, Cuban-dark and as clean-cut as Ward Cleaver.

"I need your name and destination," the guard said.

"Marcus D'Angelo," said Martin, giving his alias of the day. "I'm going to 414 Las Estacas Street, apartment 3-C."

The guard glanced up at him at the mention of the address, then back down to his clipboard and curtly said, "I'm sorry—you're not on my guest list."

Martin tipped the clipboard so he could see it, and quickly found his name. There were only a handful of names on the list—and no way the guard could have missed it.

"Funny, I could see it fine with one eye."

"You have business with Sharon Smythe?"

"My business is no business of yours."

The guard stared at him, mad-dogging him a moment more, then backed down. "Two blocks down, then make a left. If she's not home, you might try the church across the street." The guard's eyes turned to Martin's suit coat. He picked a shred of lint from Martin's jacket, rolled it into a ball in his fingers, then glanced down at Martin's rumpled slacks. "We have a dress code here," he said. "Maybe next time you'll remember to get those pressed." Then he stepped aside.

Martin crossed between the banks of the barricade, to find that the Miasma had been transmuted into an inner-city Mayberry.

Just inside the barricade, a welder worked to erect a wrought iron fence that would soon take the place of the barricade. Painters coated the gate with primer.

The buildings were of the same construction as those outside of the barricade, but here, the brick had been sandblasted clean. The hydrants were painted a cheery orange, and there was not as much as a single candy wrapper in the gutter. A man in front of an appliance store swept dust from the sidewalk. An elderly couple holding hands strolled leisurely down the street and teens hanging out on a street corner greeted the couple with a smile, tipping their caps like boy scouts. A block down, children played in a park that had probably been a syringe-mined vacant lot before Tory's cleansing presence had mutated everything caught within her sphere of influence. In a sense, a bomb *had* been dropped on the Miasma; a cleansing salvo that had sanitized the streets, the hearts and souls of those who lived here.

As Martin crossed another spotless intersection, he could see, on either side about a half mile away, other barricades keeping out the rest of the impure world. This place was an oasis in the midst of squalor. An abnormal, unnatural place. It reminded Martin why he was there, and what he had to do.

People nodded him a polite greeting as he passed, but their stares lingered on his bandaged eye a moment too long, and he could read an aftertaste of suspicion. They made it very clear that he was an outsider, unclean in some fundamental way. It wasn't just his eye, or his rumpled clothes, he realized—it was the fact that he wasn't one of them. He didn't possess their particular brand of purity. He was half tempted to go take a piss in some corner, just out of spite—but he didn't need to draw further attention to himself. Not now, when he was so close.

No one answered at Sharon Smythe's apartment, and so, following the guard's advice, he crossed the street to a church, climbing a set of wide stone steps, and entering through a partially open door.

It was a high-ceilinged cathedral. Stained glass pictorials of the life of Christ painted the sanctuary in a colorful mosaic of light, slowly fading as the sun slipped off the horizon.

A man near the entrance was on hands and knees with a scrub brush and bucket, polishing the tile floor in little circles.

"Shoes off!" he demanded as Martin stepped in. "Shoes off!" It took a moment for Martin to realize from the man's vestments that he was the priest. Martin removed his shoes and left them in a rear pew, then strode slowly down the center aisle.

There was only one congregant in the empty church—a blonde woman of forty, hair beginning to gray at the temples. She sat in the second pew from the front, as if being in the front pew would put her too deep under God's scrutiny.

"Ms. Smythe?"

The woman didn't look up. She stayed in her kneeling position, finishing whatever prayer she silently recited. Martin had little patience for it. "I don't mean to disturb you . . ." he said, loudly enough to make it clear that he *did* mean to disturb her.

Finally she looked up at him. If she was put off by his bandaged eye, she didn't show it. "I suppose you're Mr. D'Angelo."

Far in the back, the priest grumbled upon finding his shoes in the rear pew, and took them to the entrance mat.

"Don't mind Father Martinez," said Sharon Smythe. "He doesn't have much to do these days. Oh, for a while the place was packed with repentant souls and daily sermons. Now nobody comes to confession anymore. I imagine they've all convinced themselves they're free of sin."

Martin didn't care to make small talk, or linger longer than he had to within this sterile field.

"Perhaps we should go back to your apartment, Ms. Smythe—we can make the exchange."

She looked at the object bulging in his leather carrying case.

"Are you certain that those are my daughter's ashes?"

"Absolutely."

She eyed the carrying case a moment more, then she reached beneath her pew. "I have it right here." From beneath the pew, she pulled out a box, and from inside the box she pulled out an urn. It was a white ceramic vessel, much more appealing than the one Martin had brought.

"Her life was riddled with bad luck," Sharon Smythe said. "I suppose it shouldn't surprise me that it wouldn't end with her death."

Martin opened his carrying case, and removed his urn, making a point to handle it with more care than he really had. "It was a horrible time. So many had died when the dam burst."

"I suppose your business was good."

"We earn our money relieving people's misery, not creating it." He held the brass urn out to her, but she didn't take it.

"I should be heartened to find a funeral home so honest it corrects errors that no one would know about. You didn't have to tell me I had the wrong ashes—I would never have known."

He couldn't pull his eyes from her urn, and wondered if there might be some unholy magic yet in those ashes. "Some funeral homes have more integrity than others. But I give you my personal assurance that Tory has been respectfully cared for, and I regret any further suffering this mix-up may have caused." He waited for her to accept the exchange, but she still held firmly onto the ceramic urn.

"So where are the papers?" she asked.

"Which papers?"

"The ones I have to sign—the ones that state I won't sue for gross negligence."

Martin released a quick impatient breath, then regretted it. He tried to regain a sullen semblance of empathy. "You don't have to sign anything, Ms. Smythe."

"Why not?" She looked up from her urn to face him again. There was more than grief in her eyes now—more than bitterness. He could sense distrust coming into focus.

"I was only instructed to bring you your daughter's ashes. If you have any legal issues, you'll have to take them up with my employer."

"I thought you told me over the phone that you were a partner, not an employee."

"Ms. Smythe, do you want your daughter's ashes or not?"

She responded by putting her ceramic urn back down into the box, and pushing it under her seat. "It's funny, Mr. D'Angelo, but at my daughter's cremation, I didn't see you there."

Martin could feel his lies begin to fold in on one another, and he struggled to maintain the facade. "We're a large mortuary."

"Another funny thing was how her body was identified," she continued. "Her bracelet. Her father gave it to her when she was very little—when she still went by his name. The bracelet said 'Vicki Sanders.' With so many bodies turning up along the banks of the river, no one gave her name a second thought—and when they contacted me, I wasn't about to tell them who she really was—not with the way her name was plastered all over the news. But *you* just called her Tory, Mr. D'Angelo. You knew who she was."

"Perhaps I should just keep your daughter's remains, and leave you with a stranger's," he said, clinging to his story one final time.

"Do you think I'm stupid, Mr. D'Angelo? You're a reporter, aren't you? Either that or just one more nut."

Martin smiled and took a long look at this woman. He admired smart women. He had married one. And this smart woman's daughter had been an accomplice in his wife's murder.

"Are there even ashes in your urn," she asked in disgust, "or did you just fill it with sand?"

Well, thought Martin, there were times for diplomacy, and times for action. "Coffee grounds, actually." He stood without warning and swung the brass urn, connecting with the woman's cheek. She grunted with the blow, and took a breath, about to scream. He swung it again as her scream let loose, rattling the stained glass windows in the cavernous space. The second blow caught her forehead and knocked her to the ground. The lid flew off, sending a spray of earthen-smelling coffee grounds in the air. He came down on top of her as she struggled, pinning her. "This is a house of God, Ms. Smythe," he reminded her, shouting above her screams. "And I am his messenger." Then he brought the dented urn high above his head. "When you don't kill the messenger, sometimes the messenger kills you." He brought the edge of the urn down upon her head again in a final killing blow. Then he reached under the pew, and pulled out the white ceramic urn, slipping it into his carrying case. When he stood, there was someone behind him.

"My God! What have you done?"

The priest stood in the aisle behind him, mouth agape, and dripping scrub brush still in hand. Martin found himself laughing at the absurdity of the question. "The Lord's work," he answered. "Isn't it obvious?" He pushed his way past, and strode down the aisle. At the back of the church, he rinsed the blood from his hands in a marble bowl of holy water, then grabbed his shoes at the door.

17. CAUTION TO THE WIND

DREW HAD ALWAYS KNOWN THAT TORY WAS DEAD. HE HAD been there—he had been the only witness close enough to see her and Michael huddling together in the doorway on the face of the dam as it crumbled around them. There wasn't a day when Drew didn't think about it—didn't dream about it. He would relive it, trying desperately to change the outcome, but it never changed. They died, he survived. Even with a broken collar bone, he had made it to safety, but was unable to help Michael and Tory in their final moments.

Survivor's guilt—isn't that what they called it? It became the fuel of all his track victories, personal successes, and personal failures. So, yes, he knew that they were dead, but there was a strange solace in the fact that their bodies had not been found—as if they had been raptured away from a mere mortal demise.

But then they found Michael, or what remained of him after so many months, mysteriously deposited in the desert miles away from the disaster. And now, to find out that Tory was never missing at all—that she was just one of the dead, cremated and sent home a year ago . . . to Drew there was something ignoble about it. Obscene. Such an ordinary end to her extraordinary life.

There was no direct flight from Barstow to Miami. There was no direct flight from Barstow to anywhere. They managed to take a puddle-jumper to Phoenix, as Winston refused to have anything to do with the closer city of Las Vegas. From

Phoenix, they got seats on an American flight to Miami, by way of Dallas.

"So what do we do when we get there?" Drew asked Winston as they waited to board in Phoenix.

"How the hell should I know?" was Winston's response.

"Well, you're always the one with all the answers."

"This isn't *Jeopardy!*"

"Naah," said Drew. "They already have the answers. Can't win *Jeopardy!* unless you know the questions."

"I'm working on that, too."

Before boarding, Drew took out his cell phone and made the dreaded call home. "I'm taking off for a few days," he told his parents. "Drug run to Columbia," he joked. "I'll be back by Tuesday. Wednesday tops." But when his mother pressed him as to what was really going on, he told her he had to take care of "old business."

He could practically hear his mother's knuckles pop as she wrung her hands. They both knew that "old business" meant something to do with the shards—and his five unnatural friends were not discussed in their home.

When he had returned home last October, crushed shoulder and all, it had taken his parents months to be convinced that he hadn't been brainwashed by a cult. His parents were among the few, the proud, the rational, who refused to accept the bludgeoning of magic the shards had inflicted on the fragile world. What made it even harder for them to wrap their minds around was that their son was an integral part of it. After all, he still went to school, still wise-cracked, still had bed-hair in the morning—he was still their son. How could someone who cavorted with gods still be their son? To his parents, denying the shards was the only way they could keep him. So he never discussed with them his weeks at Hearst Castle, his death, his resurrection, the theft and recovery of his soul.

And so on the rare occasions that Drew invoked the "old business" clause, his parents gave him a wide berth, as a matter of self-preservation.

On the line, he could hear his mother talking to his father in hushed tones. "Does he have enough money?" he heard his father say—quite a change from his father's standard threat to shut down his credit card. But even if he did, it didn't matter. He was eighteen now, presider over, if not master of, his own choices, with enough money of his own to do as he pleased.

They didn't press, they didn't try to talk him out of going. He was both relieved and disappointed.

"Do something for me, Ma," he asked before he got off the phone. "Unpack, will ya?" He could imagine his mother still sitting there amidst the storage boxes, still seeking and believing a sensible explanation as to why she was so compelled to box and order her life. She agreed noncommittally, and Drew hung up, pondering the phone long after the connection had severed.

DREW FOUND THE AMERICAN terminal in Dallas to be like one of those nightmares where you keep running but never get anywhere. Five massive terminals boasting more than 150 gates, all of which were equally inaccessible, regardless of which gate you were connecting from. Their connection to Miami was at gate A-19. They had arrived at gate C-23, and naturally, the shuttle train was on the blink.

Moving through the terminal became a study in petit Armageddon. Sky-caps drove golf carts at breakneck speeds with less regard than usual for human life, and gate agents had long since abandoned their facades of officious geniality. The crowds around them were larger and more fractious than the normal airport hordes. There were distraught clusters of waylaid travelers caught in the growing number of flight cancellations and delays that epitomized the times. And there was also a large contingent of vagrants who had taken up residence within the terminal buildings. Sometimes it was hard to tell which was which.

"Airports are high-maintenance facilities," Winston explained as they power-walked through the terminal. "As things start to go bad, places like this get hit first."

"'Go bad'—you make it sound like the world is a container of milk that's been left out too long."

They passed a small gaggle of self-proclaimed Colists—one of countless disconnected and misinformed groups that had sprung up like crabgrass in public places, claiming to be followers of Dillon. This particular group had a Santeria flavor, and evoked blood-curses on the beleaguered security guard that tried to roust them. It seemed airport security, which had become so tight after 9/11, had now loosened to an all-time low.

"Eventually," said Winston, "as things slip further and further into chaos, there won't be enough employees to keep a place like this running. The airlines will begin to shut down."

Drew had read just a few weeks ago how United had dropped service to a dozen smaller cities. Apparently it was a sign of things to come. It boggled him to the point that he felt like burying his head in the sand, the way so many others did. "How could the Backwash be responsible for all of this?"

They had reached a moving sidewalk between terminals A and C, and they paused to let Winston catch his breath.

"Great events flow like ripples through civilization," Winston explained. "Assassinations, bombings. Acts of war. But Dillon—even unintentionally—is far too good at both creation and destruction. What he did to that dam, and that river, was the *precise* event, in the *precise* place, at the *precise* time to hit a pressure point of civilization with such power, it sent out a series of fractures, rather than ripples."

Drew tried to consider it. He supposed everyone had psychological pressure points—events that can define you, or destroy you . . . but the human race was not a single personality; it was a collection of seven billion disparate identities. To consider some cabalistic interconnectedness of the body human didn't sit well with Drew. There were simply too many people he did not want to be connected to.

"I don't know," Drew said. "It's all too Jedi for me."

"It's not just mysticism," said Winston. "There's a logic to it. Everything is a series of actions and reactions. Dillon's very presence brings order to it—lining things up in a series of chain reactions. What Dillon did—what we *all* did—not only defies rational explanation, it kills the very concept of rationality. Civilization began with rational thought. Take away that cornerstone and everything crumbles."

As if to prove Winston's point, they found their flight cancelled when they reached the gate, adding to the collective misery of the airport hordes.

"Flight crew shortages, and too many travelers," the gate attendant told them. "It's like that with all the beach cities; all of a sudden everyone's going on vacation."

And so their night was spent in the airport on a wild goose chase to every gate that promised a flight to Miami. But with so much competition, getting on stand-by was like winning the lottery. They watched three flights arrive, watched them all leave, and were no closer to getting a seat.

At 7:00 a.m. they sat in uncomfortable airport chairs on a long stand-by list for the fourth time.

"Why does it even matter if we find Briscoe?" Drew grumbled, wishing he could be home in a comfortable bed. "I mean, yeah, it'd be great if Dillon could take Tory's ashes and bring her back. But even if Briscoe does get her ashes, it's not the end of the world."

"Are you so sure of that?" Winston asked.

After a night with no sleep, Drew didn't feel like tackling the big questions. "I don't follow."

"You told me yourself—Briscoe said he's on some 'divine mission.' Maybe there's something to that—although I don't think it's anything divine."

"Or maybe he's just a psycho."

Winston considered it and shook his head. "I keep having this dream—more like a vision. There's three figures standing on a ledge and they're waiting for something. I believe Briscoe is in the dream, too—or at least he used to be. It's him they're waiting for."

Drew rolled his neck. He always knew he wasn't one of them, but neither did he appreciate being left in the dark. "You could have told me."

Winston glanced around to make sure they were unobserved, then spoke quietly. "There were six shards of the Scorpion Star, Drew. Two years ago, all six of us touched for an instant, and it was the most powerful thing I've ever felt. But now three of us are dead." Winston leaned in closer, his voice growing more hushed. "What if they weren't supposed to die? What if everything hinges on Dillon bringing them back, and the six of us coming together again?"

Drew uncomfortably shifted his shoulders, feeling the pull of the stitches on his arm, which wasn't getting any better.

"The whole has always been greater than the sum of our parts," Winston continued. "The more of us together, the more our powers multiply. With the way our powers are growing, can you imagine what might happen if the six of us came together now?"

"No, I can't." Drew said honestly. "I'm not sure I want to."

Winston nodded. "Neither does Briscoe."

THE NEXT INBOUND FROM Miami pulled up to the gate half an hour late. A short break for fueling, luggage, and mechanical Band-Aids, and it would head back to the land of gators and hurricanes. The crowds at the gate, however, made it doubtful that Drew and Winston would get seats.

They waited, eyeing the slow-moving check-in line, casually watching as passengers disembarked the jet in a panicked diaspora to catch whatever flight they were already late for.

So anxious was Drew to get on this flight that he almost missed the exiting passenger with a patch over his eye.

He saw it only for the briefest instant as he scanned the jetway exit, but once his brain registered what he had seen, he double-took to see the man's back as he strode toward the higher gates.

A dozen denials shot through Drew's mind. This could not be the same man. He looked taller; he looked leaner; what hair he had left seemed grayer at the temples. But Drew had only encountered him twice. How many men fitting that general description flew out of Miami on any given day? One hundred? Two hundred? How many with a wounded right eye? Drew felt his cool, level demeanor begin to splinter, and he shook Winston hard enough to rattle his chair.

"It's him! It's Briscoe—I'm sure of it!" His certainty swelled with his adrenaline.

"What?! Where?"

"There—just passing gate nine—do you see him?"

Their subject carried a leather shoulder bag that bulged like everyone else's carry-on—but there was an unnerving definition to the bulge, as if whatever it was, was not meant to be jammed into luggage. He turned to enter a bathroom, and again Drew caught a brief glimpse of the bandage over his eye.

"Would you know him if you saw him close up?" Winston asked.

"No question about it. What do we do?"

"What happened to the unshakeable Drew Camden I used to know?"

"I think he's about to piss his pants." Drew felt his emotions slingshot back to the scuffle on top of Michael's coffin, but Winston was there to pick up the slack, and pull both their minds into focus.

"Okay . . . okay, if it's him, we have to be careful," Winston said, as they headed toward the restroom.

"Do we storm the bathroom?"

"No—we're not even sure it's him yet. We'll separate—I'll go to the gift shop on this side of the restroom, you go to the bar on the far side—since it looks like he was headed toward the upper gates. When he comes out he'll pass one of us— hopefully you—and you'll get a better look at him. If we're lucky, he won't spot us."

"And then what? We can't make a move on him here— there are too many exits—too many chances for him to get away."

"We'll have to get him alone. Trap him somewhere."

Then something occurred to Drew. "There might be a way we can trap him," he said. "Without having to get him alone."

MARTIN BRISCOE, WHO USUALLY hated air travel, quickly discovered that airports were his friend. Where else could he vanish into a crowd so effectively? The fact that most people were on trajectories that took them hundreds of miles away made it even easier to be anonymous. He could murder some- one right there in the restroom, and by the time the body was found, any potential witnesses would be spread anywhere from Anchorage to Auckland. Not that he had any current intentions of homicide—but still, it was nice to know.

Locked in his stall, the toilet flushed as he stepped back. It was one of those automatic johns. The pinnacle of modern technology. He reached into his bag, pulled out the white urn, then opened the cap. His task was to spread Tory Smythe's ashes to the corners of the earth. And so holding the urn cradled in his left arm, he dipped his right thumb and forefinger in, extracting a pinch of ash.

He turned his eyes upward. "For your glory," he said aloud, in case the angels got off on praise—which he felt sure they did—although he also knew these were angels of action, not words. Long-winded psalms and the reciting of epistles would inspire impatience. He could sense that about them, so he pared his words of praise down to sound bytes.

Holding his fingertips close to the bowl, he rubbed them together, releasing the dusty ash, then stepped back. The bowl flushed automatically, and one more ration of Tory Smythe's physical essence was fed back to the Earth. Deep in his mind, at that strange interface, he could feel the glow of the angels' approval. But still they kept their distance, and he wondered what he had to do to bring them closer.

Perhaps when he was finished, they would come to him. Reward him.

As for Tory Smythe, she had a date with dissolution on a global scale. Even before laying waste to the offices of Eureka Dental, Martin had pulled out all of his savings, and now he had used most of it to purchase air tickets. Dallas was his first stop, then Mexico City, then Rio de Janeiro, Johannesburg, Barcelona, Tel Aviv, New Delhi, Tokyo, and a half dozen other ports of call in a massive globe-trotting itinerary. He fancied himself a Phineas Fogg of a new millennium; around the world in twenty-three days. And in each airport he would leave behind another dash of dust, until Tory Smythe had been dispersed more effectively than anyone who had ever lived.

The corners of the Earth. What a cushy assignment! This would more than make up for his failure with Michael Lipranski.

And that wasn't over, either. He would find that faggot friend of his, and julienne the truth out of him, exacting his revenge in pounds of flesh until he told Martin where Michael's body was hidden.

But why embitter himself with that now? He had listened to enough motivational tapes in his life to know that negative energy never helped the situation. Best to focus on the task at hand. So he spent a moment tracing his hopscotch flight paths in his mind, until he could see that final destination, when he would stand on the rim of Black Canyon, where he had once stood and watched his wife and son die beneath the flood, and he would hurl the empty urn into the dry bed of the Colorado River.

When he left the restroom, he felt untouchable.

Mexico City was currently not a hot destination, and his flight was only half full. Although he would have preferred his excursion first class all the way, his funds kept him mostly in coach. When the door closed, he thought he might get both the window and aisle seat to himself—but after the plane left the gate, a black kid, who reeked of travel sweat, changed seats, dropping his ass right next to Martin. Lately Martin's tolerance for minorities had declined, so he turned his one good eye out of the window as the plane taxied toward the runway, hoping that with any luck the black kid might find another empty seat more inviting. Perhaps it was just the thrill of his journey, but as the plane accelerated toward takeoff, he could feel his skin tingle. The hair on his arms, the skin of his scalp, his cuticles. It was a sensation that was familiar, although he couldn't quite place where he had felt it before. Then, as the nose of the jet lifted off the runway, it occurred to him the time and place that went along with that sensation. It was a rose garden in the shadow of Hearst Castle, where one of the self-proclaimed gods held court. His flesh had crawled then as his body hair grew, and he watched roses explode from buds into full bloom in a matter of seconds.

Before the rear landing gear left the earth, he knew who was sitting next to him.

He turned his head, exaggerating the motion to give his left eye a clear sight of the passenger to his right. It was unmistakably Winston Pell, who smiled coldly at him and said, "You need a haircut."

Martin could only stammer. "You're dead! You're supposed to be dead. Like Tory—like Michael and the others. Like Dillon!"

"Reports of my death have been greatly exaggerated," he said. "Looks like your carry-on doesn't quite fit under the seat in front of you. Mind telling me what's inside?"

"Go to hell."

And then a second face appeared looming over the seat back in front of him. "Well, if it isn't my buddy the one-eyed Chihuahua killer!" said Drew Camden.

"You both go to hell!" Martin blurted out.

"No," said Drew, "I believe we're going to Mexico City."

By now several surrounding passengers had taken notice of their exchange, but as the plane was still on a steep ascent, no flight attendants stalked the aisle.

"You should get that eye looked at," said Winston. "It's

infected, isn't it? Those bacteria must be growing at an incredible rate right now."

Sure enough, Martin could feel the flesh around his eye burn and his sinuses ache. Around him the gray cloud cover gave way to bright sunlight as they punched through the clouds. But there was another light now; a light deep in Martin's mind. Light and pain and voices without words.

It was the angels.

They were furious. He was failing them. They wanted action, not praise, not excuses. They wanted his action, they demanded his action.

"Too bad Tory's not alive," said Winston. "Infections were her thing, she could have cleaned you up in a sec. Of course, in some ways, she's still with us, isn't she?"

"So why don't you be a nice little psycho, and give us your bag," said Drew. *"Now."*

The pain in his eye grew unbearable, as did the voices, and the light. He unbuckled his seatbelt, pulled the bag out from the seat, and motioned as if to hand the bag over to Winston, but instead climbed on his seat, and leapt over its back to the seat behind him, landing on a very surprised woman. There were loud exclamations from the travelers around him, but he ignored them. He still had a mission, but now that mission had changed.

Drew and Winston came at him, but he evaded their grasp. Wrapping his bag's strap around his arm, then gripping the bag to his chest, Martin flew down the steeply inclined aisle toward the back. There were few options left to him now. He might be able to handle the Camden kid, but he was no match for Winston Pell. The freakish boy could focus his power into a surge that would shoot his growing infection down the optic nerve, routing his brain. God knew what else he was capable of. So Martin bolted to put distance between them, even if that distance could only be a dozen yards.

The aft flight attendant had seen this coming.

She had heard the escalating argument, and knew that, whatever it was about, no good could come of it—and now they had all left their seats, heading for her. What's more, the man with the carry-on had a desperate look about him that summoned her gooseflesh. She rose to intercept.

"You'll all have to find a seat now!" she said, getting between the two teens and the riot-eyed man. "You're disturbing the other passengers, and are in severe violation of—"

The black teen pushed her out of the way to get at the man, who frantically eyed the hatch.

"This can all be over now!" the black teen told the man with the bag, but the man was surprisingly strong, hurling the kid away hard enough to deliver him across the galley, knocking loose the secured cart which flew out of its niche, and tumbled on the boy.

"I need help back here!" the flight attendant shouted. By now other attendants were already running to join the melee.

The man held his pack high out of reach of the second teen—high enough for the other passengers to get a good look at the bulging, rigid shape inside.

"He's got a bomb!" someone yelled. The cabin erupted in panic, to the point that the flight attendant wondered if it were true. She hesitated, and rather than deal with the man, decided to fend off his antagonists, because whatever the situation was, they were making it worse. She turned to the black kid, who had just freed himself from beneath the cart.

As Winston rose to his feet, he saw Briscoe swing his bag at Drew's arm, the urn inside connecting with his injury. Drew wailed in pain. Winston tried to get back into the fight, but the stewardess inserted herself as an obstacle in the narrow galley.

She shouted something ridiculous about placing him under FAA arrest, while behind her, Briscoe was tugging mightily on the hatch's release lever.

"Drew! Stop him!" But Drew was already being hauled up the aisle by a steward, and two other passengers who had had enough.

Winston saw the hatch lever engage, and self-preservation suddenly supplanted all else. He reached up, grabbed a hand rail, and clenched his fist around it as a blast of sudden wind exploded in his painfully popping ears.

It was Drew who had the clearest view.

Eyes still locked on Briscoe even as he was pulled away, Drew saw the handle go down, and the instant the lock disengaged, the door crashed open, and Briscoe was gone, sack and all. At only a mile high, decompression wasn't explosive, but it was close enough. A wind sucked violently through the cabin, air masks dropped. Drew's feet flew out from under him and he hooked an arm rest with his good arm. The flight attendant who had first tried to stop them grabbed futilely for purchase, then was ejected into the void. Pressure equalized, but the roar of wind and engines remained.

"Winston!"

But Drew couldn't even hear his own voice. The jet vibrated as if it would rattle itself apart, and the screams around the cabin began to fade as passengers realized they were not going to die. The sound of the engines changed as the pilot took a new flight plan, slowing airspeed, angling them for descent and a quick airport return.

Winston, just aft of the open door, let go of the handrail, the chilling wind pummeling him, thundering in his ears. He slid to the floor, and put his head in his hands, already feeling the depth of what had been lost.

• • •

Tumbling in a cold freefall, Martin Briscoe fought to get control of his plunge. The brilliant blue sky had become a white fog as he hit the clouds, and he could no longer tell up from down. He had looped the strap of his bag twice around his arm before the door opened. But the force of being sucked into the thin atmosphere had torn the strap free from one side of his bag. Now it twisted on a tether. He fought to pull it to his chest, then gripped it tightly.

There was a sound now, even more furious, more demanding than the wind. It was the angels. *"There is one deed left to do,"* they told him, *"the one act that will avenge your family's death, and will make your life count for something."* He could hear them now so much closer than they had been before, no longer behind a window, but pressing urgently upon his mind. No faces, only voices, light, and shadow. *"Do this one last thing, and we can enter this world unchallenged. Dillon will be damned,"* they assured him, *"and you will be elevated."*

The clouds gave way to clear air, and a flat brown landscape below. Still clutching the bag under his arm, he undid the clasp and reached in. Then he grabbed the lid of the urn, and tore it off.

Tory Smythe's ashes became a funnel plume escaping the urn, like an unfurling parachute. Her dust billowed into the shredding currents of the wind, and when the urn was empty Briscoe released the pack, letting the wind take it as well.

The deed was done and he could sense the angels' satisfaction as they prepared for a grand entrance into the world. With the ground less than a thousand feet away now, he gloated, and laughed, for the shards were defeated, and the heavens appeased. Then he stretched his arms out wide to receive the earth, and his reward.

18. AN ABUNDANCE OF FISH

A THOUSAND MILES SOUTH OF DALLAS, A STEEL GATE SEVEN feet thick and weighing seven hundred tons slowly swung open, then slowly swung shut. Once sealed, the chamber was flooded. This water-step lifted even the greatest of ships more than thirty feet before the Pedromiguel Lock released them on their way toward the treacherous Gaillard Cut, Gatun Lake, and the Atlantic side of the Panama Canal.

At midday, ships bottlenecked in Lake Miraflores. Eight of them today—from the sleekest of cruise ships to the rankest rust-bucket freighters. All became equal as they waited for the locks to admit them, one by one.

The gate labored open. A freighter passed into the lock. The gate labored shut. The waters within the lock silently rose.

A small switchback path on the eastern bank of Lake Miraflores zig-zagged its way up the hill, lined with colorful flowers. Thousands of cruise passengers would see it as they passed, comment on how it resembled a great Zorro "Z" on the hillside, and then think themselves clever that they had thought of that.

The garden path, which connected a tiny weather-worn dock to a house further up the hill, was planted by Gabriela Ceballos, who died before she could enjoy it, and was now maintained religiously by her daughter.

Unobserved on that east side of the lake were three Canal Zone residents. The boy at the foot of the path, kicking his feet back and forth at the end of the small dock, the mother, who labored on the garden path, and the grandfather, who sat on the verandah at the head of the path, watching the snare of ships in the lake.

Carlos Ceballos was the patriarch of a family much smaller than it should have been. His fault, really, and his wife's, for educating their children so well, that three out of four broke out of their familial orbit, leaving Panama completely. But Carlos could never leave home. Even his job as a canal pilot never took him far from home—just from one end of the canal to the other. Still, the glimpses of the world he saw aboard the ships he piloted made him feel like a world traveler. At fifty-five he was one of the most respected canal pilots, and boasted more than twenty thousand trips through the canal. Each time a virgin ship arrived for its first transcanal voyage, Carlos was given the honor of piloting her.

But today was Sunday, his day off, and so Carlos thankfully found himself peering out across the lake from his little verandah at the mouth of the garden path, eating salted jicama as he watched other pilots maneuver the familiar contingent of ships up and down the Pedromiguel Lock—but not fast enough, for seven ships clogged the waters of Miraflores now. Four cargo, three cruise ships. Music blasted from the cruise ship decks, resounding from the hills and blending into an arrhythmic cacophony that wasn't entirely unpleasant. Such had become the soundtrack of Carlos Cabellos's life. His life was filled by the sounds from the ships, the taste of salted jicama, and the smell, that luxurious smell of plumeria blooms that swept up from the garden path, reminding him so much of his late wife. There was something missing, however. A feeling that nagged at him even in his quietest of moments. Unfinished business. It would wake him at night, and when his mind was idle, it would pull him to the front door, as if he were heading out for an errand, only to find that there were no errands to be run. Each Sunday he would sit on the verandah, wondering what this unfinished business might be.

The gate swung open. The gate swung closed. Another ship was already approaching from the Miraflores locks to take the place of the one that had been dispatched.

Cerilla Ceballos tended flowers just past the second turn of the switchback path. Cerilla had never married. A badly cleft lip had warded off most suitors. She was twenty-five now, resigned to her lot—which included an eight-year-old son. She had him at sixteen, by a schoolmate who apparently didn't care about her face, as long as he got what came with it. But he had quickly found someone else, then disappeared into the crowded workforce of Panama City, and now she had little Memo.

She had always believed that her face was a judgment for something she had done, or would someday do. The priest said she had more than done her penance for having Memo out of the sacrament of marriage, but she was never quite sure. So it became her way to turn her thoughts to God as she pruned and planted flowers, tending the garden path her mother had so loved. Fragrant lilies, and bright gold-petaled plumeria. An hour among the rich plumeria would perfume her skin with its sweet fragrance. It made her feel beautiful, and so she lingered there, waiting for forgiveness or damnation. Waiting for something to happen that might define her life in terms as vibrant as the flowers around her.

The gate labored open, admitted a ship, then labored closed.

Eight-year-old Guillermo "Memo" Ceballos often sat on the rocks by the edge of the lake, his palm spread across the stone. If you touched the stones by the shore, you could actually feel the gate closing before you heard it. Feeling the resonance of the gates through his bones connected him to this place, and he secretly longed to pilot the canal like his grandfather Carlos, although his mother wanted more for him. It's why she made him learn English, and always spoke of his uncles, and how successful they were in far-off places.

He didn't argue with her. So for now, he was content to sit at the end of the little dock and fish, watching the great ships pass, imagining himself piloting them through the canal gates. Imagining that they weren't mere oceangoing vessels, but spaceships in disguise, bound for starports far beyond the Atlantic or Pacific.

There was power in being an observer; knowing the cycle of the ships, each returning on their own schedule, but yet as regular as the phases of the moon. The ships always came back to him, on his lake. There was satisfaction in knowing that his little fishing dock sat smack in the middle of the greatest crossroads of the world.

His feet dangling over the edge of the dock, he reeled in his line to reveal that his bait was gone.

"There are no fish in Miraflores," Abuelo Carlos often told him when he spent such long hours with his line in the water. It wasn't true, of course. Certainly fish were harder to come by than in the larger Gatun Lake, but they were here. They were not good to eat, though, what with the oily sheen that covered the overtraveled lake.

"Sometime I'll take you out in the Pacific," his grandfather endlessly promised. For those were waters rich in porgy and striped tuna. This was the "abundance of fish" for which Panama was named, not the troubled waters of Miraflores.

Memo cut a juicy bloodworm in half, then wove it onto the hook, which stuck out from the end of his lure: a silver, tear-shaped sparkler. The shiny lure had been made from one of his late grandmother's old earrings. He knew she wouldn't have minded. Some fish smell the blood, Abuelo Carlos had taught him, others were drawn to the shine of the lure. The important thing was to give them what they want. Memo knew if he offered them what they couldn't resist, even the lonely fish of Miraflores could be caught. So he threw in his line, dreaming of cruise ships and starships, and waited with an anticipation that never waned.

The gate opened. The gate closed.

A point of light appeared in the air just beyond the end of Memo's dock.

The reflection off the shell of a beetle, Memo thought. Except for the fact that the pinprick of light didn't move.

A sudden breeze moved across the surface of the lake. It hit the shore, then doubled back again, picking up petals and leaves, kicking up a sweet, earthy smell. The breeze danced like a living thing; Memo watched the path of leaves and petals circling the piles of the dock, then the breeze came to him, swirling around him, slithering like a snake about to constrict. Then all at once the breeze died, and the petals and leaves fell from him to the wooden slats of the dock.

The point of light was still there, a few feet out, off the end of the dock, ten feet in the air—but it was more than just a point now. It was growing. The light fed itself, billowing out from its center, until it was an orb the size of a soccer ball, shifting with colors so bright he feared they might blind him, but so beautiful he could not look away.

"Mama," he called out. "Abuelo!"

They did not hear him call, but they were already running, for something had been stirred inside them.

Memo now stood, toes curled over the end of the dock,

leaning forward as far as his balance would allow, reaching a hand toward the growing ball of light. He had heard of ball lightning, but knew this was something else. Like the wind, it was alive. And calling to him.

"Guillermo Gabriel Cuevas Ceballos," they said—for there was more than one voice, more than one spirit within the ball of light. And then he realized it wasn't a ball at all. It was a porthole, like on the many ships that passed. An opening to another place. *"Guillermo Gabriel Cuevas Ceballos,"* they said. *"It is you we seek."*

His mother heard it, too, but it wasn't Memo's name she heard—it was her own. And Carlos, bounding down the hillside, was certain these voices were calling to him. "I am here," he shouted. "Gabriela, I am here," for he was certain that the voice he heard first and foremost was that of his dead wife.

Cerilla, then Carlos came bounding onto the dock, for this hole of light had more than just pulled their focus—it filled the absence of focus that had been building in their lives. This uncanny visitation was Carlos's unfinished business. It was his daughter's defining moment. It was the tug at the end of Memo's line that he had been waiting for all this time. How could it not steal their attention? How could they not drop everything for it?

And now the three of them stood there, side by side at the end of the dock, the shimmering hole of light filling all of their thoughts and senses, leaving no room for anything else.

The hole spread wider, the clouds in the sky beyond it distorting, straining as space stretched for the growing hole of light. Hairline fractures began to form in the space around the hole, like the aged canvas of a medieval painting.

And in that bright light, three figures began to take definition.

There was no mistaking who stood within the breach, because the boy, the woman, and the old man saw them, if not with their squinted eyes, with their minds—with their souls.

It was undeniable to Carlos Ceballos that this was the spirit of his wife, flanked by two gossamer-winged angels of light.

It was undeniable to Cerilla Ceballos that this was God the Father, with the Son on his right hand, and the holy spirit to his left.

It was undeniable to Memo Ceballos that these were the aliens he had seen in the movies, come to take him away from a sedate, fatherless world.

There was no question who they were.

"We have come to you," their voices intoned.

"To ease your pain."

"To grant you salvation."

"To take you away."

"If only you open."

"If only you invite."

"If only you grant us admission to dwell in your world, your home, your flesh."

"For we have come to you, and you alone."

"Take us in."

Their minds told them it was all they ever wanted. Their hearts told them that it was right, that it was true, and their flesh longed to be the vessels for such extraordinary light.

"Yes," they told them.

"Yes, fill me with your love."

"With your glory."

"With your strangeness."

"Yes," they said. "Enter in."

A gate flung open. The sky shattered like a windshield hit by a bullet. A blast of living light blew them off their feet. And for an instant there was surprise, and the pain of the hook. Red tendrils of living light snared them, ripping them free from themselves, and dragged them down slick gullets where nothing awaited them but death.

The dock buckled from the sudden blast of energy. A shock wave expanded outward, and then silence. Then in a few moments, three figures stood, making their way from the ruined dock, to the shore. The man, the woman, and the boy. But those three human souls were gone; devoured. Something different resided within their bodies now.

With steady, determined strides, the three climbed the switchback trail, indifferent to its beauty, or the smell of its flowers. While behind them, in the air above the twisted piles and planks of the dock, the fracture in space left by their projectile arrival slowly healed itself closed.

Part III

Anglers

19. DEEP GATHERING

A DOUBLE SHOCK WAVE SPREAD FROM THE SHORE OF LAKE Miraflores—a blast of undefined radiant energy, accompanied by a slower-moving sonic boom, like thunder after lightning. The boom echoed within the hulls of the freighters and pleasure craft traversing the Panama canal, but while its power faded with distance, the strength of the first wave did not.

Some felt the psychic blast as a visceral flash of déjà vu, gone before it could be grasped. Others felt it as a burst of mental static that momentarily derailed their train of thought. But there were three individuals whose reactions were far stronger.

On a cruise ship between locks of the canal, Lourdes Hidalgo collapsed and began to convulse in a grand mal. Since her physiology controlled all those within her immediate sphere of influence, so did all others on the vessel.

Toward the rear of a plane that had just touched down in Dallas after an emergency landing, Winston Pell began to scream uncontrollably, unable to catch his breath, and unable to understand why.

And on a two-lane interstate in rural East Texas, a stolen pickup truck flew off the road and wrapped around a tree.

• • •

HALF AN HOUR EARLIER, Dillon and Maddy had crossed from Louisiana into Texas.

Maddy had begun to liken Dillon to a shark again—a creature that could not stop moving, lest it sink and drown—so powerful, yet a slave to its own motion. He spoke little, kept the radio off, and demanded the wheel, claiming that driving kept his mind focused as they plunged West through the lush East Texas foliage. For the longest time, there was nothing but trees on either side of the straight road, until they passed a huge, incongruous blue billboard. The billboard featured a bold yellow 800 number, and beneath it the words "vasectomy reversal." Seeing that sign all by itself in the middle of nowhere made Maddy laugh aloud.

"See, Dillon," she said, nodding at the sign, "there are things in this world more bizarre than you."

"I could do the job without an 800 number," Dillon deadpanned. "And I'll bet I charge less, too."

"I'm glad to see you have a sense of humor," she told him.

Dillon considered that. "Do I take myself too seriously, Maddy?"

"You are the most somber deity I know."

He chuckled at that. It made Maddy feel a touch more powerful in the situation.

More hints of civilization passed around them, until they actually began to see homes through the trees.

"At least we're getting somewhere," Dillon said.

Maddy reached over to wipe some sweat dripping down the side of his face. He had a beautiful profile, in spite of the scars. To her he was perfect, and she wondered when it was she had fallen in love with him. Perhaps it was the first time she had touched him, reaching in through that horrible face mask to scratch his nose.

All at once she felt a sudden, uncomfortable surge in her solar plexus, and for an instant forgot what she was thinking about. Then Dillon screamed and jerked the wheel left, pulling them across the double-yellow. Maddy's shoulder slammed into the side window with the force of the turn.

"Dillon!?"

In an instant they were off the road entirely, and the feel of the asphalt beneath them gave way to airborne numbness as they flew over a ditch, toward the trunk of a huge oak.

Even before the wheels contacted the ground, the pickup hit the massive tree at seventy miles an hour.

The old pickup had no air bag, and Maddy's seatbelt tore loose from the impact. Her skull smashed the windshield. Her shoulder hit the tree. Her broken body tumbled in the dead grass.

Intense pain.

Darkness.

But no loss of consciousness.

In a few seconds the pain was gone.

Maddy was on the ground, looking up at a gray sky beyond the branches of the oak. Her hair was matted and wet with blood. It covered her clothes. She saw the bloody hole in the windshield through which she had ejected, but no wounds remained on her body. She had been healed so quickly, her battered body hadn't even had the chance to die before being restored.

Dillon was still in the pickup, pinned by the steering wheel, wailing—but his screams didn't seem to be about the pain. Maddy climbed on the crumpled hood, punching loose what was left of the windshield. "Dillon! Dillon, calm down!"

It was as if he didn't see her—his eyes were wild, like the eyes of the people he shattered.

"They're here!" he wailed. "They're here!"

"Who's here?"

He gritted his teeth, fighting the steering wheel, pushing back, and it seemed as if he made the crushed cabin longer again. Until Maddy realized that the truck was indeed stretching. She tumbled from the hood and watched in disbelief as the crumpled steel of the totaled vehicle unfolded. Shattered glass fought the pull of gravity, crawling back into place.

"My God . . ."

Another fifteen seconds and the Nissan pickup was in mint condition, its grille kissing the bark of the oak. Not a dent; not a scratch.

Dillon's power had never acted this quickly—it had never been this strong. Maddy could feel his strength now. She could always feel his power simmering beside her—but not like this. Now his presence was like the heat of a furnace. Whatever had set him screaming in the first place had charged him to a new high.

DILLON BARELY NOTICED HITTING the tree. He was faintly aware that his body had been crushed and healed at a speed unlike anything he had done before. But none of that mattered . . . *because they were here.*

He had no idea who *they* were, or why their entrance to this world was of such significance. He didn't even know why he had been dreaming about them. Even as his powers spiked, he felt weak, vulnerable, and powerless in the face of what *they* were. For a moment he saw Maddy trying to get his attention, but there wasn't room enough in his mind to hold her. She was little more than a snapshot as he ran past her through the trees that lined the highway and onto a service road, where several people had already come out of their homes to view an accident that was no longer there.

There were three homes on the street and a business with a gravel parking lot. Through an empty lot there were more buildings on what must have been the main street of this one-stoplight town.

There was a steepled building across that lot. A church. Plain beige brick. Humble and unprepossessing. He reached for the cross around his neck—the one his parents had given him when he was a boy—and remembered that it was gone—that it hadn't been there for years. He had lost it in his days of infestation, when the wrecking-hunger consumed him, and the parasite of destruction co-opted his power to feed itself. He remembered stumbling into a church during those dark times—but even the poor priest who had heard his confession had been destroyed by his presence. So helpless and confused he had been. It was the same way now. Suddenly the sanctuary of this homely church seemed the most inviting place on earth, and he longed to curl up in the protective shadow of something greater than himself.

He tried to make a beeline to the church, but found himself stumbling all the way through the field. The path of brown grass and dried autumn leaves greened like a living stream around him, spreading outward like a wake on water. As he approached the church from the back, he tripped over a waist-high wrought iron fence around the property. He found himself on the ground, facing a row of headstones. The church had its own graveyard. A sizeable one. The brown grass on the graves was already turning green. He sensed what was about to happen, and he closed his eyes, desperately praying that it wouldn't—but he had no faith in his own prayer. He knew that today his prayers would go as unheeded as the prayers of pigeons.

"Dillon, look at me!"

It was Maddy again. She grabbed him and rolled him over, pinning his shoulders. "Focus on *me!*"

"No! No—I can't be here!" But it was already too late, because he could hear—he could *feel* beneath the reviving grass, a deeper gathering of life.

HOLDING DILLON DOWN WAS like gripping a live wire. His iridescence burned through Maddy, an intense sensation her body could not decipher as either pleasure or pain, but an amalgam of both. Then when she heard the first voice, it caught Maddy off guard, and she loosened her grip on Dillon just enough for him to push her off and scramble away. He didn't get far; just a few yards, before he crumpled by a tombstone, weeping and slowly shaking his head like a bull struck by a car.

"*Hey!*" someone had shouted. "*Hey, is anybody there?*" She looked around. The voice was muffled and distant. She couldn't place the direction from which it came.

Then there was a second voice and another, and another. "*What is this?*" "*Somebody answer me!*" "*Hello?!*"

And it dawned on Maddy with a jagged, penetrating chill that these voices were not coming from the church or the woods, or nearby buildings. They came from beneath her feet.

"*What's happening?*" "*Help me!*" "*Who's out there?*"

It began as confusion and curiosity, then when some rudimentary understanding kicked in, their cries turned fearful, their fists pounding in the dark upon the satin-lined caskets that confined them. At first it was just a few, but it soon grew into a chorus of screaming for release beneath the tons of earth that covered them.

"No no no!" Dillon cried, covering his ears. "Make them stop! Make them stop!"

Maddy stood there, dumbfounded. She had no response for this. Nothing in her tactical training had prepared her for *this*.

Suddenly a rhythmic roar swooped down from above, for a brief moment overwhelming the cries of the underchorus before it passed. Maddy knew it was a helicopter even before she saw it. Generic gray, with no markings. It buzzed the tree-tops, then set down in a clearing a hundred yards away.

Then, when she turned back to the graveyard there was a flak-jacketed, rifle-armed force—at least a dozen men—storming the graveyard from two directions. Once in range, they brought up their rifles and took aim. Some were trained on her, but most were on Dillon. She went to Dillon, shielding him with her body, trying to keep him from making sudden moves, because he was still within himself, oblivious to it all. And beneath them, the chorus grew in desperate insanity.

A figure approached from the helicopter. He wore a dark suit, and had a familiar stride. Even though she had a clear view of him as he approached, it wasn't until he stepped into the graveyard that she locked on his identity. It was Elon Tessic.

To Elon Tessic, disguise was a simple trick of perception; once he became defined by his white attire, he merely had to shed it to become invisible. Even personal friends had failed to recognize him when he wore anything other than pressed Mediterranean white. Today he was just another man in a dark suit.

As he approached, Tessic found his overzealous mercenaries to have far too much firepower for his liking, so he signaled to their leader, a militia-bred mercenary named Davitt, to lower their weapons.

Even before he stepped into the graveyard, Elon could hear the distraught voices underfoot, and feel the waves of psychic energy strobing off of Dillon. It was intimidating to say the least, but not entirely unexpected. Once he had stepped over the fence, he approached Maddy, whose confusion had already taken a turn toward anger.

"Tessic!" she screamed. "You son of a bitch."

"My men will escort you to my helicopter," he said calmly.

"If they come near us, I'll break their necks."

"I have no doubt you would . . . but if you decide to stay here, I can guarantee that your military friends won't be far behind."

She hesitated, studying him. "You're not working for them?"

"I'm an independent contractor," he told her. "Today I'm here to help."

She threw a glance at the armed men around them. "Are they?"

Elon grabbed one of the mercenaries' rifles, opened the barrel, and showed it to Maddy.

"Tranquilizer darts, in case we encountered your resistance."

The moment of silence between them was punctuated by the muffled voices hopelessly calling from the grave.

"We must get Dillon away from this place," he told her. "Do you hear around you? Do you understand?"

Without answering, Maddy knelt back down to Dillon, who had been subdued by the voices of those he had called back from the dead. She helped him to his feet and threw an untrusting glance at Tessic, but in the end, got Dillon out of the graveyard, and moved him toward the helicopter that waited in the nearby field.

A dozen yards away, a scraping of concrete drew Tessic's attention. A man labored to push up the concrete lid of his own crypt, his fingertips already raw from the task. A scene from the Haunted Mansion, but far more disturbing.

Disturbing, thought Tessic, but not frightening—for these were not ghouls, but ordinary people, unable to know the cause of their situation. Not comprehending their own death, much less their call back to life.

"Help me. Please," said the man, straining against the concrete lid. "Someone's put me down here . . . someone's buried me alive. . . ."

A few of Tessic's mercenaries, now fearful themselves, looked at Tessic for direction. Even Davitt was affected by it. "What do we do?" he asked.

"Go help him!" Tessic ordered.

Two men forced off the lid of the crypt and it tumbled to the ground. They pulled out a middle-aged man in a tan, pin-striped suit that was pressed and clean. The style was at least thirty years out of date.

"Who in blazes are you?" the man asked, when Tessic approached. Since no response would have made sense to him, Tessic chose not to answer. Instead he turned to Davitt. "We'll take him with us as well."

"What about the others?"

Tessic looked around the graveyard. The voices were growing weaker. There were only two crypts with lids that could be removed. The rest were earthen graves. Even if he had had a hundred men with shovels, he couldn't have unearthed a single one of them before they all suffocated. So Tessic had his men remove the occupant of the second crypt, then forced himself to listen to the other voices, giving them at the very least, the dignity of a witness.

He could hear in their fading voices a mix of emotions. There were those who had some rudimentary understanding, and accepted this moment as a gift, and those who saw it as a curse. There were the sounds of love, comfort, and surprise between husbands and wives whose departures had been years apart. There were also wails full of the agonized loneliness of those who had no one to comfort them in this all too brief hiatus from eternity.

"Yitgadal V'yitkadash sh'mei raba . . ." Elon began. It was the mourner's *kaddish*—the Jewish prayer for the dead. He said it without the required minyan of ten. He said it alone, with the same conviction he had afforded his parents, his sisters. Loved ones who died old, and those who died before their time. He intoned the holy words with reverence, and respect. And when he was done, he could no longer hear their voices. The dead were dead once more.

When he looked up, he saw a half a dozen spectators across the street, keeping a safe distance from the armed men. None were close enough to know who or what they saw.

"What languages do you know?" he asked Davitt.

"English . . . German."

Tessic tried to hide his distaste. German would actually work to his advantage. "Go to those people. If any of them have cameras, break them. Confiscate their phones as well. Tell them to leave—but do it in German. Everything must be done in German."

Davitt accepted his orders, and took two men with him.

Tessic could only assume that the intelligence of every nation now knew that Dillon had escaped. When the authorities came, these townsfolk would tell of an unmarked helicopter, a man in a dark suit—and a SWAT team spouting German. The trajectory of blame wouldn't even come close to Tessic.

Satisfied, he strode back toward the helicopter which would deliver Dillon, Maddy, and himself, out of harm's way.

20. TANGO IN FALSE LIGHT

LOURDES WAS CERTAIN SHE HAD SUFFERED A STROKE; THAT her hedonistic lifestyle of excess had hemorrhaged an artery in her brain. Darkness enveloped her peripheral vision, and although she never actually felt her legs give out, the bruising slap of the deck against her face told her that she had collapsed. Her senses all but gone, she awaited fearfully a lapse of consciousness, and the moment when the darkness would close in, her heart would heave itself still, and her life would end. But it did not happen. Instead her heart pounded so forcefully it sent veiny streaks of lightning across her imploded vision, beat after beat. Pain in her eyes and ears crested with every pulse. Then the pain found a home in the base of her neck, and radiated from there to her temples, and out to her extremities. She lay like this in throbbing paralysis for at least ten minutes. Then gradually her vision began to return, and her muscles began to obey her commands. She brought a hand to her face, feeling the pressure of blood swelling the bruise, then pulled herself up into a sitting position. Her body felt heavy and ponderous, as it had in the days when she was obese. She had to look around to remind herself where she was; her private sun deck of the *Blue Horizon*, overlooking the lido deck. Up above the cloud-speckled sky was the same, but she knew something had fundamentally changed about the world; something intangible that she chose not to consider right now. At this moment just getting to her feet took enough of her concentration.

To her right were a pair of grossly overweight crewmen that had been waxing the wooden railing of her private deck. One struggled to his feet, the other still lay on the deck, not moving at all. A god-awful sound pulled her attention to the left, where her latest boy toy crouched on all fours. He was a twenty-year-old blond, unencumbered by intelligence—an Adonis she had taken to her bed, if only to prove to herself that she wasn't looking for a harem of dark-haired Michael Lipranski look-alikes, as Winston had claimed. Now her blond boy hunched on his knees, retching up what looked like pulverized crab meat. The sight of it quickly removed him from her list of lovers.

She stood, gripping the guard rail for balance, and looked to the pool deck below. At the far end of the deck, the breakfast buffet had been in full swing, but now it looked like a blast zone. Her frightened, moaning passengers hauled themselves to the nearest chairs, not even concerned with the plates that had broken on the ground. It was difficult for Lourdes to discern whether this devastating event had hit all of them, or if it had only hit her, and the others aboard were just mimicking her own physiological response.

A few feet away, the conscious crewman checked the pulse of his fallen crewmate, then turned to Lourdes, his eyes a study in terror.

"He's dead," the crewman said.

Although Lourdes was no stranger to death, neither did she wish to linger with it. "Take him below," she said, not sure where down below the body should be taken, only that it should be taken there. She assumed someone would deal with it, and it would cease to be her problem.

"Please . . . he needs a priest," the crewman said.

A priest? Lourdes had neither the time nor capacity for such compassion. "Take him!" she ordered.

The man obeyed without further word, dragging the body out of sight, and out of mind.

What happened to you, Lourdes? Winston's words and that doleful expression on his face came back to her, like the hint of a conscience crawling back from wherever she had banished it to. She knew full well a conscience came with heavy baggage of regret, and she was determined to regret nothing, not now, not ever. She suppressed thoughts of Winston, until they, too, were out of mind.

Shielding her eyes from the sun, she looked at the shores around the ship. By the look of it, they were in a lake larger than the first lake they had encountered in the canal, but the sea was nowhere in sight. She put in a call to the bridge, and demanded to speak with the canal pilot, whose job it was to shuttle them to the Atlantic.

"Three more locks, señorita," the pilot told her with a tremor of fear in his voice. "But the . . . the fainting spell, it set us a little off course. We need to reposition the ship before we bring her through the Gatun Locks."

Lourdes sighed, exasperated, and told him to get to it. She had grown accustomed to the open sea, and found the canal to be constricting and claustrophobic, even at its widest points. Now that sensation of being closed in was even stronger, and she was anxious to reach the Atlantic.

She left the open deck, returning to her suite. Although her cabin stewards stumbled over one another to assist her in her slightest needs, she waved them off. Her head pounded too much for her to bother with anyone right now.

Only after she had lain down on her bed and tried to relax did her thoughts settle enough for her to parse from the pain what had happened.

The more she considered it, the more she was certain; there

was no mistaking the signature of the psychic wave that had floored her. The three performers from her dreams had left the stage, taking their act on the road.

Not my problem! she told herself, summoning up a healthy dose of protective anger. *Dillon set this all in motion—let him struggle with it; I'm on vacation.*

Twenty minutes later, she was informed that a pilot ship was approaching from the Gatun station. For some reason, a new canal pilot was requesting permission to come aboard.

"One pilot," Lourdes asked the captain, "or three?"

The captain apologized, and explained that it was only one pilot, but that, for some reason, he was bringing his family along with him. "Shall we let them on?" the captain asked. After more than two months he had fully accepted Lourdes's authority over him, and deferred to her on everything.

Lourdes gave permission for the new pilot and his escorts to come aboard, knowing that the Gatun Locks would not be setting her free until she faced her trio of players.

THE S.S. *BLUE HORIZON* left the queue of ships anchored in Gatun Lake, and Lourdes put on her most festive party dress. She received her visitors in the observation lounge, overlooking the bow of the ship. She made sure the lounge was well populated and full of chatter, determined to maintain the atmosphere of a party throughout her confrontation with the three. Their meeting would be a simple chat on an ordinary cruise. She would not let it intimidate her.

When they arrived, and were shown to their table, she almost laughed. They were not even close to what she expected. A small gray-haired Panamanian man with weathered skin, a bat-ugly woman with bad hair, and a child.

"Welcome aboard the *Blue Horizon*," Lourdes said. The man

shook her hand, the woman smiled dismally through her cleft lip, and the boy's attention was lost on the view through the slanted glass window. "*Ichole!*" he said, the Spanish equivalent of "wow."

"Would you prefer English, or Spanish?" the man asked.

"English," she told him.

"Then you have to excuse the accents," the man said. "Our speaking, it is limited by the experience of . . . of . . ." He turned to the boy. "*Como diçe?*"

"Human hosts," the boy answered.

"Yes. We are limited by the experience of our human hosts."

She was stunned by how blatant they were in declaring their supernatural nature, as if it were nothing unusual. She offered to converse in Spanish, but they refused.

"We learn speak more very soon," said the split-lipped woman, who had the least command of the language.

"Although we are limited by the past of these bodies," the man said, "our future has no limit."

The cocktail waiter brought Lourdes her usual, and she stirred the white Colada into the pink daiquiri, but didn't drink. Best to keep all of her faculties. She offered her guests a round, but they declined.

"Pleasures later," the man said.

"*Alcohol es caca,*" the boy said, sticking out his tongue. "Grandpa says so."

Memories of his host? thought Lourdes. Were those memories an asset, or a hindrance? Whatever these creatures were, did their newly acquired bodies weaken them? How much danger was she in just being with them?

Since they were frank, she chose to be frank as well. "You talk of host bodies," Lourdes said. "Are you spirit parasites, or spirit predators?"

The boy giggled at the question, but none of them answered.

"Well, what are you?"

They looked to one another, and the boy reached out, gently touching Lourdes's face. She recoiled from his touch. The boy was unbothered by her reaction. "You must soon learn to love us, I think," the boy said.

"And why would I ever love you?" Lourdes sneered.

"Because," said the boy. "We are angels."

THE *BLUE HORIZON* ANCHORED for the rest of the day in the lake, drawing attention and suspicion from canal authorities, who already knew the strange reputation of the rogue ship. They were marginally eased by a spread of stalls and outright lies given them by Carlos Ceballos, their own most respected canal pilot.

Lourdes dined with the "angels" in the main dining room at her own table but surrounded by a full seating of guests, never allowing these creatures to get her alone. During the meal, she sensed that neither their breathing, nor their heartbeats were in synch with hers, or with anyone else's on the ship. Everything about the three was under their own control. It left her feeling vulnerable, unprotected.

Their conversation, which had been so direct in the lounge, lapsed into pleasantries around the dinner table. Apparently her guests had already learned the circular art of conversation.

"How did you come upon this ship," the woman asked, her English already better. "How long have you traveled in it?"

They revealed little more about themselves, but asked questions of Lourdes she sensed they already knew the answers to. Yet they feigned surprise and interest in her answers, all the while studying her as she studied them. Lourdes obliged them, joining in their gavotte, making her own glib conversation.

"What is your destination?" the woman asked, always the one pressing for information.

"I have none," Lourdes answered truthfully. "I intend to enjoy myself from here to the end of the world."

"The world won't end," the man told her. "It only will change."

"Not according to Dillon," Lourdes said.

They didn't deny knowing who he was. "His world ends," the boy told her. "Not yours."

When the food arrived, the boy shoved it into his mouth with a disregard for manners that typified any eight-year-old.

"I didn't know angels were gluttons," Lourdes quipped.

"These bodies need to eat," said the woman. "And we enjoy the pleasure of it."

"Since when do angels enjoy pleasures of the flesh?"

"We do when flesh is our temple," answered the woman, with a pious lift of her eyebrows that made Lourdes squirm.

"So, as angels do you have names I might know? Michael? Gabriel? Do any of you play a horn?"

"People give us names," said the man, "but they are not our own."

"I don't play the horn," offered the boy. "But my host would like to learn the guitar." Their little dance went on through the meal, a very civil affair. It was during dessert that Lourdes decided to change the step.

"I'd like to know why I'm dining with angels," she asked, letting some of the graciousness drain from her voice. "You've been here half the day, and still haven't told me why."

"That's easy," said the boy, sucking mousse from a chocolate swan shell. "We want you to help us."

"If you're angels, why would you need *my* help?"

But the boy seemed more interested in devouring the chocolate swan than answering, so the man took over.

"Even the best craftsmen need tools for their craft. We've

come to offer you the chance to be a tool in a task more important than you can know."

"Important to who?"

They chose to ignore that question. "You already have all the money and power you can use, but I know something is missing. Something you feel you were born to do, but what, you don't know." He leaned in closer, grinning. "But *we* know." He paused, looking Lourdes in the eye. "You were born to serve us. If you serve our needs, for the first time in your life you will truly feel contentment."

So that was it. Servitude. That wasn't a dance Lourdes knew. "I don't serve anyone."

Then the woman chimed in, oozing self-righteousness. "Do this not for our benefit, but for your own," she said. "For your own salvation."

Lourdes laughed, spraying a fine mist of mousse in her direction. "My salvation?" Their inflated pretensions grew more annoying by the moment. "If my immortal soul needs saving, I don't need the three of you as intercessors. Besides, I've grown used to the idea of going down with the ship."

Apparently they weren't all-knowing, because they had no quick comeback. Lourdes felt herself taking the lead in their nasty little tango.

"We can fill your spirit in ways it has never been filled," the man pleaded.

"I was offered that once before," Lourdes told them. "By a creature that called itself Okoya."

The angels bristled at the name, as if their spirits seethed rage deep within their host bodies. Lourdes smiled. "Ah, I see you know that particular interdimensional scumbag."

"We are angels!" the man insisted. "Don't anger us."

"So perform a miracle."

It caught them off guard. The man stammered. "What?"

"Perform a miracle. If you're an angel, make me believe; show me some magic I've never seen, and make it good, because I've seen a lot."

The boy looked at her quizzically, the woman looked down, her long hair dangling toward her food. So much for her sanctimonious airs.

"Te podría matar a hora mismo!" the man growled, his anger lapsing him into Spanish.

"Fine, then kill me." She slammed her fist down on the table, loudly enough for a dozen guests around her to turn.

The "angels" did nothing; only smoldered deep within the bodies of their hosts. Now with the upper hand, Lourdes wielded her disdain from the bottom of her belly. "You pretend to be divine, you talk of salvation, but you've forgotten one thing: I've pretended to be divine as well—made a lot of people believe it, but it didn't bring me any closer to being a god. I have no patience for your pretensions."

She stood from the table, looking each of them in the eye, daring them to lash out at her, but they didn't. *Either they can't, or they truly do need me for something*, she thought. Either way, it was a victory for her. Oddly, the boy's face began to go red, and his lip to quiver. She saw tears in his eyes; his host body reacting to the stimulus of being scolded. But in the man and woman, she saw bitter anger.

"Dinner is over," she said. "I want you off my ship." Then she stormed to her cabin and waited to see what their next step would be. Either they would leave and cease to be her concern, or they would make some move. Either an attack, or reconciliation. She waited, keeping her own anger simmering in case she needed to call on it to help battle theirs.

• • •

THE BOY CAME TO her cabin at ten in the evening, alone.

"Why are you still here?" Lourdes scoffed. "Isn't it past your bedtime?"

"My name is Guillermo," said the boy. "But people call me Memo. It is the name attached to this host body. You may call me that. The others are Cerilla and Carlos."

"I couldn't care less."

"Please, sit down."

Lourdes reluctantly crossed to her most comfortable chair, and took a seat. If there was anger, sorrow, or any other emotion in this creature before her, Lourdes could not sense it. There was a complete lack of passion to him—a direct, businesslike tone to his voice. Perhaps, thought Lourdes, the tango has ended.

"I'm listening," she said.

"We are not what we claim to be," Memo began, "and at the same time, we *are* what we claim to be."

"You've come to me with riddles?"

The boy ignored her and continued. "You would call our realm heaven, but it is a place humans will never see. We don't come here often, because human beings have never been important to us. We appear in a caul of light, becoming the one thing your spirit most desires. Some have seen us as angels, some see us as loved ones. Some see us as God. We shine with glory, turning your hope to our advantage. We lure you close with promises of heaven and love. Close enough so that we may devour your souls, and leave your shells to walk the earth."

She felt the hair on her neck rise, the skin on her arms and legs tightening into gooseflesh. His candor was almost as disturbing as his revelation. "Then you *are* like Okoya," she said, surprised to find her voice quivering. She tried to summon her anger and bitterness to use as a shield, but could not find it. She was suddenly bereft of anger, and instead found fear in its place.

"The one you call Okoya is the least of us," he said. "A criminal spirit, weak, worthless, and unimportant."

Lourdes wanted to push herself away, but the chair sat in a corner. She wanted to expel this boy-thing from her suite, but sending it away now would be a show of weakness.

"Do you want me to go on?" he asked.

Every ounce of her soul said no. "Yes," she told him, and he continued in the same easy, forthright tone.

"Humanity," he said, "has always struggled to learn its purpose. We know the answer, and always have. Your purpose is to feed our appetites. You are food of the Gods. You've never been anything more. And never will be."

His dispassion made it sound like a simple fact of life, as if the ramifications were insignificant. As if humanity was insignificant. She wanted to deny his claims—she was always so skilled at strategic denial, but somehow this boy had sliced through her defenses. That was, after all, his skill. But instead of showing her spirit the thing it most desired, it showed her instead the thing she most feared, capturing her just as effectively. She felt her soul bare and open to this child-faced predator. This was the vulnerability she had sensed within herself; these creatures knew ways of shoving a hook deep within one's soul.

"You can see why it would have been much easier if you had simply accepted us as angels when we arrived," he said. "We didn't want our meeting to have to come to this."

"Stop . . ." Her voice now came as a faint whisper. "Please, for the love of God, stop."

"God?" said Memo with the sweetest of voices. "Everything your world has ever seen as divine has been our hand at work. We are *pretenders*, you could say, showing the world a false light, so that we can feed."

Lies lies lies . . . everything it says is a lie. But that voice in her was fading, what little faith she had was extinguished beneath the boy's thumb.

"More of us are coming," he said. "We need you to help us prepare."

Lourdes was crying now, bawling uncontrollably. Could all this be true? Could the universe be such a hostile, loveless place that this vile blasphemy could be true? In spite of herself she found herself infected by him, accepting every word he said, like it was gospel.

"Do you believe me?"

But why did he have to ask? He knew she did. He had snared her, and she longed for him to devour her soul. She longed now for the death of her consciousness, so she did not have to live with the knowledge he had forced down her gullet.

But it didn't devour her, instead it took a step closer. Then, the boy suddenly seemed no more than a little child again, frightened and lonely. She didn't understand the change in him, only that it served to shift her even further off balance.

"Abrázame," Memo pleaded. "Hold me. My mother—she never does. It is her ruined face—she feels she is unworthy to hold me. But you can, Lourdes. Hold me. Hold me now."

Her arms swung open. He stepped forward, her arms swung closed, enveloping him, and in that embrace, her last failing ember of faith was snuffed into darkness. With nothing left to cling to, she held him tightly, and cried, rocking him back and forth. *Let my life end. Let the world end. Let every last human vanish from existence, for what does it matter now? What does it matter now?*

BY MIDNIGHT, THE *BLUE HORIZON* had moved through the Gatun Locks, and was sailing into the flat blackness of the open sea.

21. SANCTUARY

DILLON AWOKE ON A LOUNGE CHAIR IN PARADISE. HIS EYES focused, revealing a flagstone patio within a colorful flower garden, surrounded by a grove of wild-limbed, white-barked trees. A large, free-standing umbrella shielded him from the sun.

Although his mind still struggled to fit together his memories he was fairly certain that none of them would logically lead him here. He remembered driving along the Texas highway, and then came the flash of sudden awareness of an unearthly arrival so disturbing it sent him flying off the road. He recalled his unintended stunt in the graveyard. And Tessic. Tessic was there. Why was Tessic there?

As he lay on the lounge, he could still feel the threat of the strange trinity that had infected the world, but it felt distant now. Whoever they were, *what*ever they were, their arrival had changed something in him, amping up his power to a new extreme.

Dillon heard footsteps, and turned to see that Elon Tessic approached through the knotty olive trees that stood only a few feet taller than he.

"Good to see you awake," Tessic said, and sat in a chair beside him. "I was beginning to wonder if you'd come out of it today at all."

"Where am I?" Dillon asked. "Where's Maddy?"

"Lieutenant Haas is perfectly fine. Off entertaining herself, I think." Tessic studied Dillon for a moment. "What do you remember?"

A bit more was coming back to Dillon now. There was the helicopter, the relieving sensation of being spirited away from the graveyard.

"I remember an extremely large needle," Dillon finally said.

Tessic laughed. "You might also remember I gave you the choice of being sedated or not. You chose sedation."

"I must not have been in my right mind," Dillon said.

Tessic raised an eyebrow. "No, you weren't." There was a small table between them, and a bowl of fresh fruit. Tessic picked through the fruit until he found a few dark, shiny cherries. He popped one into his mouth and spit out the pit. He offered the bowl to Dillon, but Dillon declined.

"I'd like to know how you found me," Dillon said.

"Trade secret," Tessic answered. "But rest assured, no one else searching for you will find you here. Not even our friends in the military."

"You still haven't told me where 'here' is." But Tessic only grinned. Dillon took a deep breath and tried to get a sense of his surroundings. More often than not, his ability to reach out and sense distant subtleties in the world around him was a distraction, but there were times it helped to orient him. Although he could feel the olive grove around him, he felt nothing beyond it. It was a discomfiting feeling.

"Are we on an island?" he asked. But if it were an island it must have been the Dead Sea, because even on an island, he'd be able to feel life and currents within the water.

"Come and see for yourself," Tessic answered, getting up. He offered Dillon a hand, but Dillon wanted no assistance. He stood, expecting his balance to be clumsy, and his knees to be weak, but apparently the rest had done him good.

Tessic led him slowly through the olive grove. "This garden was designed by a feng shui specialist," Tessic told him, "for maximum harmony and vitality."

A dozen yards farther and the grove came to an abrupt end at a glass wall seven feet high; a dramatic barrier separating Tessic's world from everyone else's. Beyond the glass wall was a city, stretching out beneath them.

"An ounce of perspective begets a pound, yes?"

"So we're on a rooftop?"

"Sixty-seventh floor."

"I don't recognize the city."

"Houston. We are atop Tessitech's southern headquarters."

But there was something wrong. Dillon closed his eyes, and tried to sense the patterns of the city. He had learned to avoid cities, because their intensity overloaded his thoughts. The world shouted at him enough without him having to feel the blare of a city. But, oddly, there was none of that here. All he could feel were the faintest of echoes of the city patterns below.

Tessic tapped on the glass wall. "Three inches of crystal inlaid with twelve micro-fine layers of lead mesh," he explained. "Wonderful stuff—a neutron bomb could go off, and you wouldn't get a sunburn." He beamed. "I own the patent."

"Why am I here?"

"That is for you to find out."

"I'm not in the mood for guessing games."

"You misunderstand," said Tessic. "I mean this literally. You see, all five floors of this penthouse were built with you in mind. The entire place is lined, floors and walls, to contain your energy and sensory field. It keeps you from being overwhelmed with what lies outside, and will keep those on the outside from sensing you. This place can serve whatever function you choose. A retreat, perhaps, as it is for me."

Dillon got the gist. "Just another cell. Only prettier."

Tessic bristled at the suggestion. "There are no locks here. You can leave whenever you please. My hope is that you will see the wisdom of staying."

"And Maddy?"

"She is my guest as well. In fact, she told me you needed a place like this to settle your mind. That you lacked a certain clarity."

"She said that?"

"In so many words."

Dillon put his hand to the glass, then turned to look at the olive grove. An oasis in the sky. A world apart. He turned to Tessic. "I don't think I was meant to live a life of leisure."

"None of us are," Tessic said. "We are all called to action in one way or another. But sometimes we need a place to regroup, and to stage our operations. Even Superman had his Fortress of Solitude, yes?"

Dillon chuckled at the thought. "If you saw me in the graveyard, then you should know I'm not a man of steel."

"There are substances more useful than steel."

Useful, thought Dillon. Yes, for a man like Tessic everything had to have utility. There would always be something for him. "So what do you want from me?"

Tessic pondered the question, but didn't respond quite yet. "Come, I'll give you the grand tour." They strode back into the grove, taking a different flagstone path that led to an artificial stream. Hidden speakers pumped the sounds of birds and other wildlife into the air, adding to the illusion. By the time they reached the steam, there was no telling they were on the roof of a skyscraper.

"Until a few years ago," Tessic said, "I was arrogant enough to think I was the greatest man of our time. Then you appeared on the scene."

"Jealous, Elon?"

Tessic shook his head. "No. Envy never brings a man true success. Certainly there are men like Bussard in the world, who are threatened by anything more powerful than themselves. But I am not Bussard. To me you are not a threat. You are . . . an opportunity."

The path wound them back to the garden where the two lounge chairs sat. But this time, Dillon saw the vine-covered wall behind it, and the opening that led to an elevator. "Opportunity for what?"

Tessic paused, picking up his bowl of fruit, popping a few grapes. "I have so much money, I can't find enough things to do with it—and the curse of wealth can be as potent as its blessing. You see, when money ceases to be an issue, a man can either become a slave to his passions, or buy his freedom from them, seeking more worthy objectives."

"Meaning?"

Tessic patted Dillon on the cheek, and offered up a wry smile. "Simply put, Dillon, I am helping you because you're good for my soul."

Dillon glanced at the oasis around him. There was something tempting about it, and somehow that made it feel dangerous.

Sensing Dillon's reluctance, Tessic reached over and twisted a twig from the tree beside him. "This has always been a symbol for hope and peace," he said. "I hope you'll accept my olive branch."

When Dillon didn't take it, Tessic placed it on a boulder beside them, and turned the key that opened the elevator doors.

THE MULTI-STORY PENTHOUSE WAS part office and spa, part museum, and part spiritual sanctuary. "Not exactly Hearst

Castle," Tessic commented. "I like to think my tastes are not so garish."

Perhaps not, but every last amenity seethed excess, from a reading room that featured a priceless collection of medieval Jewish artifacts, to a four-story indoor rock-climbing wall, which towered above Tessic's personal gym. Maddy clung to the top of the wall, focused on her climb; "entertaining herself," as Tessic had said. Dillon chose not to disturb her.

The sixty-second floor, the lowest floor of the penthouse complex, was set aside for what Tessic called his "professional hobbies." It housed his private office; an uncharacteristically modest space, with some shelves and a simple cherrywood desk, within a larger gallery of high-tech toys. Some projects were complete, others still works-in-progress. In one corner sat an elaborate model train that ran on magnetic levitation. Nearby was a drafting table overflowing with schematics for a large-scale version, that Tessic was clearly drafting by his own hand.

"The stuff of dreams," Tessic told him. "Or at least my dreams."

There was a workbench full of computer viscera, reminding Dillon of the hands-on inventiveness that was Tessic's calling card, even before he became known for his business acumen. It was comforting to see that the man was still elbow-deep in nuts and bolts.

"Let me show you my latest interest." Tessic led Dillon to a Lucite-covered display case that held a matchbox city. Row after row of three-inch high-rise apartment buildings.

"Another dream?" asked Dillon.

"Reality," Tessic answered. "We're already on the third phase."

"I didn't know you were a developer." Dillon's eyes blurred

as he looked at the three-dimensional grid of towers. "There's got to be a hundred buildings here."

"A hundred and twelve. The largest single housing complex ever conceived—and it's just one of several I have planned."

Dillon moved around the box, to view it from another angle.

"It interests you," observed Tessic.

"I'm just a little stunned. I mean, it must cost billions. No matter how rich you are, I can't believe you can afford this."

"I have no one to leave my money to. So I intend to exit this world penniless."

"This is a good start."

"Besides, money's not quite the same over there."

"Over where?"

Tessic drew Dillon's attention to a map on the wall, pinned up between artists renderings of one of the buildings. "I have purchased several large plots of land in Belarus and Poland. The labor's cheap, and so are the raw materials. Some leverage with a few friendly European banks, and my out-of-pocket expense is under fifteen million."

"Oh, is that all," Dillon scoffed.

"Of course they're not the most beautiful of structures, but form follows function. The goal is to get them up quickly. We can always beautify them later."

"What's the rush?"

"I'm nothing if not efficient," Tessic answered, then added, "And besides, as you're the author of world chaos, you should know how little constructive time is left."

Dillon shifted uncomfortably. Tessic was prodding him, gauging his reaction. "I may be responsible for what's happening in the world," Dillon said, "but I won't take credit as its author. I never intended it."

"You have plans to repair it, then?"

Dillon found he couldn't look Tessic in the eye.

"Hopes, then," Tessic prompted. "Hopes in search of a plan."

"Yes, you could say that."

"Perhaps I can help you there," offered Tessic. "Strategy is one of my specialties." Tessic exuded confidence like a musk, and Dillon found himself half believing Tessic really could help. He wondered whether or not it was just wishful thinking.

Dillon studied the lattice of model buildings, which was more like a starburst than a grid, the buildings radiating outward from an octagonal park in the center. A bold design, like the man who conceived it. "So, are these housing complexes part of some strategy?" Dillon asked. "These people obviously can't afford this type of housing, unless you give it away. What could you possibly get in return?"

Tessic paused. "Always with you, I must have some angle."

Dillon waited, and Tessic looked away. "The great wall of China is the only man-made structure visible from space," Tessic said. "I intend to add to the tally."

Dillon nodded, but knew that Elon Tessic was not so shallow a man. He served more than just his ego. "That's a nice cover story. Now tell me the real reason."

Dillon refused to back down, and, cornered, Tessic sighed. "You read me too well."

"One of *my* specialties."

Tessic looked at his miniature city, and gently stroked its Lucite lid, as if it were a lover. "You can call it my *mitzvah* project," Tessic said quietly. "A holy deed in a faithless world." Reflexively, Dillon's thoughts ricocheted to Deanna. It irritated him that the mere mention of faith could bring her to haunt his thoughts. But if nothing else, it helped to sober him.

"We could go there," Tessic offered. "I could show you the site."

"Why would I want to go there?"

Tessic had no immediate answer.

Dillon looked around the workship. If this was Tessic's sandbox, Dillon didn't want to play. "I appreciate your hospitality, Elon," he said. "But I can't accept it. I'll be leaving in the morning."

Although he thought Tessic might deflate with the news, he showed no signs of it. "That is, of course, your choice to make."

Dillon nodded. "I'll tell Maddy." He turned to leave, but Tessic called to him.

"You've always spoken of your desire to pull back your energy field—contain yourself. Do you still believe you'll ever be able to do that?"

"Yes, I do." Although he was no closer now than he had been in Hesperia.

"Has it occurred to you," said Tessic, "that perhaps I was brought to you as your means of containment?"

Dillon hadn't considered that. It was a seductive thought, for it implied a grand design, and if there was anything that Dillon longed for, it was grand designs. Perfect patterns. An ordered universe.

"From the moment I was brought in to build your prison," Tessic said, "I knew that our meeting was *bashert*. Fated. I built you this sanctuary, knowing fate would bring you here."

Dillon maintained his distance, keeping a buffer zone between himself and Tessic's persuasive intensity. "Fate didn't bring me here; *you* did," Dillon reminded him. "In a helicopter, backed up by your own personal army."

"If it wasn't meant to be, I would have failed."

Dillon laughed. "What? Elon Tessic? Fail?"

Tessic hesitated, becoming quiet. "It has happened more often than you know."

There was deep sorrow to his words. Dillon found himself trying to decipher the source of the sorrow, and found the path convoluted and clouded. Dillon knew if he pushed himself, he could decode Tessic's complex patterns and truly know the man, but Dillon didn't have the heart to do it. He much preferred Tessic as an enigma.

"Do you know how I became successful, Dillon?" he asked.

Dillon shrugged. "You're a genius. Everyone knows that."

"Most geniuses starve," Tessic reminded him. "I succeeded because I took the time to listen. I learned to be still. But you—you spend your time running. Running away, running toward, but always running."

Tessic paused, perhaps waiting for Dillon to defend himself, but there was no defense. Tessic was right.

"Be still," Tessic said, his voice soothing and calm. "You are like some beacon that is never in the same place twice. What good is that to anyone? What good is that to you? Imagine yourself, for once at the center of the universe, Dillon, and the shadows you chase, your purpose here—everything you seek will be drawn to you. And in that stillness, when your fate does come to you, you will be ready to seize it."

ON THE ROCK-CLIMBING WALL, Maddy was already seizing what Tessic had to offer. She had earned it. Years of busting her ass to gain admittance to a military machine that stuck her with the likes of Bussard, then created a backspin of lies that turned her into America's Most Wanted. AWOL and disgraced; a fugitive only six months after a high-honor West

Point graduation—yes, she had earned the right to luxuriate in Tessic's penthouse.

As she scaled his magnificent rock-climbing wall, she thought back to easier times; Bryce Canyon, two summers before, when the only challenge in her life was the stone faces of the rocks she climbed, and her stone-faced instructors come fall. This had once been a predictable, rational world she could sink her teeth into.

She reached up, deftly inching her way higher, trying to block out everything but the wall. Tessic called it his climate-controlled Everest. He called the entire penthouse complex his "urban cottage."

"You'll find it pleasant," he had told her while their helicopter was still en route. He took pride in his ability to understate.

She didn't know what to expect of the place before she arrived. Somewhere in the back of her mind were images of a pleasure dome replete with large-breasted, iron-thighed amazons running the whole operation. But instead she found, to some disappointment, a staff no more exotic than any other. A plump Midwestern woman ran the penthouse staff, and went on about how the military had stonewalled her husband after Desert Storm, "so I can sympathize, honey." Maddy wasn't sure how much she knew of their situation, but she knew enough. It could have been a security problem, but the woman's loyalty to Tessic was unwavering. "Elon paid all of Jimmy's medical bills, when the Pentagon SOBs were still denying Desert Storm Syndrome," she had told Maddy, as she led her to a lavishly appointed bedroom suite.

She was introduced to the gardener, a small Asian man with a nominally effective artificial eye that Tessitech Labs had designed. It appeared that for everyone here, Tessic had descended upon their particular misery, assuaging it with some well-conceived act of kindness. It was the most effective security measure she had ever seen.

While Dillon still slept off a massive sedative, and before she attempted to climb the wall, Tessic had visited her in her room.

"I wasn't certain of your sleeping arrangements," he told her, "so I prepared you and Dillon separate rooms."

"That will be fine," she said. If he were fishing for the state of her and Dillon's relationship, he would not find out from her. She briefly wondered if he might try to seduce her—after all, he did have a reputation as a playboy, but there was nothing in the penthouse to suggest he was a womanizer. "So, are we your guests, your prisoners, or your experimental subjects?"

Tessic laughed and wagged a finger at her. "Still you only trust me as far as you can throw me."

"Actually, I can throw you farther."

"Well, perhaps I will give you that opportunity in the gym later on."

She hated that he was always so disarming, deflecting her barbs with the facile skill of one of his weapons systems. "Good," she said, trying hard to hide a smirk. "I think I'd enjoy putting you in traction."

Tessic opened the blinds, bringing in the afternoon light, and a spectacular view of Houston. "I must confess, I've taken a liking to you, Lieutenant Haas."

"You can drop the Lieutenant," she told him. "I think we can assume my military career is over."

"Then may I call you Maddy?"

"Miss Haas will do fine."

"Very well, then," he said. "A minor victory in our little cold war." Then he paused for a second, contemplating her—

not looking her up and down, but simply considering her as a whole. "Perhaps, Miss Haas, if things ever settle down, you might consider working for me."

"That depends. Is hell freezing over any time soon?"

"We'll have to ask Dillon," he said. She laughed in spite of herself. "You know," said Tessic, "you might have a problem in trusting me, but after what I've seen you do for Dillon, I trust you implicitly."

She sighed. "So . . . what about Dillon?" In spite of their cushy sanctuary, nothing had really changed. Dillon was still at the center of events raging out of control. They weren't free from the hurricane, they were merely in its eye.

"Yes, what about Dillon?" echoed Tessic, waiting to take her lead, rather than pushing forward with his own ideas. She had no answer for him. She was still grappling with the events of the past few days. A graveyard resurrection—a spirit that devours souls. Before knowing Dillon, she had never been truly convinced of the existence of souls, much less the possibility of them being ripped away. This past week was enough to process; she was light-years away from considering tomorrow.

"No one knows him better than you," Tessic reminded her. "You know what he needs, perhaps better than he does himself."

Yes, she did know him, and while Tessic's motives were still in question, she and Tessic shared the common goal of Dillon's well-being. That was reason enough for detente, even alliance. And so, in the end, it was Maddy who suggested that Dillon be allowed to wake in the garden; a tranquil environment where Tessic might be perceived more as a friend than a threat.

She found herself avoiding Dillon for the rest of the day. After the rock-climbing wall, she took a massage at Tessic's suggestion, then retired early to her room for a long bath in an oversized tub. After spending so much time tending to Dillon's needs, she had forgotten she had needs of her own. She had never been one to pamper herself—that was her sister's style—but perhaps it was time.

Her sister! It had been so long since Maddy had even thought of Erica. No doubt the FBI had found her in Brooklyn and was harassing her no end about her psychotically homicidal sibling. She wondered what Erica made of all this, and whether or not she believed the lies being spread about Maddy. She didn't even want to consider what her parents might be going through. Perhaps Tessic could arrange to get messages to all of them. She would have to ask.

Dillon came to her that night. She had hoped he would, and yet at the same time dreaded being read by him, before she could really read her own feeling about being there.

"I thought I'd see you at dinner," Dillon said, when she let him in. "Are you all right?"

"Just tired," she told him. "Too much for one day."

Dillon threw her an impish, scarred grin. "Ah, you're such a lightweight."

"I can see you're feeling better."

He hesitated for a moment. "Maddy . . . what you saw in the graveyard . . ."

But Maddy put a finger to his lips. "We'll sort that out later."

He kissed her, then she took his hand and led him to her bed. Being with him was different now. That radiant fire she had felt pulsing from him in the graveyard was still there, so strong that she feared being near him would push her threshold of pain. But she quickly found that being with him now was like slipping into that hot bath. Her spirit and flesh had to grow accustomed to the intensity of his aura, but once they had, it was marvelous. Discomfort gave way to hypersensitivity of touch, and she could feel herself entirely enveloped by him. It was wonderful to be lost in him, but there was a sadness in knowing that it could never truly be mutual. That there would never be a time she could envelop him.

DILLON FOUND ONE QUESTION plaguing him. It was a question he was afraid to ask Maddy, because any answer would be just as troubling.

"Do you trust Tessic?" Dillon finally asked in the silence as he lay beside her. He didn't expect her to answer the question, but after his conversation with Tessic that afternoon, he had to ask. As he suspected, she sidestepped the issue, pulling back slightly from his touch.

"Whatever his agenda, it doesn't seem to be hurting you."

"You think he has an agenda?"

"Everyone has an agenda," she said. "Whether they know it or not."

"So what's yours?"

She answered him with a passionate kiss.

"I hope that's always on the agenda," he said.

He moved in to kiss her again, but she held him off for a moment. "Dillon . . . if Tessic's offering you a safe haven, there's nothing wrong with taking it."

Dillon pulled away, frustrated by her words. "You don't believe that—even in the dark I can see it in your face."

"I have a suspicious nature—you'd be stupid to hang your decisions on me."

"Well it doesn't matter, anyway. I've already told him I'm leaving in the morning." He turned to her and gently touched her face, and when that didn't seem like quite enough, he kissed her, but now the kiss felt forced. "I'll understand if you don't want to come with me."

"Of course I'll come." But it was resignation he read in her voice. As if to stem off any further discussion, she shifted closer to him, and held him. "I love you, Dillon." He knew it was a simple truth that transcended their tensions.

Sometime later, he told her he loved her, too, but only after she was asleep. Why? he wondered. Why couldn't he say it to her face? Did he love her? He loved who she was; he loved the feel of her body; he loved that *she* loved him.

But she's not a shard.

Damn it! He didn't know why that should matter. He had seen how Michael and Lourdes had been so close in the dark days—just like he and Deanna had been—but once their parasites were gone, they no longer clung to one another with the same desperation. In the end, Michael had spurned Lourdes. Who's to say that Dillon and Deanna might not have suffered the same fate had she survived?

He had a dozen logical rationalizations, but none that made him feel any better.

Let yourself love her, he told himself. *Maddy is good for you. Learn to be still, and let yourself love her.*

Dillon didn't leave her room until dawn, but he didn't go back to his own room. Instead, he crept quietly up to the garden to watch the sun rise, turning the glass towers of Houston into spires of fire.

Stillness. It was an amazing thing to Dillon. He had forgotten what it was like to have a barrier between his mind and a tumultuous world. Even a barrier of lead-lined crystal was better than no barrier at all. Perhaps this *was* a retreat worth lingering in for a few more hours. A few more days. Perhaps Tessic's containment was the only containment he'd ever know.

From the garden, Dillon went down to Tessic's workshop, passing the sketches of towers and trains, until coming to Tessic's desk. In the center of Tessic's desk, Dillon left an olive branch he had taken from the garden. Then he returned to Maddy's bed, pressed against her until he could feel her heartbeat, and finally released his resistance, letting stillness infuse him.

22. CHAMBER OF HORRORS

DREW BRUSHED AN UNCOMFORTABLY LONG LOCK OF HAIR back from his face, then took a second Suprax and a third Vicodin in the hotel lobby before taking the elevator back to the room he shared with Winston. The antibiotic was a one-a-day deal, but he figured he could use all the protection he could get. As for the painkiller, he suspected he was developing an addiction, but it was worth it to numb the pain that now shot up his entire arm. He imagined his long, straggly blond hair and uneven facial growth already made him look like an addict.

The Dallas Galleria Westin was supposed to be an upscale establishment, but the hotel's infrastructure was in an accelerated decline. Only three of six elevators worked, the bell counter was permanently unmanned, the granite floors were unpolished and every corner bred forms of trash that no one bothered to remove. As service was the first thing to go these days, Drew found himself grateful for whatever services remained. Housekeeping, room service. Hotels were closing their doors at alarming rates, and once housekeeping decayed it was impossible to stay open for business. All else considered, the Westin was holding its own.

As he rode up in the crowded elevator, he thought about the last few hours. Four hours of waiting at an understaffed clinic, on Halloween morning. Under other circumstances, it would have been hell, but instead it was a welcome respite from Winston.

"That's some infection you got there," the doctor had said with the weariness of a man who had little desire left to practice medicine. He studied the curved line of dark stitches across Drew's forearm. "How'd this happen?"

Since Drew was already losing track of the lies he had to tell, he simply said, "Graverobbing accident."

The doctor chuckled, assuming it was just Halloween humor. Turned out the truth solicited fewer questions than any lie he could have told.

The wound looked awful. Rings of purple swelled around the gash, and streaks of red shot all the way down his wrist into his palm, which was also swollen. "How bad's the infection?" Drew asked.

The doctor poked at his stitches gently, but not gently enough. Drew grimaced from the pain. "Looks like it goes pretty deep. Did the nurse take your temperature?" He looked at the chart to answer his own question. "101. Hmm." He felt Drew's glands, looked down at his throat, then returned his attention to the wound. "There's an odd pattern to it," the doctor commented. "Mottled rings around the trauma, as if . . ."

"As if the flesh keeps dying and regenerating over and over?"

The doctor raised his gaze to catch Drew's eye, but only for an instant. "As if it wasn't getting proper circulation." And then he added, "Besides, flesh doesn't regenerate the way you suggest."

It does around Winston Pell, he wanted to say, but instead was silent, and endured a diatribe about cleanliness and maintenance of the wound. The doctor asked about other symptoms, then palpated his spleen. "Normally this kind of a bacterial intrusion would trigger an alarm in your immune system. The pus around the wound is actually a good sign . . .

still . . ." He glanced once more at the chart. "Are you allergic to any prescription medications?"

He redid the stitches, then gave Drew an antibiotic injection and the two oral prescriptions, then sent him on his way, with instructions to return if his fever wasn't gone in two days.

Now, as the hotel elevator rose, nearing the twenty-fifth floor, he could already feel his arm, which had grown mercifully numb, begin to ache again. He could feel the new flesh regenerating to replace the dying, gangrenous flesh around the wound—but not fast enough to battle the bacteria that had also begun to grow and reproduce at an unnatural rate. Winston's broadcast of growth was not selective.

Winston's effect on Drew's wound had been bearable before, but something had happened that day on the plane. Something had inexplicably changed him. It was a change for the worse as far as Drew was concerned, because the last thing Winston needed was an increase in power.

Winston was exactly as Drew had left him that morning; curled up on his bed, curtains drawn. He slept while the TV flickered a god-awful 70s cop show on an off station. Drew's bed was made, but only because he had done it himself before he left.

Drew pulled the DO NOT DISTURB sign from the outside doorknob. "Dude, what good is maid service if you never let them in?"

Winston groaned and stirred beneath his covers. Drew reached into the bag he was carrying and threw a 7-11 po' boy at his head.

"I've checked us out, so get your sorry black ass out of bed."

Winston glared at him. "Eat me."

"Another place, another time," Drew said with a wink.

Winston grunted, and rolled over, so Drew grabbed the

covers with his good arm and tore them off. "I'm not kidding. We're outta here."

"Why the hell would you go and do a dumb-ass thing like checking us out?"

"A final act of sanity," Drew answered. "Maybe you've grown used to it, but this room smells like roadkill in a rainforest." Drew pulled on a peeling piece of wallpaper, revealing the flaky mildew that had taken hold of the drywall beneath. No doubt all the adjacent rooms were suffering from Winston's effect as well. "Welcome to the petrie dish. A few more days and the mold in these walls is gonna demand the right to vote."

"You're exaggerating."

"Am I?" He reached up, flicking up the ends of his shoulder-length blond hair, for Winston to see just how long it was. "I don't think so."

"You look like Jesus," Winston commented.

"Well, I did come back from the dead once," Drew commented, "but that's old news." He found Winston's socks on the floor, and tossed them to him. "I don't even want to know what's growing in there."

When Winston began going about the motions of dressing, Drew went into the bathroom. "Better watch out," he called to Winston, "this morning there was a bedbug under my pillow the size of a Volkswagen." Drew studied his face in the mirror. He barely recognized himself anymore. "What the hell are we doing here?" he asked his reflection. He didn't expect an answer, either from himself or from Winston. Four days ago, Drew had spirited a hysterical Winston out of the unfortunately ventilated airplane, and calmed him down enough to get him here. He wouldn't discuss what had triggered that seizure on the plane—offered no explanation for the quantum leap in his power. It was, of course, just like Winston to keep such things to himself, but with Tory's ashes thrown to the wind, Winston had also lost all direction, all motivation. *That* was unlike him. Winston was always up to something in his own abrasive, antagonistic way. To see him beaten left Drew treading water. He couldn't leave him like this, but being in Winston's presence was poisoning Drew with an aggravated infection. At the very least, Drew wanted to point them both in some hopeful direction, but Winston wanted to do nothing but sleep. Now he cultured futility like bacteria, and it was contagious.

Grabbing a can of shaving cream from the bathroom counter, Drew lathered up, as he had done every day for four days. He began with his face. His scant facial hair had come in fuller each day. Now he had straggly mutton chops that didn't quite stretch to his chin. He shaved them off, losing every last bit of sideburn, and higher still, until the razor began to clog with longer hair. Even though the throbbing of his arm made it hard to concentrate on even this simple task, he found the slow, smooth strokes of the razor soothed him, provided him a Zen-like focus. The shaving ritual had begun to take on a monastic flavor. He cut away his long locks with scissors, then lathered his scalp, picked up a fresh razor, and brought it back and forth in short strokes, clear-cutting inch by inch until his entire scalp was shaven and smooth. He was getting used to the shaving ritual, and that frightened him.

When he was done, he studied his shaven head in the mirror—a reflection as unfamiliar to him as the one he had first seen entering the room. The only thing that seemed the same were his eyes, glassy from his growing fever. He watched his reflection for a minute or two, until he could see his clean-shaven scalp begin to fill with fine peach fuzz. For an instant, a wave of anger overcame him; a sudden surge of hatred. He closed his eyes, inundated by it. *It's just the pain,* he told himself. *It's just the fever.* He didn't go back to Winston until it subsided, but the undercurrent was still there.

Winston, still in his underclothes, had made no move to get dressed. Instead he studied a particularly nasty spot of mildew on the wall near his bed. "We need Tory here," he said longingly. "She'd sanitize the place. Maybe even kill the mold, too, who knows. Her power added to mine. It was really something, you know?"

"Yeah, but she's not here," said Drew, with hostility he didn't expect. "She'll never be here. She's fertilizing half of Texas by now, okay?"

Winston turned to look at him. "You're an asshole," he said, and used it as an excuse to get back into bed.

"That's it, I'm outta here. You can lie there until you're eaten alive by athlete's foot for all I care."

"Close the door behind you," was all Winston said.

He would have left. He had every intention of it, but as he neared the door, he felt his legs go out. He landed on his knees, and gripped the doorknob, but only to keep himself from flopping to the ground. He could feel the fever in every joint. It had skyrocketed in the few minutes he had spent in Winston's presence. *Damn Winston. Damn him.*

He tried to get to his feet and complete his exit, but found he was just too dizzy. When he turned, he saw that, wonder of wonders, Winston had actually gotten out of his bed, but he kept his distance.

"I had a life, you know?" Drew found himself ranting, grimacing through the chills and body aches. "I mean, yeah, friggin' high school track, not very important, but it was *my* life, *mine*, and I was happy keeping my head in the sand like everyone else, pretending the world wasn't falling apart."

Winston took a step closer. "Let me see your arm."

"Just stay away. The closer you are, the worse it gets."

Winston didn't listen, and Drew didn't have the strength to ward him off. As Winston came closer, the pain in Drew's arm exponentiated. He could feel the pull of the stitches, smell the sickly stench of infection. He felt it would explode. The room now spun faster, the floor and walls switched places. A trap door sprung in his mind, and he found himself slipping away from consciousness. He offered no resistance.

There was nothing to mark the passage of time. If he had dreams, they were lost. When he came to, he was on his bed, and the curtains were open. Winston was gazing out at the late afternoon sun, fully dressed. Their backpacks, that carried what little they had brought with them, were packed and resting on a chair.

"The front desk already called," Winston said, "wondering why we haven't vacated the room."

Drew's left arm felt curiously light and numb. He raised it to find the dressing around the wound was gone. So was the wound. No stitches, scar or discolored flesh, no hint that his arm had ever been wounded at all!

"Winston . . ." Drew continued to stare at his arm. He turned his wrist, as if perhaps the wound could have switched to the other side. Although he did still feel a bit weak, his fever had broken as well.

"Winston, how did you do this? You can't heal a wound, or fight an infection."

"No, I can't," Winston said calmly.

There was a pillowcase in the corner, overstuffed and tied closed with a shoelace. "What's that?"

"Towels, mostly," Winston answered.

"Mostly?"

Drew got up to inspect it more closely. As he neared the overstuffed pillowcase, he could see there were some stains on it. Blood stains.

Winston can't fight an infection, thought Drew, *his art is growth, and regeneration. The regeneration of flesh. And bone.* Drew reached for the shoelace to open the mouth of the bag, but Winston grabbed his arm, before he could.

"I'm asking you not to look inside," Winston said. "I'm asking you not to question what I did. Not unless you really want to hear the answer."

Drew looked at the back of his left hand—his perfect left hand. It was a bit pale—substantially less tanned than his right hand. Drew felt a brief instant of nausea, but chased it away. "Trick or treat," he said. This was a little bit of both, perhaps.

"I think I saw that bedbug you were talking about," Winston said, grabbing the pillowcase with one hand, and his backpack with the other. "If it's all the same to you, I'd rather not hang much longer."

They left the key in the room, the bloody pillowcase in a Dumpster, and drove out into the melee of All Hallow's Eve.

THE STRANGENESS OF THE times only fueled Halloween. Usurped from the children, the holiday had fallen even further into the hands of adults. This year, the parties began early, for people were, now more than ever, eager to lose themselves in masquerade and alcohol. For those not satisfied with partying, the streets offered other recreation. It was amazing the things that would burn.

Winston saw eerily costumed commuters in the cars around them as he and Drew attempted to leave downtown Dallas. He supposed the fetid state in which they left their hotel room qualified as a particularly macabre Halloween prank. With nowhere else to go, and most roads clogged with partygoers and traffic accidents, Winston drove them to Cowboys Stadium, where the Packers played the Cowboys in an under-attended game. Winston was not surprised by the lack of attendance. Since random acts of violence were no longer isolated incidents but a veritable plague, attending any large public gathering was taking one's life into one's hands. The most die-hard sports fans were leaving their season tickets in the drawer. "All part of the big picture," Dillon would say— as if the hammer on every gun was just a cog in some cosmic Rube Goldberg machine.

Winston and Drew didn't watch the game. Instead they stood on the abandoned top concession circle, looking out over the parking lot and suburban Dallas beyond, counting the plumes of smoke.

"Hell night," Winston explained. The fires had begun even before the sun had set, and now, as the last light of dusk slipped from the sky, the night was aglow with distant pockets of flame.

Drew shook his head. "They don't do this in Southern California."

"They will this year."

Winston glanced at the space around them. The entire concession level was closed, and lit only by the stadium lights spilling through the access tunnels that led to the stands. Most everything else on the level was cast in shadows. It was as good a place as any to privately bring Drew up to speed. Winston told Drew everything that he had kept from him. All that he knew, or at least all he *thought* he knew.

Rather than being distressed by the news of the three intruders, Drew appeared relieved. Perhaps knowing the face of doom was better for him than waiting for it in the dark.

"And these three . . . phantoms you're talking about—you think they're looking for you?"

"No," answered Winston. "They're *not* looking for me. That's the problem."

"Three ghouls out there, and they're not looking for you. Maybe I'm a moron, but I don't exactly see that as a problem."

Winston sighed. "It means that whatever they're up to, I no longer figure into their equation. They've completely dismissed me."

"So, you think there was a point when you *did* mean something to them?"

"I know there was."

"You were a threat to them?"

"Not just me," Winston said. "Dillon, Lourdes—Tory and Michael as well. Maybe even Deanna."

"Fear of the dead?" asked Drew.

"Fear of their recovery," Winston answered.

"But you're not a threat anymore?"

Winston shook his head. "We're nothing to them now. I can sense it." Winston gave Drew a few moments, watching him piece it all together.

"They had to make certain one piece of the whole was destroyed forever," Drew concluded. "So they sent Briscoe to destroy Michael's remains, but he failed, so he went after Tory instead!"

"And the moment Tory's ashes were scattered to the sky," added Winston, "it was safe for the three to enter this world."

Drew pursed his lips, shaking his head. "There's still something that I don't get. You're not a threat to them, yet your powers increased the moment they arrived. Why?"

"I don't know. It's as if their intrusion triggered something. Like an alarm."

"Or an immune system," offered Drew. It was an offhand comment that almost slipped by. It took a moment for both of them to really latch onto it. Drew turned to face Winston, and Winston caught an intensity in his eyes. Excitement, fear, both beginning to blossom together. *"Like an immune system,"* Drew said again, slowly, like a spell. Winston could feel the spell open a door, and the scope of what was beyond it gave Winston vertigo.

A shadow moved in the dim service lights of the closed concession deck. They turned to see a figure approaching, something terribly wrong with the face. Only as the figure got closer, did they realize that he was wearing a latex mask over his head. The mask, a Halloween staple, featured a bloody, lopsided face, cleaved down the middle by a rubber hatchet. He smelled the part—a stench of organic decay as if he hadn't washed for weeks.

"You boys looking to score some dope?" said a muffled voice behind the mask. "I got something for whatever ails you. Only the good stuff, guaranteed."

"Get lost," said Drew.

"C'mon, I got your number," said the drug dealer. He turned to Winston. "You boys are looking to shoot up. Let me inoculate you against your pain."

"Get the hell out of here before I put a real hatchet in your head," Winston said.

The dealer put up a pair of dirty hands, and backed off. "Suit yourself. If you change your mind, I'll be around." Then he strolled off looking for fresh customers.

Sign of the times, thought Winston. When the dust finally settled, the only ones left would be the cockroaches and the drug dealers. Winston looked out over Dallas. There were more fires on the horizon now. The distant echo of fire engines blended with the sounds of the stadium behind them. A handful of fire-fighters, battling to break a fever raging out of control.

"Do you know how an immune system works, Drew?"

Drew shrugged. "The marrow and spleen kick out white blood cells. The white cells surround the foreign body, and kill it. Hey, man, didn't you ever see *Fantastic Voyage*?"

"There are also antibodies," Winston reminded him. "Different kinds, each with their own specific properties. Their own special charm. They lie dormant until triggered by either a disease, or a vaccination."

Let me inoculate you against your pain.

Winston glanced around for the split-faced drug dealer, but he was nowhere. He shivered, holding the thought in abeyance. "The thing is, it takes more than one antibody to do the job. To fight the most dangerous threats to the body, it takes specific types, in specific quantities working together."

Drew considered it, and nodded a deeper understanding. "A quantity of six, maybe?"

"Maybe." A roar from the crowd signaled that one of the two teams had scored, but neither Winston nor Drew ventured onto the field to find out which one. Winston scanned the deserted space around them, until spotting the nearest ramp leading down. "I do believe we have to find ourselves a drug dealer."

THE HATCHET-FACED DEALER HAD left the upper concession level, and they did not spot him on the lower levels either. He could have taken off his mask and vanished into the crowd, but somehow Winston doubted that.

"The guy was dog crap on bad news," Drew reminded him. "Why are we looking for him?"

Winston chose not to answer that. Instead he asked, "Are you familiar with fractal theory?"

"No, but I'm sure you are."

"Only what I've read." Of course, they both knew the library locked in Winston's head had grown rather extensive. "The theory says that the smallest particle of something is just a smaller version of the whole."

"You lost me."

"A boulder on a mountain will, on some very basic level, contain the pattern of the entire mountain inside it. The way an acorn holds the pattern of the oak. The way every living cell contains the pattern of the whole organism."

"DNA."

"Right. But what if it doesn't stop there? What if the organism is the blueprint for the species? And what if the species is the blueprint for the cosmos?"

Drew laughed the idea away. "Winston, I don't doubt that you see yourself when you look at the stars."

With the fourth quarter winding down, and their masked marauder nowhere in sight, they headed out into the parking lot.

"All I'm saying," Winston continued, "is that if a star can be alive, and its death be the birth of six souls here on earth, what else might be alive out there? How much bigger is the picture?"

"And what does all this have to do with a ballpark pusher?"

Winston slowed as they neared their car. "I think we're about to find out."

Drew turned and caught sight of it, too. The elusive drug dealer sat on the hood of their car. The parking lot lighting cast a dark shadow of the rubber hatchet across one side of his face. Half in shadows, the mask was even more menacing.

Drew grabbed Winston's arm. "I don't like this. Let's get the hell out of here."

"He's on our car," Winston reminded him. "Where are we

going to go?" The hatchet man watched them, his face like a portrait that always held one's gaze. They stopped a good five yards from the car.

"Leaving so soon?" the dealer said.

"Looking for you," Winston answered, reigning back his own fear. "We were wondering what you had to offer. And what it might cost."

"It just so happens I'm running a special today," the dealer said. "Crystal Nova. Powerful stuff. Just a small piece of it is guaranteed to grow hair on your chest—and just about everywhere else, for that matter."

Winston took a step closer to the car. "Take off the mask."

The "dealer" slowly reached up, and peeled off the latex mask to reveal the sickly face of a Hualapai Indian nowhere near as beautiful as it had been a year before. The voice had lost its musical timbre, but the face was unmistakable. It was Okoya.

Winston should have warned Drew, for now Drew's fear spiked suddenly. "Oh, crap—I thought Dillon took care of that thing."

"Dillon did take care of me," Okoya said. "He took care of me so well that I had no choice but to come back."

"You have five seconds to start making sense," demanded Winston.

"It will all make sense soon enough. Trust me."

"Trust you?" Drew took a step forward, his initial shock transmuting into rage. "You left four hundred people worse than dead, and left Dillon to clean up after you. He might take the blame for what's going on in the world, but you're the one who caused it."

"Me, responsible for what's going on in the world?" Okoya mocked. "I'm flattered you think me capable of such large-scale atrocity."

Drew lunged at him, but Winston held him back. "Save it," he told Drew. "Save your anger until we need it."

Okoya hopped off the car. Winston could see his body was frail, barely clinging to life.

"Drew has more reason to hate me than you realize, Winston. You could say Drew and I have an intimate history."

"You have a sick definition of 'intimate,'" Drew said.

"I tore his soul from him during that unpleasantness at Hoover Dam last year," Okoya explained.

Winston turned to Drew, shocked by this disclosure, but before he could jump to conclusions, Okoya continued.

"Oh, he got it back, of course. When I tore his soul from him, I didn't feed on it myself, I tried to serve it to Michael. But instead of devouring it, Michael gave Drew back his soul."

Winston could feel Drew shudder.

"Rest easy," Okoya told Drew. "While it was personal for you, it was tactical for me. However, troubling with you now would serve me no purpose." Then he threw a mischievous gaze in Winston's direction. "It's more likely that Winston would chop off your arm, than I would devour your soul."

Winston had to look away, and it made Okoya laugh. How long had Okoya been shadowing them? How close had he been? "No matter what you choose to do, and not do," Winston said, "we'll never see you as anything but evil."

The smile quickly drained from Okoya's sallow face. "If so, I am the least of many evils. There are three creatures out there—I'm sure you've seen them in your mind's eye. They prey on souls, but are much more powerful than I ever was. If you send me away, I promise you, this world—this universe— will fall into their hands."

"Why would you help us?" Winston asked.

Okoya held out his hands, palms up. "I've made an enemy

of them. I have no choice but to side with you."

Winston nodded. A matter of necessity. Practicality. For once Okoya's unfailing self-interest gave them the upper hand, and had turned him into a staunch, if somewhat sinister ally. The question was, did Winston have the stomach to deal with the devil?

"What would you want in return?" Winston asked.

"The right to exist. Nothing more."

"And devour souls?" asked Drew.

Okoya sighed. "I've found I can get by on other forms of subsistence in this world, if I must. The modest life-force of animals, plants." And then a broad smile. "Perhaps I'll become a vegetarian."

Drew threw up his hands. "He's playing us for fools. You know that, don't you?"

Winston kept his eyes on Okoya. "All I know is that the immune system is failing. Isn't that right, Okoya?"

Okoya raised his eyebrows. "I'm impressed. Figured that out by yourself, did you?"

"Drew did."

Okoya threw Drew a smirk. "An insightful soul. But I already knew that."

While Drew didn't exactly warm to Okoya, he seemed to step down his defenses a bit. "How do we know you won't start feeding your old hunger?"

"When I broke through into this world, I had to feed once," Okoya told them, "just to survive the shock of passage. Since then I've abstained. You could say I've been testing my newfound virtue." He grinned, but no matter how mollifying he tried to be, his grins had all the warmth of a crocodile.

Winston dared to step close to him. He looked Okoya over, Winston's nose clogging from the stench. Okoya's muscles had atrophied, leaving swollen joints, and a belly beginning to distend. Apparently without his feasts of souls, he could not sustain his host body. "You're starving that body," Winston told him. "You'll need to feed it to survive. Our kind of food."

"I've been neglectful in that area," Okoya admitted.

"What's the matter," taunted Drew, "afraid you'll enjoy our primitive tastes?"

"There was no such nourishment where I've been. And lately I've been too busy tracking Dillon and the two of you to bother serving needs of the flesh."

"Dillon?!" It was Winston's magic word. "You know where Dillon's at?"

"That depends," said Okoya. "Do we have an understanding?"

Winston looked to Drew for support, but Drew wouldn't meet his eyes. "We'll see what your help is worth," Winston answered.

Okoya considered it, and accepted. "Yes, I do know where Dillon is," he said. "We'll talk about it on the way to California."

"He's in California?"

"No—but there's something we'll need before I lead you to Dillon."

We, thought Winston with a wave of discomfort. *He talks as if he's one of us now.*

"You really want to do business with this thing?" Drew asked quietly, but not so quietly that Okoya couldn't hear.

"I can't see as we have any more choice than he does," Winston answered.

Okoya took a step closer. "This universe is about to be infected by hundreds of thousands of my kind," Okoya told them. "But sometimes an ounce of the disease can be the cure."

23. GRAVITY

CAYMANAS PARK WAS HERALDED AS THE PREMIER HORSE racing track in the Carribean. Nowhere near as exotic as the flamingo-laden turfs of Florida's Hialeah, Caymanas was like most everything else in Jamaica: functional, but badly weathered by tropical storms that came one after another.

The track was frequented by locals, made up of native Jamaicans and America retirees, as well as tourists who had had their fill of palm trees and tropical beaches. They would all come to wager on thoroughbreds whose bodies frothed in the oppressive Jamaican humidity. The racing season at Caymanas never ended—there were races every Wednesday and Saturday, as well as holidays, but without the luxury of night lighting, races always ended at dusk.

By Saturday's ninth race, the last of the day, the sky was already bruising the colors of sunset. The horses paraded a loop on the homestretch, studied by a crowd that had gathered on the asphalt apron between the track and the grandstand. The apron filled up as post time closed in, and the horses were led to the gate. For many, part of the thrill of the race was pressing up against the homestretch railing and feeling the thunder of hooves in their own bodies as the horses powered toward the finish line.

Within that crowd was one American girl of Hispanic heritage, whose interest was not in the horses at all. Her interest was in the crowd.

Although no one noticed, by the time the gate crashed open

and the race began, everyone standing up in the homestretch was breathing in unison, and their hearts followed the same adrenaline-pumped beat. Although everyone shouted different things, exhaling various words of encouragement and dismay at their respective horses, there was a silence on the inhale, leaving the shouts to come in a strange wave pattern.

The horses came out of the clubhouse turn, and flew down the backstretch. A bay horse named Eagles Dare had the lead by a length. With tight attention on the distant pack of horses, no one noticed as the American girl closed her eyes, finding her center in the midst of turmoil. The horses went into the far turn, the lead horse falling back, surpassed on the outside by a spotted stallion with an aggressive jockey, whipping his horse into the lead.

That's when Lourdes Hidalgo lashed out, imposing herself on the crowd.

It began with the people immediately around her; a man waving his racing form in the air suddenly found his arm heavy by his side; a woman screaming for Calliope to move up from last place suddenly found her mouth no longer forming the words; a man with a cigar stub in his hand found he couldn't discard it even as it began to sear his index finger.

The horses came out of the turn, hoofs pounding, dirt flying. By now the crowd at the rail had fallen eerily silent, and the grandstand quickly followed suit. Even the announcer, who barked the race like an auctioneer, found himself, for the first time in his career, speechless as the horses came into the homestretch.

A powerful impulse swept through the crowd, latching onto each nervous system, usurping control. It was an impulse to move. To gather. The spectators found themselves turning from the race, becoming a circle pushing inward toward the girl who had suddenly become their center of gravity.

For Lourdes, it was like screaming into darkness, for the place was so dense with bodies, she had no clue what the response would be. She feared her bid for control would be so diluted, it wouldn't take hold. But as more and more faces turned to her, she realized she had succeeded in seizing them, just as her three "angels" had instructed her to do. She thought it a victory, until she realized that the crowd wasn't just focused on her. They were pressing toward her, tighter and tighter—and it wasn't just the crowd standing by the rail.

On the track, as the horses tore past the tote board, they veered from the finish line, bearing right, following a new command. Lourdes could see the wild eyes of the animals; neither the horses nor their jockeys able to control their tons of flesh. Like the curl of a breaking wave, the horses hurdled the rail and came down on the crowd. Spectators were trampled beneath their hooves, and crushed beneath the weight of their falling bodies.

Lourdes panicked, struggling to release the crowd from her grasp, but she had gripped them so tightly, she could not release them. A woman in front of her pressed up against her. Squeezed by the crowd behind her, the woman began working her mouth, trying to draw a breath of air, but her chest had collapsed under the pressure of the crowd. Lourdes, constricted and unable to move, craned her neck toward the grandstand, where people found themselves climbing down over rows of seats against their own will until reaching the front. Dozens upon dozens of people hurled themselves from the upper level like lemmings, their bodies obeying the command to draw close to Lourdes, even if that command resulted in death.

This was not what she wanted. She had meant to call the

mob to crisp attention, but instead they were moths drawn to her flame.

"Stop!" screamed Lourdes, her voice a faint warble. She could barely breathe now within the growing pressure of the crowd. "Help me!" She knew the angels were somewhere watching, but if they heard, they did not lift so much as a finger to help her.

The woman who pressed painfully against Lourdes's breast now showed no signs of struggle, although her eyes were open, there was nothing there. She was dead. The men to her left and right were dead. She was surrounded by a minion of corpses crushed by the press of the crowd, unable to fall. In less than five minutes a simple day at the races had become an ordeal surpassing her worst nightmare, and although she tried to scream her terror, she found her own breath squeezed out of her.

Then she realized there was a way to stop this. She had pulled the crowd to her, and she couldn't simply turn off that physical impulse: it had to be replaced by another impulse equally persuasive. So she closed her eyes and pushed forth to everyone under her control a simple physiological imperative: the irresistible urge to sleep.

It took hold immediately, and bodies began to drop. Soon the pressure around her eased, and the dead pressed so tightly against her slid to the ground, like petals falling from a flower. She gasped a deep breath, filling her lungs over and over again until she was dizzy from hyperventilation.

In the orange glow of sunset, Lourdes regarded her personal Armageddon. The grandstand was almost clear, bodies piled beneath, too deep to count. A dozen yards away, the head of a jockey protruded from beneath the carcass of his horse. Eagles Dare. The favorite. The lethal weight of the horse had forced a deluge of blood from the jockey's nose and mouth.

Only three figures remained standing. A man, a woman, and a child. Cerilla, Carlos, and Memo, or at least those had been the names of their human hosts. They waited in the winners' circle.

Lourdes stepped over the carnage. It was impossible to know how many slept, and how many were dead—trampled by horses, or suffocated by the press of the crowd. She leapt over the obstacle course of flesh, crying at the magnitude of the disaster.

"I can't do it!" she screamed at her mentors. "I can't—look at this, I can't do it!" The boy came forward and dispassionately smashed the back of his small hand across Lourdes's face. It came as a shock, and hurt more than she expected.

"She's a disaster," said Carlos.

"Worthless," said Cerilla.

But Memo said, "She'll do better . . . won't you, Lourdes?"

She had once flawlessly controlled half a dozen people on a volleyball team. She had turned a group of twenty into a kick-line for her own amusement. She had forced dozens to dance, and kept a shipload of beautiful people emotionally dependent on her, irresistibly drawn to her magnetic personality. But all that was child's play. She had never stretched herself as thin as this task required.

"There were too many people!" she told them. "I'll never be able to do it!"

"You'll practice," Memo said calmly. "You'll get better. You will master your control of fifty, then a hundred, then five hundred, then a thousand."

"But why?" she demanded. "Why have you asked me to do this? How many people do you need me to control?"

"When you succeed, you will understand," Memo told her.

"And once you understand, you will revel in it."

Cerilla shook her head, her chilly look made arctic by the grimace of her cleft lip. "She won't succeed. We need to find another way."

Carlos nodded his agreement, but little Memo waved them both off dismissively. "That's for me to decide," he said.

The other two nodded in reluctant acquiescence. If it had not been clear to Lourdes who was in charge among them, there was no longer a question.

Faint groans and cries around them indicated that Lourdes's sleep was wearing off. "We should do something," she said. "People are dying."

"Since when did you care about human suffering?" asked Carlos.

She had no answer for him. For a year now, Lourdes had cultivated insensitivity and indifference. Compassion was never her strong point, but she still had to work hard to purge it, clothing herself in an attitude of disdain. It took a calamity such as this to remind her that she was human, or at least once had been. Perhaps it was easy for these creatures to see humans as nothing more than fodder, but it wasn't so easy for Lourdes.

There were other people approaching now—people who were blessedly beyond the rim of her event horizon, and were not under her control; late arrivals, and curiosity-seekers who had heard the commotion and came to investigate.

Memo glanced at the people wandering in, then turned to Lourdes. "I'm hungry," he said. "Gather us some dinner." Then he left with the two others, heading toward their limousine waiting behind the grandstand.

Lourdes took a deep breath, and released it. For days she had watched these angels dine, trying to desensitize herself to it, trying to see their feast of souls as something other than awful. There was a higher purpose to all this—or if not a higher purpose, a practical one. Why align herself with humanity, she reasoned, when she could align herself with something higher on the food chain? If the universe was indifferent—even hostile—what end was there besides self-preservation? No, it wasn't easy to see people as cattle, but she was working on it.

A woman clinging fearfully to her husband approached Lourdes. "Did you see this here?" she asked in a rich Jamaican lilt. "Do you know about it? Were you here?"

"I was right in the middle of it," Lourdes said.

The woman began to shiver. "This a dark happening here," she said. "A dark happening."

"It gets worse," answered Lourdes. Then with a flick of her head, she took control of them, sending the couple marching toward the limo, where the angels waited to devour their souls.

Part IV

Syntaxis

24. SINS OF OMISSION

THERE WAS ONLY SO MUCH RECREATION MADDY COULD take, and although she knew she was free, in theory, to leave the building, both she and Dillon had grown accustomed to the security of Tessic's high sanctuary. She found herself losing track of the days, and feeling more and more a prisoner of the tower.

Dillon, on the other hand, luxuriated in his newfound freedom. With all of Tessic's resources left completely at his disposal, Dillon was like an overstimulated kid in a toy store. Much of his days were spent in Tessic's media room, scouring five hundred some-odd stations for news of the world, analyzing patterns and trends of the decline, but now from a detached, enlightened distance.

Maddy found herself absorbed in Tessitech's computer network. Tessic had given her enough access to his computer system to tempt her to look, and enough restrictions to tempt her to look deeper. In two weeks she had racked up enough information about his organization, in both R & D and trade secrets, to be either a substantial threat, or qualify for a high corporate position. It annoyed her to no end that she was beginning to fantasize about the latter, and she wondered whether or not Tessic had planned it that way.

Toward the end of the second week, Dillon called Maddy down to Tessic's sixty-second floor workshop.

"This is great, you're going to love this!" Dillon told her as he led her down three flights of stairs, not patient enough to wait for the elevator.

Tessic had been gone for three days, jetting abroad to take care of business, but had left Dillon a whole arsenal of gadgets to toy with. Today's objects of fascination were two glass cylinders filled with brown sand, which he pulled out of a heavy metallic container. Both were about a foot high, on a heavy base, like two high-tech blenders. A closer inspection revealed that the sand was, in fact, colored granules blended into a homogenous muddy mélange.

Maddy crossed her arms. "So what am I looking at?"

Dillon set them at the two ends of a large work desk. "Tessic had me working with these before he left." He grabbed a remote control, backed away, then positioned himself about five paces away from the table, equidistant from both cylinders. "Watch." He clicked the remote and the two glass cylinders began to vibrate in unison. The sand shifted, and the blend of colors began to separate from one another until what remained were two cylinders filled with rainbow strata of sand that would no longer blend, no matter how much the cylinders vibrated. Dillon hit the remote to shut them off.

"I came down to watch you do sand art?"

"No—see, look." He pointed to a timer at the base of each cylinder. "This measures the time of separation. It's a way to quantify the strength of my field. The closer I am to the device, the faster the color separation occurs. I can place myself behind different objects, and test what inhibits my field, and what amplifies it!"

"Interesting," she said with a smirk. "A Dillonometer."

"But here's the really exciting thing." Dillon pointed out the two timers again. "The right one is two-point-three seconds slower than the left." Dillon looked at her proudly.

"And?"

"Don't you see? I was able to control it. When I first started, both times would be identical, but I've been able to alter that. I've been able to control and focus my field."

There was something unpalatable about Dillon's enthusiasm, and even though Maddy was impressed, she found herself downplaying it. "It's just sand, Dillon; sand in a perfectly controlled environment. It has no bearing on the real world."

"It's a start." Dillon grabbed the colorful cylinders, returning them to their metallic case, which was no doubt some shielded material that would allow the sands to mix. "Before, it took a damned vault to contain me. This is one step closer to containing myself."

"If that's what you want, I hope you succeed."

Dillon took a good long look at her, his enthusiasm over-ripening into irritation. "What's wrong with you lately?"

She shook the question off. "Maybe I'm just tired of watching you putter your days away."

"What would you rather have me do? Live in shadows, playing hide and seek with the FBI?"

Maybe, she thought. There was an intensity to him then; a wildness that had now been tamed. But then, wasn't it she who told him to slow down and accept Tessic's hospitality?

Maddy sighed and turned to see how far she was from the stairs. "Listen, just forget it. Forget I said anything." She kissed him on the cheek, and made her way toward the stairs, hoping to get there before Dillon spoke, and knowing she wouldn't.

"You need me helpless," he said.

She found her feet slowing in spite of herself.

"You prefer me locked in a chair, or running from the Feds, or tormented by thoughts I can't control. It's the only way you can deal with me. If I'm helpless."

"That's not true," she said, forcing herself to turn to him.

"Of course it's true," Dillon scoffed. "I know you—don't forget that. I can see right through you."

"Well, maybe I don't enjoy being transparent."

The back door to the workshop opened with a conspicuous squeak. They turned to see Tessic standing there, feigning to have just arrived. There was no telling how much he had heard, and Maddy wondered why she cared.

Dillon spared one more look to Maddy before hurrying to Tessic as if he were Daddy home from work.

"Elon! I've had some breakthroughs while you were gone."

"How was Poland?" Maddy asked, flatly.

"Cold." Tessic pulled out a stack of pictures from his pocket. "The Ciechanow construction site. Would you like to see?" Tessic spread the photos out methodically on the work table. The images showed a swarm of more than one hundred building all much closer to completion than Maddy had assumed. Little more than landscaping remained.

"The first twenty buildings are ready for occupancy. The rest will be done in a matter of weeks. Then we repeat the process at identical sites in Belarus and Lithuania."

"Any takers?" asked Dillon. "Anyone moving in?"

"Not yet." Tessic finished laying out the pictures. Maddy noticed how he avoided looking Dillon in the eye. "Marketing has not matched the pace of construction, but I'm confident Ciechanow will fill quickly."

Maddy wondered why, if she could read Tessic's evasiveness, Dillon could not. Or perhaps he did read it, and chose to ignore it.

"I'd very much like you to join me on my next trip," Tessic told Dillon. "Photographs do not do it justice."

Maddy watched Dillon's response closely. He took his time before answering, studying an aerial view of the sprawling complex that looked eerily similiar to the model across the room.

"Sure," Dillon said, tossing it off like it was nothing. "Sure I'll go." Then he turned to her as an afterthought. "Maddy?"

"Well, since a winter coat magically appeared in my wardrobe a few days ago, I assume I'm to go as well."

Tessic put an arm around both of them as he led them to the stairs. "I assure you, you will both be better for the experience."

TESSIC JOINED THEM FOR lunch, listening avidly as Dillon went into detail describing the various tests and experiments he had done in Tessic's absence. Then, while Dillon buried himself channel-surfing for news of the world, Maddy took to her own analysis, delving once more into Tessitech's mainframe. Tessic called this Polish construction project a "sideline," but from what she could see it was, aside from Dillon, his primary concern. It didn't bode well with her that such a shrewd businessman would put all his attention into a money pit, and leave the rest of his business on autopilot.

In the computer, she found that Tessic's personal jet was scheduled for another trip abroad in two weeks—but it wasn't what she found that surprised her; it was what she didn't find. It brought things into sharp focus.

Late that afternoon, she approached Tessic on the roof garden. He was having what appeared to be a heated conversation in Hebrew with himself, but as Maddy got closer, she could see he was talking into a Bluetooth. A man who spoke with his hands, Tessic's motions resembled a kind of kinetic art. A corporate t'ai chi.

When he saw her, he cut the conversation short, and removed his Bluetooth, but his anger remained. He grabbed a glass of iced tea from the nearby table. "It's falling apart, you know. In corporations everywhere, there are executives resigning at the highest levels, nightmares in productions, funds disappearing."

"Thank goodness for 'sidelines.'"

"Yes." Tessic took a sip of his drink, and then another, calming down.

"It's amazing those buildings of yours still go up with all that's going on in the world."

"Eastern Europe is used to chaos," he answered. He poured her a glass, and offered her a seat, but did not pull it out for her, as he knew her aversion to such social niceties. "I can't help but notice the trouble between you and Dillon," he said.

Maddy gulped, and grimaced. "Not everything can be as sweet as your tea."

"Our roles are rarely what we want them to be," Tessic said, slipping from businessman into philosopher mode. "Have you considered that perhaps your place in each other's lives lies outside of the bedroom?"

Maddy laughed at his audacity. "Are you trying to provoke me, or are you always this callous?"

"Do not misunderstand, Miss Haas. I think what you and Dillon have is wonderful. But a relationship requires a joining of mind, body, and soul. If you can live with two of the three, my blessing to you. But if you find your own soul lacking, overwhelmed by his . . ."

Tessic hesitated, reconsidering his words. "I don't mean to offend . . . but for both of your sakes, please be certain of your purpose in Dillon's life. For when you are certain, your choice of action will be as clear as it was on the day you rescued him."

"I like to think I make my own purpose," she told him, coolly.

Tessic sighed. "There I go again," he said. "I give you another reason to hate me."

Maddy considered that, and shook her head. "I don't hate you, Elon." And then, with more sincerity than she thought she had in her, she said, "The truth is, I think you're a great man, with more vision than I gave you credit for."

The admission caught him by surprise. "Such a change!" he said, gloating a bit in the new light she cast him in. "What brings this about in a skeptical young woman like you?"

She looked down to the table, preparing herself, then returned her gaze to Tessic. "Over the past two weeks, I've spent a lot of time studying your business dealings."

"Really," he said, crossing his legs, knee over knee. "Perhaps you found something interesting?"

"Oh, it's all interesting," she said. "But what I found most remarkable is your marketing plan for the Ciechanow project."

"Oh, that." He attempted to conceal a grin behind his tea. "And what interested you most about it?"

"The fact that there *is* no marketing plan. None whatsoever."

Tessic sipped his tea, neither confirming nor denying it. He always said he was a man of honesty. She supposed that was true—she had never caught him in a lie. His were all sins of omission.

"All that living space, in the middle of nowhere," Maddy said, "and no one invited to the party."

Tessic didn't try to hide his grin anymore. He leaned in

closer to her. "I anticipate a need," he said. "But you've already figured that out, haven't you?"

"I wish I hadn't."

"And do you approve?"

Maddy deliberated on her response, and answered truthfully. "I think it's brilliant. I think it's terrifying."

"A powerful combination."

"And when were you going to tell Dillon what you're planning?"

"I'm not planning anything," Tessic insisted. "It will be Dillon's idea, and he will plan it himself. I am merely laying the groundwork for when he does."

"What makes you so sure he will?"

Tessic put his glass down, and studied her. "You're not a woman of faith, are you, Miss Haas?"

"It's hard enough to believe what I see, much less what I don't see."

Tessic took a long draught from his glass, until the tea was gone, and the color drained from the ice, leaving it clean and clear. "Time will ease your doubts."

"I can live with doubts," she told him, "and once in a while even do the right thing. But it's your lack of doubt that frightens me."

25. BODY BUILDERS

TESSIC GOT A CALL AT EIGHT O'CLOCK THE FOLLOWING morning that Security was detaining two visitors. The security officer apologized profusely for disturbing him in his private penthouse, and the intruders would have been summarily expelled, had they not claimed to be relatives of Tessic's guests. Since building security had not been informed that Tessic even had guests, it warranted his attention.

He found the two teenage boys in the security office, double-teamed by four guards. The guards were all unsettled—it was in their eyes and their stances; discomfort in the way they looked to one another, scratched their arms, necks, and heads, complaining about the heat regardless of the fact that the air was overly conditioned with a breezy Freon chill. Tessic knew the reason for their discomfort. There was a field of presence here, like the one Dillon exuded, but this one was different. A variant flavor, a different charm.

"Are you Tessic?" said the black teen, all attitude. It only aggravated the suspicions of the good ol' boys with security badges.

"Get out!" Tessic said. The lead guard promptly advanced on the two teens, just as Tessic knew he would. "No," Tessic said, stopping the guard in his tracks. "You and your men. Get out."

The men looked to one another, clearly suffering some testicular trauma at their dismissal. The guards began to slink out, and Tessic took guilty pleasure in watching them go.

When he was seventeen, all long hair and torn jeans, he would have been cast out of an establishment like this as well.

"In the future," he told the exiting guards, "I expect you to treat visitors with common courtesy and respect—even the ones you expel."

Once the door had closed, Tessic turned to the black teen. "Do I have the honor of addressing Winston Pell?"

Winston cracked the slightest smile. "Expecting me?"

"Not at all—but your presence is a welcome surprise." The fact was, Tessic had an entire staff of private detectives searching for Winston and Lourdes, and they had come up empty-handed. That Winston had just fallen into his lap was just further indication of how *bashert* his endeavor was. Tessic could feel the hand of the Almighty in this. He offered Winston his hand, and Winston looked at it for a moment before committing to shake it. As their hands clasped, he felt Winston's current move through him, making the hair on his arms and neck stand on end. Tessic laughed, a bit giddy from the sensation.

"So how come you dress like that?" Winston said, pointing to Tessic's white suit. "I've always wanted to ask that."

"Image is everything," Tessic answered, "or at least my public relations staff tells me."

The blond kid stood up behind Winston. "Excuse me," he said, "the non-entity requests an introduction."

"Drew Camden, Elon Tessic," Winston said.

Tessic raised his eyebrows. "The biographer!"

Drew's eyes lit up. "You know about that?"

"With the amount of airplay your videos of the shards received over the past year, you should have been a rich man."

Drew sighed. "Yeah, too bad I left them in the desert, for some low-life from Vegas to find. He hit the jackpot, I got nothing."

"Ah, well, I imagine living it was worth all the money in the world."

"Give me all the money in the world, and I'll tell you which I like better."

"So," said Winston. "I've heard it from a reliable source that you've got Dillon locked away like Rapunzel in your tower."

Tessic considered his response, and said, "The Talmud says a man's own chains are the strongest."

To which Winston responded, "A man's own chains might be the strongest, but the Talmud also says, 'A man who puts his brother to the test is not to be trusted.'"

Tessic shook his head, impressed. "Extraordinary! Your gift of growth has turned your mind into a sponge for knowledge." Tessic laughed with pleasure, in spite of all of his attempts to maintain a cool, suave demeanor. "I only ask one thing: that I be in the room for the reunion."

Winston shrugged. "Hey, it's your tower."

DILLON WAS AWAKENED BY what he thought was an alarm clock, but when morning replaced his dreams, he realized nothing was ringing. Still, there was some energy in his room he could not name, just at the edge of perception.

Maddy had left the room at dawn for her regimen of exercise, and Dillon found himself relieved that she was gone before he awoke. They had shared a bed but not each other the night before. He didn't know who was to blame, and he wondered if their relationship had become so fragile that a single change in their pattern could cause the fabric to unravel.

He scratched an annoying itch on his lip and cheek. Maddy still needed to come to terms with the fact that Dillon had found himself again. He was no longer a boy who needed rescue, but a man, more comfortable with himself than he had ever been. If Maddy truly did love him, she would come to accept that.

There was a knock at the door, and Dillon opened it to Anselm, Tessic's valet, a good-natured Swede who had suffered to learn Hebrew. He had pledged himself into Tessic's service after Tessic led a campaign to find the man's daughter a marrow donor.

"Mr. Tessic asked that I should bring you this." He gave Dillon a hand-held mirror. When Dillon looked up for an explanation, Anselm only shrugged. "It is my understanding that it is a gift to you."

Once Anselm had left, Dillon turned it over to see if it said anything on the back, but it did not. Well, Tessic was nothing if not enigmatic. Dillon had come to find the puzzles he posed entertaining.

Dillon put the mirror down, and dressed for breakfast. As he pulled on his polo shirt, he felt the smooth flow of the fabric over his face. There was something different about it, and it registered only faintly in his mind. It was as he slipped on his socks that it occurred to him that the shirt wasn't different at all, it was his face. Then he looked down to the mirror he had left on the edge of the dresser.

In an instant he knew, even before he picked up the mirror to look.

The face he saw reflected in the oval was not the face he had gone to bed with. That face had been shredded and paved with scars from one cheek to the other, across his lips, down to his chin. Those scars were mere shadows now, and as he touched his face, he could feel them dissolving as good skin regenerated to replace it. There was a growing ache in his mouth as well. Blood began to spill from the corners of his mouth, and by the time he reached for a towel to wipe it away, new molars had sprouted from the empty sockets left from Maddy's bullet.

There was only one explanation for this, and now he could put a name to the presence he had felt upon waking. Forgetting about Maddy and Tessic, he raced out of the room, his shoes barely on his feet.

He hurried down the hall toward the winding staircase that led down to the penthouse living room, hearing voices below. But as he neared the stairs, his enthusiasm took on a flavor of apprehension.

He took the stairs slowly, letting the room below move carefully into his view. Maddy was there, and Tessic. Neither had seen him yet. He was surprised to see Drew Camden there, and finally Winston. Drew, the first to notice Dillon, rapped Winston on the arm, and Winston turned toward the stairs.

Dillon found himself frozen on the last step as Winston saw him. Things were changing again for him. This controlled equilibrium Tessic had so painstakingly prepared would be violated by that final step into the room. Dillon opened his mouth to speak, but found nothing to say, and he could read the same uneasy ambivalence in Winston as well. This long-awaited reunion had brought with it an unexpected fear.

"Where the hell have you been for eight months?" Winston asked, the first to break the silence.

Dillon shrugged. "Out of sight," he answered. "And out of mind."

And then Winston gave him the hint of a smile. "No surprise there—you've always been out of your mind."

Dillon took that final step down into the room, and crossed the floor to Winston, as Winston came toward him. Caught off guard by their own momentum, they nearly toppled one another in a bruising hug. Dillon felt a charge within the embrace—a surge of energy as Winston's power added to

Dillon's, their harmonics fitting together like a major fifth. The tingling sensation in Dillon's face peaked, then vanished, and he knew that the last of the scars were now gone. "I was starting to think I'd never see you again," Dillon said.

Winston pulled away at the precise moment Dillon expected he would. "All right, let's not get all touchy-feely about it."

Dillon laughed. Whatever else might change, some things would always stay the same. He turned to Drew, offering a quick greeting, then returned his attention to Winston. "The army had me in lockdown like King Kong," Dillon said, and went on to explain his months of captivity. Then Winston filled him in on his travels, but it was obvious that he was dancing around the things that were really on his mind, as was Dillon. Finally Dillon said, "Okoya's back."

Winston looked away for a moment. "I know." Dillon sensed there was more he knew, but Winston just said, "We'll talk about it later. Tell me how you wound up here."

Maddy watched the two of them in the center of the large room, feeling uncomfortably voyeuristic. This was a relationship she had no place in. For as long as she had known Dillon, he had been alone and unique. But now the dynamic had changed. He and Winston spoke as if no one else in the world existed—as if the two were part of their own private universe. They belonged with each other, and Maddy wondered if it would be this way if they came together with Lourdes, too. Would their confluence serve only to push Maddy further and further away? It was small and selfish, this kind of jealousy, but she couldn't purge herself of it.

Make sure you know your purpose in Dillon's life, Tessic had said. Now, as she watched Dillon and Winston, she wondered if she had any place in Dillon's life at all. Tessic, however, didn't appear to have any doubts of his own tenure among the starshards. Across the room, he watched in silence, content, for the time, to be an observer.

Drew, who apparently shared the curse of the periphery, came over to introduce himself to her.

"Do you live here with Tessic?" he asked.

She wanted to be angry at the suggestion, but what was the point? "No. I'm a friend of Dillon's."

"Ah," said Drew. The two watched Dillon and Winston for a few more moments. Winston was relating an encounter he had had with Lourdes. Something about a cruise ship. Dillon hung on his every word. Then Drew said to Maddy, "You can't get close to them, you know?"

"Excuse me?"

"It's like you're always on the outside. Believe me, I know. I tried to get close to Michael once—it got me killed."

Maddy turned to Winston and Dillon, both connected to the exclusion of everything else around them.

"They started as a star," Drew said. "And I figure in lots of ways they still are. They catch people like you and me in their orbit. We can't get away, but we can't get too close, or we burn. Best we can do is keep our orbit stable."

Drew's ruminations tugged enough of her focus that she missed something key in Dillon and Winston's conversation, because Dillon now showed an expression of surprise, and suddenly turned from Winston, shooting a look to another body currently in orbit: Tessic.

"You mean here?" Dillon asked Tessic. "In this building?"

"In the infirmary," Tessic said. "We'll go, when you're ready."

"I've been ready for months."

Maddy turned to Drew. "What are they talking about?"

Drew paused before answering. "What have you seen Dillon do?"

"Everything," she answered.

"You haven't seen this," Drew answered. "No one has."

AMONG TESSITECH'S VARIOUS EMPLOYEE perks was an infirmary and small medical clinic on the mezzanine. But today the clinic was closed and guards were posted at the doors.

In radiology, several leaded X-ray aprons covered an undefined mass on the X-ray table.

"He's in pretty bad shape," Winston said, as he and Dillon peered in through the window of the X-ray room. "And I suppose being around me didn't help. Bacteria, algae from the lake—anything that was still alive in that foot locker grew out of control as we drove here."

"Jeez, do you hear this conversation?" said Drew, to no one in particular. "I gotta find myself some new friends."

The door opened, and two medical technicians who had the grim task of preparing the body exited the room. "What are we, friggin' forensic examiners now?" one grumbled to the other. He stifled himself when he saw Tessic, who had them led out, never to know the nature of their task.

"One thing I learned from Bussard," Tessic told Dillon. "Don't let anyone see the whole picture."

"Does that include me?" Dillon asked.

"You? Who do you think is painting the picture?"

Dillon thought to the first time he had repaired the ravages of death; the recomposition of flesh, the reanimation of spirit. It had been so difficult at first, taking such a profound focus of his will. It had always been a lonely, solitary act, both selfless and self-indulgent at once. But things had changed. Now his will was secondary, his presence dragged order from chaos whether he chose to or not. Yet even in the graveyard, a victim of his own power, he knew his limitations. He knew there were those among the dead who did not revive—those whom he could never reanimate alone. Organ donors, perhaps, and others who were buried incomplete. Dillon could not give them new kidneys, eyes, or a heart any more than he could fill the scarred gaps in his own bullet-torn face.

But Winston could.

And no matter how little of Michael remained on that table, if they could somehow get the teeth of their curious gears to mesh, he could be restored. It would require more than their simple presence in the room. This task would require precision and control.

Dillon pulled open the door, and the stench hit him instantly, registering in his gut. Tessic quickly tugged out a handkerchief, holding it over his nose.

"You weren't kidding, were you, Winston?" Maddy said.

"You don't have to come in," Dillon told her, but as he and Winston entered the room, Maddy, Drew, and Tessic followed in their wake.

Three video cameras had been positioned in the room, already recording.

"What are we, on satellite feed to the world?" Winston asked.

"I wish to keep a record of this," Tessic explained. "To document what you both accomplish here."

"Like a videotape at birth," suggested Winston.

"Exactly."

Winston scowled. "I hate people who videotape births."

Dillon shuddered as he approached the table. The mass on the table had so little definition beneath the lead aprons, it was hard to believe there was anything remotely human there.

"Ready to rock?" Winston asked.

"Only if you are."

It began the moment they pulled back the lead radiation aprons.

The broken frame on the table before them was a collection of brittle human bones, caked with rancid mud, and glistening with a dense hair-like pelt of green lake algae. That algae was the first thing to start growing again in Winston's presence, appearing to slither around the bones. Winston, having not actually seen the body before this moment, launched off into full-scale panic.

"That's not Michael!" he said. "It's not him! We got the wrong body, it's not him!"

"Shh."

Dillon put his hand on a broken thighbone, half of which was missing. The bone, a dead gray beneath the algae, began to blanch to an eggshell white. "Winston!"

Winston shuttered his panic and reached out, touching the bone as well. Its jagged end began to stretch, marrow bubbling up from the hollow within, until it became enclosed within the smoothly curved end of the bone. The algae peeled away and slid to the table.

The process picked up speed, the two of them matching each other's rhythm. Dillon touched the skull, healing its many fractures. Winston moved the jaw into place, teeth growing to fill the empty sockets.

"Yes, I see it now!" said Winston. "It *is* Michael!"

They moved to the midsection. Crushed ribs rose into place, defining a chest cavity. From the decay that clung to the bones, Dillon was only able to re-integrate bloody fragments of organs—but with Winston's touch, those fragments cultivated, cells dividing into complete structures, until Winston and Dillon both found themselves wrist-deep in it.

They now moved at an accelerated pace, time dilating itself around them. To those behind them, their hands moved with the agility and grace of virtuosos: four hands at the same instrument, perfectly synchronized.

All at once blood began to pulse, splattering the walls. A heart now beat at the center of an open circulatory system. Connective tissue sprouted like spider webs from joint to joint and muscle mass thickened the legs and arms, rising like dough, encasing the bones beneath. Winston pressed his fingers on empty eye sockets, and when he pulled his fingers away, a pair of eyes filled the space, lids growing closed over them. The bleeding stopped and on the flayed, red figure before them, islands of translucent skin began to grow like clouds in an empty sky, growing denser, thicker, joining one another. A scalp grew back from the forehead, darkening with hair follicles. Skin stretched to cover the body, pushing the last of the algae away, until only the midriff remained open, like a gaping abdominal wound, but dermal tissue rushed in to fill the void until the gap became a crevice, became a crack, became a navel, leaving the fully realized body of Michael Lipranski, his chest rising and falling in slow, metered breaths.

Then Tessic suddenly bolted, flying from the room with uncharacteristic speed, but he was barely noticed as all eyes were on the body before them that had formed in less than a minute's time.

Covered with blood, Winston backed away, but Dillon did not, for there was still one thing left to do. Although Michael's body was there, there was an emptiness within. Calling back the spirit of others had been an instantaneous and automatic result of bringing life to the flesh. But Michael was a shard; a soul with such huge inertia that he had to be ignited like a furnace. Dillon pushed his thoughts forward, seeing Michael's being in his mind. Into Michael's flesh, into his cells, deeper still to the space between molecules, Dillon forced his own spark, and finally felt Michael ignite! A wave of intensity imprinted itself on every cell of his renewed body, aligning the life within into the service of a single consciousness.

MICHAEL FELT HIS OWN ignition.

Void of thought or reason, knowing nothing but his own existence, he was a bullet flying down the barrel, suddenly in motion, exploding forward into a body. He felt every bit of himself at the same instant, from the tips of his toes to the tips of his fingers. He felt his shape, settled into it, and seized control of a familiar mind, remembering who he was, accepting all that went with that knowledge.

Michael opened his eyes, feeling as if he had just been hurled from a carnival ride. He didn't know whether it was he who was spinning, or the room. Dillon stood over him, out of breath and flushed as if he had just climbed a long flight of stairs. Michael tried to speak, but only gasped at first, coughing until he hacked up a bitter, foul-smelling green wad that only slightly resembled mucous. In fact, he was lying in the stuff; green muck mixing with blood, like some bizarre birth caul. And he was naked.

Reflexively, he rolled to his side, away from Dillon, floundering in the slippery mire.

"Easy, Michael." Dillon grabbed his shoulders to keep him from sliding off the table. Dillon took off his own shirt and handed it to Michael to cover himself. Then Michael heard Winston speak. Until he heard his voice, Michael hadn't even known there was anyone else in the room.

"The temperature's dropped ten degrees in thirty seconds,"

Winston said. "Yeah, Michael's back all right."

Back? Back from where? Michael closed his eyes tightly, searching for a memory of the moment before, but there was none. He had no idea where he had just been, or how he got here. The past was piecing itself together now, bit by bit like the present. He remembered the dam collapsing around him and Tory. He remembered their terrified leap into the updraft which had carried them both into the sky. But Michael's control of the wind had broken down. The updraft failed them, and gravity dragged them down through the thin, icy air. Although he had clung to Tory, the force of the wind had torn her away. The last half mile he had tumbled alone. Brief pain. A blackout. And now this. It seemed many hours had passed since his last memory.

Shivering, he sat up, and turned around on the table, to see there were even more people present. Standing farther away stood a woman Michael didn't know, and Drew. Drew had an odd, lobotomized expression on his face.

"Hey," said Drew.

"Hey," Michael answered.

The woman beside Drew stood wide-eyed and rigid against the wall, staring at him. Michael suspected if the wall wasn't there to hold her up, she'd be on the ground.

Michael felt the temperature continue to drop as his uneasiness grew. "Toto, I don't think we're in Vegas anymore."

"You're in Houston," Dillon answered, with more deadpan seriousness than Michael cared for.

"I survived the fall?"

Dillon hesitated. "Not exactly."

Only now did his mind allow him to see that both Winston and Dillon were covered in blood. The sticky mess coated their arms to their elbows, and had splattered on their clothes.

All right, thought Michael, *I can handle this.* It was, after all, what he had hoped for. That Dillon would find his broken body in the Nevada desert, and bring him back.

He shuddered in the cold, his breath now coming in puffs of steam. "So what's this stuff I'm lying in? Some kind of ectoplasm?"

"More like pond scum," Winston answered.

Across the room, the girl wouldn't stop staring at him. Even with Dillon's shirt clasped over himself, her stare was seriously unnerving.

"What's the matter? You've never seen a resurrected naked guy lying in green slime before?"

"Sorry." She turned her eyes away.

"Hey, where are my clothes anyway?"

Winston offered an apologetic shrug. "Animals got 'em long before they buried you. Tough break."

"Buried? Holy crap, they buried me?"

Dillon turned to the girl. "Where's Tessic?" he asked. Michael was sure he didn't hear him correctly.

"Gone," she answered. "I'm amazed he actually got his legs to move. I couldn't."

Michael struggled to capture more of his bearings. He was on an X-ray table. Was this some sort of hospital? Dillon said they were in Houston—how did he get all the way here?

"I must have been offline a few weeks, huh?" he asked.

No immediate answer. Then as he regarded Winston and Dillon, it struck him how much different they both looked. A bit taller; a harder edge to their facial features. Suddenly he knew the gist of what they were about to tell him, and thunder rolled ominously outside. He wanted to deny it all. If only for a few moments, he wanted to believe that it was just a joke.

"It's been over a year, Michael," Dillon said.

He didn't even try to consider all the ramifications of it now. It was so overwhelming all he could do was ride it, like a wave. "Damn. Now my movie rentals are *really* gonna be overdue."

Drew had scrounged up a hospital gown for him, and approached with it.

"What happened at the dam?" Michael asked Dillon. "Did you hold back the water? What about Okoya?"

"You'll get cleaned up, and we'll get you some clothes," Dillon said, trying to wipe the blood from his own arms with a paper towel. "Then we'll talk."

Dillon turned but Michael grabbed him before he could go. "How about Tory? Did you find her, too?"

Dillon slid out of his grasp. "Like I said, we'll talk later."

Dillon left with the girl. Winston caught the door before it closed.

"Good to have you back, Michael," Winston said, and left as well.

Now it was just himself and Drew. Drew held out the hospital gown to him. "You know the drill; slip this on, open to the back."

Michael forced a grin. "So they left us to play doctor, did they? You gonna grab my balls and ask me to cough?"

"Ooh," Drew said. "That's low, even for you."

Michael stood up, and let Drew help him into the gown. The moment was uncomfortable, but then, how could it be otherwise? Whatever else had been resolved between them, it didn't change the fact that Drew, Michael's closest friend, had wanted to be more than just friends. Michael hadn't handled that well, and the year gone by hadn't changed Michael's discomfort. To him it had only been a few hours. The temperature in the room continued to fall, telegraphing Michael's apprehension better than words or body language. He didn't want to start his new life by treading on eggshells, so Michael chose to smash the shells with the bluntness that had always typified their friendship. "So what's the deal with you?" Michael asked. "You still hot for me? And if so, would that be considered necrophilia?"

Drew laughed, tying the strings to Michael's hospital gown. "To tell you the truth, Mikey-boy, dragging around your moldering bones wasn't exactly a turn-on. Sorry to disappoint you, dude, but couldn't we just be friends?"

Michael smiled. He had to remember that Drew had had a whole year to heal from old wounds. It suddenly struck Michael that Drew was a year older than him now. They all were.

"Fine with me," Michael said, then pointed to Drew's short, unevenly shorn hair. "But as your friend, I gotta tell you, I don't like the do."

"Yeah, well, wait five minutes," Drew answered.

WRAPPED IN A SILK prayer shawl, Elon Tessic offered prayers to the God of Abraham, Isaac, and Jacob. Prayers that he could retain the courage of his convictions. Prayers that he might regain his composure. He had called for a minyan of ten from among his employees to pray with him, but could not wait for them to arrive, so he began alone, reciting the *Sh'ma* and the *Amidah*, two seminal prayers of his faith. Surely today would be a day to humble himself in prayer, for he had already been humbled by what he witnessed just a short time before.

It was one thing to know the scope of Dillon's and Winston's powers, but another thing entirely to witness dust become flesh. It was nothing short of the creation. The way it must have been when God breathed life into man.

His Judaica study, filled with artifacts from all eras in history, was a sanctuary within a sanctuary for him. But today the framed parchments and silver adornments that had always brought him comfort and connection to the past held only accusations. Condemnations. Who was he to take such miraculous beings into his own hands? But then, who was any man called upon to do the will of the Almighty?

Maddy Haas, as perceptive as she was, had been wrong about one thing. Tessic had doubts. Not about Dillon's purpose, but about his own ability to complete his role in it. And so Tessic had removed himself from the sight of the revived Michael Lipranski, retreating to his library, and cloaking himself in his *talis*. He had bought the ancient silk prayer shawl at an auction, authenticated to be more than seven hundred years old. Until Dillon arrived it had been kept in a climate-controlled case, but now the crumbling yellowed silk had a fresh, white sheen, renewed like everything else that fell into Dillon's presence.

The door opened behind him. He expected it to be members of the prayer minyan he had called for, and was surprised to see that it was Dillon. Tessic put his prayer book down and kept his hands beneath the prayer shawl so that Dillon could not see how they were shaking.

"My jeans are a little long on Michael," Dillon said, "but they'll do until we can get him his own clothes."

"Yes. Good. We'll take measurements and whip him up a wardrobe right away."

Dillon was bathed and clean, but he still smelled faintly of blood. He took a few steps closer. "Are you all right? You left the infirmary in a hurry."

Tessic couldn't meet his eyes. "The job was done, I saw no reason to linger."

A gesture of his hand knocked the prayer book from the

table. Dillon quickly bent over to pick it up. He handed it to Tessic, and Tessic brought the book to his lips, kissing the spine. "Customary," Tessic said. "When something holy falls to the ground."

Dillon looked around at the artifacts and parchments on display around him. "These things mean a lot to you, don't they?"

Tessic looked to the artifacts he had been so proud to have amassed. "They are only things," Tessic answered. "What matters are the hands that shaped them. Poor men, mostly. I expect when all this is over, I shall be a poor man as well. What then will I have but my faith?"

The door creaked open, and a gaggle of businessmen entered, awkwardly pulling folded yarmulkes from their suit pockets. Tessic sighed. "What is the value of a minyan when they come at my beck and call? It should be a gathering of devotion, not a gathering to please one's employer."

The men respectfully greeted Tessic. And went to retrieve a set of prayer books across the room. Dillon became uncomfortable, clearly troubled that he might somehow be recognized. Tessitech's employees were not the trustworthy cadre that typified Tessic's personal staff. Before the men returned with their books, Tessic gently led Dillon to the door, and spoke so that the others could not hear. "You must convince Winston to join us in Poland."

"Winston goes nowhere Winston doesn't want to go."

"I trust in your ability to persuade him." Tessic gently closed the door, and returned to the nine other men who had gathered in the center of the room. He could already feel his composure returning.

26. INERTIA

WINSTON: NO ONE EXPECTED WHAT HAPPENED WHEN THE dam collapsed.

Dillon: I thought it would all end right there. I was wrong.

Michael listened. He didn't judge, he didn't think, he didn't try to make an emotional connection to the things Winston and Dillon told him. He had only "arrived" an hour ago, was quickly stuffed into some of Dillon's ill-fitting clothes, and now sat shell-shocked in the suddenly overgrown roof garden of industrial icon Elon Tessic. He found it all too surreal for comment. As he sat there, Winston and Dillon spouted the year-in-review in matching couplets.

Dillon: I could have held the water of Lake Mead back, but I didn't.

Winston: He let it flow, hoping it would become a disaster that would heal more than it destroyed.

The way they explained it, sending a flood sweeping down the lower Colorado River was the only way to stop the world from seeing the five of them as gods. Dillon's death would paint him in ignominy, and the scope of the disaster would shock the world back into stride, like a broken bone being set. Thousands would die, but civilization would go on, back on its steady track, as it had been before. The only thing that would collapse would be the dam.

Dillon: But I didn't die, and the flood waters never reached Laughlin.

Winston: Instead, Dillon's presence reversed the river's entropy. The flood slowed, and began to flow backward.

Apparently, in the wake of the Backwash, the shards were feared, revered, and worshipped on a global scale. The world believed them to be dead, which elevated them into martyrdom. In the face of that, everything rational and reasonable fell into decline. It was, in effect, the shattering of civilization, just as Dillon had feared from the beginning. The shards had been the agents of the shattering—not the solution.

Dillon: I was imprisoned and used by the government for almost a year.

Winston: I lived like a fugitive, hiding my face, afraid I'd be recognized.

In a way, Michael was grateful for his hiatus, having never had to witness all this with his own eyes. They told him how Lourdes abandoned them, taking refuge in her own bitterness, setting sail on a hedonistic voyage of excess. Michael could hardly blame her. Had he been alive, he might have done the same, isolating himself on some island in the calm eye of a perpetual hurricane.

Winston: There are three spirits out there now. Their arrival is the beginning of the end.

Dillon: But we're safe from them here.

Michael caught the look Winston threw Dillon, belying some unspoken tension. Even before he was told of the three spirits, Michael had sensed something. Even now, within the supposedly shielded confines of the penthouse, Michael knew there were three—but he didn't sense them so much as spirits. They were more like living coordinates. Markers of dimension; the axis of a three-dimensional grid. He might have shared his take on these creatures with Dillon and Winston, but they began to tell him about Tory, and how her ashes were dumped out over the skies of Dallas.

It was this news of Tory that finally reached him. Sorrow mushroomed within the numbness, a cumulus threatening rain. Acoustics in the garden dampened as the air pressure lightened in a sympathetic response. Although the sky over the rest of Houston remained clear, a single cloud now lingered above the Tessitech building. Apparently Tessic's shielding had a unique effect on Michael's power, focusing his mood into a narrow beam, sending it skyward, like a searchlight. In the rooftop garden, and nowhere else, it began to drizzle.

Michael knew a remedy to this mournful little cloud. It would be simple first aid, temporary and superficial, but it would hold him, if only for a little while.

"There's a year's worth of new music I haven't heard," Michael told them, as they stood from their chairs. "Get some for me."

The drizzle became a downpour before they reached the elevator.

WINSTON DIDN'T TELL MICHAEL everything.

He kept his secret, the same way he kept it from Dillon. Dillon had not yet asked how he and Drew had found him. Winston still didn't know how to answer without telegraphing a lie. But eventually both Dillon and Michael would have to be told about Okoya's part in this. He intended to keep the secret as long as he could.

Dillon disappeared after Michael's little emotional outburst, and Michael had since returned to the garden, stationing himself on a lounge chair in the rain. Equipped with an iPod and a mood-altering armada of tunes, he used the sky above him as biofeedback, determined to either disperse the cloud or suffer in the storm.

Winston found himself exploring the multi-level residence, losing track of why he was there. Tessic's penthouse was a tall drink on an empty stomach. Refreshing, inebriating, addicting. Dillon was already hooked, and that made Winston's task all the more difficult.

He came across Drew in the workout room, pounding a rapid pace on a treadmill.

"Dillon's acting normal," Winston told Drew. "I don't like it."

"He's not entitled to be normal?"

"You know Dillon—he's all gloom and doom."

Drew hit several buttons on the high-tech treadmill, but failed to find the off switch, so instead he let the momentum of the conveyor belt carry him off the back. "The change in Dillon could be a good thing. Maybe he's starting to feel all his dire predictions are wrong."

"Or maybe he's just running away from them."

Winston looked at the treadmill. It was, like everything else here, state of the art, with a curved screen that projected a path through a lush sequoia forest, or whatever environment you felt like jogging through. Simulated progress, when all you're doing is looking at a wall.

"He's even got a girlfriend now," Winston said. "Could you ever imagine Dillon with a girlfriend?"

"Well, there was Deanna . . ."

Winston waved it off. "That was different. The two of them . . . they . . ."

"Completed each other?" offered Drew.

"Yeah, something like that."

Winston looked out of the window, which, like every window in the penthouse, offered a view of downtown Houston, and the flat suburbs beyond. It would be so easy to remain here, aloof, and above. "Now that we have Michael back, I'm beginning to worry if we've lost Dillon. If we lose him, we lose everything."

"*Now* who's gloom and doom?"

"I'm just picking up the slack," Winston said. "And it's pissing me off."

And then a voice from the doorway. "You didn't show up at lunch."

It caught them off guard, jarring Winston's train of thought. They turned to see Maddy Haas. "I was hoping we could actually be introduced," she said.

"I know who you are," said Winston. She was, as far as Winston was concerned, part of the problem. Until this morning, he had only known her from news reports. The papers all featured the same pale headshot that didn't do her justice. She was, in fact, beautiful. But wasn't that requisite for a femme fatale?

She strode into the room with a confidence Winston found unnerving. "You should know that Tessic has an intercom system that could pinpoint the location of a mosquito from its buzz."

"Tessic's been eavesdropping?" asked Drew.

"No. *I've* been eavesdropping."

Winston wasn't surprised. "Did Uncle Sam train you in surveillance?"

"I'm trained in a lot of things." She flicked off the treadmill, the hum of the belt died, and the sequoia forest resolved to a flat, neutral gray. "As a matter of fact, I got straight As in BS detection. And you're standing in one hell of a dung hill."

"Dillon's usually the one who detects BS," Winston said. "But for some reason his antenna's offline. Any idea why?"

"Dillon only sees what he wants to see. What he's *ready* to see."

"And so you're an advocate of these blinders he's got on?"

"I never said that—but I don't think just ripping them off is going to help him. Dillon's fragile right now."

Winston laughed. "Fragile? Dillon could be at ground zero at Hiroshima, swallow the whole goddamned bomb, and walk away from it with mild indigestion. I can think of lots of words to describe Dillon—fragile isn't one of them."

"Then you don't know him as well as you think."

Drew pushed his way between them, putting his arms on their shoulders. "Can't we all just get along?"

"Sure," Winston said. "We'll all put on a big purple Barney smile. I love you, you love me." Winston shrugged out of Drew's grip.

"I see why Winston needs you to travel with him," Maddy told Drew. "Nice of you to be his referee."

"Yeah, well, the pay sucks, but there's a good medical plan."

Winston threw an annoyed look at Drew, but said nothing, since anything he said would just make her point.

Maddy strode over to the wall, and turned off the intercom, then came back to Winston, speaking to him quietly, a little too close for his personal comfort. "There's something you're keeping from Dillon," she said. "I want to know what it is."

He only had one thing to say to that. "Go shave your legs."

Drew laughed. "Can't argue with that logic." He reflexively scratched the itch of his own uneven beard stubble.

"You know, we don't have to like each other," Maddy told Winston, "but it would sure help if we could be civil. After all, I'm a part of this now, too."

The suggestion made Winston bristle. "Getting a piece of Dillon doesn't make you a part of anything."

It must have stung, because she took a sizeable step into his airspace, balling her hand into a fist. For a moment he thought she might hit him, but in the end, she backed off. "You're a real disappointment, Winston. The way Dillon always talked about you, I expected more than this. I thought you were supposed to be the wise one."

She strode off with much more dignity than Winston felt at the moment. Once she was gone, Drew turned to Winston, wearing one of his best smirks.

"It didn't take her long to find your secret 'asshole' button, did it," Drew said.

"Ah, shut up."

DILLON HAD NOT EXPECTED the others to warm too quickly to Tessic's overtures of friendship. The events of their lives had inscribed for each of them the same boilerplate of distrust that Dillon carried. He had hoped, however, that when they saw Dillon at ease in Tessic's company, they might soon relax their defenses, but they were far from disarmament.

Dinner that night was an exercise in strained civility. Dillon and Maddy sat on one side of the table, Drew and Michael on the other, with Winston and Tessic facing each other from either end, like opposing goalies.

"Have you ever flown on a private jet?" Dillon asked just after the main course was served.

Winston stared at Dillon as if he were speaking in tongues. "Excuse me?"

"We're flying to Poland next week," Dillon told him. "There's room for everyone."

"Cool," said Michael, then gauged Winston's eyes, and hedged. "Isn't it?"

Winston crammed a large piece of steak into his mouth, and worked it, effectively dodging a response.

"You shall all be my guests," Tessic said with a gesture of his fork. "Friendlier skies you will not find."

"Well, Mr. Tessic," Drew said. "I can't speak for Winston, but after almost getting sucked out of a plane two weeks ago, air travel and I have ended our relationship."

"Perhaps seeing another part of the world would lend you some perspective." Tessic's comment was directed specifically at Winston.

Winston swallowed his meat, and Dillon braced for the response. "If I need someone to loan me perspective, I'll let you know."

Tessic deflected it with a laugh, then threw a grin at Dillon, as if the two of them shared some secret, although Dillon wasn't certain what that secret might be.

Winston excused himself just as dessert arrived. "I can't remember the last time I ate so well," Winston said, then chased the compliment with, "I can see how one could grow complacent with fine food like this." Winston left, and his exit opened the door for Drew and Michael to follow.

After dinner, Dillon considered Winston's departing barb. Had Dillon grown complacent? Well, perhaps—but Dillon had a hundred reasons why complacency was exactly what he needed in this place, in this moment. To be a body at rest was a luxury he could never afford, and as Tessic had predicted, Dillon had found clarity in his hiatus from anguish. He felt, for the first time in many years, simply human. Here, his power was neither feared nor worshipped. He need not concern himself with its effect on the world around him, or the world's effect on him. Such contentment deserved to be prolonged, and so he told himself it was all part of some positive metamorphosis and he would emerge from this cocoon far better than he arrived. *I'll leave after we get back from Europe,* Dillon told himself, or at least he'd consider the possibility of thinking about leaving.

Winston, however, had no such moratorium on desertion.

At nine in the evening, Dillon found Winston alone in the living room, punching combinations into the digital lock on the residence elevator.

"Going somewhere?"

Caught in the act, Winston did not try to hide what he was up to. "I thought you said Tessic had an open-door policy."

"Maybe he got tired of the draft." Dillon punched in the code, which Tessic had given him on his first day there, although he had never chosen to use it. The elevator door opened to a cherry wood interior, then closed again, empty. "I'm sure he would have told you the code himself, if you hadn't skipped out during dinner."

Winston looked around, making sure they were unobserved. Even so, he spoke in a whisper. "You can't stay here, you've got to realize that."

"I'll leave when I feel it's time," Dillon told him. "And it's not time."

"Like hell it's not! You, Michael, and I don't get the cushy way out—there's things we've got to do."

"And you have no clue what those things are."

"I know a lot more than you think," Winston said. He hesitated, then took a breath. "I know who the three spirits are. And I know why they're here."

That caught Dillon completely off guard. He had been arrogant enough to think his was the clearest vision of all the shards. "Then why haven't you told me?"

"Because we can't talk about it here."

Dillon turned at the creak of footsteps on the stairs. Drew and Michael. Drew carried their travel bags. Seeing Dillon there, Drew stopped short, looked to Winston, then completely misread the situation.

"Glad you decided to come with us," Drew told Dillon.

"No one's going anywhere," Dillon said. "Especially not Michael. He's not ready to leave here."

"Why don't you ask him yourself?" Winston said.

And suddenly Michael was the center of attention. He stood on the bottom step of the winding staircase, just as Dillon had that same morning when he first saw Winston.

"You're staying, right, Michael?" Dillon said. "You know you need time to adjust."

Michael offered Dillon a half-hearted shrug. "I figure it's best to dive in before I really know what the hell is going on out there. Because once I know, I might be too scared to go. Like you."

Dillon started to protest the suggestion that he was afraid, but was cut short by the sound of the elevator door sliding open. Winston had remembered the code.

"Could you just stop for a minute and think!" insisted Dillon.

"I already think too much."

Drew and Michael pushed past them into the elevator. "Sorry, man," Michael said. "Tell Tessic I like his place."

Winston followed them in, and Dillon found himself stumbling over his words. "There's no point in leaving—nothing makes sense out there; it's full of images and noise for us now. What we feel out there is panic—the only sanity is here."

Winston wedged his foot against the open elevator door to keep it from closing. "Has it ever occurred to you that sanity is our worst enemy? That maybe we need a little insanity, or we'll never be pushed to do what we need to do?"

"And what might that be?"

Winston responded by handing him a slip of paper with an address. "This is where we'll be. Meet us there later tonight, and I'll tell you everything I know."

"I'm not leaving here!"

"I'm not asking you to. Just slip away for a couple of hours."

Dillon looked at the piece of paper. A three-digit address and a cross street.

"You want us to come back, that will be your last chance to convince us," Winston said. "Promise me you'll be there."

"I can't promise anything."

Winston nodded and back-stepped into the elevator with the others. He said nothing more as the elevator door slid quietly closed.

Dillon closed his eyes. The sensation of being robbed of Michael and Winston's presence as they dipped out of Tessic's insulated domain almost made him physically ill. He waited for his own sense of self and autonomy to return, but it was slow in coming. Their exit was sudden, unexpected, but Dillon knew he should have expected it. He should have sensed the pattern leading up to this. It was after all, his talent. It troubled him how easily he could unconsciously snuff his own intuition and he wondered what else he might be preventing himself from seeing.

When he finally turned from the elevator, Tessic was coming up the stairs from his workshop.

"Did you give them the code, or did Maddy?" Tessic asked.

"You heard them leave?"

"I didn't have to. Security informs me when there's unauthorized use of the express elevator. My door may be open, but no one leaves without my knowledge, one way or another." Dillon expected him to be furious, but he wasn't.

"You could have stopped them in the lobby," Dillon said.

"What kind of host would I be then? I told the officer on duty to open the door for them, with my regrets that I couldn't see them off personally."

Tessic went over to the wet bar, stocked with Amaretto, Crème de Menthe, and a dozen other sweet liqueurs, crystal-lined decanters glistening in every color from orange to violet. Tessic once told him he couldn't abide alcohol without a healthy dose of sugar to go with it. But Dillon suspected there was no sugar in the world sweet enough to make this medicine go down.

"I'm sorry," Dillon said. "*I* showed Winston the code. I thought by showing them they *could* leave, they'd no longer feel they had to."

Tessic poured himself an amber liqueur, then poured a second snifter. "Would I be contributing to the delinquency of a minor if I asked you to drink with me?"

"Probably."

Nevertheless Tessic brought the second glass to Dillon. "It's called Benedictine. I've been to the monastery in France were it is distilled."

Dillon took the glass, and sipped it; the sweetness overwhelmed his taste buds, the sharpness burned his lips. The smallest sip left a whole series of subtle aftertastes.

"The recipe is five hundred years old, and is flavored with twenty-seven different botanicals that you would never expect to find together. Cinnamon and saffron, lemon and myrrh.

Whenever I feel troubled by circumstance, I have a glass of Benedictine to remind me that the greatest things are forged from the most disparate of elements." He swirled the snifter, watching the way the Benedictine coated the glass. "Life is much the same. Events both serendipitous and unfortunate combine together in the end."

"There's always a chance they'll come back," Dillon offered.

"Of course they'll come back." Tessic appeared so unconcerned, Dillon wondered whether or not it was a facade. Although he did sense turmoil in the man, it didn't seem to be about this particular point.

"How can you be so sure?"

"Their presence is required, and therefore I trust it will be provided."

"Required for what?"

Tessic smiled. "For the greatest of works, Dillon. The greatest of works."

A heavy downpour began to pelt the living room windows. Now that Michael was out in the world unprotected and unconstrained, the skies over Houston resonated his turbulent state of mind.

Tessic held up his glass. "To the return of old friends," he said, and touched his glass to Dillon's. Behind them, a silent flash of lightning lit the room, chased quickly by a slow roll of thunder filled with as many haunting flavors as the Benedictine.

MADDY SHAVED HER LEGS in the shower, disgusted by the effect Winston had had on her body, and the effect Michael had had on her mood. There was no way to tell how much emotional tension was her own, and how much was projected upon her by Michael. Even in isolation, she felt she could not be alone, irradiated—violated—by their strange incandescence.

When she stepped out of the shower, the sound of thunder caught her by surprise. Wrapped in a plush robe thick as a parka, she stepped into the bedroom suite. The room had grown warmer than it had been all day, while outside, rain sheeted down the glass wall, obscuring the lights of the Houston night.

"They're gone."

The sound of Dillon's voice made her jump. She turned to see him in bed, sitting up against the pillows, halfway beneath the covers. "You must be disappointed."

"Are you coming to bed?" he asked.

"I have to dry my hair."

She retreated to the bathroom and set the blower on low. All day she could get by with attributing her mounting sense of discomfort to events outside of herself. First there was the shock of witnessing Michael's resurrection, and then there was the pervasiveness of Michael's emotional presence. But now Michael was gone, outside of their shielded world. Her emotions were now her own, and she didn't like what she felt.

When she stepped out of the bathroom again, she found the lights off. Dillon was a flow of satin contours lit only by flashes of distant lightning. She hoped he'd be asleep, but knew he was not.

She slipped on a nightgown, and slid beneath the covers of her side of the bed. Dillon's hands were on her instantly, stroking her shoulders and back, urgently importuning. His hands were colder than usual. His caresses mechanical and forced. When she didn't respond, he became more insistent. Maddy knew that tonight this was not about love. It wasn't even about passion.

She rolled toward him, but grabbed his wrist, moving his hand away from her.

"What is it?" he asked.

He sounded so young when he said it, it made the four-year

gap of their ages seem like a canyon. Yet even as she considered it, she knew that wasn't the reason for her discomfort. It was her "orbit," as Drew so incisively put it, which so dismayed her. The expanse was unbridgeable. They could be together, holding one another, and still she would be in a distant orbit. Maddy would never truly be with him, and that knowledge was getting harder to bear each time she felt Dillon's body against hers.

"Do you think of her when you're with me?" She found the words were out of her mouth before she knew she would say them.

"Who?" Dillon asked.

"Who do you think?" There was something she had heard over the intercom earlier in the day. Drew and Winston talking about how Dillon and Deanna "completed" each other. Maddy knew she did not complete him in this way, for even in their most fulfilling moments, she sensed a depth of longing in him that her spirit was not large enough to fill. "Well, do you?" she asked again.

He reached over again to touch her, gently stroking her hair, which had grown longer in Winston's presence. "Only sometimes."

She spat out a laugh at his response, hating him for the answer, yet loving him for being incapable of a lover's lie.

"Please, Maddy," he said. "It's been awful today. I need you to be there. Nobody else is."

A flash of lightning lit his eyes, pupils wide, pleading. It was consolation he wanted. She was nothing more than his consolation prize. And she did want him, but now she knew what it was she *truly* wanted. Stifling her own tears, she reached up to his face, gently tracing the curves of his cheek and nose. She kissed his lips, for the first time feeling his kiss free from the scars she had given him.

"All right," she said in a whisper. "But you have to do something first."

"What?"

"Tell me that I complete you," she said. "Tell me, and make me believe it."

She knew how Dillon could find words to heal hearts and minds. Surely he could cut through the truth, and make her believe a lie. *Please, Dillon,* she prayed. *Lie just this once, and shatter the truth. The truth that I can never be the companion you need.*

But Dillon said nothing. And in time, he took his hands from her. She rolled over, facing away from him, and let her tears soak silently into the pillow. For the first time, she found herself truly wishing they were back in the Hesperia lockdown. Back then she could be exactly what he needed. A human contact. The hand that fed him; the source of his survival. In those days they could cling to the wonderful illusion that titanium and steel were the only obstacles keeping them apart. Maddy would have done anything to have that illusion back.

Some time later she felt him get out of bed, and heard him dress. She watched him move in the shadows and the strobing flashes of lightning as he opened the closet door, pulling out the designer overcoat Tessic had given him for their trip to the cold northern reaches of Poland.

"Going out?" she asked.

"Something I need to do. I won't be long."

He opened the door to their suite, letting in the hallway light. He lingered there for a moment before he left, silhouetted against the door frame, looking toward her.

"I love you, Maddy," he said.

"I know you do," she answered. But it was only a shard of what she needed to hear.

27. THE DYING VOID

THE WINDSHIELD WIPERS METERED OUT THE TIME IN DILLON'S taxi like a metronome.

"I hate storms like this," the cabby said. "They make me nervous."

Dillon had taken the stairs down sixty-seven flights rather than alerting Tessic by using an elevator. As soon as he had descended away from the penthouse, a sudden sense of the outside world hit him. Dread and paranoia, a panicked call to action, with no hint of what action to take. *Do something,* his spirit cried. *Do anything.* He immediately realized that his time convalescing under Tessic's protection had changed nothing. He was no more equipped to face things now than he had been when he first arrived. If anything, the sense of panic had intensified.

Already drenched by the downpour, he had called a taxi from an all-night coffee shop three blocks away.

"Got caught in a flash flood once," the cabby said as they drove to the address scrawled on the slip of paper. "Sumbitch washed my car away. Lotta power in them there things."

The taxi was brand-new. Dillon was certain it hadn't started that way. He wondered how long it would take for the cabby to notice the change. Hopefully not until after Dillon left the cab.

Halfway there, the rain turned to sleet, pummeling the roof in a metallic clatter. "Yeah, this is a weird one," the cabby went on. "Pattern of a hurricane, but it ain't got no eye. Stretches all the way to San Antonio."

That was almost two hundred miles. A year ago the radius of Michael's influence was only ten, maybe twenty miles at its peak. This knowledge only added to Dillon's sense of foreboding.

"I don't like it," said the cabby. "Don't like it at all."

The address was a warehouse in a deserted industrial district. "Sure this is where you want to be?" the cabby asked, obviously nervous, yet not knowing why.

Dillon double-checked the address. It was right, and he could feel Winston and Michael close by. Having no money to speak of, Dillon told the cabby to wait, knowing he would not. Michael's icy sphere of emotional influence would repel anyone from its epicenter—and sure enough, as soon as Dillon stepped out into the sleet-filled street, the cabby spun off, his back end fish-tailing until it found traction.

Dillon took in his surroundings. The place would have been dismal even in bright summer sunshine. Up ahead, a red Durango straddled the curb, as out of place in this bleak circumstance as he. The headlights of the Durango flashed on and off, and as Dillon approached, the driver's-side window rolled down. Drew sat behind the wheel of the otherwise empty car.

"They're inside," Drew told him, pointing to the warehouse entrance.

"How come you're out here?"

Drew hesitated before responding. "Hey, ignorance is bliss, right? Some things I don't want to know. Some company I'd rather not keep. Go on, they're waiting for you."

The window closed before Dillon could question him any further. Dillon went to the door of the warehouse, and pushed it open.

Inside, the warehouse had been plunged into a deep freeze.

Ice coated the walls; it hung in massive icicles from the high ceiling, like stalactites. The few lights that worked flickered in and out, casting the ice cavern in shifting shadows. Dillon lost his footing on the slick floor, and fell to one knee.

"He's here," he heard Winston say.

Carefully rising to his feet, Dillon followed the direction of the voice to a far corner, where several chairs sat. Three were occupied, one awaited his arrival.

Three? Was Lourdes there, too? Was that Winston's secret?

But as Dillon approached, hopefulness gave way to apprehension, and then to despair. Even before he saw the mystery guest, he knew who it was.

"The prodigal son returns," Okoya said. "So happy you could grace us with your presence."

Dillon felt his feet threaten to slide out from under him again so he stood still, holding his distance. The sense of betrayal was more overwhelming than the cold.

"It's not what you think," Winston said.

"I'm not sure what I think."

"Winston says we have to listen to him," Michael said. "I don't like it any more than you do."

Every human instinct told Dillon to turn and run . . . but, like Michael's ice storm, Dillon knew it was a reaction of fear. He would let Okoya have his say. And when he was done, Dillon would leave. Alone, if he had to.

He took his place with Michael and Winston on either side, across from Okoya—who looked less emaciated than when Dillon had last seen him, but just as depraved. Speckles of frost dotted his long dark hair, and he wore heavy layers of old clothes like a vagrant, but the clothes were quickly renewing, their colors brightening, their tattered threads redarning.

"I want to talk to you about destruction," Okoya told

Dillon. "It's important that you understand the level of devastation you've caused."

"I already do understand."

"No," Okoya said. "It goes beyond anything you've witnessed—anything you've imagined. But within that destruction lies your salvation."

If Okoya had bitterness and vengeful intents, they were no longer evident. In fact, Dillon sensed a hopefulness in the dark creature. And so he forced himself to suspend judgment, listening to everything Okoya had to say. He began by talking about home.

"As I'm sure you've surmised, the place I come from has a different reality from this universe, with its own natural laws," Okoya said. "There is no physicality; all is spirit and energy. And in our dimension, my kind is supreme." Dillon shifted, irritated by Okoya's species's arrogance. "The best way I can describe our existence to you is that of a single pod of interconnected spirit-beings—about three hundred thousand in all. We exist on a grid of three dimensions, moving in unison along simultaneous vectors of depth, width, and time, but these three vectors, like everything else in my universe, *are alive*. They are three powerful entities—the greatest of our kind. The vectors determine the course and momentum of the pod, as our species impels through the universe."

Michael laughed nervously. "Great. Extra-dimensional off-roading. Why do we have to know this? Will we be tested on it?"

Dillon considered what Okoya had said. "I think I know why. These three 'vectors'—are they the spirits we've been sensing?"

Okoya nodded. "They are."

Dillon felt his own vector of fury building within him, and

it took all his control not to launch himself at Okoya. "Why did you bring the leaders of your soul-sucking species here?" Dillon hissed.

Okoya met his scorching gaze with ice enough to douse the flame. "It was *your* actions that brought them here, not mine."

Dillon turned his gaze to Winston, who only looked away.

"This world of yours," Okoya said. "This entire universe has always been insignificant to us, but we do occasionally make ourselves known, angling for sport or amusement. In our natural form, we are, to human eyes, whatever those eyes wish to see. Glory and wonder; lost loves; sacred memories. Wherever your emptiness—wherever your *need*—that is how we appear. Call it the natural lure of a species of hunters. The problem is that humans are too weak to resist the lure, and so there's no challenge to the hunt. Fortunately for you, the effort it takes to break through to your universe is rarely worth the reward."

"Then why did you come?" Dillon asked.

"The lure of power can be irresistible as well," Okoya admitted. "But trying to elevate myself in this world earned me immediate condemnation by my own kind. I was therefore a pariah from the moment I first arrived here."

"And the three vectors, as you call them—are they lured by power as well?"

"They came here out of necessity." Okoya tossed his long hair which had become caked with white rime, and the flakes fell from him like dandruff. He turned to Michael. "I wish you'd warm up to me, Michael; this frosty welcome gets tedious."

"Maybe you're right," Michael said. "Maybe I should broil you instead." But the temperature retained its deep freeze.

"You still haven't explained why the vectors are here," Dillon said.

Okoya turned back to Dillon, pointing an accusing finger. "It all comes back to what *you* did last year. Your cunning ploy to get rid of me."

"It couldn't have been too cunning if Okoya came back," Michael said. "So what did you do, Dillon?"

"I . . . infested him," Dillon explained. "Okoya had confronted me, and offered me a bargain. He offered me the chance to reclaim and revive Deanna . . . in return for my servitude. Then he punched a hole to the place where we left Deanna's body."

"The Unworld?" Michael said. "Okoya can get to the Unworld?"

Dillon nodded. "I agreed to his terms, but when I crossed into the Unworld, I never went after Deanna. Instead I went looking for our parasites—the two that were still left alive, but trapped in the Unworld."

Dillon had tried to put it out of his mind, but now brought the vile memory back. He explained to Michael how, in order to defeat Okoya, Dillon was forced to invite those two unclean spirits into his soul. His own parasite had evolved into a winged gargoyle that still hungered for destruction, and Deanna's was a vermiform serpent that thrived on fear. They were as complementary and codependent as he and Deanna had been— and far too powerful, for they had been nurtured well. While the other shards had faced and killed their parasites, these two had survived, trapped in that place between worlds, waiting for a soul to crawl into. A soul that could take them out.

"I stood on the sands of the Unworld until they came," Dillon said. "Then I took them into myself, letting them leech onto my soul. And I brought them back into this world."

"I was not expecting it," Okoya said. "The moment Dillon came through, the creatures leapt from him, and burrowed deep into me. I could not free myself from them, and in a panic, I punched a hole into my own universe. I withdrew back to my own world, taking the two parasites with me. And in so doing, infested my entire universe."

"They were only two parasites," Michael said. "That's not exactly an infestation."

"You saw the damage they did when they were here," Winston reminded him.

"They infested *us*," Michael said, "not our universe."

"Such limited thinking." Okoya turned to Dillon. "When I escaped, you caught a glimpse of the place I came from. What do you remember of it?"

Dillon closed his eyes, trying to find a way to put it into words. It wasn't so much what he saw, it was more a feeling spilling through the breach. "Like you said, there was nothing solid; everything was light and shadows. It seemed to me that the light was somehow alive . . . and not just the light. The darkness was alive as well."

"The living void," Okoya said. "Sentient darkness. It fills our universe like water fills an ocean. It's what my kind thrives on. We move through the living void, consuming the darkness."

"I think we have a name for this place," Winston said. "We call it hell."

Okoya turned to Winston, considering his little insight. "Very well," said Okoya. "Then consider yourselves warned that the gates of hell are about to open."

Dillon's body gave in to the cold, and he began to shiver uncontrollably. "And why would the gates open?"

"The moment I returned with the parasites, they left me, and inhabited the living void. Their host became the void itself, and it became rancid. The void was alive now with destruction and fear, feeding on itself, consuming itself until our universe could no longer hold, and began to collapse. As great as we are, my kind cannot survive the death of our universe." Okoya kept his eyes fixed on Dillon. "And so they've chosen to come here."

Dillon pulled his overcoat tighter, and clenched his teeth to stop the shivering. A malevolent species facing its own extinction. Dillon wasn't sure how to feel about that.

"The arrival of the vectors is a prelude to a mass migration," Okoya said, "for where the vectors go, my species will follow. It is a physical law of my universe."

"We could coexist," Dillon suggested. "We could offer them—"

"*You can offer them nothing!*" Okoya stood, and paced the frozen corner, his voice growing angrier. "They have neither compassion nor patience for humanity. You are vermin to them—*less* than vermin—and nothing will change that. Rest assured they will come; they will steal almost three hundred thousand of your bodies to use as hosts. Then they will enslave you, then they will devour every soul on earth, and when they are done they will burn your bodies, keeping only enough of humanity alive to breed a new generation of souls. This is the fate of your precious world."

Dillon shut his eyes, wishing he could erase what he had heard. This was the face of his dread, and it was hideous. "No," he said, "you've lied to us before. I won't believe this."

"Disbelieving it won't change the truth."

An icicle the size of a human leg plunged from the ceiling in the center of the warehouse. It shattered, radiating a vibration that shook sheets of ice from the walls, like the calving of a glacier. When the room fell silent again, the silence remained for a good long time before anyone spoke.

"Why," mumbled Michael, "couldn't I just be left at the bottom of Lake Arrowhead?"

And although no one expected an answer, Okoya said, "Winston knows why."

Dillon and Michael turned to Winston, who had said very little during Okoya's revelation. "What else is there, Winston?" Dillon asked. "What other secrets have you been keeping?"

Winston couldn't look up at them. He kept his eyes lowered to the ground. "It's no secret. It's something Drew and I came to understand."

"Enlighten us, O wise one," said Michael.

Winston took his time before he spoke. Finally he said, "For years we've wanted to know the reason behind our lives. Why did the Scorpion Star explode? Why did we inherit its fractured soul? Why have our powers been growing? What are we?" Winston looked to Dillon, then to Michael, then back to Dillon again. "How ready are you for the answer?"

Suddenly Dillon found himself no longer wanting to know.

"Okoya talks about his universe being a living thing," said Winston, "but what if ours is alive as well? Not a living void, but a lifeform of matter and energy stretching across space—a single organism, thirty billion light-years wide?"

Michael threw up his hands in exasperation. "Oh, gee, that's just wonderful. So what does that make us? Universal sperm?"

Winston ignored him. "If we see the universe as a complex organism, how do you think it might protect itself from invasion—from *infection*?"

Dillon fought his own resistance, and let the idea begin to sink in. When he finally spoke, he found his own voice cold and hollow. "You're saying we're some sort of defense? A kind of metaphysical immune system?"

"Dillon gets a gold star," Okoya said.

Dillon considered it. The idea was too large to grasp, and yet simple at the same time. He found himself looking at his hands—which he had always seen as an interface for his powers. Healing hands; hands held up to hold back a flood, or to release one. Instruments of creation and destruction. If Winston's conjecture was true, it would reify what was always just a vague sense of purpose. It would explain why the shards were so attuned to one another, and to rifts in the "skin" of space. All the questions he posed now had obvious answers when factored through this new equation.

"If this is all true, then why would you help us?" Dillon asked Okoya. "What could you possibly have to gain?"

"My kind views me as a hated fugitive," he answered, far too casually for Dillon's comfort. "If their plan succeeds, what do you think will happen to me?"

"You would sacrifice your entire species for your own survival?"

The question gave Okoya pause. His demeanor clouded, bitter and resentful, as if the question were an insult. "Loyalty is as foreign a concept to us as compassion."

Dillon held his astringent gaze, more comfortable with Okoya's hostility then with his congeniality.

Winston leaned closer to Dillon. "Okoya agreed to give up his appetites, in return for a kind of political asylum."

Michael let loose a cackling laugh. "Asylum?" he said. "I agree. Let's all find an asylum. We can tell people how we're actually T-cells in disguise, and they can tell us how they're really Queen Victoria, and Alexander the Frigging Great."

Dillon thought to say something to shut him up, but noticed that the frost around Michael's chair had melted. In spite of Michael's derision, the truth was setting him free.

Dillon turned his attention back to Okoya.

"So if we face this 'infection' the moment it happens . . . you think we'll be able to stop it?"

Okoya raised his eyebrows, and shifted in his seat. "Sometimes an immune response succeeds, sometimes it fails."

"Where will it happen, and when?" Dillon asked.

"Yes, are you ever going to tell us that?" said Winston. "Or don't you know?"

"I suspect they will tear their way through a very large, very old scar, in the last moments of their universe," Okoya said. "My best guess is the Greek Island of Thira, on the seventh of December, 7:53 a.m."

Winston gasped. "Pearl Harbor! The same date and time as the attack on Pearl Harbor."

"And the Mongol invasion," said Okoya, "and the siege of Troy, and the fall of Jericho. Even before your calendar, and the measure of hours, all these events took place on the same date, at the same time."

Winston nodded in an understanding Dillon had yet to grasp. "Each fraction of creation is a reflection of the whole," Winston said.

Okoya nodded. "But you'll need more than a fraction of a response to stop it. The three of you alone will fail; all six of you must come together again."

Winston looked at him in surprise. "You never told me that!"

"Until you had Dillon, there was no point in discussing it."

Winston shook his head. "Impossible. Even if we somehow won Lourdes back, there's Deanna . . ."

Okoya smiled. "Leave Deanna to me."

The suggestion sent a surge of adrenaline through Dillon's body, warming his chilled extremities.

"And how about Tory?" Winston said. "You know what they did to her. There's no way."

Okoya seemed more sure of himself than Winston did. "The vectors have made a critical error in underestimating you, just as I did a year ago," Okoya said. "Don't make the same mistake, and underestimate yourselves."

"Winston—what did you mean by 'win Lourdes back,'" Dillon asked. "Don't you think she'll help us once she knows?"

Winston looked to Okoya, then back to Dillon. "We believe the vectors have turned her to their side."

"What makes you think that?"

"Don't you get the news up there in Tessic's tower?"

"Of course I do—I've been keeping track of everything."

"Well then, you should already know what happened in Daytona."

But Dillon hadn't heard a thing, so Winston explained.

"Ten days ago, hundreds of people in Daytona Beach, Florida, suddenly left their beach blankets and drowned themselves," Winston said. "As if an irresistible force took them over, and they had no control over their bodies—how could you not have heard about this?"

"I don't know." The truth was, with the hours he spent scanning the news, he should have known. He could only assume that some events—events that might pull him away from Tessic's comfortable sanctuary—were screened out. "There's no question it's Lourdes, but what the hell is she doing?"

"I would guess she's flexing her muscles," Okoya said. "Preparing herself."

"For what?" Dillon wondered, but Okoya didn't answer.

BY THE TIME THEY left the warehouse a few minutes later, the sleet had turned to rain and Dillon had to ask Michael how their little summit could possibly have affected his mood for the better.

"If I have to be hit by a train, I'd rather see it coming," was all Michael said of it.

They piled in the Durango, waking Drew, who slept across the front seat. Dillon wondered how much of the picture Drew knew, and concluded that he was smart to ration his own awareness.

"Still want us to drop you off at Tessitech?" Winston asked.

Dillon searched for the Houston skyline, but it was obscured behind the clouds. He could imagine himself sneaking back in, sliding into bed with Maddy, forcing himself to ignore everything he had learned tonight. Then morning would come, Tessic would greet them for breakfast, and life would be as sweet, and as intoxicating, as Tessic's liqueurs. It would be easy to give in to that temptation. So easy that he knew he could not return, not even to say good-bye to Maddy. If they succeeded, she would come to understand why he had left. And if they failed, well, it wouldn't matter anyway.

"If we leave now, we'll reach Dallas by nine," Dillon said, and slid into the front passenger seat. As they drove off, Dillon closed his eyes, and warded off his regrets by counting the metronome beats of the wiper blades, until they were far out of Houston.

THE FOLLOWING MORNING, FIVE thousand miles away on the island of Bermuda, an accountant and his wife were escaping from it all. These were unpalatable times, and it didn't take a number cruncher to see the unlucky arithmetic of the days. As he lay there poolside, beside the cellulitic form of his wife, who burned a mottled pink beneath the ultraviolet rays of a midday sun, he ogled the more shapely figures on the beach, longing for his slimmer youth. He dreamed of himself sur-rounded by a harem of such beautiful women—not so far-fetched a thought, he concluded. These were, in fact, strange days. The unusual had become commonplace; inexplicable mischief and miracles were rules rather than the exceptions. Take that bizarre mass suicide in Daytona Beach. Five hun-dred people, without forethought, without reason, suddenly plunged themselves into the ocean. The Coast Guard was still fishing out the bodies. The accountant had laughed and his wife had been angry.

He yawned, and tried to roll over to sun his back, but found that gravity had shifted. No, it wasn't gravity; it was him. He was no longer lying on the lounge chair, instead he was stand-ing in front of it. He did not remember getting up. When he turned, he found his wife standing as well. In fact, everyone around the pool was beginning to stand like a reluctant ova-tion.

At first he found this merely curious, not threatening, for his life experience gave him no way to distill a threat from this aberrant occurrence. He didn't realize he was walking until his third step, because he had not told his feet to do so—yet they were impelled to move. Soon he was jostled by the bodies around him—a mob as surprised by their sudden migration as he. He tried to crane his neck to see his wife, but he couldn't move his neck at all; the most he could gain control of was his eyeballs and they darted back and forth with growing concern. He smashed his shin on a chaise lounge and tumbled over, hit-ting his head on the concrete. He couldn't even scream from the pain, for his vocal cords were locked as tight as his jaw.

The man got up and moved from the pool, then down a set of stepping stones to the beach, where he realized it was more than just those lounging at his hotel caught in this wave of motion. They were coming from all directions—from all the Bermudan resorts within his line of sight. They ran from restaurants and lobbies, they abandoned their cars, and now in this moment of absolute helplessness, the terror and panic truly set in, for he was on the beach now, marching with thousands of others toward the surf.

And he was in the front line.

Now he understood the terror of the mob in Daytona— understood how their limbs could be torn from their control—how their bodies could rebel and drown them, leaving no survivors to tell how it had been. His feet sank into the wet sand at the edge of the surf, but he kept on moving, the mob pushing behind him. The water rolled across his toes, churning a cloud of foam and sand. He knew the bottom dropped off suddenly a few feet out and although he could swim, he knew his body would continue walking even as his lungs filled with water. He would die and no one would understand.

But then his feet stopped as quickly as they had begun moving, and he stood at attention with the water lapping at his ankles, and there he stayed. The sun beat down on his bald head for more than a half an hour that way. He felt the sunburn on his forehead, nose and shoulders. He felt it would burn him through, but still he could not move. And then came a different kind of radiance; a type of magnetism tugging at his being. He knew, even before she moved into his line of sight, that she was the one who had seized control of his body and the thousands of other bodies lining the beach, as far as the eye could see. She strode before him, ankle deep in the surf surveying the crowd. Not as if looking for someone, but rather taking it in as a whole. *Like a general*, he thought. *A general appraising his troops.*

She was a young woman, attractive and formidable in

both stature and presence. She caught his gaze for an instant and in that instant he could feel her heartbeat. It was his own heartbeat. He could feel the pace of her breath; it was his own. And he knew this powerful girl could end his life; shut down his heart with a single errant thought. But in an instant her eyes moved on, and he knew he was nothing to her—not even worth the thought it would take to kill him. He didn't know which was worse—the pain of his will usurped, or the pain of his insignificance.

Ten minutes more and he was released. The entire beach was released. People fell to their knees, crying, whimpering, but still alive. She had brought them to the edge of the surf and had stopped them, then released them. For what reason he didn't know.

Could she have been one of the—but he cut the thought short. No. That freakish gaggle of teens all died when Hoover Dam fell. But now he wasn't so certain, for he could still feel a hint of the girl's presence like static in the air.

He went to find his wife, so they could tend to each other's sunburns, and they did not speak of it. Not even that afternoon when they chanced to see a cruise ship heading across the Atlantic, and felt the girl's pervasive aura fade as the ship fell off the horizon.

28. THE MEMORY OF DUST

THE EMPTY FIELDS FIVE MILES NORTH OF DALLAS/FORT Worth airport had browned and died more than a month ago. Although the weather was clear, the temperature stayed a brisk thirty-five. At one o'clock in the afternoon, a red Durango turned off a sparsely traveled two-lane road, churning up dust. Then it stopped at no place in particular, letting out its five occupants. Three of them walked farther out into the field, the dead brush beneath them turning green and growing denser beneath their feet. Wild mustard bloomed yellow around sudden pockets of bluebonnet and red cosmos.

Drew and Okoya stood beside each other back at the Durango watching the greening of the field—and although Drew swore he'd never allow himself to be left alone with Okoya again, neither did he want to be out in the field with Dillon, Winston, and Michael. Getting here had been an undertaking in and of itself. While the storm over southeastern Texas had ended, so many roads were washed out between Houston and Dallas, that a four-hour drive had stretched into eight.

Up above, a United jet screamed its way heavenward against the pull of gravity. When Drew looked back from the ascending jet, the field before him was almost entirely green.

Dillon was quite aware of the field renewing around him. He also knew there would be no disguising it from anyone who cared to notice, so he didn't worry himself with it. Like smash-and-grab robbers, they would accomplish this deed by brute force, rather than subtle scheming. There was no time for anything else.

Dillon looked around, realizing that he was a pace ahead of Winston and Michael. As had been the case so many times before, they were following him.

Winston realized this as well, and knew he could have taken the lead. A part of him wanted to, but there was something very natural about being a wing to Dillon's center. Winston had long since learned that whatever came naturally to the shards was not to be fought.

Michael, on the other hand did not care who took the lead. He had no time for such thoughts, because his task had already begun. He knew what he had to do, and kept telling himself that he was up for it, bolstering his confidence, and thereby bringing clarity to the skies. Compared to Winston and Dillon he felt like a novice, for their skills were so exact and precise; fine brush strokes to Michael's sloppy finger-painting. Every few moments a doubt would invade his confidence, reminding him that what they were about to attempt was like seeking a single grain of sand in a hundred miles of beach. Such negative thinking was a formidable enemy for him now, because everything depended on his ability to manipulate his own emotions on cue, like an actor.

Dillon stopped about two hundred yards away from the car. "This is as good a place as any."

"So what do we do now?" Winston asked. "How do we begin this?"

"It has to start with Michael," Dillon said.

"No pressure." Michael closed his eyes and took a deep breath. "How far away do you want it to start?"

"I don't know," said Dillon. "Fifty miles? Can you do that?"

"Let's find out." He took off his jacket and held his hands out wide as if to receive an embrace, but kept his eyes closed. In the cold, it was easy for him to feel the fine hairs on his arms and legs rise, tightening into gooseflesh. He concentrated on the feeling, bringing his attention to his extremities. Then he began to generate turbulence. He thought of bad times and brutal fights from his past; arguments at home; acts of violence directed at him, and acts he directed out at the world. Some were memories, others fabrications, but they had the desired effect. He could feel his fingertips and toes begin to tremble with anxiety, and slowly, slowly he let the anxiety sweep inward.

Two hundred yards away, Drew and Okoya stood beside Drew's car, watching and waiting. Drew couldn't feel the slightest change in the breeze. All he felt was . . . unsettled. "Nothing's happening."

"It would seem that way," Okoya agreed.

After fifteen minutes, Drew saw Michael put his hands down, too tired to hold them up anymore. Now he just stood there, with Winston and Dillon pacing behind him through an ever-increasing tangle of brush. At twenty minutes Drew was close to panic. "It's not working," he said. "He's not ready, it's too soon!"

"It's *his* anxiety you're feeling, not your own," Okoya reminded him. "Which means it *is* working. Why don't you turn on the radio."

Desperate for any diversion, Drew powered up the Durango, and turned on the radio.

"Now find a local news station."

Drew searched the AM band until finding one. The big news of the hour was a weather advisory. A wind storm. Gale force gusts had already swept west through Dallas, east through Fort Worth, and appeared to be zeroing in on the airport in between. Callers from the north and south reported winds as well, again moving in converging directions. The winds and accompanying dust storm had shredded signs, torn down traffic lights, and brought the twin metropolitan areas to a standstill. Drew turned to see Okoya smile.

"Michael doesn't know his own strength."

Now when Drew looked toward the horizon, he could see it had taken on a strange amber shade in all directions.

Meanwhile, out in the field, Michael concentrated. He didn't look to the horizon, he didn't open his eyes. He focused on his anticipation and turmoil, letting his heart rate increase, feeling his heartbeat in his fingertips, then his wrists, then his elbows. Tension bubbled within him. He had no idea how far away the wind was, until he felt a hand on his shoulder.

"Michael," Dillon said. "Get ready to brace yourself." Dillon's voice cracked as he spoke.

Then Michael opened his eyes, and saw his creation. A tumbling wall of dust, hundreds of feet high. A brown tidal wave bearing down on them from all directions. Michael closed his eyes again, his anxiety closing in on his heart.

Back at the Durango, Okoya laughed with glee at the sight, and Drew could only stand with one hand on the open door of the car, staring at this mountain rolling toward them, engulfing the earth.

A jet, perhaps the last one with departure clearance, fought its way heavenward on a trajectory taking it directly toward the dust storm. It looked as though it might clear it, but then the plane disappeared into the cloud's roiling head. Drew didn't know what became of it, because now there was a roar in the air, and the ground began to shake like an earthquake.

Suddenly Drew realized they were out in the middle of nowhere. There was no structure they could run to. No place they could go.

In the distance a farmhouse vanished beneath the dust. A string of telephone poles disappeared one by one, measuring the distance. It was five poles away.

Drew practically threw Okoya into the car, and threw himself in after him. When he turned to reach for the door, the leading edge of the dust storm was upon them. He pulled the door closed just as it hit.

Two hundred yards away, Winston saw the Durango disappear and he panicked. "Slow it down!" he screamed at Michael. "It's coming too fast!"

"I can't!" he screamed back. "I'm trying, I—"

It hit them from all directions at once, banging them into one another, lifting them off their feet and tumbling them through the shredding brush.

Michael felt his flesh abrading away and regenerating. He could have died a hundred times in those first few seconds, before self-preservation kicked in. He bore down, held his breath and found, in the middle of it all, a seed of peace in which he now centered his awareness. Almost instantaneously the wind pushed outward, leaving a gap in the center of the maelstrom; a ten-foot bubble of still air, an eye in his storm in which the three of them now huddled, coughing and trembling.

Dillon was the first to stand and assess the situation. The violent sands that raged around their air pocket kept shifting and changing—but it wasn't random—nothing in Dillon's presence ever was. The dust now swirled in shifting moiré patterns. Spirals within spirals, like galaxies revolving.

Now the burden was on Dillon.

This was by far the most difficult task Dillon had ever been asked to perform. It was not just reconstructing a life out of cinders, but sifting out those ashes from a trillion particles of dust—and although Okoya told them this was possible, Dillon's own faith was sorely lacking.

To Dillon's right, Michael hunched on all fours, straining to keep the winds churning around the low-pressure eye. To Dillon's left, Winston tried to tell him something, but Dillon couldn't hear a thing over the roar of the wind.

The particles of dust churning in the air were already coalescing into a rougher grit, taking on texture and color. Particles of leaves, bits of bark and feather down. The memory of the dust over Dallas.

Dillon reached a hand out of their protective bubble, feeling the grit sift through his fingers, and he began to concentrate his thoughts on Tory; the way she looked, the sound of her voice, the feel of her cleansing presence—every memory he could find. The patterns of the wind changed as he thought of her; slim dust flares snaked down through the swirling clouds.

And when Dillon pulled back his hand, his palm was ashen gray.

He brushed the dust from his fingers onto a spot he cleared in the brush, then thrust both hands into the maelstrom, and repeated the process, again and again, each time brushing the milligrams of dust from his hands until the dust become a small pile. How much would it take to substantiate her? How much of Michael's body had they needed for Winston to bridge the gaps?" Dillon knelt down to Michael and screamed in his ear. "I think we're going to need water!"

Michael nodded. He didn't open his eyes or change positions, but in a moment the air around them fogged and the brush grew heavy with dew.

Dillon reached his hands into the dust cloud again, thrusting them up to his elbows, while on the ground, the pile of fine ash condensed into tiny particles of bone.

• • •

IN THE DURANGO, DREW and Okoya waited the better part of an hour in the swirling winds, isolated, with only static from the radio. Okoya was hardly a comforting presence. He made no conversation, and spent much of the time grooming himself, brushing his hair and admiring his reflection in the vanity mirror, obviously pleased with the effect Dillon's presence had on his tartared teeth and mangy hair. His motions were so feminine, it reminded Drew that he was in fact both genders at once—that their subjective designation of Okoya as a "he" was for convenience. He recalled that Tory and Lourdes had both considered Okoya a woman.

Finally Drew heard the sound of the wind diminish; a long, slow exhale, and the direction of the wind changed, blowing back to the north. Dust flowed across the windshield but the dust began to thin, giving way to something else entirely. A storm of leaves and flower petals of every color now blew across their line of vision, until the wind died, leaving the car draped in a floral blanket. To the north Drew could see the wind storm retreating, trailed by a swarm of leaves and petals. The telephone poles reemerged from the cloud, then the farmhouse and the trees beyond it.

He opened his car to a fresh organic aroma pervading the air. Sap and chlorophyll, magnolia blossom and rose.

Out in the field a small oasis had bloomed. Saplings and shrubs were woven together by ivy and brightly colored trumpet vines. A shock wave of rats, rabbits, and field mice exploded outward, while above every bird from blue jay to crow took to the sky. A menagerie of life drawn back from the dust.

Drew took to the field, stomping through the thick dew-covered brush, kicking up swarms of insects, anxious to see with his own eyes what was now hidden within the heart of the oasis.

· · ·

SHE WAS AWARE. She was aware, but only barely.

She could hear several people asking questions, voicing exclamations, but her mind had not congealed enough to attach any meaning to the words. The voices were ones she recognized; their timbre and rhythm familiar enough to set her at ease. She tried to open her eyes, but a grit of sand beneath her eyelids made opening her eyes painful, so she kept them closed. She felt hands brushing dust from her and she laughed at their touch, a bit intoxicated by the unexpected tactile sensation. She did not even attempt to dredge up how she came to be here. For once, if only this once, she was content to be in the inebriating now.

She tried to open her eyes again, and this time found it a bit easier, although her vision was still clouded. Someone had slipped a robe around her, and now she was being carried through a lush field.

Michael was the first face she locked on to and identified. "Hey," he said gently, when he saw her gazing at him. "How've ya' been, Tory?" His voice sounded tired, strained, as if the simple phrase took great effort to push out. She opened her mouth to speak, but found her throat clogged. She coughed, spouting a flurry of flower petals. How odd.

Her legs and arms were still exposed to the cold day, and she could feel her fingertips and toes chill. It wasn't an unpleasant feeling. She wiggled her toes, to find a fine grit between them; indeed, the fine sand covered her body, as if she had been rolled in the white sands of a gulf beach. But it wasn't just *on* her, the grit was *in* her—deep in her, but migrating outward, expelled in a powdery smoke with her breath, exuded through her pores.

Up ahead was a red car. An SUV. She was pushed in, and by the time everyone else had piled in and the doors had closed, her level of awareness had tuned itself enough to start formulating the fundamental questions of where, how, and how long.

She knew all the faces around her. Michael to her left, Winston to her right. Drew and Dillon in the front seat, and behind her—

Okoya!

She flinched, throwing Michael a panicked glance. "No! We have to tell the others! Warn them about Okoya."

"Easy," Michael said. "Okoya's not the problem now."

"Okoya's not the problem now," she repeated, trying to make the absurd suggestion stick. "Then what *is* the problem?"

Dillon spoke up next. "Ask again later," he said flatly, as if she had hit the null response of a Magic 8-Ball.

She accepted his advice, not really caring to know what could be worse than Okoya. "I'm hungry," she told them.

Winston chuckled. "Death must be like sex," he said. "Makes you hungry."

"How would you know?" teased Michael. Winston burned him a glare, and Tory grinned. Just like old times. But the times weren't old, were they? And did someone say death?

Drew started the car and the heater came on. In a few moments it was pouring warm air over her. The SUV rocked uneasily over the dirt, then climbed a slight embankment up to the road. As Tory's lucidity continued to grow, she did remember the collapse of the dam, and the way she and Michael had tumbled through the sky.

She turned once more to glance at Okoya, who offered her a nod, and the faintest of smiles. Her downy sense of contentment almost completely gone now, she found the questions mounting faster than she could process them.

"Where's Lourdes?" she asked. "Why isn't she here, too? Is she dead?"

"Might as well be," grumbled Winston.

Drew pulled from the narrow shoulder, and onto the two-lane highway, accelerating to sixty-five. He took his eyes from the road for a moment to scan through local stations. *No stations are programmed*, Tory thought. *Does that mean we're far from home? When did Drew get a Durango?*

Michael put his arm around her, and she found herself sliding deeper into his grasp, wanting to be up against him. She looked at him, and he only smiled. *Were we in love?* she thought. No, but perhaps they should have been. Tory closed her eyes, and forced the questions away, allowing herself to enjoy her growing sense of well-being.

DILLON EXPECTED THEIR POWERS would surge again with the addition of Tory. What he didn't expect was what Okoya called "syntaxis." It began as a subtle thing; none of them really noticed the visceral pull toward one another at first. There were too many things to think about as they drove from Tory's birthing place. Drew, for instance, who suffered to sustain himself within their spiked fields of power, his hands shaking as he gripped the wheel. "I should be wearing lead underwear," he quipped, "or maybe a radiation suit altogether."

"Yeah," said Winston. "That won't draw any attention to us."

It wasn't that Drew was looking ill. After all, in their presence—and with Tory there—he couldn't be. His eyes appeared sharp, indeed, his senses must have been piqued. But too much of any good thing was never good. When one's entire being was sharpened to a rapier edge, it was hard to handle; bound to leave unexpected incisions.

"It burns like holy hell," he told them, finding no other way to describe the sensation. Yet he dutifully skewered his attention to driving, until the moment they parked, then he bolted from the driver's seat, just to gain a few feet of distance.

They were at a clutch of roadside motels, and, exhausted from the ordeal of prospecting the winds for Tory, Dillon chose to take a room, if only to have a few short hours to close their eyes. It irritated Okoya to no end, as he was constantly berating the human body for its never-ending need for rest. "Lourdes has sailed out of range," he insisted. "She's probably crossed into the Mediterranean by now, and you're just going to sit here?"

But Okoya was not in charge—and Dillon made sure he was reminded of that. "If this battle we're facing is what you say it is, this may be the last chance we have to recuperate."

Okoya grumbled acquiescence, and went off to sit on a fencepost, facing stalwartly toward the horizon, like an Easter Island statue.

"Did you say battle?" asked Tory, who was still in the dark about all of it. "Haven't we had enough of those? Can't we just lie out on some beach for a while?"

"Haven't you heard?" said Michael. "Lying on a beach these days can be lethal. Ask the people in Daytona."

Drew lingered in the parking lot, checking international flight schedules on his cell phone, happy to leave the shards to themselves. They retired to a cheap motel room, and the moment the door closed—the moment they relaxed, and allowed themselves a moment of downtime—the gravity began to take hold. The four of them began in separate corners of the room: Dillon in the desk chair, Winston sitting up in the solitary bed, and Tory and Michael on the floor, leaning back against the wall—Dillon had a disquieting sense of the distance between them; he felt he could measure it down to the millimeter, and wondered why such a thing should cloud his thoughts. "We need to bring Tory up to speed," he said, then scooted his chair a bit closer to Michael and Tory.

"I was dead, wasn't I?" Tory said. "I've figured out that much. And most of the license plates I've seen are from Texas, so I take it we're a long way from Hoover Dam."

"You weren't just dead," Winston told her. "You got yourself cremated. You were harder to put together than Humpty Dumpty. It was a real bitch."

Tory grinned. "I'm a bitch, even postmortem."

By now Michael had come up behind her, and began massaging her neck. "That's not the worst of it. You did a little sky-diving, and got dumped out over half of Texas."

"So what are you saying? You pulled me back out of thin air?"

Michael pulled her closer, wrapping his arm around her. "Hey, we're Houdini, babe."

By now Winston had migrated across the bed, closer to where Tory and Michael sat on the floor, and Dillon once more found himself pulling his chair toward the three of them, closing the distance between them.

Together they tried to deliver for Tory, in as small a capsule as possible, all that had transpired, and what they were called upon to do. By the time they were done, Dillon noticed that Michael and Tory were all over each other, taking turns massaging each other's necks, or backs; a hand on a thigh, an arm over a shoulder, touching in as many ways as they could.

Dillon found himself leaning forward on his chair toward them, almost to the point of losing his balance, as if the floor itself were tilted. "If Okoya is telling the truth, and we provide the only immunity against this . . . this invasion, infection, whatever you want to call it, then we have no margin for error. Everything we do from this moment on is crucial. Like strategy in a war."

"*If* Okoya is telling the truth," said Tory. "That's a big 'if.'"

"It feels true," said Winston, who now lay across the bed, letting his hand dangle down, gently touching Tory's shoulder.

"What if it's only because we *want* to feel that it's true?" Tory suggested. "Because we're so desperate to know why we got spat out into this world with these powers. What it Okoya knows how desperate we are for an answer, and is using us again?"

"What if what if what if," said Michael. "I never wanted to know 'why,' so that theory doesn't hold with me; I just wanted to survive—live my life in spite of the power. I don't want this responsibility," he said, "but I'm with Winston; it *feels* true."

Winston slipped off the bed, and sat on the floor beside Tory, leaning against her. Without realizing what he was doing, Dillon had shifted from his chair, to the ground as well, even closer to the others.

"What troubles me," said Dillon, "is that to fight a disease, antibodies have to die."

Only now did Dillon realize that something was happening. That they were pulling toward one another with an unconscious magnetism as irresistible as gravity itself. Winston clasped Tory's hand, Michael had his arm over Winston's shoulder, and Dillon ached to close the distance between himself and them.

"Let's not talk about dying now," Tory said. "Not when I've just been brought back."

Dillon found he couldn't resist the pull. He reached out and touched the closest bit of exposed flesh he could. His hand wrapped around Michael's ankle, and in an instant he felt himself pulled in. Tory lifted a hand to receive his, Winston reached out to grab him as well, pulling him into this awkward four-way hug. Dillon found himself, as he always did, as the center; the linchpin that kept them connected.

The sensation of the four of them in physical contact was overwhelming, but it was more than mere contact—it was an irresistible yearning to meld with each other's spirits and to be as they had once been: a single soul in the heart of a brilliant star. The powerful yearning defeated any concept of personal space. When they were touching, they were one.

"Do you remember when we held each other like this?" Tory asked Dillon. "In that field in Iowa—in that open corn silo, looking up at the stars?"

"He wasn't there," Winston reminded her. "It was the three of us and Lourdes."

"I never knew . . ." was all Dillon could bring himself to say. It was, for Dillon like nothing he had ever experienced before.

No, that wasn't true. There was one time he had felt this.

One fraction of a second more than two years ago. All six of them were falling through a portal in space. Holding one another. Touching. Connected. Complete. They had never once come into physical contact since then—certainly not during their tenure at Hearst Castle, or in the Nevada desert—Okoya had made sure to keep them divided against one another.

Although Dillon was losing a sense of his boundary between himself and the others, he forced himself to pull away.

"Not yet."

"Stay here."

"Stay together," the others pleaded, still clinging to him. But now Dillon was sure there was something off about this; something he couldn't quite place.

"No," Dillon told them, and tried to put his feeling into

words. "There's a . . . a *perfect* joining," he said. "A perfect pattern—that we haven't found. . . ." He stood, pulling free from them, feeling their fields fall slightly out of alignment as they individuated once more. He turned to them as they stood from the floor, and regarded them, trying to see beyond sight. He was the great seer of patterns, and he could sense that their pattern was more than just a random intertwining. They fit like a crystal—like a molecule. There had to be a physical form to match the pattern by which their spirits connected.

He held up his right hand, thought for a moment, then put it down again. Then he held up his left hand and stretched it toward each of them. He felt the greatest gravity toward Michael.

"Michael," he said. "Hold up your left hand." Michael did, and it seemed that his hand pulled Michael forward almost against his will. Their hands touched, their fingers intertwined, their knuckles became white with the strength of the grip.

"Where do you feel Tory?" Dillon asked Michael.

Now that he understood what Dillon was after, he didn't even have to think to know the answer. "I feel her pressed against me, my right arm wrapped around her."

Tory stepped forward, and folded into his grasp, then she looked at her own right arm, and at Dillon, then smiled. "Have I ever told you, Dillon, that I've often had a strange urge to spread my fingers across your chest?"

"Do it."

She reached forward, her hand connecting with Dillon's chest at arm's length.

"Winston?" Dillon asked.

"I . . . I don't connect directly with Michael," he said.

Michael laughed. "That's nothing new."

Winston took a step closer, examining the tableau in which

the three of them now stood, trying to find his place within it. "I think I connect to Dillon . . . Tory . . . and to Deanna."

"I connect to Dillon, and Tory," Michael offered.

"I connect to Dillon, Michael, Winston and Lourdes," Tory said.

"And," said Dillon, "I connect to everyone."

Winston approached Dillon's right hand, but Dillon pulled it back, curling his fingers away from him.

"That's not for you."

Winston nodded. He came up behind Dillon, knelt, put a hand around his leg, then with his other hand stretched out toward Tory. Michael shifted to allow them contact, and Winston's hand landed on her hip.

The moment he completed the circuit, a memory exploded within them, crisp, clear, and timeless.

Thought before words.

Consciousness before flesh.

A memory of eternity.

This was what Dillon had been seeking! If they had felt connection before, now it was perfect. Their heartbeats, their breaths came not in unison, but in succession; a living arpeggio. Their power was magnified now, their own unique harmonics resonating in tune so that the walls themselves bowed inward as space visibly curved around them, stretched by the same gravity that had impelled them to one another. Their intensity was surely lethal. If anyone came too close now, they would suffer death a thousand times and yet be unable to die.

They could have stayed like that forever. They would have—for in this joined state only Dillon had the power to dissolve the pattern. It was the bareness of his empty right hand that did it. He was perfectly connected to the others, yet still disconnected from the one whose bond with his own was the strongest. Deanna. Her absence was a wound, and this great linking meant nothing without Deanna, so he broke contact, pushing the others away.

For a moment they looked at him in a hurt anger that quickly faded as their individuality asserted itself once more. Still, they lingered within a few feet of one another, not wanting to let it go. They stood silent—words seemed to have little point in the wake of this communion. Finally Michael spoke.

"Wow," he said. "If we could bottle that, we'd be richer than Tessic."

OKOYA WAS FACING EAST, appearing to stare through a berm that obscured the view. As Dillon approached, Okoya's stalwart resolve infuriated Dillon, but then anything would infuriate Dillon now.

The alignment between him and the others had filled him with contentment, but had left him with a state of spiritual withdrawal once they had separated. He wanted more, feeling less complete now than before they had touched.

As Dillon approached, Okoya turned to him, looking him up and down. "I see you've achieved *syntaxis*," he said. "Good for you." The tone in Okoya's voice was both congratulatory and disgusted all at once; a sentiment as ambiguous as his gender.

"Syntaxis—is that what you call it?"

Okoya returned his gaze east. "Your alignment with one another will give you the strength you need to defeat the vectors. Without that syntaxis you won't stand a chance."

Annoyed by the way Okoya looked off, Dillon moved into his line of vision. "It's time to bring back Deanna."

That got Okoya's attention. He pulled his focus back from the unseen vanishing point, and trained his owlish eyes on Dillon, studying him, not responding.

"We've got Tory," Dillon said. "We'll soon be on our way to tackling Lourdes. Now's the time. Open a portal. I'll go and bring her back."

"Do you assume that's a simple matter? Opening a portal?"

"Isn't it?" Dillon had seen Okoya rend a hole in space before. Twice, Dillon had crossed through himself, into the desolate buffer-zone that existed between the walls of worlds. The first time Deanna had died there. The second time Dillon was too busy trying to defeat Okoya to bring Deanna back. And each time the portal to the Unworld closed, Dillon could feel the infinite distance fall between him and Deanna. Once that doorway was gone, she was further from him than the furthest star in the universe. But having Okoya here, as much as he despised and distrusted the creature, put Deanna within tantalizing reach.

"Not now," Okoya told him dismissively. "Another time." He tried to return his gaze to the hidden horizon, but Dillon grabbed him tightly by the shoulders.

"I want a reason!" he demanded.

Okoya shook him off. "Your syntaxis is a beacon for the vectors. They will know Tory has been gathered back."

"All the more reason to bring back Deanna!"

"All the more reason not to! They know you're not capable of tearing a hole to the Unworld. If they sense Deanna's presence here, they will know I'm helping you, and will alter their strategy. Bring back Deanna, and we lose the element of surprise."

But Dillon knew Okoya well enough to know the deeper reason. "Once she's back, we have no more need of you. And you'll have no control over us."

Okoya regarded him with enough hatred to fill an abyss. It was the same deep hatred Dillon sensed in Okoya back on the

diving platform, when Dillon refused to have any part in his
plans. Now Dillon wondered if that was the better decision.
Tory was right. There was no proof that anything he said was
true—and as long as he held the key to Deanna's prison, he held
Dillon hostage as well. He thought back to his incarceration at
the Hesperia plant. He would much rather be held captive in his
own body than to have his soul shackled by Okoya.

"Do it now!" Dillon demanded.

Okoya smiled. "You ache for her, don't you? For both her,
and Lourdes, but especially for her."

Dillon didn't answer, but he didn't have to—it was obvious.
It was the syntaxis—it had made Deanna's absence unbearable to him. So close to completion, their spirits yearned for
the consummation that could only come when they were all
together. The craving was overpowering. He felt he would do
anything to sate it. Anything.

"You knew this would happen!" Dillon shouted. Okoya must
have known the longing would become maddening. Then Dillon realized that this had been Okoya's strategy all along. The
more unbearable it became, the higher Okoya's ransom could be.

Dillon would not allow it. He would not allow this wretched
router of souls to hold them hostage one moment longer. "Open
the portal, or I'll kill you with my bare hands and find a way
to make it stick."

And to Dillon's surprise, Okoya said, "Very well."

Okoya sighed, then closed his eyes, concentrating. Dillon
felt adrenaline begin to flood his capillaries, turning his fingertips warm.

It began as it always began; a twinkle in the air like an
ember, then a sucking of wind, as atmospheres tried futilely to
settle the differential. But there was no change in the light, as
there always had been before—because this portal was less of a

doorway, and more like a peephole. Okoya had opened a hole only four inches wide, and when Dillon peered through it, it was like looking through a telescope.

Even in diminished tunnel vision, the Unworld was there, ever unchanged. He could see the crumbling palace carved into the granite of the mountain many miles away. The place where Deanna lay—the place Dillon was forced to leave her two years ago, alone and unreachable. Until now.

The sight of the mountain through the small hole was enough to cloud Dillon's judgment. He thrust his hand through the hole, thinking he could just stretch it wide, squeeze himself through. Then it snagged his wrist like a rabbit trap. With a sharp sting he pulled his hand back to reveal that his hand was gone! The portal had sliced shut with the unforgiving finality of a guillotine, taking his hand and three inches of his forearm with it.

He yelped in pain, staring at the raw, pulsing stump in disbelief—but the wound closed in an instant, scar tissue bubbling forth, pinching the veins and arteries, closing in the raw flesh, until it looked like he had lost his hand years ago.

"Pity," Okoya said, relishing his own indifference. "That was a nice watch, too."

"Y-Y-*You son of a bitch!*"

Okoya stood from his fence post and approached Dillon, only so he could push him back like a schoolyard bully. "Do you think tearing a hole in your universe is an easy thing to do? It takes more energy than I can dredge forth from the pathetic greens and animal flesh you've forced me to eat."

"What are you saying?"

"I think you know."

As much as he wanted to deny it, Dillon did know. It had to do with an appetite. An old, ineffable appetite. So this was the wage for partnering with Okoya—this was the ransom: Deanna, in return for more souls to devour.

"I've let myself grow weak," Okoya said, becoming more coy, more feminine. "In order to gain enough strength to punch a hole large enough, and hold it long enough for you to retrieve Deanna's corpse, I'll need a nice healthy feeding. A hundred souls, at least."

"No. No, I won't let you!"

"You're a stupid child."

Dillon gripped his wrist, feeling his whole being thrown out of balance by the absence of his hand. He tried to grab a fencepost, but found there was nothing to grip with, and he stumbled. Okoya advanced on him again. "Compromise is the great constant—in your universe as well as mine. Deanna is worth a million common human souls. You're getting the better part of the deal; all I'm asking for is a few thousand."

"You said a hundred."

"I'm entitled to a profit margin, am I not? After all I've done for you? And then there's fair restitution for the trouble you've caused me."

"I'll kill you before I let you take a single soul."

"Then everyone will be devoured, and you'll die along with the rest of your kind."

"You'll die with us!"

"Perhaps not. After you're dead and the infection takes root, the vectors can afford to take pity on me, and allow me some sort of existence."

Dillon looked away. Above everything, Okoya was a master of manipulating his options.

"The choice is yours," Okoya said. "Souls in exchange for salvation . . . or the spirit-death of humanity."

Although the pain in Dillon's arm was little more than a memory echoing through his nervous system, the pain of this choice lingered. It had been one thing to flood Black Canyon, and kill the soulless shells of the four hundred Okoya had already devoured—but to give this dangerous demon his blessing to devour more innocents? He couldn't bring himself to do it.

Okoya reveled in Dillon's anguish. "Decisions, decisions. Your moral integrity, or the survival of your species."

Dillon could only stand there, impotent within his own power.

Okoya sauntered away, as always without any hint of conscience. "Better have Winston see to your hand. I suspect you'll be wanting it back."

Dillon strode back toward the hotel room, wondering which would be worse, telling the others, or bearing the burden himself.

Winston's sphere of influence was now such that the strip of motel rooms was already being forced off its foundation by undergrowth. Dillon didn't even have to look down to know that his hand had fully regenerated even before he reached the room. He simply used it to open the door.

As he joined the others again in a tightly bound syntaxis, he silently wished for some godsend—a monkey-wrench that could plummet from the heavens into Okoya's plans—for that could be the only way they could scrape back some self-determination within the events unfolding around them. He now knew they were no match for Okoya—either joined, or separate—they had never been. Dillon could see the pattern of their future now. If they did the job Okoya set before them, and defeated the coming "infection," then Okoya would be the last of his kind. He would then find a way to dominate the shards, rising to power over them. In the end he would seize control of this world.

If, as Winston was fond of saying, everything was just a reflection of the larger whole, then Dillon had to concede that scripture could wind up being an accurate mirror; for Okoya was most certainly a Prince of Darkness, and, if he had his way, would be the star of Armageddon.

As WITH SO MANY things in the shards' lives, the monkey-wrench Dillon asked for fell heavy and hard. It happened as they left the motel, and pulled onto the deserted highway late that night.

Tory was the first to see it.

Dozing in back seat, peering out of the window, she thought she saw a ghost of a car veering over the double yellow line just ahead of them. She hesitated a moment, and never had the chance to warn the others.

The car sideswiped them hard, threw their back end into a fishtail, and then the Durango flipped. The earth and sky revolved around one another for a long graceful moment, and then the world exploded.

Drew and Winston, who were in the front seats, were killed once, then again, and again with each flip of the car, but thanks to Dillon's presence behind them, death never lasted long enough to be anything more than flickers in their persistence of vision.

Tory felt herself an observer, out of body, watching the car flip away from her, over and over again, tumbling through the field, sending glass and gears and hubcaps spinning free. Then she realized she *was* an observer, lying in the mud, thrown from the car. The pain only now registered in her body—but it faded almost as quickly as it had come. The Durango came to rest upright, wheels deep in the gouged mud of the field, a mangled ruin—but when she cleared her eyes and looked again, the damage didn't seem quite as bad. Still lying in the mud, she forced her head around to see that the car that had struck them had never left the road. Several of its passengers were now running out into the field, no doubt to assess the damage, and help them. A woman approached her, and stopped a few feet away.

"So you're Tory," the woman said.

Before Tory could ask how this person came to know her name, the woman raised a rifle. "I hope we can be friends." Then she fired.

As for Dillon, his experience was different. The initial impact jolted another memory into his mind. A grand piano crashing down through a crystalline roof. It had been annihilated by its own weight when it finally hit the floor, leaving behind splintered wood, with its last atonal gasp. It was a moment from his destructive days almost forgotten, but as the car tumbled to rest, he saw that his life had always been echoes of that moment. Unmanageable, disastrous, absurd.

And he laughed.

Even before he saw Maddy shoot Tory; even before Maddy pulled open the car door, and trained the rifle on Dillon, he laughed—because he knew that he was, once again, that erratic instrument plummeting toward its end.

29. GABRIEL'S TRUMPET

A TRUCK RATTLED BY AT DAWN, JARRING DREW AWAKE. HE opened his eyes to find the light hitting them triggered an explosion in his head, translating down to his gut. His stomach constricted, forcing him into a dry heave. When the wave of nausea ebbed, he opened his eyes again, forcing himself to bear the migraine pain. He was in the driver's seat of his Durango. For a hazy moment he remembered an accident. Squealing tires. The shrieking of metal on metal. The car wasn't damaged in the least. In fact, it was sparkling new, right down to the new-car smell. There was a pain in his left side, and he looked down to find a serrated blue flag protruding from a small brown bloodstain on his shirt. He tugged it out, grunting at the pain as a large needle slid out from between his ribs. It was the kind of tranquilizer dart they used on animals, and no one had bothered to remove it.

It was dawn. He was alone in the car. Okoya was outside leaning on the bumper. Drew opened the door and stepped out into a muddy field, about thirty feet from a two-lane road. The last thing he remembered for certain was driving that road, but now the car was in the field, which was scarred with deep gouges between himself and the road. Drew felt his stomach begin to contract again but this time he fought the nausea down.

Okoya spared him a quick look, then returned his gaze to the Eastern horizon, where the sun had yet to make an official appearance. "I was wondering when you'd come out of it."

"What happened?"

"You died, but it didn't take," Okoya said. "So they tranquilized you."

"Who?"

"They knocked me out also, so I can't be sure."

"And the others?"

Okoya pointed. "That way."

Drew squinted, but saw nothing but the road and fields beyond.

"Don't bother trying to see them, they're too far away for that, and moving quickly. I can barely detect their presence at all."

"We'll go after them," Drew said.

Okoya slowly turned, his head rotating with the eerie smoothness of an owl. His eyes were dilated. "*We* won't do anything."

"What do you mean?"

Okoya advanced a step, and Drew took a step back. Those eyes were more than just dilated, they were piercing and predatory. Drew had seen Okoya take on this countenance before. When he was hungry. Okoya came even closer, and Drew backed up against the car. Drew could see a flash of red deep within Okoya's dark pupils. He wanted to run, but the sedative had turned his legs to rubber.

"Dillon isn't here to protect you," Okoya said coldly. "And the next time you die, he won't be there to bring you back." Suddenly Okoya's hand was at Drew's neck, holding him pinned against the car. Paralyzed by fear, Drew couldn't move. "Therefore you will get into your shiny new car, you will drive me to the airport, and then you will drive yourself back to your beautiful home on your beautiful beach."

"I . . . I can't do that," Drew said.

"You can and you will." Okoya tilted his head slightly, studying the apertures of Drew's face, almost as if he zeroed into the pores of his skin. "The consequences of not leaving now, Drew, could be . . . severe."

Okoya sniffed the air around Drew, as if smelling the scent of Drew's soul on his breath. And then he backed off, his demeanor changing, his hunger reined in. "You've helped them all you can. You can only be a hindrance to them now." Okoya opened the driver's side door for him. "Go home, Drew. Put your affairs in order." Then he went around the car, sliding into the passenger side, and waited.

Drew didn't know whether his fear or his anger was more powerful at that moment. He wanted to bail on the entire thing. Leave Okoya and his car, and run. But he didn't. Instead he got in the car, and started it up, riding the rough course back to the road.

"You'll find them?" Drew asked as they turned onto the road. "You'll help them do whatever it is they need to do?"

"As my survival depends on it, I assure you, I'll do my best."

"You'll need cash," Drew said.

"I can find what I need."

"What are you, so powerful that you have to make things hard on yourself? Open the glove compartment."

Okoya pulled open the glove box to a clatter of old cassette tapes.

"Now find the one labeled 'Eddie Money.'"

Okoya pulled out the Eddie Money cassette box and opened it to reveal a roll of bills instead of a tape.

"There's more than a thousand dollars there," Drew told him. "Take it."

Okoya considered the roll of hundreds, and slipped it into his pocket, saying nothing.

As they got on the Northwest Parkway, heading toward DFW, Drew dared to ask the one question that had been on his mind since he stepped into the car. "Tell me one thing: You had every opportunity to take my soul back there. Why didn't you?"

Okoya chuckled bitterly. "Are you worried I've acquired a human conscience?"

"Have you?"

Okoya's voice grew cold again. "Your friends know the look of me when I'm well fed. They are more likely to trust me if I stay hungry. Otherwise I'd be here talking to your soulless shell."

He said nothing more. And after Okoya was left at DFW curbside, Drew took the first highway west, flooring his accelerator to 95, openly daring any cop from Texas to California to pull him over. But none did.

DILLON'S SENSE OF HEARING was the first to return. A high-pitched hiss and a deep rumble in his ears resolved into the atonal groan of an engine. He was wrapped in a cocoon. No. Not a cocoon; a shell. It was a sensation familiar and unpleasant. Déjà vu washed through him, leaving him nauseated. He opened his eyes to a narrow swath of vision; a horizontal strip of light, and when he tried to turn his head to see more, he found his head would not move.

He was back in the chair.

After all he had endured, he was seated once again in the infernal device that had held him in check in the Hesperia plant. For a moment he felt he was back in that awful place, but in a moment he realized that this couldn't be the same chair—it was a duplicate—and the slim image before him was not that of his cell. There were several plush leather chairs in his field of vision. One held Winston, another Tory. No doubt Michael was there as well, somewhere out of his limited range of sight. They were slouched, unconscious, their hands and ankles in shackles—bonds far less elaborate than Dillon's chair, but then the others didn't need the complex restraints that Dillon did. Beyond the chairs were several small oval windows in a curved wall. They were on a plane. A private jet.

Someone moved into his line of vision. A pair of familiar eyes peered in at him, heavy with sympathy, and Dillon looked away, not wanting to meet those eyes.

As Maddy crouched, looking in on Dillon through the faceplate of the restraining chair, she was filled with a strange aggregate of emotions. He was once again helpless, a victim of circumstance, unable to effect his own destiny. But this time she was not his lifeline to the world, she was one of his captors. There was sorrow in this, and yet it was seasoned with a comfortable sense that things were as they needed to be. Things were best this way with her outside of his faceplate, looking in. He would need her now. Need her to explain, need her to calm his angers and fears. Dillon, she had decided, was at his best in chains.

"You're awake," she said. "Good. We were hoping your tranks would wear off first."

She got down on her knees to stay in his line of vision, and when he closed his eyes, she took his hand, gently, lovingly massaging his fingers. She could feel him try to pull away, but his wrist was shackled to the chair.

"Listen to me, Dillon," she said. "This is not what it looks like."

"No? You've kidnapped us, and locked us up. That's what it looks like. Is there something I'm missing?"

Maddy sighed, still holding his hand. "We had to. You were . . . you were out of control."

"Out of *whose* control?"

Maddy found herself angry at his bitterness. "Don't throw this back on me. You were the one who left without a word." He had promised to be back, hadn't he? Instead he left, abandoning both her and Tessic, forcing them to become allies in corralling him again. She looked to Tessic, who stood silently behind Dillon, out of his view. Yes, Dillon had brought this on himself by his own irresponsibility.

"Are you going to tell us why you left?" she asked. "What could you possibly have been thinking, going out there alone?"

"I wasn't alone. And if I left, then I had reason to."

"You have no idea how dangerous it is for you out there, do you? You have no idea how many people want to use you—the way Bussard did."

"Don't pretend I'm here for my own protection."

Maddy wanted to argue with him—to tell him that, yes, he was here because he was incapable of taking care of himself—incapable of giving direction and purpose to his own powers.

"I'll talk with him now," Tessic said, making his presence behind him known.

Before leaving them, Maddy asked if there was anything she could do for him. To which Dillon answered, "You could scratch my nose."

And so she did.

THE COCKPIT WAS THE only place she could go to get away from Dillon, and as much as she wanted to be with him, she wanted to be miles away. It was the strange nature of Dillon's charm that it repelled almost as much as it attracted. Or maybe it was that she had no way to deflect his anger. Let Tessic talk him down and enlighten him as to why they were halfway across the Atlantic Ocean. It was, after all, his inspiration, not hers.

She closed the door, and although it shut out their voices, it didn't close out the strength of the field that surrounded each of the shards. She was used to it by now—eventually she could tune it out like the background drone of the jet engine, but never, never when Dillon was close enough to touch.

"Come sit," the pilot offered in an Israeli accent even stronger than his cologne. His name was Ari, and he had also piloted the helicopter that spirited her and Dillon from the graveyard a few weeks ago. From what Maddy knew, he was once the most decorated pilot in the Israeli air force. Now he served as Tessic's own private aerial chauffeur. Only the best for Tessic.

"Come, the co-pilot takes a crap. Sit down, I teach you to fly."

Maddy ignored the invitation. She looked through the windshield to see darkness. Flying east, the sun had plunged behind them quickly. Now there was nothing before them but night. "How much longer?"

"Four more hours." He looked her over. "Teach you to fly some other time then? Just two of us? This I will enjoy."

Maddy wasn't sure if he was serious, or whether flirting was his only lexicon for communicating with American women. "Do you have any idea what's going on here?" she asked.

Ari shrugged. "The big man says ask no questions, I ask no questions, and I sleep at night. The ones who do ask—they don't sleep so well."

Maddy had to laugh. Ignorance was indeed bliss where Dillon was concerned. Still, she caught Ari pondering the hairs on his arm; the way they had grown denser since picking up their new passengers. Dillon's effects might have been more pervasive, but they were subtler among the living; the straightening of teeth, and a sort of cellular detox—but you couldn't miss what Winston did to those who hung around him too long. Ari caught her watching him. He brushed his hand across his arm. "I make a hairy man today," he said, confident in his misspoken English. "Like a wolfwere. You like wolfwere men? Hair give you something to grab onto. This you will enjoy."

Maddy laughed, and he laughed as well, feigning that he was only joking. "Do me a favor," she told Ari. "Ask me no questions, and I won't throw you the hell out of the plane." To think only a few weeks ago, Maddy might actually have entertained such a panting proposition. Dillon had undone in her that need. But he hadn't truly undone it, had he? He had merely redirected her wandering desires, focusing them all toward him. There was the cruelty in the kindness. But better not to consider that; momentous things were happening here. If she kept that at the center of her focus, perhaps she could find a bliss that was somewhat closer to ignorance.

"You're here because you fell victim to your own folly," Tessic told Dillon, back in the cabin of the plush jet. "Consider this an intervention."

Dillon found Tessic uncomfortably close to his face mask. "Not exactly a divine intervention, is it?" Dillon said.

"No—that would be presumptuous. But time will tell."

Dillon strained against the titanium exoskeleton, knowing it would not give. "You told me I could come and go as I pleased—that I was not a prisoner."

Tessic leaned away and sighed. "You and I were not meant to travel the easy path," he said. "God has a vision for you, Dillon. You must come to accept this. If it takes me locking you down long enough for you to come to your senses, then that is what I must do."

"I will not be used against my will."

"It won't be against your will. You'll choose what's right. I have faith in your choices."

Dillon wondered what choices Tessic could possibly be referring to. His choice to leave Tessic's protective bubble? His choice to listen to Okoya, and get a glimpse, however fragmentary, of why he and the others might be on this earth? No matter how far the aura of Dillon's spirit extended out beyond the fuselage of the plane, how much choice in anything did he have when he couldn't move as much as an inch?

"I could shatter you," Dillon threatened. "It would only take me a moment to look inside you and find the words to destroy you."

"But you won't," Tessic said, so unconcerned it infuriated Dillon. "You won't because deep down you know I have a perspective that you lack. You, with all your power of life and death are blinded. You needed Maddy to help you escape from your cell. You need me to help you escape from yourself. Because I see a larger picture that you've yet to grasp."

Dillon thought to the duplicitous Okoya. Okoya, too, had a larger picture. A picture so large, it was beyond Dillon's scope of comprehension. But Okoya was self-serving to the last. Everything he told them might be nothing more than a well-conceived lie. If, in the end, his fate was to be used by someone, would he rather be used by Okoya, or Tessic?

"What do you want with me, Elon?"

Tessic offered him a joyless smile. "Have I been so good at hiding myself from you, Dillon? Or is it that you never wanted to see?" He knelt deeper until his eyes were level with Dillon's. "Look at me now, Dillon. Tell me what you see in the patterns of my life. I've been keeping something from you. Holding it until it was ripe for you to know. I open for you now, my friend. See into me and you'll know where we are going, and what is to be done."

Dillon's vision was filled with the aspect of his eyes; the

care lines and crow's feet. A world weariness beneath a muscular mind built by the wielding of heavy power. Dillon probed deeper, finding genuine intentions, sullied by the pain of something lost. Not something but someone. A person. People. Many people. On Tessic's shoulders rested an unbearable weight, that levied itself upon him the moment Tessic became aware of Dillon's existence. Because Dillon could undo unspeakable crimes. Now Tessic's weight became Dillon's, and he understood.

Tessic backed away. Perhaps he, too, had some level of clairvoyance and saw into Dillon's mind as well. Dillon's fury of being kidnapped left him. What remained was a spiritual vertigo, and a heady fear, like skydiving into a storm.

Tessic hit a button and the shell of the chair split open. Dillon didn't move. Barely dared to breathe.

"I can't do what you're asking."

Tessic laughed and clapped his hands together in sheer glee. "Of course you can. It's why all of you are on this good earth. You must know this by now."

Dillon closed his eyes. Although the chair no longer embraced him, he felt every bit as enslaved—not by Tessic, but by himself—because Tessic was right. Just as they had sifted Tory from the dust, they could do it again. It was simply a matter of scale.

Dillon shuddered.

If you could save a life, was it a crime to let that life end? If you could restore a murdered life, was it a crime to walk away? What if it were more than one life? What if it were millions?

"When the others awake, you will explain," Tessic told him. "And they will come to understand, just as you have, this glorious thing you have all been called to do."

Yes, thought Dillon. There was a glory in this, but there

was also infamy. There was something right and holy, and yet something almost profane. The violation of a violation. He no longer knew what was right or wrong, all he knew was that somewhere out there the "vectors," as Okoya had called them, were using Lourdes toward a disastrous end. He had to stop them, but how could he turn from this?

Dillon found no yardstick to measure his choices. Then he realized he didn't have to; Tessic had mercifully left him with no choice. Because nothing short of the world's end would stop them from soaring across the Atlantic, toward places whose names had become synonymous with death.

Treblinka . . . Buchenwald . . . Auschwitz. The death camps of Europe.

Part V

Reveille

THE OLD WOMAN OF MAJDANEK PULLED HER BROOM ACROSS THE weed-choked pavement of the square. Beyond the leaves and dust, there was never usually much to clean. Few of the candy wrappers or bottles that plagued other tourist spots littered the ground here. But then, the visitors here never came for their pleasure—either then, or now.

The snows were late this year. They would usually come in November, first dusting the concrete slabs of the square with a white quilt that would soon thicken into a pearlescent blanket, far too beautiful for a place such as this. A shroud of snow to hide a multitude of sins.

When the snows would come, the old woman would lay down her broom until the spring. There would be much to do then, for the square would be filled with the layers of fall leaves entombed in the drifts, now decayed into a sinewy mud that the rains would not wash away. For that she used a stiff whisk broom, spreading the mud out until it dried into a thin silt that she could sweep into the April winds. The dust and chaff would then be carried back to the town of Lublin and the forest beyond. She fancied herself an active participant in the cycle of life, and it was a comfort to her.

No one paid her for her labors in the square. She was not part of the grounds crew, and yet she predated anyone else who worked there. She was simply there, like the barracks and statues. Like the fences and the ashes, moving her broom across the square every morning her joints allowed.

Visitors would take notice of her on their way to view the memorial and the crematoria. They would snap pictures. She would neither pose for nor demur from their cameras. Occasionally people would approach her in the square to ask her why a woman of such advanced years would labor so to clean a vast concrete square. They would ask in many languages. Although she spoke only Polish, she understood the question in most languages now, and could answer in a few of them as well.

"You see that house there," she would tell them, pointing to her small home just beyond the outer fence of the camp. "I lived there seventy years ago, watching from my backyard, and I did nothing. So now I sweep."

A stroke of her broom for every time she closed her window to the stench of the smoke. For every time she pulled vegetables from her garden, and ignored the sounds from the death chambers. For every time she took Sunday communion, and went to bed in silence. For each of these things there was a stroke of her broom. And she could only hope that the millions who visited Majdanek would see the respect she now gave the dead . . . and perhaps they in turn might once again find the respect for her and her people that had also burned in the death camps of Poland.

The leaves of fall had gone through their spectrum of color, and now, brittle and brown in these early days of December, they longed for their grave of snow as they tumbled on the concrete, pulverizing as they cartwheeled in the wind. The sky was a cloud of gray, pulled from horizon to horizon like a faded linen. It was a snow-sky. But no matter. If it snowed, then it snowed. She would not leave her task this morning until the flurries multiplied into a true fall of snow. So she pushed her broom, churning up leaf *fragments and bird droppings, pushing back the tide of disorder to the edges of the square. When the sun struck her cheek, she thought it was something imagined, until she looked to the southern sky.*

A hole had opened in the clouds to the south.

An elliptical spot of blue opened before the sun, spreading wider. Her sight and hearing had peaked long ago, and it took a few minutes until she heard the heavy beating of blades against the air, and saw the approaching shapes that soon resolved themselves into three helicopters descending toward her. They were shiny and white—nothing like the military monstrosities she had seen before. They came down in the square, creating a downdraft that cleaned the square far better than her broom. But she held her ground, holding her kerchief on her head, watching in the center of the square, beside the stone monument to the Holocaust. In all her years of tending to the square, she had never seen activity such as this. Instinctively she knew that she was about to be a witness to something wonderful, or something horrible—she did not know which.

An hour later, she found herself on her knees in the church she had frequented all her life, bowed in dire supplication, her broom abandoned forever in the square.

30. MAJDANEK

As the shards stepped down from the helicopter in Majdanek, Dillon could feel their influence settling upon the stark place of death. The evil of so many years ago still lingered here like an oil slick, permeating the rocks, coating the leaves, worming into the lungs with every breath. Yet Dillon could swear the evil receded with their presence, leaving the Earth prepared to give back what it had stolen.

"We should *not* be here," Winston said. He had been repeating it like a mantra since he regained consciousness and learned their destination. "We should not be here at all."

Back in the plane Dillon had stated the case quite simply. They were hijacked. They were captive, and that, if nothing else, made them obliged.

"Do you believe we should do this?" Tory had asked. "Instead of seeking out the vectors?"

Dillon found himself borrowing some of Tessic's faith for his own. "If there's a God," Dillon said, "then I refuse to believe that Okoya is his messenger."

Now, as they stood on the concrete square, a sense of foreboding took root. Up ahead stood a concrete dome that, for more than a generation, held a mound of ashes raked from the ovens when Majdanek was liberated. Now those ashes were being hosed down into a silty mortar for them.

"Instant resurrection," said Michael. "Just add water."

"We should not be here," said Winston.

Tessic led them as far as the dome's entrance, where a team of triage workers waited—but Tessic and the workers remained outside, Tessic deeming the act of creation inviolate, not to be seen. And so Dillon, Tory, Winston, and Michael went in alone, while Tessic and his workers waited for a sign of the miracle.

Faith had brought Elon Tessic to this precarious pinnacle of his life, but to propel it to completion, that would take business acumen. This, he knew, was why he was chosen for the task. Who but one of the most successful businessmen in the world could orchestrate such an event? Everything was a clockwork now; a massive, interconnected machine fitted by Tessic, and powered by the divine gifts of Dillon Cole and his three friends. More than thirty thousand were in Tessic's employ, clearing, building, setting the stage. Most workers knew nothing. They received their paychecks and went home, the knowledge that their families were fed was enough for them. Others knew bits and pieces—saw a corner of the grand design—but only Tessic saw how it all fit together, and as he watched his great machine of revival grind into motion, even he was stunned by how precisely the gears turned.

He had begun a year ago—the day after the Colorado River Backwash—the event that introduced Dillon to the world. He knew Dillon could not have died and, once he was found, Tessic maneuvered himself into a position as Dillon's jailer. Then he put much of Poland's builders to work, constructing the first of Tessic's personal megapolises. The nation was more than happy to lay the infrastructure at their own expense—including the very roads that would connect the complex with the rest of Poland.

Tessitech had placed an order with a German bus company

for three hundred coaches, with plush velour seats. They were the kind of tour buses that moved millions in and out of tourist attractions around the world. The bus builder's simple assumption was that Tessic, who dabbled in everything from art collection to construction, was planning to open some sort of travel enterprise. He hired three hundred bus drivers. They had been collecting salaries for weeks now, and had yet to be called to work. Until today.

Once it began there could be no turning back. The clockwork would grind to its inexorable conclusion; a final solution to the Final Solution—and now Tessic knew why the Almighty, in his wisdom, had seen fit to make Tessic into a manufacturer of weapons. He had at his disposal enough firepower to decimate anyone who tried to stop him.

It was nothing short of hell.

A pit of muddy ash soon became for the shards a place beyond the reach of nightmare.

It began even before they stepped over the railing that separated the living from the dead. Then, as they stepped into the pit, they lost their balance, sliding down the slick concrete slope until they were waist deep in the wet, ashen soup.

Things began to move.

The homogenous mixture began to differentiate, bubbling like a brew in a massive cauldron, turning brown, then red, and taking on the smell of blood.

"Syntaxis!" shouted Dillon, for to be alone and disconnected now would be unbearable.

"Hurry, hurry!" cried Tory.

Dillon reached his left hand out to Michael's. Tory pressed herself against Michael, thrusting her hand to Dillon's chest. Winston insinuated between Dillon and Tory, and syntaxis swept through them. They thought it would shield them, but as their power magnified, their perception expanded, as if they had a dozen new senses at their grasp.

It happened quickly.

In a matter of minutes the bubbling brew began to transubstantiate, and they were immersed in bones and blood; a crucible of flesh consuming its own decay, swelling, soaking up the moisture.

Dillon didn't know if the others screamed, for he could only hear his own as that first hand grabbed at his leg; a woman as terrified now as she had been at the moment of her death. Then there was another, and another, until their wailing voices drowned out his own. The resurrection of flesh was not a glorious process, gilded in a sacred light. It was bloody, and violent. It was like birth itself; traumatic and painful until the cry of life filled the room.

The living differentiated themselves from the dead, pulling themselves from the pit, staggering toward the light at the entrance, where Tessic's workers would clean them, and spirit them away—their lives processed with the swift efficiency that their deaths had been.

Soon the tangle of desperate arms and legs pulled the shards down, and Dillon felt something within himself give way. He felt his mind drop through a trapdoor like a snail pulling into its shell, around and around, spiraling deeper into itself, until reaching the center of his soul, where time and self mercifully vanished into sweet nothingness.

A STEADY STREAM OF the awakened flowed from the monument dome. They were rinsed with warm water, and wrapped in plush robes. "You've been liberated," was all the workers were allowed to tell them. Explanations, Tessic knew, were secondary. That they were alive was all they needed to know; enough to grapple with for now. Their names were taken down, and they were walked to the line of buses that would shuttle them three hundred miles to the Ciechanow housing complex.

After four hours the line of the awakened slowed, then stopped. Only then did Tessic go into the dome. There he found the shards lying in a vascular miasma that was not quite alive, not quite dead. A dense membrane thick with blood vessels had grown up from the pit and onto the walls; flesh that could not find its form, but was obliged to find some form. It became a womb that filled the cavity of the monument from the bottom of the pit to the apex of the dome. Some of the workers who followed Tessic in became ill, but Tessic began to pray, reciting the *Sh'ma*. It was the same prayer he had uttered when his plane hit clear air turbulence and took a five-thousand-foot dive. The same prayer he had intoned when terrorists put the muzzle of a pistol to his head, then capriciously spared his life. It was a prayer he said daily, but only on certain occasions did it become a lifeline to sanity.

Three others followed Tessic down into the center of this terrible womb, where the four shards lay unconscious, almost fully encased by the membrane, their bodies touching in what seemed a very specific way. He tore them from it, and blood spilled from the membrane. It was already beginning to peel from the walls and drop from the dome as it died. He left, carrying Dillon in his arms, focusing all his attention on Dillon's catatonic eyes, refusing to look at the dying walls of the womb, for he could swear within the veiny patterns of flesh, he could still see faces.

It was deep into the night by the time Dillon spiraled out of himself, coming back from wherever it was he had gone.

When he did return from that void, he returned slowly, expanding his perception in increments. First he was aware of his own heartbeat. Then he felt the shape and form of his body. His extremities. Fingers and toes. He knew that he was covered in some thick fabric. A quilt, warm and comfortable.

He had never quite lost consciousness. Some part of him was aware of all that happened, because even in his state of detachment, he remembered being pulled from the pit. He remembered that he was in Tessic's private *dacha* on the outskirts of Ciechanow. He knew that five thousand had been brought back from a death camp known to have snuffed almost half a million.

And he knew that their powers had given out before the rest of the job was done.

The shards had simply shut down, emptied. Now it took a great measure of his will just to move his arm. He wanted to sleep—truly sleep, but he could not. He wondered if he'd ever be able to sleep again.

"You're back with us, then?"

Dillon pulled himself up enough in his bed to see Tessic keeping a vigil beside him.

"Is it still Monday?" Dillon asked.

"Barely. You slept for more than twelve hours."

Dillon shook his head. "I didn't sleep."

"No," Tessic admitted. "Your eyes were open."

"Where are the others?"

"Resting, like you."

"Things didn't go the way you had expected."

"Things rarely do. But all in perspective. Today five thousand murdered souls have a new claim on life."

"You expected more."

Tessic stood and paced to the window.

"Next time there will be. Today you flexed your muscles. You were bound to exhaust yourself. This is how we build ourselves up. Next time you'll be twice as strong."

"This isn't a marathon."

"I think that perhaps it is." Tessic crossed the room to a familiar device Dillon hadn't noticed in the room before; two canisters of colored sand.

"The Dillonometer."

"When we brought you here," Tessic said, "the sands took half an hour to differentiate. Now it's down to five minutes. Tomorrow it will be back to ten seconds—maybe even less." He let out a confident sigh. "You see? You have recovered quickly. The Majdanek dome was only an auspicious beginning."

He waited for Dillon's reaction, but when Dillon gave him none, he said, "Maddy should be back soon. Shall I send her in?"

Dillon shifted in his bed—feeling every joint, every tendon. "What makes you so sure I want to see her?"

"Do not be so hard on her," Tessic said. "You owe her your life a dozen times over."

"I know that."

"She is in love with you."

Dillon looked away from him. "I know that, too." After what his mind had been exposed to that day, he didn't know why sorting out his feelings for Maddy should seem such a monumental task. He *did* care for Maddy deeply; this girl who had the strength to fire into his face to save him; this girl who threw away all that she had to be a companion to him, longing for a syntaxis of their own that would never come.

"I don't want her to see me like this," Dillon said. A blanket escape, he thought, from having to think about it any further. But Tessic replied, "She's seen you worse." He turned to leave, but before exiting, he turned back to Dillon, and smiled as if in admiration. *What's to admire?* thought Dillon. *Right now I'm a helpless lump on a featherbed.*

"I know you don't feel it yet, but this day in Majdanek has made you stronger. It has given you stamina. Soon you'll have enough stamina to face Birkenau."

Dillon had never been a student of history, but he knew that when people spoke of Auschwitz, they really meant Birkenau; Auschwitz's back-factory of death. Dillon closed his eyes, feeling his lids weighty as a sunset.

MADDY WENT IN AT about midnight. She expected—almost hoped—she'd find Dillon asleep, but his eyes were already fixed on her when she cracked the door.

"You missed the first game of our little World Series," Dillon said.

She stepped in, her ambivalence preceding her. "I was in the outfield," she told him. "I was in Ciechanow, making sure everything went smoothly when the buses arrived."

"And did it?"

"Like silk." And in that, there was no exaggeration. For eight hours she had helped to supervise the handing out of apartment keys and groceries. Four people per apartment, one bag per person, families kept together when possible. These refugees were not ones to look this mysterious gift horse in the mouth. "Three buildings are at 100 percent occupancy."

"A hundred and nine to go," said Dillon.

"At least at this site." She leaned forward and kissed him gently on the lips. He didn't return it, and she couldn't tell whether it was a judgment on her, or if he was simply too weak. She found her spirit wilting and it angered her that her feelings for him could affect her so.

"I suppose not everything can go like silk," he said. When she looked at his eyes, she could tell he had just read her. But why should she care? What could he learn now that he didn't already know?

"I never thought I'd get caught in that old romantic loophole," she said, "wanting what I can never have."

"I never thought of you as a romantic," said Dillon.

"No. Until recently, I thought of myself as a realist."

He tried to smile, but it came out slim. "I guess now you're a surrealist."

She looked at him a moment more and then shook her head quickly, trying to break the spell he cast even at his weakest moments. "Here we are in the middle of undoing the greatest crime in recorded history and I'm going on about broken hearts." She stood from the edge of the bed. She had no illusions about her purpose in his life anymore. She was nothing more than a facilitator. She trusted that her disciplined mind would force her to accept this, and if not, she'd simply endure the pain like a good soldier. "Winston and the others are in the living room, warming themselves around the fire. You should join them. As I'm not quite so superhuman, I'm going to bed."

"You can stay here," Dillon offered, but it came out as an offer of mercy. Lukewarm compassion.

"Tessic gave me the best bedroom in the place," Maddy told him. "Even better than yours."

Maddy retreated to her room, thankful for her mental and physical exhaustion, for it hammered her into sleep and kept her from dwelling on the things she could not change.

THE FIREPLACE GLOWED AN eerie bluish-green, and the logs were not consumed by the flames. Dillon found Michael, Tory, and Winston around the fire, drinking from mugs as if this were some sort of cozy retreat—but the worn looks on their faces were anything but cozy.

Winston saw Dillon first as he entered the room and threw him that we-should-not-be-here kind of gaze.

"Don't say it," Dillon said.

"I ain't saying nothing," Winston answered, too tired to sublimate his Alabaman drawl. "I'm just gonna sit here and sip my egg nog and pretend like it's Christmas."

Dillon got close to the fire to find its blue glow gave off no warmth. Instead, what little warmth there was came through the furnace vents around the room. This cold could not be kept outside. Dillon glanced out of the window. The fog was cotton dense, and showed no sign of lifting. A mirror of Michael's state of mind.

"At first," said Michael, "I thought Tessic was bringing us to lower Manhattan." The fog outside grew a bit dense. "It scared me to think so big. But Tessic thought bigger."

Dillon couldn't help but think that was also somewhere in Tessic's plans. Where others saw sacred ground, Tessic saw opportunity.

"At least Okoya will know where to look for us now," Dillon said.

"How can you be sure he's even looking?" Tory asked.

"I doubt that Okoya is biting his nails in Texas," Dillon said. "And no matter how much of a media blackout Tessic tries to impose on this, Okoya will know where we are—and remember we're closer to the island of Thira than we were two days ago."

"You have a thousand reasons to stay, don't you, Dillon?" Michael grumbled. "A thousand reasons why we should keep dragging up the dead."

"You say it like it's something terrible. It's not like we're bringing back empty shells—these people are coming back complete, in perfect health, and with their souls intact. What we're doing is incredible! It's *important*."

"It's immoral!" Tory moved closer to the fire. "Hell, everything we do is immoral because we're unnatural."

"No we're not," Dillon insisted. "We're just a side of nature that's rarely seen." He watched Tory rub her arms for warmth, but now the flames had turned from blue to green and were actually drawing heat from the room. Dillon knew it was his presence. As his own power recovered, the logs were unburning, adding to Michael's chill.

Wintston put down his mug with a shaky hand. "We're outside of morality now."

"Careful, Winston," Tory warned. "We put ourselves above morality before, and you know what happened."

"Not *above* morality," he explained, "outside of the framework entirely. I mean, is bringing back people who never should have died an ultimate justice, or an ultimate wrong? Morality's got no answer for the things we do. It's got no answer for *us*."

Michael spat out a resigned laugh. "And you know what they did to the last person who brought back the dead."

Dillon shivered at the thought. There was a time a year ago that he might have felt up to the comparison, but not anymore. "I don't want to be crucified or worshiped."

"Oh, I think we're gonna catch ourselves a whole lotta both," Winston said.

"Yeah," added Michael. "I'm sure a thousand years from now they're going to have whole universities and seminaries devoted to studying every stupid little thing we did."

Tory paced to the nearest heat vent, giving up on the fire.

"Can we not talk about a thousand years from now and just get through today?"

"You have to understand how it is for Tory and me," Michael said. "For both of us, the disaster at Hoover Dam is just a few days old. We never had time to recover from that, and now we're in the middle of this. I don't know about Tory, but we're working on my last thread of sanity here."

"I wouldn't worry, Michael," said Winston. "You gotta have a mind to lose it."

"Yeah, yeah, so I hear."

"I feel like everything's resting on Okoya and I don't like it," Tory said. "'Is Okoya going to find us?' 'Is Okoya going to show us what we're supposed to do?' The more wired in he becomes, the more likely he'll turn on us again, trying to use us like he did before."

"He already has," Dillon told them. It was a wrinkle none of them wanted to hear, but still they turned to him, waiting uneasily for an explanation.

"We need Deanna to defeat the Vectors," Dillon told them, "but Okoya won't bring Deanna back. Not unless we give him free rein to feed his appetite."

Winston put down his egg nog. "This is gonna be one helluva holiday season."

"I told him we would never agree to it," Dillon said. "I told him I'd rather let Deanna stay where she is."

He expected them to be just as adamant as he, but Michael shook his head, and laughed bitterly. "With all that moral fiber, you'll never need a laxative—the crap never stops flowing."

Dillon looked to Winston, then Tory. Neither of them would meet his eyes. "So you think we should give him our blessing and let him devour as many souls as he wants?"

"No," Michael said. "I think we should give him our blessing and then renege the moment Deanna is back."

"Cheat the devil and the devil gets mad," Tory warned.

Michael stood and paced to the window, watching the fog as it thinned ever so slightly. "What's he gonna do? Hurl us into some bloody abyss? We've already been there today. Sorry, but this devil doesn't scare me anymore."

"Tessic scares me more than Okoya," Tory said.

Dillon waved the thought away. "Tessic's a good man."

"So was Oppenheimer before he built the bomb," Michael said. "Just because what we're doing here is good, that doesn't mean it's right. We've got a power that's raging out of control—and just because he's got money and an idea doesn't mean he's got all the answers." The window rattled with a sudden gust, punctuating his point.

"Actually," Tory said, "Oppenheimer was a creep."

"No," Winston corrected, "he was a romantic. A man in love with the beauty of his own power. Just like Tessic."

Tory joined Michael at the window, apparently finding in him the warmth that the room failed to give. "It's *our* power, not his."

"It's his," said Michael, "as long as we give it to him."

Tory looked around to the corners of the room. "For all we know, he's got bugs and cameras everywhere, listening to everything we're saying, laughing at us."

Tory lowered her voice. "Why does he want to *do* this, anyway? Yes, we can bring these people back to life, but we can't give them the lives that they had. We can't undo the *aftermath* of the Holocaust. We can't take away the pain of those who survived it."

Then Dillon saw an expression crossing Winston's face; something so unsettling, he could almost see it like a shadow.

"What if we succeed," Winston said. "What if we succeed

in bringing them all back . . . *and we undo the effect the Holocaust had on the world?*"

It was something Dillon, and most certainly Tessic, had never considered. If they bring back the dead, will the world eventually forget it ever happened? What if that's more devastating than the Holocaust itself, because without the pain of that memory, the next time it might take a billion lives?

"In the end which is more important," posed Winston, "the millions of lives lost, or the memory of the atrocity?"

The question lingered and no one even attempted an answer.

"I don't want to sit here discussing this like we're in some highschool debate class," Tory finally said. "We're neck deep in something real, in case everyone's forgotten where we were today."

Michael pulled away from her. "You know what? I'm not big enough to face what we did today, so yeah, maybe we should play high school for a while—I just want to pretend that I'm a normal guy, and that the whole universe doesn't rest on my bad decisions."

"What decisions?" said Winston. "We're not makin' any."

And that, Dillon knew, was the trouble.

Winston directed his words right at Dillon. "All this time we've been afraid to, so we let everyone else go makin' our decisions for us. First Okoya, now Tessic."

"Tessic's got us trapped!" insisted Dillon.

"Keep telling yourself that, Dillon, and you'll never have to make a decision."

Michael sat back down, holding his temples between his hands as if they were the only things keeping his head together. "All I know is that if we were *meant* to revive the victims of the Holocaust, then we wouldn't be coming out of it feeling so drained."

Dillon sat beside him, all but melting into the plush sofa. Drained was not the word. Poured out, spent—but drained? That was too mild. Tessic believed it would make them stronger, but what did Tessic know, really?

Winston gently put down his mug with a shaky hand. "We're being used up. You know that, don't you?"

It was a simple statement with a bitter ring of truth. Could they be "used up"? Dillon wondered if there was some conservation of energy when it came to their powers. Nothing came from nothing—how much more life and limb would the shards renew until their power was drained? Or was it a bottomless wellspring, fed from some infinite source, with no reckoning ever due? Dillon suspected that Winston was right. Someday very soon, they might turn up completely empty. And then what would become of their "great purpose"?

"Michael's right," Tory said, coming back to his side, sitting beside him, rubbing his back. "Whether it's right or wrong to resurrect the dead here, we're meant to do something else, and we've been afraid to take responsibility for it." Then she added, "If we really wanted to get away from Tessic, we could. But what do we really want?"

Dillon paced across the room, knowing it all came down to him. He was the fulcrum on which they all turned. But abandoning Tessic's dream? The man was so certain about it, and it was so easy for Dillon to use Tessic's faith as his own anchor—but was it an anchor keeping him grounded, or one that dragged him down? "Tessic feels he's on a mission from God. He feels it so strongly, it makes me wonder myself. How do we know he's not?"

And then Tory asked. "Do you believe in God, Dillon?"

Dillon found himself stumbling over the question. "Since I found out about my own powers the question scares me too much to answer. I believe we have a purpose. I believe it's unique in the history of mankind." Then he turned to Michael—an easy target to cast the question off of himself. "How about you, Michael? What do you believe?"

Michael kept his head in his hands, and didn't look up. "I believe it's time to go to bed."

Tory shook her head. "You'll never get a straight answer out of him."

"Because he doesn't believe in anything," scoffed Winston.

But Michael looked up and surprised them all. "That's not entirely true," he said. "Three years ago if you told me we'd have proof of human souls, I would have laughed, but now I know there are souls and that they can be robbed from us. So maybe I believe in a lot more than I used to. Or at least I don't *disbelieve*."

It was sobering to hear Michael voice something other than sarcasm. Perhaps too sobering.

"Our faith in our decisions has to be as strong as Tessic's," Tory said, "if we're going to defeat the vectors."

The vectors. Dillon had tried so hard to put them far from his mind. That was the reason he went along with Tessic, wasn't it? Anything so that he didn't have to consider those dark, inscrutable spirits. "Faith was Deanna's gift," Dillon reminded. "Not mine."

"And that's where we're lacking." Winston stood up, gathering himself some energy for the first time all evening. "We've got everything but Deanna's faith, and so we're clinging to everyone else's. If Deanna were here . . ."

"But she's not," Michael was happy to remind him.

"But if she *was*, that faith of hers would leave us with no question of what it is we're meant to do. We'd have the conviction to carry it out and everybody around us would trust enough to let us."

Winston was right. This is what had been missing all along—this was why everything they did misfired, blowing up in their faces. One element was missing. In this new light, there was no question in Dillon's mind the direction their actions had to take. "Then we have to get Deanna back at all costs."

"Yes," the others agreed, "at *all* costs."

So, if it meant bargaining with Okoya—if it meant deceiving him into cooperating—it had to be done. It wasn't the right thing, but it was the necessary thing, and if their integrity had to be a casualty of this war, then so be it.

"What about Lourdes?" asked Tory.

"We'll get to her, somehow," Dillon said, finally finding a sense of self-determination that he hadn't felt for a very long time. "I'll make sure of it." Now he didn't care if Tessic was listening. No matter what Tessic heard, it would not change things now. "We have five days to get to Thira," Dillon said decisively. "I'll come up with a plan to get us there."

"Better get cracking, Entropy Boy," Michael said. "Open us a magic door, because we sure as hell can't find our own way out of this fun house."

TESSIC WAS AWAKE BEFORE dawn. He was a man who required little sleep, his mind so busy, even his dreams were productive. That night he dreamt himself at the right hand of God. The Almighty's most beloved.

He had awoken from barely three hours of sleep feeling as invigorated as a child. His office in his *dacha* was identical to his offices in his various other residences, down to the paperwork on the table. There was an assistant whose job it was to make sure that, wherever Tessic went, his desktop went with him. For a man who worked and traveled as much as he did, he deemed that if his office could be consistent, everything else could be transitory.

There was much work to be done this morning. Pages and pages of reports to pore over from the various teams. Polish police had pulled over several of the buses, but each bus had its own private slush fund for such unfortunate occurrences. Polish police were not entirely unfamiliar with bribes, and even if it only kept them quiet for a day, the money will have served its purpose. By the time the serious questions would start being asked, they would be further along in this great revival and Tessic would have a dozen other smoke screens to throw at them, keeping the authorities as confused and divided as the Nazis had kept the Jews.

His four special guests needed at least one more day to recuperate. That was unfortunate. He would have to repace the operation. He could only hope their recovery time would be quicker with each successive reveille his four musicians played.

He was surprised to see Dillon at his office door, soon after sunrise. Tessic quietly motioned for him to come in. Dillon sat down across from him and Tessic showed him what he was looking at.

"These pictures are from our next endeavor," Tessic said, fanning out the photos before Dillon. They were pictures of a road; an old one, no longer used. It had almost disappeared in the undergrowth and towering oaks. "A service road that leads to Treblinka," Tessic explained. "Portions of it were built using the ashes of the dead."

Dillon raised an eyebrow, but didn't say anything.

"I have workers crushing the road into gravel for you," Tessic told him.

Dillon put the pictures down and shook his head. "Pointless

to crush it. I'll end up pulling the road back together before I pull anyone out of it."

Tessic took a moment to process what Dillon had said. "Yes, of course." He was surprised. Not at what Dillon had said, but by the fact that he hadn't recognized this himself. "I'll have them stop the demolition at once."

"It can wait, we have something more important to discuss."

Tessic smiled. "More important than what you and I are doing here in Poland?"

"Something that's important, because it's crucial to our success."

Tessic leaned back in his chair, feeling its springs comfortably buffer him. "I can't wait to hear."

Dillon put down the photos. "I know something that can maximize our efficiency and increase our output."

"Go on."

"I know a way to turn the five thousand we revived today into fifty thousand tomorrow."

"Go on."

Dillon leaned back in his chair almost mirroring Tessic's relaxed demeanor. "Her name is Lourdes," he said. "Lourdes Hidalgo."

Tessic found his balance failing and leaned forward putting both hands on the desk. "Hardly plausible at this moment in time."

"But worth the effort?"

Tessic stood and moved to the window—fading back, hoping not to be read too quickly by Dillon on this matter.

"Something wrong?" Dillon asked. "Why would Lourdes make you uneasy?"

He turned back to Dillon, but kept his distance. "Yesterday, the Italian navy sank a cruise ship just off of Sicily. The *Blue Horizon*."

Dillon did not react as Tessic had expected. He greeted this news with a wicked grin. "I didn't know Italy still had a navy."

"She went down quickly. None of my sources talk of survivors."

Still Dillon was unperturbed. "So you've known about Lourdes's whereabouts all along?"

"I knew she was on a ship. I suspected it was the *Blue Horizon*. I sent three operatives to find it. None of them came back."

Dillon picked a candy from the dish on his desk, and slowly unwrapped it, popping it into his mouth. "She's not dead," he said.

"You're so sure?"

"If she were dead, I would know. We all would. We'd feel as if part of ourselves had died with her."

"Then I'll send a team to find her." Tessic was already eyeing the telephone. "A team professionally trained for—" But Dillon put his hand over the phone, keeping Tessic from lifting the receiver.

"No," Dillon said. "You'll send *us*. All four of us."

"Out of the question."

"This isn't a negotiation," Dillon said. "We're asking you as a courtesy."

As a man whose marching orders were rarely challenged, Tessic found his anger taking hold. "I released you from your security chair," he said, "because I thought you had become reasonable. Perhaps, I was premature."

And then Dillon did something.

Tessic wasn't sure if it was in his gaze or in his voice. Maybe it was just in his focus; the lens of his spirit brought to a burning convergence on Tessic.

"It stems from your mother," Dillon said.

And Tessic was transfixed.

"Everything about you—your will to succeed; your faith; your anger. Everything."

"So Freud would say," Tessic answered, with less deflective aplomb than he wanted.

Dillon shook his head. "This goes even deeper than that." He cocked his head, taking in the pace of Tessic's breath; the set of his jaw; the almost, but not quite, dominant position of his stance. *"There was a child before you. Your mother's child, but not your father's. A child that died in a death camp years before you were born."*

"This you could have learned from many places," Tessic snapped, but his voice was weak and wavering. He knew Dillon hadn't learned it; he had divined it. Tessic had always thought he was somehow immune to Dillon's invasive power. He was now well aware that that had been his own arrogance at work. In the end, he was an open book to Dillon, just like everyone else.

"I believe it was a sister," Dillon said. *"This is the spirit you want to bring back more than any other—this innocent child . . . and yet, the camp where she died is our last destination. You see her as your reward when all others have been revived. No one knows this but you."*

Tessic could barely move or breathe. "Stop," he tried to say, but his lips wouldn't form the word.

"Shall I go on?" Dillon asked.

Tessic had no idea what Dillon was about to say. Until this moment, he didn't think there was anything that could make him vulnerable, but now he instinctively knew that the next words out of Dillon's mouth, whatever they were, would either make him whole or destroy him. He did not know which it would be. Then he realized that it didn't matter. Either way, Dillon would win. Nothing in Tessic's own personal arsenal could defend against this weapon Dillon now wielded. Until now Tessic had not truly understood this power of Dillon to affect the world with a whisper. Simple words, nothing more. But from Dillon's mouth even the simplest of words could be devastating.

"M-M-Michael and Tory," he said, stunned to find himself stuttering—something he hadn't done since the earliest days of his youth.

"Michael and Tory, what?"

Tessic forced volume into his voice. "Michael and Tory may go seek out Lourdes. But I need you and Winston to stay. You two are the ones crucial to this effort."

There was a hesitation on Dillon's part. Perhaps for the first time since he came into the room.

"Please, Dillon. I need you."

Dillon considered his plea for a moment more, then nodded. "All right. But I want them to leave immediately."

Tessic let his shoulders relax. So, it was a negotiation after all. "Yes. Of course—with an escort, a jet—whatever they need."

"Make those your first calls." Dillon stood, handing Tessic the telephone receiver, then glanced at the pictures on the desk. "Once they're on their way, Winston and I will be ready to take on that road."

Dillon left and Tessic collapsed into his chair, forcing a few deep breaths to regain his composure. Perhaps it was worth losing Michael and Tory temporarily in a gambit to bring back Lourdes. He quickly got a paper and began to jot down notes. Their progress would be slower without Michael and Tory, but Michael's moods and weather patterns were more of a hindrance than a help. And although Tory's was a medicinal presence, they could do without her; there were medical supplies enough to treat anything the dead brought back with them.

Within five minutes he had retuned his thinking to this new business environment. He was nothing, if not adaptable. And he put out of his mind how, for a moment, Dillon had extracted the fragile core of his existence, and pinched it between his fingers.

MICHAEL AND TORY WERE more surprised than anyone that Dillon had negotiated their release.

"I could have forced him to let us all go, but I sensed that it would shatter him," Dillon told them.

"And why is that such a bad thing?" Winston grumbled.

Certainly Dillon had many reasons for not shattering Tessic, not the least of which was admiration, and some level of love for this man who had, in a strange way, become Dillon's surrogate father. But these weren't the reasons he gave them. "You don't want to shatter the richest arms manufacturer in the world," he told them, and the others were quick to agree—after all, Tessic probably had more fingers on more buttons than all of NATO put together.

Dillon had played the situation, just as they knew he could. He let Tessic believe he had negotiated, but in truth, this was the arrangement Dillon wanted all along. Michael and Tory would be their ambassadors to the vectors. "Yeah, because we're expendable," Michael complained—but they knew why it was best this way. Dillon could not be allowed to face the vectors until they were at their strongest—because if they defeated him, then all was lost.

Michael and Tory were gone, spirited to Katowice International Airport by helicopter before breakfast was served, bound for Sicily, and the cold embrace of Lourdes Hidalgo, who they all agreed was more than merely AWOL.

If they were shards of the Scorpion Star, then she had become the venom in the tip of its tail.

31. SEA OF DEATH

SCORES OF ROTTING FISH WASHED UP AGAINST THE CLIFFS OF Taormina, Sicily, sending up an uncompromising stench to the Cliffside Greek Theater. It was a constant reminder to Lourdes of her many mistakes and missteps under the tutelage of her three Angels of Death.

The disaster at the Jamaican racetrack had only been the beginning. Following orders from Memo, thinly veiled as suggestions, Lourdes had gripped and controlled one hundred people in Miami, then three hundred farther up the Florida coast, marching them this way and that like a cracker box army. There had been no major mishaps. Then when their ship reached Daytona, she had tried to commandeer five hundred—and had succeeded, her skill sharpening with practice, as Memo had said it would. She was able to grip their bodies and their wills, propelling them in an orderly and efficient manner to the beach. But their inertia proved too much for her. The wave of their motion had direction but no destination. They couldn't stop moving. They drowned.

For the media, it became just one more nasty event in a disintegrating world—and although it would have been analyzed ad infintum by the public a year ago, there were so many unconscionable events from one day to the next, it was quickly submerged in the collective consciousness. Lourdes thought she would feel worse about it—tormented by the helplessness her victims must have felt, and yet she was amazed at how well she slept that night.

"You've grown beyond caring about them," Memo, the child-demon, had told her. She didn't know whether to be pleased or horrified by her ability to dissociate from a human context. Did it make her a cold-blooded killer, or transcendent?

Still packed with her hedonistic throng, the *Blue Horizon* had cut a course to Bermuda. There, she had gripped ten times as many—but this time did not leave her impulse open-ended. She clipped it, focusing her attention on the shoreline. Five thousand fell under her control, impelled to the edge of the surf, where they stopped at her command, holding themselves at attention until she released them. Success—and yet in this success there was still no satisfaction.

"Five thousand, or fifty thousand," the bat-faced woman, Cerilla, had said. "It doesn't matter. It isn't anywhere close to what we need."

"Give her time," Memo had insisted. But time was running out—yet they wouldn't tell Lourdes why this needed to be accomplished on a predetermined schedule.

"If you are leading this invasion," she had asked, "why can't *you* decide when it will happen?"

"The water must boil," Memo told her. "My *abuela* used to tell me, you can't put the spaghetti in until the water boils. But if you wait too long, the water boils off."

When they crossed through the strait of Gibraltar into the Mediterranean, that water began to simmer. That's when she sensed two revivals, falling only a day apart. They were distant—back in America. She could only assume that Dillon had brought back Michael and Tory, as Deanna was unreachable. At both moments, it had evoked in her old feelings of an unbreakable connection between all of them, but those feelings were quickly snuffed by the vacuum in which her spirit now dwelled.

So, the Fantastic Four were together again. Well, good for them. Let them obsess and confer over the fate of the world. She had no interest in being part of that. She knew her three new malefactors must have sensed their revival as well. Perhaps that's why they continued to be so displeased with her progress.

Then, on December first, with only seven days left until the greatest performance of her life, their pleasure cruise became the Voyage of the Damned.

It was the Captain's fault. He had chosen to take the ship north of Sicily rather than south, forcing them into an ambush in the Strait of Messina. Perhaps he was in collusion with the ships that attacked them. She could not be sure, and she could not ask him because he had died in the attack, along with most of her guests.

Three warships had attacked the *Blue Horizon* without warning, under cover of darkness. One torpedo would have done the job, but apparently they weren't taking any chances. After the third torpedo shredded the hull, Lourdes's little floating oasis was sent to the bottom of the Mediterranean in less than twelve minutes—not long enough to launch more than a handful of half-empty lifeboats.

But this wasn't the loss that weighed on her. It was the loss of her brother and sisters. They had not made it through the smoke-filled hallways to the lifeboats before the *Blue Horizon* coughed up her ghost in a greasy spill of diesel fuel.

She thought she was impervious to that kind of pain, and found her sorrow quickly putrefying into fury, as she foundered in a flooded lifeboat with her three angels, who were content to hurl others off the boat to keep themselves afloat.

Lourdes could kill the entire population of Italy for what they had done. Every village, every town, every beggar on every lousy cobblestone street. She could kill them all—and made a concerted effort to do so from her lifeboat, sending an angry impulse across the surface of the waters.

This was perhaps her worst mistake of all. It was stupid. Unproductive. Because when the impulse of her anger faded, there was silence in the waters around them. Silence, and bodies. That silence sat in stronger accusation even than her victims in Daytona. She knew what she had done. She had gripped every beating heart within her reach, and shut them all down. Not only were the seamen on the three attacking ships killed by her anger, but the survivors of her own ship were extinguished as well; those in the water, those in the lifeboats. All of them.

Only she and her three "Angels" were immune. Even more, she sensed death in the sea beneath her, running to its very bottom. How far had the impulse gone? Five miles, perhaps, until it fell beneath a lethal threshold? She knew her influence would be felt for many miles beyond that. A sudden spasm in the chest of every living thing for a hundred miles in every direction. For those far enough out of range the spasm would pass. Maybe. She didn't know her own strength anymore, and until that moment, she had never considered herself a weapon of mass destruction.

Her angels were quick to remind her that the sinking, which they could have turned to her advantage, was only a disaster because of her rash action. She could very easily have commandeered one of the naval vessels and continued their crusade, but now without a living crew to manipulate, they were just as dead in the water as those ships.

They made shore just before dawn. Then Carlos and Cerilla took some rope from the lifeboat, and tied her to a tree. She tried to stop them, but their anger was more powerful than her ability to fight them off.

"This," Carlos told her, "is something you've earned," and then they both beat her with their bare hands, until their fists were as bruised as her face, relieving their anger on her the way she had relieved hers on the world. Lourdes tried to counterattack, by gripping their muscles with her mind, but their immunity to her was complete. Just as they could not devour her, she could not injure them. There was a balance of power, delicate though it may be.

All the while, Memo sat nearby, not lifting a finger to stop it. He was the leader of this trio of wolves—one word from him could have ended their beating, but he let it go until his cohorts' human bodies were exhausted, and their inhuman spirits satisfied.

Memo came to her when the other two left, untying her bonds while whistling a pop tune dredged from his host body's memory. Once one hand was free, Lourdes pushed him hard enough to send him flying across the beach on which they were marooned. He stood up, looking at her with hurt and surprise.

"You let them torture me, and you expect me to follow your orders?"

He came back to untie her other hand. "Using your power against those warships was a bad thing," he said, sounding more the child than the demon. "They are angry."

She had grown used to his manner now, but still it unsettled her the way the personality of the child host-body had merged with the seriousness of the creature who commandeered it. At times almost innocent, and at other times evilly calculating.

But there is no evil, she reminded herself. The angels had taught her that. Was the fisherman evil for catching fish? Was the hunter evil for feeding his family? There is no evil, the angels told her, only power and weakness. The weak see power used against them as evil.

If I see them as evil does that make me weak?

It was simply easier to ignore the question than to answer it.

"Mama and Abuelo are very angry," Memo said as he untied her. "But if they hit you enough now, they won't kill you tomorrow."

"I thought you didn't suffer from human emotions," Lourdes snapped.

"We feel what these bodies feel," Memo answered. "Me, I find anger the most useful, don't you?"

Lourdes rubbed her swelling face. She couldn't find the use in their anger or in her own. It had landed them on this wretched shore.

"Anger must be used, though. Directed," Memo said.

"And what if I direct it at the three of you?"

Memo stood on his tiptoes looking closely at her swelling face. "More of the same," he answered, then kissed a bruise above her eye. "A kiss will make it better, *verdad?*"

She pushed him away again. "Not that easy."

"Still, you will do the things we ask of you."

"How can you be so sure?"

"Because," he said quite simply, "you wish to be with greatness. And we are the only greatness there is."

She grunted but refused to admit how well he had her pegged. For months she had taken all this world had to offer and found it flavorless. Then to learn that everything the world perceived as divine was merely the work of these predators had crushed her. Crushed her, then freed her. This new, bleak view of creation left her unencumbered by troublesome human ethics.

But your brother and sisters are dead, her atrophied conscience whispered from its hiding place. *They are at the bottom of the Mediterranean because of you.*

She would have cried, but refused to let Memo and the other two seraphic ghouls see the depth of her sorrow. These creatures did not care about her sorrow. They simply needed her to accomplish their goal. To know that beings greater than herself needed her was its own reward—and in spite of their constant disapproval, she would serve them, because they were, as Memo had said, the only embodiment of greatness she'd ever know. She longed to be party to the power they would soon unleash. How odd, she thought, to finally find fulfillment in the slavery of "Angels."

SHE SET UP COURT in nearby Taormina, in the ruins of the Greek Theater, because it reminded her of those spectacular, but brief, golden days beneath the faux Greco facades of the Neptune pool at Hearst Castle. But *these* ruins were real, from a time before Sicily became a kicking toy for the toe of Italy. It had once been claimed by Greece, and in some fundamental way, Lourdes felt connected to it.

The view from the theater was stunning: snow-capped Mount Etna to the south, and to the east, the tranquil, azure waters of the Mediterranean—but as they made preparations for the next leg of their journey, it was the north that drew Lourdes's attention. Something happening to the north.

The other shards. They were closer. They were . . . *doing* something. Now they were not just together, but connected in some new way, and the sense of their connection deepened her own sense of isolation. She closed her eyes, hating them for making her feel this way, but longing to know what it was they were doing. She closed her eyes, trying to feel more clearly what they felt. Whatever they were up to it was both wonderful and horrible at the same time.

"Forget them," Memo said, seeing this new direction of

her attention. "Come look at the sea. We are not that far from Thira."

When she looked across the ocean, she imagined she could see the island out there, waiting for her arrival, and it chased the irritating sense of the other shards out of her mind.

"There is a scar running through Thira, from the sky to its bowels," Memo told her with childlike enthusiasm. "We get to tear it open again."

Lourdes knew if they succeeded, it would mean a slow and painful end to the human condition, as if afflicted by some terminal disease.

A disease, thought Lourdes, *is that what these creatures are?* She couldn't shake the thought, and yet when she dug down to mine her feelings about it, she found she did not care. To her, the human race was already dead. In that, perhaps she was not all that different from these creatures of darkness posing as light—for if she was a luminous spirit, why did she feel so black at her core?

Up above a reconnaissance plane flew past, toward the three dead warships that had run aground ten miles up the coast.

"Tearing open the sky . . ." Lourdes said. "I can't wait." Then she effortlessly gripped the hands of the pilot in the low-flying plane, forcing them forward, and she and Memo watched as the plane plunged into the sea.

32. WEB OF SHADOWS

MICHAEL AND TORY'S FLIGHT TO SICILY WAS A LESSON IN European geography. What Michael expected to be a brutally long flight aboard Tessic's jet was a mere puddle jump. Two hours from Warsaw to Palermo and by late afternoon they were received at Tessic's villa on the north shore of Sicily.

"Is there a place where this guy doesn't have a villa?" Michael had asked as the housekeeper walked him and Tory through, pointing out the many amenities. There was no fog here—and although a chill filled the air when they had arrived, it had become a sullen breeze. Now that the weather was permitting, the glass wall of the living room was slid open, leaving a vast Mediterranean view as their fourth wall.

Michael and Tory sat out on the verandah, taking a late lunch, feeling guilty about it—but not too guilty. This was, after all, the first real reprieve they had—not just since being revived, but since the nightmare at Hoover Dam, and the heady hell of being addicted to their own power. "Who says we have to find Lourdes," Michael said, devouring some delicious Sicilian dish he could not name. "Let's just stay here, sponging off of Tessic, and watch the world end from our balcony." He was only half kidding.

"Won't work," Tory told him. "World's ending to the east; the balcony faces north." Tory wasn't eating. Instead she was still examining the silverware, too embarrassed to complain to the help about the spots, but too obsessive to use them. *Well,* thought Michael, *our experiences left us all with some quirks.*

"Lourdes is on the island, east of here," Tory told him. "Not all that far."

Michael did not want to be reminded.

"She's up to something horrible," Tory went on. "I can feel her like a short circuit."

Michael had to admit her presence did feel different. One of them, and yet not. Winston had warned them about her—that she was not the girl they remembered—that she had let herself become evil. Michael thought to when he had first met Lourdes. She had been a bitter outcast, so frighteningly obese, she inspired fear rather than sympathy. Hatred and anger were not new emotions to her—she had hated with a riveting, heart-stopping intensity even back then. She could have killed any number of classmates and teachers with the intensity of her hatred. But then, for a time, anger gave way to self-indulgence, as it had for all of them. What then of Lourdes's self-indulgence? Had that matured into something worse? Had it fused with her anger into something even more lethal than the gluttonous parasite that had once enslaved her?

"They say she kills people," said Tory. "Hundreds at a time. For pleasure." She shivered at the thought. "I can't imagine it."

"Keep talking and you'll ruin this wonderful warming trend." And indeed, Michael could feel the temperature dropping. It wasn't just the presence of Lourdes that bothered him—it was the vectors. Everything inside him was screaming panic—but he was strong enough now to box those emotions. And so, when sunset came, he streaked the sky with wispy cirrus—a trick he had perfected back at San Simeon for his adoring throng a week—no—a *year* before. The swatches of clouds soaked in the colors of sunset, painting the whole sky in vivid oranges and blues, resolving to violet. When the spectacle was done, Tory led him to the bedroom for a syntaxis of two.

"We'll set out to find her in the morning," Tory said. "But we owe ourselves this one night."

They lay down on the bed, fully clothed at first. Michael had hoped that the right set of circumstances would ignite his scarred libido, but it wasn't happening, and as she pressed against him, slipping her hand into his shirt to feel his heartbeat against her palm, he grew uneasy.

"I want to be with you," she whispered to him, and although he felt his heart pouring out, the passion moved no lower.

"I can't," he told her, taking her hand from the lip of his jeans. "I used up all my lust a long time ago. Didn't save anything for a rainy day . . . or a starry night."

She giggled, as if she were drunk. *Is she drunk on me?* he thought.

"I still want to be with you," she said.

"I don't think you understand."

"Yes, I do." Then she undressed herself, and undressed him. He was glad it was dark, so she couldn't see the humiliation in his face at his own flaccidness.

"I told you," he said. "DOA."

"And I told you, I don't want it anyway."

She moved her hand up his thigh, and although it brushed past his groin, it continued past, never her destination. She ran her hands across his chest, his neck and shoulders. She sifted her fingers through his dark hair, and in a moment his hands were on her as well. Like her, he found his hands had no destination; the path itself was the pleasure. It was as if she were teaching him how to touch a woman all over again—and he who had seduced more girls than he could count from the earliest days of his volcanic pubescence. Those were days of a dark fire—when he was enslaved by his own parasite beast, feeding on a lust that consumed him, drove him. His whole being had wired itself to feed that lust, and everything he did and thought was filtered through the beast's glowing turquoise eyes. When he had finally killed it, it exacted a heavy price. It stole from him not only his lust, but his passion, leaving him as asexual as a eunuch. Seventeen, and never to be a whole man.

But here he was, naked in Tory's arms, and somehow she had found a way to turn his impotence into a virtue. Love without lust. She made his jaded spirit feel clean and pure.

She kept running her hands over him until there was not a spot on his body left untouched. Her touch coated him now like a second skin, and although he could still feel the looming threat of Lourdes and the vectors, for this brief moment, they felt muted and distant.

"I love you," he told her. He could not remember ever telling anyone that.

She kissed him and rested her head on his chest. "Hold me," she whispered. "Hold me like you did when we died."

He did, and this time he was determined not to let go.

THE FIRST INDICATION THAT something was amiss was the state of traffic. The main Sicilian highway that led east toward Taormina was flooded with traffic heading west. It seemed to Tory that she and Michael were the only ones going against the trend. Their driver stopped to ask what the trouble was, but everyone had a different story. Some said a battleship had run aground and was leaking radiation. Funny, because battleships were not nuclear powered. Another spoke of disease—smallpox, Ebola, and even a new invention; *il Morte Aspettare*—the standing death—something downright medieval for this new dark age. Yet another spoke of poisoned earth. *She's become poison. Isn't that what Winston had said?* Tory thought. Apparently the driver, who was on Tessic's payroll, was not paid enough for this. He abandoned the car and thumbed his way in the other direction, leaving Michael to take the wheel. The weather stayed clear, but the winds blew chilly.

"I'm not ashamed to tell you that I'm scared," Tory said. Which was probably not what Michael wanted to hear. After all that had happened between the two of them, she knew he considered her the brave one.

"Come on," said Michael. "It'll just be like any other family reunion. Blood; violence; medical triage."

"So what do we do when we find her?"

"We're in Sicily," Michael said, and put on his best Vito Corleone. "I'll make her an offer she can't refuse." Tory laughed in spite of herself.

By the time they could see Taormina in the distance, both sides of the road were deserted. Then once they wound their way up to the cliffside town, the situation became far clearer than they wanted it to, for while homes and businesses on the outskirts were deserted, there was a point closer to the town's main gate where the population remained, but they weren't talking much.

Michael slowed the car for a man crossing the street, only to find the man stuck in mid-stride, not moving, like a toy whose batteries had died halfway across the street. On the cobblestone street, people were frozen in place.

"Lourdes . . ." said Tory. This time Michael had no quick retort. Lourdes had seized control of these people—but there had apparently been an event horizon. Those who had seen the immobile victims from just outside that horizon could not have understood what they were witnessing. Some would have crossed over and been caught themselves, like insects on flypaper, until enough had gotten the general idea, and would run, beginning that panicked exodus. The road narrowed into a pedestrian-only street, so they left the car and continued on foot. They strode around static figures until reaching a very literal tourist trap; a spot in the road clogged with frozen pedestrians. Although they were not subject to Lourdes's field as these people were, they could still feel it, making it a chore to move their own muscles as if the air were thick and gelatinous.

Tory stopped to examine one woman. Although she wore a hat, her arms and shoulders were exposed by a strapless dress. Most of the exposed flesh was red and peeling with a sunburn that went down to second degree. Tory took off her own sweater and covered the woman's shoulders.

"Lourdes must have grabbed them in the middle of the day yesterday," she said, "and just kept them here." *For what purpose?* Tory wondered. *She was holding them in abeyance, in a sort of psychic stasis, but for what?*

Then the woman suddenly started moving, and Tory yelped and jumped back, stumbling on the uneven street. This woman wasn't the only one moving, the others on the street were as well. They came out of shops and galleries, villas and flats, adding to the numbers on the street. Although their footfalls fell at different paces, they seemed to be of one mind when it came to their direction—downhill, toward the sea.

"Looks like we're just in time for the brunch of the living dead," Michael said. But these people weren't exactly zombies. The marching throng had more grace than Tory and Michael expected.

"Shall we join the party?" asked Michael. And so they did, for today, in the town of Taormina, all roads led to Lourdes.

At the bottom of the winding street was a marina, quaint,

but sizable. People made their way down the docks and boarded boats. Some were just passengers, others seemed to own the boats and have keys. Other keys were pulled through the smashed ruins of the marina office. This made it clear that Lourdes's power had gained a new sophistication; she wasn't merely controlling their bodies, but she had commandeered their wills like a persuasive post-hypnotic suggestion. In every way, these people now belonged to her.

"Those people who got away weren't all that wrong," Tory said. "I can feel her hatred like radiation."

Tory saw her first. She was at the entrance to a small gazebo, in a park overlooking the marina. She stood there watching her private civilian navy take shape, but Tory knew she was also watching them.

"Remember," Michael reminded, "we're just as strong as she is."

"Except that she has the vectors on her side."

"They're like Okoya," Michael said. "They can manipulate, but they have no direct power over us, except the power we give them."

But it did nothing to ease Tory's sense of dread, as they approached Lourdes.

LOURDES LEANED ON THE railing of the gazebo, her arms crossed and her eyes fixed on them as they came across the park toward her. The latticework of the gazebo cast weblike shadows across the floor. She stepped back into the gazebo, letting the web of shadows fall across her clothes and her face. They would have to enter into this open-air lair. They would not want to get that close, but she would make them.

"Hello, Lourdes," Michael said, stopping just a few feet short of the gazebo. Tory stepped forward first. *Coward,* thought Lourdes. *He's a coward. What did I ever see in him?* She remained toward the back of the structure, making no move toward them. *Come into my parlor, said the spider to the fly.* "What a surprise," she said, making it clear she was not surprised at all.

And then her eyes shot down to Tory's hand. It had clasped Michael's. Even in their apprehension, their hands came together with such casual ease, she knew there was something more between them now than there had been before. As they stepped into the gazebo, Lourdes found her jealousy, which had seasoned so many of her days, was now bitter arsenic in the back of her throat.

"Where's loverboy?" she asked Michael, with such enmity in her voice, she barely recognized it as her own.

"Excuse me?" said Michael.

"Drew," she said. "Your lover."

Tory turned to Michael more curious than shocked.

"You're mistaken, Lourdes," Michael told her. "Drew and I were never lovers." And then he added, "Any more than you and I were lovers."

She felt the barb twist in her gut. "I know what I know," she said. In fact she knew nothing—only suspected, but she was loath to admit it.

"Would you mind telling us what you're doing here?" Tory asked.

All right, she thought. They were no more interested in small talk than she. "My vacation came to an unexpected end. I'm here making myself some new friends." She gestured toward the marina, where tourists as well as locals flooded the docks, squeezing themselves onto whatever boats still had room. Lourdes noticed their progress had slowed since her attention had shifted to Tory and Michael. This gathering required focus, and she resented that her focus had been pulled. She had thought she was supposed to be stronger in the presence of other shards, but their fields were working against her own, hopelessly out of sync.

"I suppose I should thank you," she said to Tory. "The stench from the beach has been unbearable in this heat. But the second you got here, the smell went away. Now the whole place is minty fresh."

She took a step toward Tory. "'*The Goddess of Purity*,' isn't that what Okoya had called you? Is that why you like her, Michael? Because her crap doesn't smell? I'll bet she doesn't even have morning breath, does she?"

"You're one sick bitch," said Michael.

Lourdes laughed, and the laugh was echoed back a hundredfold by the mob in the marina, sounding like the cackling of geese.

"Did it feel good to kill all those people in Florida?" Michael went on. "Is it a thrill to pull planes out of the sky?"

She thought to tell them that Florida was an accident—and that she *had* to pull reconnaissance planes from the sky to keep them from finding out what happened to the three warships. But telling them this would serve no one. Their disgust, on the other hand, was something she could relish.

"We know about the vectors," Tory said. "We know what they plan to do."

"*Vectors?* Is that what you call them?"

"Why are you helping them?" Tory grabbed her, and for a moment she felt that long-lost connection between them.

Lourdes pushed her away, not wanting to feel it. "Because there's nothing and no one in this world worth saving."

"So you'd rather fill it with demons?"

"They're not demons!" She turned away. "They're not

angels either. But they're the closest thing there is. If I have to choose sides, I choose them."

Michael looked at her, not with disgust, or horror, but with pity. It was a look Lourdes could not abide. "What have they been telling you?" he asked.

"Only the truth," she said. "That there is no God—there are no miracles—there is no meaning to anything we do; that the universe isn't just indifferent, it's hostile, trying its damnedest to get rid of us."

Again that look of pity from Michael. "And you believe this?"

Lourdes felt her hands close into fists, and she knew if she wasn't careful, she'd send another lethal pulse of anger out through the crowd she had gathered.

Just then, the three "vectors," as Tory had curiously called them, stepped out from their hiding places; behind a tree, behind a shed, behind a truck. They converged on the gazebo at a steady but unhurried pace.

"They're going to kill you," Lourdes told Michael and Tory. "You must have known that when you came here."

And indeed Michael and Tory did know. They knew these creatures were formidable enemies. They knew they would most likely have their own brief candles snuffed once more—perhaps this time for good, but they also knew they had to come.

If we die together again, thought Michael, *then it will be okay*.

But Tory, on the other hand, was not thinking about dying. She was running through her mind every possible way they might live.

She and Michael said nothing, only took in the faces of the three approaching creatures. A child, an old man, a cleft-lipped woman with witch-long hair. Tory could laugh at the hosts they had chosen to inhabit.

temporal
lateral
leading

The identities of the vectors were projected into her mind. Not so much names, as assignments. Each one was an axis of dimension. The child—he was the leading vector, and most powerful. The old man was temporal, the woman lateral. Then as they approached, they changed. They drew out from their hosts their true being, letting the false light flow around their bodies.

Tory almost fell to her knees with a very personal revelation of glory. "What do you see?" Michael asked. Tory couldn't answer, the image was so vivid. It was a young girl with flaxen hair running through a cotton field. The girl kicked up wisps of cotton that drifted high into the air, as if pulled toward the sun. "I see myself as a child," she said. She saw the same image in all three of the vectors. It surrounded her no matter where she looked.

Michael, on the other hand, saw his mother, who had walked out of his life when he was ten. The woman Michael saw now, however, was not as he remembered her, but as he *wished* he remembered her. Not the cold, bitter woman she was, but a woman with such inner warmth it could fill any needy child. This was a fun-house mirror distortion that took the ugliness of his memory and bent it into something so desirable, he could barely resist. It was something he didn't realize he needed until now.

"They'll make it easy for you," Lourdes told them. "They will make you feel fulfilled. Complete. It will be the most wonderful moment of your life."

"And then they'll kill us," said Tory, unable to reconcile the thought with the visions of happiness the vectors put into her head.

"You're shards," Lourdes said, "so they can't devour you like they devour others. Your souls will go . . . wherever the souls of shards go. Where you went before, the first time you died."

But they had no memory of where that might have been.

The vectors came closer. They were at the entrance to the gazebo now.

"Come," Michael heard them say deep within his mind in that gentle voice of his fantasy mother. *"Come and I'll rock you to sleep. Come, and I'll make you believe once and forever that I loved you."*

"Come," they said to Tory. *"Come play in the field the way you used to. This is your heaven."* So innocent and so compelling were the images they put forth, that the blade they each held in their sweet little hands hardly seemed to matter at all. *"Just let me bring this across your neck and you can stay here forever."*

Both Tory and Michael wanted to, so overwhelming was the lure—but a lure was all it was. Tantalizing, enticing—irresistible. But a lie.

"Hold on to me, Michael," Tory said. In an instant she felt Michael's hand around her, linking her to him. Then Tory reached out toward Lourdes.

"You should feel this," Tory said, "before we die." Then she grabbed Lourdes by the shoulder.

Syntaxis was sudden and powerful. At last their mismatched fields fell into place. This was a new variation for Michael and Tory—a different harmonic from syntaxis with Winston and Dillon, but every bit as satisfying.

For Lourdes, who had not experienced this before, she found her mind had no way to interpret the feeling. Time seemed to cease as all the darkness within her nurtured by the vectors soaked in this new light. She could feel her own field multiplied by theirs. She could feel at once the beating of every heart within her sphere of influence. Not just in Taormina, but miles beyond, to the countryside; to the north shore; across the Island of Sicily. Finally when she could stand no more, she broke free and saw Cerilla taking Tory into her arms, then turning her around, bringing a knife to Tory's neck.

"Wait!" Lourdes shouted.

The woman looked at her as if she might turn her blade on Lourdes instead.

"These two can help us!"

"They'd much rather die," said Carlos. "And we'd much rather kill them."

"Kill them and you'll never gather enough hosts," Lourdes told them. That stopped them and got them to listen.

"When I connect with them I can seize the wills and bodies of a thousand times what I can do on my own." Then Lourdes smiled. "Take them with us, and we can use them to gather the three hundred thousand you need."

The pity Michael had shown before transformed into disbelief and horror. Good, thought Lourdes. That was an expression she could live with.

Free of the vectors' spell, Tory and Michael tried to run, but Lourdes turned a dozen people in the marina against them. They were tackled and tied with such unceremonious ease, she almost wished the vectors had killed them. At least in that, there would have been some dignity.

THE FLEET OF NINETY-THREE boats—everything from sailboats to speedboats, fishing boats to yachts—set out from Taormina. After more than a year of unbridled luxury, Lourdes took a curious liking to a well-seasoned fishing boat. The fact that it was named *La Fuerza del Destino*, after the Verdi opera, clinched it for her. She wasn't much for opera, but how could she not sail on The Force of Destiny?

With more than eight hundred bodies and souls trained into her gravity, they sailed east from Sicily to the southern shore of Italy, the sole of Italy's boot. As the fleet grazed the shoreline, Lourdes let her influence drag along the fishing communities they passed like a rake pulling up leaves. In each town a dozen new boats were added to their number as their owners were impelled to join them. However, as they set off across the Gulf of Taranto, trouble set in—not with the power of Lourdes's control, but with the boats themselves. The Gulf of Toronto was ninety miles wide and many of the boats simply didn't have enough fuel to cross it. Engines stopped; dozens were set hopelessly adrift in the water—and the fact that Michael kept the winds raging against them didn't help. By the time Lourdes reached the far side of the gulf, all but the largest boats were running on fumes, and they had lost more than half their numbers.

Of course, the vectors were furious. For all the acuity of their grand spirits, there were some simple things they could not grasp about this world of matter.

"The boats need fuel," Lourdes explained to them.

"So get them fuel," they insisted.

But the town of Gallipoli, where they had landed, did not have enough fuel for a fleet the size of hers, and even if it had, the logistics of bringing in each boat for fueling would take a half a day. What then when her fleet grew to be thousands? How would she move them to the Aegean sea? When connected to Tory and Michael she could pull an army of three hundred thousand and more, but she could not make them fly. Ultimately, they were all bound by the limitations of terrestrial mechanics.

"If we use sailboats . . ." Carlos suggested.

"I can't direct the wind," she replied.

And in fact, Cerilla's hair was a wispy mess from the capricious winds blowing up from the Ionian Sea. "*He* can direct the wind," Cerilla said, pointing down to the aft cabins of the fishing boat. There was so much animosity in her voice, it could have doused the sun.

"Michael won't do it."

"You'll make him do it," insisted Carlos.

"I can't make him do anything," she had to admit to them, and to herself. Then she added, "And if you kill him for not obeying you, you'll cut the number of your army in half."

The two older vectors turned away from her, casting their frustrations over the side.

Memo approached her. "We will get them there if they have to swim." Unlike the others, there was no vitriol in his words. It was simply a statement of intention, but intention or not, no human being could cross the five hundred miles from Italy to the Island of Thira. Such an attempt would only make her death count multiply again. But she didn't tell him this.

"I'll work on it," she said. She left the boat and paced the dock, returning all her focus to the fractioned control it took to move her masses into fueling for the next leg of the trip across the strait of Corfu and the western shores of Greece.

The gas was already running out, as she knew it would, but those under control had their wills so completely supplanted by her own, that they continued to pump from empty tanks in a bizarre compulsive collective consciousness. It was getting dark when she returned to her fishing boat. The vectors were nowhere to be found and that was just as well with her.

Every inch of the boat, from top to bottom, smelled of sea salt, diesel, and fish, but the rancid odor that used to permeate the corners had vanished the moment Tory had arrived. *This would all be sparkling new if Dillon were here*, she thought. It was the first time she could remember thinking of Dillon in anything but the most negative terms.

Then, as she stepped onto the boat, she heard Carlos scream. It was a horrid sound that went on and on, then ended with sudden silence. Lourdes went down below into the narrow, dimly lit hallway of the worn fishing boat.

Carlos wasn't in his cabin, only Memo was there, sitting by himself. Blood had splattered on the walls, and lay in pools on the floor. When he saw her, he ran into her arms and cried.

"Abuelo is dead," he cried. "Abuelo is dead."

Lourdes caught sight of Cerilla, who peered at her ferally from a dark corner.

"Abuelo is dead," wailed the boy-thing. She pulled him away to see that his hands had left red prints on her blouse. The boy's palms were covered in the old man's blood. As for Carlos, his body was nowhere to be seen, but there was a small open porthole. Lourdes shivered. "You killed him! You killed the host."

"He was weak," Memo said, wiping away the tears, as the leading vector forced control over the host-child's emotions. "Abuelo was too weak to hold the temporal vector."

"So you killed the old man, and found a better host?"

But the vector refused to answer; instead, he shielded again behind the child's distress, allowing the host-body to bawl. It was an effective tactic, because Lourdes comforted him in spite of herself. *This is not a child*, she tried to convince herself. *This is a monster that murders without hesitation or remorse*. But then, how did that differ from herself now?

"Where is he?" Lourdes asked. "The . . . *temporal vector?*"

"He seeks his new host on the shore," Cerilla answered. "He'll return once he's found the best one."

"Tell him not to hurry back."

She left them to their bloodbath, lingered at her own cabin door momentarily, then passed it by and went to Michael's—

who was kept on the opposite end of the boat from Tory. He knelt in the center of the room, but then, all he could do was kneel; his hands were handcuffed above his head to a hook in the ceiling. The ceiling was too low for him to stand, but the chain of the cuffs did not allow him the comfort of sitting, so he was forced to find this compromising position in between. The vectors had done this to him.

No, thought Lourdes, *I was the one who bound him at their request.*

"Where are we now?" he asked weakly.

"Southern Italy," she told him. "A small town called Gallipoli."

"Gallipoli," said Michael. "There was a massacre there in World War I. The British kept sending waves of soldiers into enemy gunfire. Another low point in human history."

"Now you're starting to sound like Winston," Lourdes said. "A walking encyclopedia. Or should I say kneeling."

"Nope," said Michael. "Can't accuse me of knowing anything. I just saw it in a movie once." And then he hesitated. "So is this history repeating itself today?"

She didn't answer him. She didn't know. "I wanted to tell you that I'm sorry things turned out this way."

"But not for anything you've done?"

Lourdes shook her head. "I swore to myself I'd never live to regret the things I do."

Michael offered her an ironic smile. "You probably won't." Then his expression became serious. "You never answered my question."

Lourdes turned from his gaze. "Which one?" although she knew precisely what he meant.

"Why do you accept their bleak view of the universe? That everything's pointless; that everything's hostile?"

"What happened, Michael?" she snapped. "Did you die and find God? You were never one to believe in anything."

"I believe in keeping my options open." Then with uncharacteristic patience, he waited to hear what Lourdes had to say. For a long bloated moment Lourdes said nothing. The sense of the boat rocking on the water, and the sound of it shouldering against the dock, filled the gap between them until Lourdes could no longer stand the silence.

"I've seen the vectors pose as angels," she said. "I've felt that glow of glory they put off before swooping in for the kill, dozens of times." Lourdes felt her cheeks redden from anger as she thought about it. "I've seen them take people into their arms, making them believe they were raptured to heaven, and then suck their souls right out of the marrow of their bones."

She realized she did hate these creatures for being what they were, but she hated human beings more, for believing these monsters were something divine. Lourdes thought to her childhood. All those years under her parents' wing—church every Sunday, Midnight Mass at Christmas and Easter. She had once felt the residue of holiness. She had believed in miracles back then, and knew in her heart that the blood and body of Christ fed her when she took communion. But now these shadowy creatures made her believe it was a lie.

Then Michael said: "If everything they do is built on lies . . . how do you know they're not lying to you now?"

The very suggestion took the wind out of her. It unlocked a door that had always been right in front of her, but hiding in her blind spot. "What?"

"They've told you that faith is a sham—that it's a tool they've invented with their visitations for thousands of years. But how do you know it's not just another lure—something to lure *you* into their service?"

Lourdes found she couldn't answer. Could it be true? They were false light. Deception was their art by their own admission.

"And even if what they say is true," Michael went on. "Even if every 'divine intervention' in the history of the human race has been them trying to consume their souls . . . *How do you know that they are all there is?* How do you know there's not something out there greater than them? Something beyond them that they hide with their darkness?"

Lourdes found herself stumbling over her own thoughts, wanting to close her mind to Michael's voice but unable to.

"They want your faith to be in hopelessness," he said, "because you'd never surrender to them unless you had no hope."

Her cheeks red from anger and confusion, her head pounding, she latched on to her anger, the only companion that was stalwart and consistent, and spat her words at him. "When you died, Michael, did you see the face of God? Did you get lifted up to heaven or dragged down to hell?"

Michael looked away. "I don't know."

"HOW COULD YOU NOT KNOW?!"

Michael took his time in answering. "Maybe memory is something stored in our flesh. We don't take our memory with us when we die, and nothing comes back with us when we return."

"Wishful thinking!" she shouted. "You remember nothing, because there *is* nothing."

"I didn't bring anything back from death," Michael finally admitted, "except for this: I'm not afraid to die anymore. Maybe that's because my soul knows something my memory doesn't."

She tried to dismiss the thought, but found that Michael's words lingered. Lourdes was no stranger to death. She was, in fact, its jaded comrade now. But she recalled her first unhappy introduction to it. It was when her grandmother died. Lourdes was all of seven. Her mother had put her to bed that night, and told her how Grandma was in a better place. Reunited with Grandpa. Lourdes had pictured them there together running through the clouds; the old woman free of her crippling arthritis, still the same person she had been, only somewhat more transparent.

Then, when Lourdes had become fat, pitied, and hated, she had dismissed heaven out of hand. People dressed in white, playing harps in the clouds. Ridiculous! A Bugs Bunny cartoon without a punch line. That's all, folks. With heaven gone, God wasn't far behind. It was harder to dispense with hell, however. That idea lingered until she decided her own life fit the description.

The thought was so hideous it forced something out of Lourdes—something she had no idea she would say. "You were the only damned thing I ever really wanted. Why couldn't you have just loved me?"

"Because we don't connect to each other, Lourdes," Michael told her with far too little passion one way or the other. "You connect to Dillon, and to Tory, but you don't connect to me."

In defiance of the words she reached out to him. She intended to grab his neck in her hand, but found herself cupping his cheek gently in her palm. And although she felt some connection between them, it was only an echo of what she wanted to feel.

WHEN LOURDES WENT BACK on deck night had fallen. The moon was a full blue beacon overhead. She could see the hills painted in subtle indigo tones, and in the harbor, her minions continued to hopelessly pump invisible gas from empty tanks.

Lourdes closed her eyes, took a deep breath, then released it . . .

. . . and let go.

It took every ounce of her own will to do it.

It was harder letting go than it was grabbing these people and holding them.

She watched in the moonlight as the disoriented masses found their bodies and spirits under their own control once more. For a minute, there was quiet confusion, and then the fear that should have gripped them in the beginning, gripped them now. They ran from the docks; they leapt from the boats. Anything to get away from Lourdes Hidalgo.

"What are you doing?" Memo's voice was so commanding it was hard to imagine it came from the body of an eight-year-old boy.

She turned to him. In this dim light, she could imagine him for what he was. An ancient spirit that moved in a singular, relentless trajectory. Self-serving, manipulative, but never changing course. It was this she so admired in the vectors. And hated in them as well.

"We can't bring these people to Thira," she told him. "It's too far away. We'll travel south to Crete, and I'll collect your army on the shores there. From Crete's north coast it's only eighty miles to Thira."

And for the first time Memo deferred to her judgment. She wondered if he noticed that this was also the first time she called the army *his*, and not her own.

33. BIRKENAU BLACK

Auschwitz was no longer run by the Third Reich. Now it was administered by the Polish Ministry of Parks.

It was preserved as a museum; hundreds of barracks, the execution wall, Mengele's chamber of death. But Auschwitz II, also known as Birkenau, was a different story. The heart of darkness where more than a million and a half people were murdered was left exactly the way it was found, untouched—untouchable. Crumbling barracks stretched farther than the eye wanted to see, behind the remains of the three massive crematoria and gas chambers, now no more than skeletal factories of death. Although the SS tried to blow the crematoria up before the liberation, they were not entirely successful. The twisted rubble that remained still testified to the atrocity.

The current curator was a middle-aged man who had not lived through the horror, but was born in its aftermath. His deepest personal connection was the coldness of his childhood winters, because his parents refused to burn wood in their fireplace, the stench of the smoke reminding them of the stench that blew across the miles from Auschwitz-Birkenau for four long years.

On the morning of December fourth, the curator ate his standard ham and eggs breakfast, kissed his wife and children good-bye, then headed out in his aging Citroen over the snow-dusted road connecting the town to Auschwitz, twenty miles away.

The "Facility" (which was the accepted euphemism among the administrators) did not open until ten o'clock, but he found the road already crowded with buses. There were always buses on the road. Buses coming, buses leaving and on his weaker days the curator often wished that the abandoned railway that had once brought so many across the border from Hungary to their death, could be used now for the shuttling of tourists back and forth.

It was only after riding between two buses for ten minutes that he realized that they were both were empty. In fact—they all were. Drivers, yes—but no passengers.

This did not bode well. A fleet of empty buses was unnerving in and of itself, but that coupled with the bizarre rumors from some of the other memorials left him in a deepening state of dread. Rumors that they had been seized by foreign forces. Rumors that mystics were disturbing the bones and ashes of the dead.

He now recalled that several weeks ago some workers had come to his Facility from the Ministry of Public Works, with high-tech equipment. They claimed to be checking the state of the watershed, but when he phoned the Ministry they denied sending a team of workers. He hadn't been concerned at the time—he knew that when it came to government, the right hand rarely knew what the left hand was doing.

But now, as he drove into the parking lot, he suspected that those workers had not been state workers at all. Buses already filled half the lot—at least thirty of them. All identical. All empty. What's more, there were teams of laborers waiting at the gate. Their beige uniforms suggested some utility, but was nondescript enough to defy any definitive association.

"We were sent by the Ministry of Health," the curator was told by a young woman as he approached the gate. "We believe your aquifer is contaminated, creating a risk to public health."

"Funny that a representative from the Ministry of Health would talk to me in English," he told the young woman, whom he took to be an American even before she had opened her mouth, by the way she held herself.

"Would you like to see our permits? I think you'll find everything in order."

She held out some official-looking documents. "No doubt," he answered and waved the papers off. She folded them and put them away.

The night guard, who had his own unspoken suspicions, had refused to let them in. Now the guard meandered behind the protection of the double fence, refusing to get any closer to these visitors.

Other workers, who should have been inside by now, lingered in the parking lot, smoking, making small talk, but keeping one eye on the curator, waiting to see what he would do.

"Do these buses have anything to do with decontaminating our aquifer?" he asked.

"The buses must be for tourists," the young woman said without changing the stone in her expression. "Isn't that what tour buses are for?"

By now the entire lot was full, and more buses were forced to pull off to the side of the road. Every one of them empty, save for the drivers.

The curator thought to say something about it, but instead just motioned to the day guard, who was waiting patiently to unlock the gate. He did so with shaky hands that dropped the keys twice, before the lock came undone.

The American woman passed some instructions to a team leader, who then translated them into Polish for the others in their company. The curator grabbed her before he went in. Maybe all the rumors he had heard were unfounded, but he felt compelled to know the truth. She shook his arm off, but waited for his question.

"The American boy," he said. "That Cole boy—the one who *did* things." He hesitated, almost afraid to ask—almost afraid to know. "Everyone says he died, but he survived the breaking of the dam, yes?"

He thought he caught a glimmer of something in the young woman's face, but he couldn't be sure what it was. "Why, yes," she said. "I believe he did."

"And he is coming here?" the curator asked, but it wasn't really a question at all. He knew. He knew without her saying anything—and her silence was deeply intimidating.

Finally she said, "Stay and find out for yourself."

It was the most compelling invitation to leave he had ever heard. He stood there as her teams of workers flowed around him and in through the gates as if he were a stone in a fast-moving river. Once they had gone inside he was left with his staff who looked at him, wondering what to do.

"Go home," he told them, then he went to his old Citroen, and started it up, thankful that the engine was warm enough for him to drive off without lingering.

Perhaps he would visit his children's classrooms today. Perhaps he would take the family off on a winter holiday. But whatever he did, he knew that he would not be returning to the Facility anytime soon.

STILL TEN MILES OUT, a wedge of helicopters beat across the belly of the clouds.

Without Michael, the skies over Poland slipped back to their natural state, which was not all that different from the atmosphere Michael had imposed on them. The fog had lifted to become a colorless blanket that stretched from horizon to horizon, as if God had created the Earth, but had forgotten to create the heavens. Flurries of snow dusted the ground and all eyes looked to the blank sky that was blizzard-heavy and ready to burst.

Dillon and Winston maintained their silence in the lead helicopter with Tessic, who watched them as if they might leap out of the helicopter at any instant. He was, in fact, pondering the tally of days ahead, and portents the past few days held for the future.

The road to Treblinka had yielded only thirty-seven hundred souls over a two-day period. This time Tessic's curiosity had gotten the better of him, and he watched the making of the miracle. As Dillon had predicted, the road that had been broken down for his benefit mended the moment he arrived. Gravel became chunks of asphalt, chunks became slabs. The cracks zipped closed, and the worn texture of the road darkened, unseasoning into a black slurry as new as the day it was paved. Only then did the real work begin. Dillon had gotten down on all fours, slowly rocking back and forth, moaning, feeling the pain of the dead, resonating with it until the road began to break apart again—not in random chunks, but in a perfect pattern. An octagonal grid. The road kept dividing and dividing, until the fragments were no larger than grains of sand. Water trucks had already saturated the roadside and now the moisture seeped back into the black sand. Tessic had watched as Dillon sank into it about six inches. Still on all fours, grunting, bearing down, Dillon sent ripples of force out through the thick tar. He had called for Winston in a guttural voice, and Winston came up, kneeling as well, grabbing him around the waist. They looked like two wrestlers in starting position, and the moment they made contact, Tessic, who was only twenty feet away, felt a surge shoot through his body beginning at his feet, and exiting his eyes, ears, and mouth, like an electric current.

I'm feeling their life, he thought. *I'm feeling their souls called back into flesh.*

And all this time Dillon was sobbing, absorbing the pain and horror. Like a sponge he leached death from the earth, and with death gone, life had no choice but to replace it and find its form. The black quicksand turned deep maroon, growing brighter; bubbling. Then when distinct shapes that could only be bones began to appear, Tessic turned away.

Hour by hour, Dillon and Winston had inched their way forward through that road-turned-river, the revived peeling away in their wake into the arms of Tessic's retrieval crew. But it was different than at Majdanek. After four hours, Dillon and Winston got up and left. They demanded a bath. They demanded food. They demanded privacy. And then four hours later, they returned to continue their task. For two straight days it went on like this; they pulled six shifts at the road of death and although they revived fewer and fewer with each shift, they never reached a level of exhaustion they had at Majdanek. Then after the sixth shift, Dillon came to Tessic.

"We're done here," Dillon said.

Tessic shook his head. They had barely covered a mile of the road and what remained was a river of organic debris. Bones that had fused in misshapen unnatural ways in a red river as thick as a lava flow.

"No," Tessic told him, and quoted Frost. "We've miles to go before we sleep."

"Not today," Winston said. "Today *this* is the road not taken."

He could sense that they were holding back—that if they stayed, there was more life they could squeeze out of this place. Perhaps, thought Tessic, the drawing of life was like the pressing of olives. The first pressing yielded the purest of oils, but each pressing beyond it became harder and harder to accomplish. Still, if it could be done, why not do it? Why not double the effort and press the road for all the life it could deliver?

But Dillon refused, with no further explanation. It infuriated Tessic.

"Do you think you can just indiscriminately choose where, when and who to resurrect, on a whim?"

And Dillon had laughed aloud in his face. "This has all been on a whim," he had said. "But now it's *our* whim, instead of yours. And besides, isn't it your plan, to hopscotch from one site to another and back again, to keep the authorities confused?"

Tessic wanted to push it, but held his tongue. With Dillon as well, there was a point at which pressing yielded less and less. Dillon was there by his own grace, and by Dillon's grace, Tessic remained in charge. Tessic was a lion tamer now, in the ring with no protection. He was in charge, only because the lion allowed it. Tessic knew not to push, for the fangs could cut deep.

In the end, Tessic ordered bulldozers in to bury the undifferentiated remains beneath darker earth, gathered a minyan to recite the mourners' *kaddish*, and left. Now, in the helicopter, he stared across at Dillon and Winston, making sure his prize lions made no unexpected moves.

Dillon, on the other hand, had no interest in studying Tessic. He had to put all his attention into coming to terms with the new destination toward which their helicopter inexorably flew. Dillon had put the gruesome nature of the past few days out of his mind. He found dispensing with the past a powerful defense mechanism to keep him moving forward and not spiraling down into himself, as he had in the Majdanek memorial dome.

I will not dwell on whether this is right or wrong, he told himself. *I will not make that judgment. I will bide my time, performing these miracles, until the time is right to stop.*

He felt sure he'd know when that time would be. He'd feel the pattern of cessation in everything around him. He'd know when it was enough. And perhaps this is what Tessic was most worried about.

"We've heard nothing from Michael and Tory," Tessic told Dillon, which was no news to him.

Dillon didn't answer. Didn't even shrug. He waited to see where Tessic would go with this.

"Are they still alive?" Tessic asked

Dillon nodded. "Yes, they are."

"You'd tell me if they had died?"

"Yes," Dillon said honestly. "I would."

"Then why have they not returned?"

This time Winston answered him. "Maybe they've decided to go and resurrect the Minoan Civilization."

This piqued Tessic's interest, and Winston grimaced, realizing the information he had just leaked.

"Minoans," said Tessic. "Why would they be going to Crete?"

"No reason," said Winston, poorly covering. "I just hear the Aegean Sea is beautiful this time of year."

"Thank you, Winston," Tessic said, miming a tip of the hat. "Not only do I know where they are, but now, thanks to you, I know where they're going. I'll be sending a search and rescue mission by seaplane. A whole squadron if necessary."

"I wouldn't," Dillon said. "Lourdes can pull them out of the sky."

"So I've been hearing."

"If they are meant to be back—they will be back," Dillon told him. "What's fated is fated. *Bashert*, isn't that what you call it?"

But Tessic's smile was forced.

"Your faith has given way to your ego, Elon," Dillon told him.

To which Tessic answered, "Faith only goes so far."

Their helicopter turned, and Dillon gripped his gut, feeling their destination before he could see it. When he looked out of the window, he could see down below, among the low, barren hills, two huge square patches, about two miles apart. The work camp of Auschwitz and, looming behind it like a tidal wave, the massive death camp called Birkenau. He could hear Winston hyperventilating—he could feel the presence of death, too; even from a distance it was exponentially worse than Majdanek or the road of the dead.

"So cold," Winston said. "So cold."

Dillon tried to speak to him, to calm him down, but found he had no wind in his lungs. It was as if the atmosphere had been sucked away from the planet, leaving beneath them this barren moonscape of gray rubble. Death was already screaming out to them and they were still miles away.

"We won't be able to control this," Winston hissed. "Once we're there, once it begins, it's going to swallow us like the millions it swallowed before."

From here they could see that the road leading there, and the visitor's parking lot, were clogged with buses. Since many of the bus drivers had deserted after that first day, a fair number of the drivers were now men and women raised from

Majdanek. Tessic took pride in the poetic justice, for just as these masses were forced to assist their own extermination, now they were given the chance to assist in their resurrection.

They set down in a clearing beside the Auschwitz guard tower, the downdraft of the helicopter blasting away the snow, which scattered like ghosts from a grave. When the other copters had landed, Tessic opened the door to let in the bitter cold. But it wasn't only the cold that came in. There was a presence, almost sentient, that peered in through the open door. *When you look into an abyss*, thought Dillon, *the abyss looks into you.* It was the eye of old murder.

"Dillon," Winston said in a panicked whisper. "I'm scared. I'm so scared."

"So am I," he admitted.

"Why don't we just leave? Why don't we just—"

"Shhh," Dillon said. "It's going to be all right."

"But you don't know that, do you? You don't *know* anything, do you?"

Dillon closed his eyes. Even that vile sense of the vectors was gone here, obliterated by the static field of earthly evil that now enveloped them.

"Why are we here?" Winston whined.

Why are we here? thought Dillon. The easy answer would have been to blame Tessic—but Dillon could have delayed this visit. He could have detoured them to any number of sites, but he hadn't, because deep down he *wanted* to come here. Could Tessic be right? Could they have been meant for this? Was this his own intuition telling him so?

"We have to face Birkenau," Dillon told Winston. "We have to face it."

"Why?"

"I don't know yet."

• • •

Tessic walked them through the oppressive Auschwitz gate—the wide brick arch through which a thousand trains of the condemned had once passed. Tessic pointed to red posts marking the ground. "We've used sonic imagery to locate the"—he broke off, his mind tripping over the thought—"to locate the spots most likely to yield new life. Begin wherever you wish."

But Dillon did not need sonic imagery to know where the dead were. He could feel them, and they were everywhere. He could read their history in every inch of ground he crossed. There had been so many ashes, so many bones, there had been no way for the Nazis to dispose of it all. It was spread into creeks until the creeks choked. It filled ponds until the ponds were dry gray sores on the face of the countryside. And toward the end, the Nazis didn't even try to conceal it. Within the camp and in the surrounding countryside were unnatural ash mounds that in the summer would sprout with weeds and wildflowers, but now in winter were as bald as granite, revealing their true nature.

They were led by Tessic and his entourage through the double fence, and into Auschwitz. Maddy was there supervising teams of workers that waited to assist. Dillon thought to say something to her, but changed his mind. What was there to say now? She had, in a strange way, fulfilled her military destiny, becoming a key cog in Tessic's machine. He felt an intense pang of regret as he caught her gaze, but it was quickly taken under the cold waves of death rolling in all around him.

"Begin wherever you wish," Tessic repeated.

Dillon turned from Maddy, and picked up his pace rather than slowing down. He could sense the dead already beginning to gather around him—but not like in the other places he had been. Here, it was unfocused—diluted. A million souls, each grasping a tiny, tiny fraction of his power all at once. Not one had yet been revived, and already he felt drained.

This place will swallow us.

He felt himself a single grain of salt dissolving in a sea. So he didn't slow his pace, for fear that he would dissolve entirely.

The rear gate of Auschwitz opened to a road that led to Birkenau, three kilometers distant, its guard towers clearly visible through the flurries of snow. To the right, in the open fields, were storehouses of stolen memory. "The Fields of Plenty," the Nazis had called them. Each structure was still filled to the brim with eyeglasses, photographs, shoes, watches. Anything and everything that could be stolen from the victims, down to the hair on their heads, shaved and awaiting shipment to German textile mills.

They made their way down the snow-dusted path. One kilometer. Two. With each step, the overwhelming presence of Birkenau grew stronger, making his knees feel weak with burden. There was a veil of darkness surrounding Birkenau that went beyond a mere absence of light. Dillon could feel this palpable pall of oppression—he could see it when he closed his eyes, darker than pitch; a pigment of black that could not be manufactured anywhere else on earth. Birkenau Black. It robbed the color from the countryside, washing everything in shades of gray.

"Like hell I'm going in there," Winston said, but they both knew that he would walk through the gaping maw of the guardhouse arch right beside Dillon. A wind blew against them now, through the arch, and it was hard for Dillon to shake the feeling that the place was breathing.

Places had personalities. Dark deeds and cruel intents lingered, soaking into the porous soil, leaching into the rocks, until the place became permeated with it. This, Dillon knew, was the most evil place on Earth, where even the blades of grass that grew in the spring had an unnameable malevolence about them. This place was indeed alive, not with any kind of life Dillon understood, but with a living shadow. Darkness that consumed light. A place not full of the souls that had died, but filled with the shadows cast when they were murdered.

The living void.

And as he neared that horrible guardhouse gate, Dillon finally knew. He understood why he and Winston had to come here. This was a place as close to the living void of the vectors' world as there could be on Earth.

If they could face this then maybe—just maybe—they could face the vectors! But what did facing Birkenau mean? Did they have to complete the task Tessic set before them? They would not be able to—it was too great. They would truly be swallowed if they tried. It had to be something else they needed to do here.

The gates of Birkenau were swung open before them to reveal the ruins beyond. As he stood there beneath the entry arch, Dillon could feel himself pulling together the molecules, the atoms that once made up those who had died here. They were beginning to resonate with the powerful call of his own soul as if his body were an instrument—Gabriel's trumpet— the horn of the ram blown long and loud, awakening the dead.

He clenched his teeth as he and Winston stepped through the gate, twenty yards in, and no one followed. No one would cross that border into that horrible place now. Dillon closed his eyes, feeling the weight of death encroaching on his soul, and the ground around them began to change; the broken concrete healing, the crumbling bricks of the massive crematoria pull- ing themselves back into place. This place of horror would rise again. Its gas chambers and ovens would renew before the dead could be brought back—and the thought of restoring Birkenau made him so sick to his stomach that he leaned over, gripping his gut. He strained to rein in his power so that he didn't lose everything that he was to this field of death. He felt he would shatter like a vessel in a vacuum, his soul exploding like a supernova once more, leaving only smithereens spreading out across these fields, giving the tiniest hint of life to these million souls; their bodies never brought back from dust, their spirits held intact only long enough to be faintly aware of their own existence before fading. This time Dillon and Winston would fade with them, both lost in the blackness of Birkenau. If he let his power go. With his eyes still closed he heard a desperate whisper from Winston, who had doubled over on the ground.

"Syntaxis," he whispered. "Please, Dillon, please. Take my hand. Join with me." Anything so he didn't have to face this bitter place alone.

"No," Dillon said. Even as he lost control of his body, feeling his bladder release, saturating his pants, running down his leg. Even then he refused to touch Winston. For he knew if he did, there would be no containing themselves. They truly would shatter.

"Contain yourself, Winston," he said. For to give in to the need this place had for their life energy would surely mean death, and their only defense was to hold their power back, within themselves—something they had never been able to do—but before now their lives had not depended on it.

"Syntaxis will kill us—we have to face this place alone," he told Winston. If they could contain themselves, they'd survive this place—and if they did, it would prime them to face those black creatures that would soon come spilling through the dying void. Dillon had to believe that.

Tessic was right about one thing—this foray into death *would* make them stronger, but it wasn't their strength of resurrection that needed to be tempered and reinforced. It was their fortitude in facing the darkness.

They both held on. They held on until they knew they had the strength to hold on as long as they had to. To hold on forever.

Something deep within Dillon changed, and for the first time, Dillon miraculously felt his field pulling back! Finally, after all these years his powers obeyed his will, drawing into his flesh, instead of radiating outward!

Winston curled into the fetal position, and Dillon stood there, arms by his side, fists clenched. He held within him now the wellspring of his luminous soul, and the sensation was different from anything he had ever felt—as if his senses and emotions were charged to a new high, and he could at last sense the boundary between himself and the world. He still felt the horror of this place, but now he was aware of something bright beyond the darkness, something eternal, that fueled in him a compassion for those who died here as immense as his power. But rather than stir them with the depth of his compassion, he would hold it.

When he opened his eyes he saw that the buildings had ceased their renewal. Nothing had renewed to the point of making a difference in the bleakness of the death camp, but the difference was in him. Something wonderful would be taken from this horrible place, and he marveled that the souls he had intended to bestow the gift of life upon had given him a gift instead. They had given him the ability to contain himself, and a knowledge that there was something beyond the dark places.

It took Winston a few moments longer, then the look of

pain and fear dissolved from his face as well. He took a few deep breaths and struggled to stand. He, too, had triumphed. Mind over matter. Will over wonder. He, like Dillon, was finally contained.

"Are we there yet?" Winston asked.

Dillon nodded. "I think we are."

THE AIR OF THIS place was getting to Tessic as it had every time he made a pilgrimage here to mourn for his people, and for his family that could have been. Today the hope, the fear, the expectation and the desperation roiled in him, churning up unexplored places within his mind. Had he been Michael, he thought, his storm would rage all over Europe.

Tessic waited outside the gate with growing dread. Then, not five minutes after walking in, Dillon and Winston came back, and they brought no one out with them. The look on Dillon's and Winston's faces was unreadable and something felt different about them, too. It took a few moments before Tessic knew what it was.

It's that my hair isn't growing, Tessic thought. *It's that my bones are once again subject to the slow decay of age. Dillon and Winston have shut down their own powers.* Tessic found this more frightening, more distressing, than anything he had seen or felt before.

"What do you think you're doing?"

"We're leaving now," Dillon told him.

Tessic found himself stammering as he had several days before when his lion first defied the whip.

"You will go in there," Tessic demanded. "You will wake them."

"They're not asleep," Dillon reminded him. "They're dead. They've been dead a very long time."

"Why should that matter to you? To you death means nothing!"

Dillon's calm stood in harsh relief against Tessic's growing agitation. "I won't invalidate their suffering. Let them rest."

Tessic grabbed him by the shirt, practically lifting him off the ground. *He's just a boy*, Tessic thought. *A scrawny child, stupidly naive.* "Do you think they *want* to rest here in this place?" Tessic screamed. "Is there justice in that?"

And then Winston spoke, his voice as calm as Dillon's. "The evidence of injustice is sometimes as important as justice."

Tessic let Dillon go, pushing him away. "Rhetorical garbage," he sneered. "You two will be the criminals if you leave this place untouched. Hitler's accomplices." Tessic wanted to hit them, hurt them, to smash into their brains the importance of this. The *necessity* of it. How could they question the validity of his cause—of his *calling*, and of their own place in this glorious undertaking? How could they do this to him?

"I will lock you in your chair," Tessic yelled, a froth of spittle building in the corner of his mouth. "I will lock you in your chair and force you."

"No you won't," said Dillon with such unexpected empathy in his voice, it derailed Tessic, sending his thoughts flying for cover from his own anger. He stomped the ground like a child, he threw his hands up. He screamed to the colorless sky. Tessic's entire life had been for this moment. Building up to it only to have the prize torn from him just inches from his grasp.

And then Dillon reached out and put his hand on Tessic's shoulder, speaking again in that tone of understanding so deep, Dillon's voice could have been the voice of God himself. "Listen to me, Elon: it was never your responsibility to bring back the lost. You truly were meant to be a maker of weapons;

defensive weapons, that would protect. Today you've made your great work in me, and in Winston. We were never meant to be tools for the undoing of this Holocaust," Dillon told him. "We're weapons to defend the world against a coming one." And then he leaned forward and whispered gently to Tessic, like a kiss upon the ear.

"Their weight is off your shoulders."

Those were the words that healed him. He had always known of Dillon's power to do this. To find the key to someone with simple, whispered words. But knowing and experiencing it were two different thing. Tessic felt his completion come to him like the final number of a combination turning into place. It was as if the shell of his own restraining chair had popped open, leaving him in a naked state of release. He felt a weightless joy that stood out in such stark contrast to the bleakness of Birkenau. And he cried. He cried for the joy that came with the completion that Dillon had given him and he cried with sorrow for every life here that would neither be avenged nor restored.

"Go," he told them without looking up at them. "Take anything you need. Do whatever it was you are meant to do. Just go."

And then he turned from them, looking out over the ruins before him. *"Yitgadal v'yitkadach sh' mei raba."* Alone he recited the mourners' *kaddish*, for all those here, and the millions of others whose bones and ashes were spread across the fields of Europe. The millions whose lives were sacrificed so the world could know the meaning of injustice.

MADDY HAD KNOWN EVEN before Tessic did that their little endeavor ended here. She had been within Dillon's field enough to know the instant his influence ceased. She had feared, at first, that he had died. But then he came out of that gate with Winston, wearing that beatific grin—an expression both leaden and weightless. Moses descending Sinai. One look at his face, and she understood. Whatever he was on this earth to do, whatever his so-called "purpose," he had finally been primed. His will had triumphed over his power, and he had finally reined himself in. She found herself unexpectedly angered, but not for the same reason Tessic was. Maddy had always known that Dillon had a spark of something divine— but to see that spark kindle and her not be caught up in the flame—to be just another outsider like the rest of Tessic's revival crew—it was too much to bear. The only thing that kept her from running AWOL right there was Tessic. Damn Tessic, crying at the gate of the camp after Dillon had denied him his final victory. Someone had to tend to the man.

Maddy had prepared Dillon's way at Majdanek, then here, going before him like John the Baptist, preparing the way for the lord. In doing so, it connected her again, making her more a fulcrum than a gear in Tessic's grand machine of revival. It was heady and glorious . . . but in the end it wasn't meant to be.

As she watched Dillon walk away from Tessic, away from her, she suppressed her own emotions, and filled her mind with the reality that it was over. It was all over.

I will not be a victim of this.

She had to find the opportunity here.

My life will not rise and fall with the coming and going of Dillon Cole.

Tessic would need someone to clean up this mess. He would need someone to dismantle his machine and assess losses. She had to look out for herself now. Her strength had always been in crisis control. Intuitive improvisation in dire circumstance. Her only future now would be in Tessic's organization, and if she succeeded in damage control and got Tessic out of this mess unscathed, surely she'd be set for life. Dillon be damned—she was tired of the big picture. Life larger than life left her depleted. It was time to enjoy the simple pleasures of being small, selfish, and petty. Yet imagining herself as Tessic's right hand in the world of arms manufacture only added to the chill of this horrible place.

They all followed in Dillon's and Winston's wake back through Auschwitz I, to the parking lot, and the waiting gauntlet of helicopters. Dillon and Winston went to one of the helicopters—not the lead one that had brought them here—that was for Tessic's personal use. Instead they approached one of the support helicopters, but Ari, Tessic's personal pilot, began beckoning them back to the lead copter like a sideshow barker.

"Come," she heard him say, over the confusion that now rose in Tessic's ranks. "Come, I take you where you want to go. Come."

There was something markedly off about his overtures. Before this moment it seemed all Ari had wanted to do was fly Tessic around and get into Maddy's pants. Hearing him now—*feeling* the way he pulled Dillon's attention—filled her with an unsettling vertigo. It was the sensation strong enough to send her to intercept.

She reached Ari before Dillon and Winston did.

"You're *Tessic's* pilot," she reminded. "You need to get him out of here. Don't go volunteering your services without his permission." Then he smiled at her—a grin that crossed well over the line from mischievous to lascivious. If the time were different she might have put him in the hospital for such a demeaning, objectifying look.

Dillon called from somewhere behind her, and she didn't

turn to look. "One of the other pilots will do fine," he told Ari. "You take care of Tessic."

Again that grin from Ari. He didn't meet Dillon's eyes—he appeared to turn his face away intentionally. Instead he kept his gaze fixed on Maddy. "I fly you then," he said. "Fly you to the moon, like the song. This I will enjoy."

"Get in there, start it up, and wait for Tessic," she told him, disgusted.

He broke his discomfiting gaze. "Of course," he said. "I was only trying to do the good thing." He sauntered off toward his helicopter calmly, as if they weren't standing at the mouth of Auschwitz in the middle of three hundred empty, idling buses.

When she turned, she bumped into Dillon, who had decided to offer her a single shining moment of his time before disappearing into the blue.

"What will you do now?" he asked.

"Same as you," she answered. "We'll all get the hell out of here. You don't linger at a failed mission."

"And then?"

"Sorry, that's as far into the future as I'm willing to think right now."

Dillon glanced back at a helicopter where Winston was already giving instructions to another pilot. Tessic had arrived and was nodding his approval. With Tessic's carte blanche, the two of them really could have hitched a rocket to the moon if they wanted. But apparently they had another destination in mind.

"Winston and I have a date in Greece," he told her.

Greece, she thought. *Do I want to know what this is about?* She decided that she didn't.

"For someone who's supposed to bring order, you left a hell of a mess."

He kissed her. It was tender, it was sincere, and she hated him for it, because they both knew it was a kiss good-bye. She was now a part of his past, and there was no chair she could lock him in to change that.

"Go," she said. "I'll clean up."

"I'm sorry," he said. She didn't know which of the hundred things both large and small he was sorry for, but it didn't matter. He was what he was. As Drew had said, he was a star. Stars burn, stars blind. Stars trap lesser bodies in perpetual orbit. This was the way with Dillon. Space curved around his luminescence, keeping him forever at the center of her longings, and still a million miles away.

She watched as his helicopter ascended and the sound of its beating blades dissolved into the wind.

When she turned, she saw Ari still lingering, watching her. Tessic was already in the helicopter, but Ari didn't seem to care. He took his time in the turmoil building around him, smoking a cigarette.

"Do your job!" she told him. "Get Tessic out of here."

He flicked his cigarette to the ground, tossing her another unseemly grin, then got in the helicopter.

There's something wrong about him, she thought in the back of her mind, but brushed the thought aside. After all, everything here was wrong, twisted, and schizophrenic. Isn't that what was happening to the world? Minds and emotions were disconnecting everywhere—why should Tessic's pilot be different?

Much later, she would regret that she hadn't taken this bit of intuition more seriously.

Part IV

The Shattered Sky

34. THE SHELL OF ATLANTIS

NINETY NAUTICAL MILES DUE NORTH OF CRETE, THE ISLAND of Santorini fought a losing battle to return to its traditional name of Thira. The crescent form of the island and its huge circular bay came by no ordinary means. Had the Minoans survived to tell it, there might be more records of the rumored isle where wondrous things occurred—where the god Zeus and his compatriots spent their summer through the harvest, because its beauty rivaled Mount Olympus. Had the Minoans survived they might have told of the day the earth ripped open and tore the heart of Thira from the world along with the gods themselves. They *might* have told, but so great was the cataclysm on Thira, that a wall of water a thousand feet high washed halfway across Crete, killing every last Minoan and leaving little more than broken pots, tumbled walls, and the legend that was stretched and chewed like a piece of gum until truth, rumor, and miscommunication molded it into a legend now called "Atlantis."

Of course modern science knows that the volcanic mountain that once stood where Thira's bay is, blew stratosphere-high in an explosive eruption; a somewhat rare thing, but not so rare when you take into account the grand sweep of time. One might think the evidence of this explosion would litter the floor of the Aegean Sea; massive chunks of volcanic rock blown from Thira. But no such mountain fragments exist. Perhaps because the center of Thira didn't blow up. It was surgically removed from the world. It had plunged through a tear in the foundation of the universe, and now had the distinction of being the only mountain on the endless red plain of that lonely place that existed between the walls of worlds.

There was a palace on that displaced mountain, and in that palace were the dusty remains of twelve star-shards born to the Greek isles three thousand years ago, who had grown too arrogant to be allowed to live. And also in that castle rested another star-shard, her remains not quite as well seasoned, but her untimely death just as unpleasant. Her name was Deanna Chang, and her death, by the unwitting hand of her love, was a valiant one. For in her final days, the fear that had enveloped so much of her life had given way to a faith so overpowering, it had to be taken with her when she died. A faith that all things would run their proper course, and that time would balance the tide of unhappy circumstance to her brief life, and to the world.

OKOYA HAD NOT DEVOURED a single human soul, as he had promised.

He had instead suffered through hideous airplane food in a ridiculously cramped seat between fat businessmen, whose throats he would have slit on a better day. It disgusted him how in this absurd world of matter, the small-minded inhabitants were forced to burn the distilled remains of previous inhabitants just to power unshapely, cumbersome objects that carried them uncomfortably from point A to point B. Ridiculous. Had his own survival not been in question he would have thought nothing of someone obliterating this world with a well-placed comet.

His first flight ended in Amsterdam—as far as the money Drew gave him could get. He found, however, that a hermaphrodite could earn money in various ways in the back streets of the debauched city. By the end of the second night he had earned enough for first-class travel to Athens and then on to Thira. He found himself both satisfied and yet disappointed that he got there using human guile alone, and didn't have to kill anyone to do it.

Once there, he knew he need not do anything but wait. He was in the epicenter now; the focal point of all things to come. So he took himself a hotel room overlooking the stark white hillside buildings and sat out on a terrace, gazing out over the near-bottomless bay, and waited for the vectors and the shards to converge.

On December fifth, while Dillon and Winston faced Birkenau, a wave of influence swept slowly across the Greek Island of Crete. It began on the northwest shore, then penetrated deep into the hills and mountains, saturating the cities, towns, and farms. It was a call to action that refused to be ignored, and took all prisoners.

Believing in the autonomy of their own free will, people stepped from their homes and workplaces, all the while believing that it was their choice to do so. Cars, bicycles, and buses made their way north. Boats sped around the coast. Those who could not squeeze into a vehicle walked, greeting friends on the way, as if this dawn were any other moment in time. What a nice day for a walk; a run; a drive, they would say. Doors were left open and livestock left unattended as the population of Crete impelled toward the northern shore.

By the time rural dwellers reached the north shore town of Hania, they knew that their hearts and minds had been seized by something they could neither explain nor fight. Here, so close to the source, the force of the gravity that pulled them from their lives was so strong, they could feel it like a tone in their ears—a frequency oscillating just above their hearing, creating unbearable pressure deep in their limbic systems; a place that knew only instinct and impulse. On the rare occasion that a man, woman, or child was willful enough to buck the spirit that controlled them, they found that their arms and legs still obeyed the marching orders, their bodies following the silent tune of this pied piper that sucked them all from home and hearth.

Why are we here? they asked. Where are we going? And they laughed at the incomprehensibility of their own answers as they grabbed their loved ones so they were not lost in the raging mob moving toward the shore.

We're here for the ferry! Which ferry? Any ferry—and in Crete there were many to choose from. Come, one, come, all! Today all ferries are free, and when the ferries are packed to an inch of sinking, there are fishing boats and sailboats and barges. Today everyone is welcome.

They could not know that their bodies and their wills were under siege by one girl who had forced a powerful syntaxis upon her two comrades in chains. It was this link between the three of them that allowed her to create this moving wall of leverage, every bit as devastating as the tidal wave that had wiped out the Minoans. Although the skies above churned with resistance, it made no difference. Not even the heavens could escape.

When every last ferry, boat, and barge had set sail, thousands were still left on the shore. Those thousands now pushed eastward along the shoreline like a swarm of locusts, plundering every town in their path for anything that would float so they could join the growing fleet that swept east across the coastline.

By the time the call came to the city of Rethimno that evening, Hania was empty save for the stray dogs wandering in and out of abandoned restaurants. By midnight, when the call reached further east, to Heraklion, Rethimno was burning, with no one left to put out the fire. And by the next morning, when the odd armada was complete, it sailed due north across the Aegean from Heraklion, it contained more than half the population of Crete. Nearly three hundred thousand were jammed into every floating vessel the island had.

Bit by bit as the fleet sailed north, the impulse lifted from the land, leaving thousands left behind to mourn—not for the loss of so many sons and daughters of Crete, but for themselves, and the fact that they had been too crippled, too infirm, or just too slow to be a part of this great rapture that was surely headed for some kind of glory somewhere across the Aegean, at a place just off the horizon.

WINSTON WONDERED WHY HIS life suddenly seemed to revolve around airports—and each time he found himself in one, he couldn't help but notice how much worse things were. These terminals had become a yardstick for him to measure the state of the world.

Athens-Ben Epps Airport was in a state of complete disarray.

"Things will fall apart," Dillon had promised. Here, as in the airports in the United States, squatters had taken up residence in the hallways. The stench of urine permeated every corner of every gate. Travelers who still had enough sanity and sense of direction only kept it by turning a blind eye to the chaos around them, pretending that it was normal, or

460 • NEAL SHUSTERMAN

that it didn't exist. That it was somebody else's problem.

When they had landed, Winston had caught sight of a burned-out wreck of a plane abandoned on a taxiway. No one had bothered to remove it. The edge of the tarmac was crowded with derelict planes—so many it was almost impossible to maneuver. Airlines that had shut down; jets without enough fuel to go anywhere else. This great European hub had become an airplane graveyard. A flood of arrivals, but fewer and fewer departures. "The planes just keep coming in, but there's not enough jet fuel left to get them out," Dillon explained. "Airports in this part of the world are seeing more arrivals than they ever did, because of what's going to happen here."

"Because of what's going to happen here?" Winston asked. "How the hell does anyone know what's *going* to happen here?"

"Foreshocks," said Dillon. "Intuition. People feel their attention drawn to a place and they don't know why. Pretty soon people start to feel the need to come. To see the ruins, they'll think. To walk on the Acropolis, but that's just their mind trying to make sense of a feeling they can't understand."

The Athens airport, notorious for slipshod security, for some mystical reason had chosen this, the twilight of time, to detain all suspicious-looking persons. Of course, these days everybody was suspicious-looking so they had a wealth to choose from. On the morning of Tuesday, December sixth, they chose Winston and Dillon. Had Winston any sense of humor about it, he might have laughed. To think they had survived and triumphed over all they had, only to be harassed by yet another cast of rent-a-cops. The fact was, Athens Airport had become a hot spot of activity, intrigue, and violence over the past few months, and so, naturally, two teens arriving in a corporate jet was bound to catch someone's attention. Security collared them immediately, shunting them to a 10x10 windowless room with bad fluorescent lighting that flickered like a disco strobe.

The walls were peeling institutional green that clashed with the faded maroon linoleum floor that peeled up in the corners. Two guards stood by the door like fixtures, theoretically waiting for someone to come and interrogate Winston and Dillon. The one to the left had given Dillon a black eye, smashing Dillon as soon as they got here. He claimed that Dillon had resisted arrest, but the truth was he hit him because he was American.

Winston watched the floor for a few minutes, waiting for it to renew like everything always did in Dillon's presence. It took him a moment to realize that Dillon's field was so well contained that the room remained unchanged. Containing themselves was, Winston realized, like holding one's breath. Saving his own powers for a better purpose was both exhausting and invigorating at once, and just when he thought he couldn't hold it in anymore there always came that second wind, like a burst of adrenaline giving him the strength to pull back, suck in, and keep his own skin the boundary between himself and the world.

"You're so calm," Winston commented. "Like you expected this."

"I didn't expect it," he said, "but I understand the pattern. It doesn't surprise me, that's all."

"You have a plan for us getting out?"

"My plan is to watch and listen," Dillon said.

The two guards in the room with them didn't speak English. As Greek was one of Winston's many languages, he thought that by conversing with them in their native tongue it might make things go more smoothly. But a black kid who was an American, and flew in on a private jet of Israeli registry, became even more suspect when he started spouting perfect Greek.

Finally, the security chief who had been so good as to put them in this comfortable, well-appointed cubicle came back in, smoking a cigarette, which he held turned in, in a European way. He was gray with thinning hair. His lips were pursed in a perpetual smirk, earned through years of interrogation and professional disbelief.

"Don't worry," Dillon whispered to Winston. "Interrogation rooms are my specialty."

Their interrogator dispensed quickly with any niceties.

"So your plane is owned by Tessitech, as you said."

"Took you long enough to find out," Winston said.

Dillon said nothing.

"Your pilot tells us you were coming from Poland." His smirk broadened. "You must be rock stars on a world tour." Winston so wanted to punch that smirk away.

"We're meeting our parents here," Dillon said. "For a vacation."

"In a Tessitech jet?"

"My father," Dillon said patiently, "is Vice-President of International Relations for Tessitech." He nodded toward Winston. "And his mother heads the Greek office." Then Dillon imitated the man's smirk. "And they're going to make sure you lose your job." The security chief's expression took a turn toward sour. He pulled out the fake ID he had confiscated from Winston. "You should know better than to fly without a passport, Mr. Stone," he said, and turned to Dillon. "And you without any ID whatsoever."

"Listen," said Winston. "Our parents are waiting for us on

Thira. Let us go and we won't cause any trouble."

"Thira," said the officer. "A popular vacation spot these days. I'm glad to hear you call it by its traditional name. Most just call it Santorini."

"What is it you want?" Dillon asked.

And the officer dropped something on the table. "What I want," he said, "is for you to explain this." It was a plastic bag containing a sizable amount of white powder. Dillon saw it and snickered. Winston just let his jaw drop. "We found this in your jacket," the officer said to Winston. "The inside pocket."

"What kind of garbage is this?"

"The most severe kind," the officer said. His smirk narrowing into a frown. "Do you know what the penalty is for bringing drugs into this country?" he asked. "It starts with twenty years in prison and goes up from there."

And still Dillon snickered, but Winston was in no mood to laugh. "You planted that! What, did you see it in some old TV movie? What kind of morons are you?"

The officer snatched up the bag. "You two boys have yourself a problem. I suggest you think of how it might be resolved." And he left the room, closing the door, leaving with them the mute, Greek guards.

When the door had shut and the silent guards resumed their Green Giant positions, Winston turned to Dillon. "Any more of this and I'm going to start siding with the vectors," he said.

To which Dillon responded, "We'll call our parents; they'll bail us out."

Winston looked at him about as dumbfounded as he had been when the bag of white powder had been dropped on the table before them.

"Run that one past me again?"

This time, Dillon stepped on Winston's foot. Firm pressure on this toes—a signal—and spoke deliberately. "I said, our parents will bail us out."

Winston looked at the silent guards; they didn't appear to speak English, but that didn't matter, did it? The room could have been wired. Hell, there was probably a hidden camera. They were left there to stew and give information.

"Our parents," said Winston. "Yes, my mom will get us out of this. She'll get us out easy," and then he added, "I don't know which is worse though, a Greek prison or facing your dad."

Dillon laughed, a fake laugh, but real enough to anyone who might have been listening.

Winston laughed, too. "You *do* know what you're doing?"

Dillon nodded, but Winston noticed that he wasn't laughing anymore.

A few minutes later, their grand inquisitor came back in, conveniently porting a cell phone. "It's an American custom to grant you one phone call, is it not?" he asked. "I think we can do that for you."

"And what if we wanted to call the American Embassy?" Winston taunted.

"Very busy time of day there," he answered suavely. "Best if you made a call of a more personal nature."

Winston wondered if this corruption had always been here or whether this was nouveau sleaze brought on by these crumbling times. *Things will fall apart.*

Dillon took the phone and dialed something totally random. Then he turned and smiled at the big cop that had given him the black eye. Winston watched as Dillon released the tiniest faction of his immense power, which he had so successfully contained within himself since Birkenau. The puffiness around Dillon's eye shrank and the motling faded until it was gone completely, all the while he was smiling at the green giant who suddenly didn't seem so smug. Dillon then turned to the security chief.

"By the way," Dillon said, "see that guard over there?"

"He wouldn't have hit you if you didn't resist arrest," the inquisitor said, defensively.

"It's not what he did to *me* that I'm worried about," Dillon said, "it's what he's doing to *you*." And Dillon leaned forward to the inquisitor, cutting the distance between them in half—and although they were still about two feet apart Winston could swear that in some way Dillon was closer; pressed against his face, deeper still, into the man's brain.

"He's been with your wife when you've been working late," Dillon said casually.

His eyes were locked on Dillon's now. He couldn't move if he wanted to.

Dillon continued. "And you know what," he said, *"she does things with him that she would never do with you."*

The man's cheek twitched. A strange whine came from the back of his throat like the death cry of a small animal. When he broke Dillon's gaze Winston could see how the pupil of one eye had spread, voiding out the iris completely, and how the other pupil had collapsed to a pinpoint. All at once the light above stopped flickering and shone bright. The walls became a brighter green and the scuffed floor renewed. Then Dillon pulled his field back into himself once more, and he and Winston watched as the shattered security chief reached with a shaking hand for the gun beneath his jacket coat and turned to the green giant guard, who spoke no English and had no idea what was about to happen to him.

• • •

IN TWO MINUTES DILLON and Winston were hustling down the terminal building. The melee that had followed Dillon's surgical strike had left not one, but two guards dead and their grand inquisitor putting the barrel of the gun in his own mouth, pulling the trigger over and over and over again, refusing to believe that he hadn't left a single bullet for himself.

Winston had passed through the wake of Dillon's destructive power before—but had never witnessed it firsthand until now. It was as horrible as his power of creation was beautiful. Now Dillon had drawn in and contained his power once more, just as Winston had, but it didn't change what Dillon had unleashed in there.

"You enjoyed that, didn't you?" Winston asked after they disappeared into the milling mob of the failing airport.

"I did what was necessary."

"You still didn't answer my question."

"Yesterday I told Tessic that we were weapons," Dillon said. "I believe that's true. We were put here to save the human race with the violence of our power. No, I don't enjoy it, but I've come to accept it, and all that comes with it."

They reached a baggage claim so stuffed with luggage the carousel flatly refused to turn. People had crawled into some of the larger luggage and made them into nests, their faces turned into a stranger's clothes, their bodies curled up so tightly, as if they were trying to implode upon themselves. Things were falling apart at such an accelerated rate, there'd be no telling what this place—what any place—might be like tomorrow. Here before him minds were shattering before his eyes. Perhaps not with the detonating flash with which the security chief's mind had shattered, but the end result was the same. The spirit of man was losing its integrity in the face of a coming "infection." But was preventing that infection enough to justify what Dillon had done in there? Blowing out that man's mind?

"Some things can never be justified," Dillon told him, "but we have to do them anyway. In the past few years, I've managed to kill at least a thousand people—some of them intentionally. Does the fact that I brought back ten thousand stop me from being a mass murderer?" Dillon asked.

"Are you asking for forgiveness?"

"Not anymore. There was a time when all I wanted was to be forgiven, doing penance, longing for redemption. And then I wanted to be damned—because I was certain it was the only way to save the world. Now all I want is the one thing I can give everyone but myself."

"And that is?"

"Completion." He took a deep breath and let it out slowly. "Let's go to Thira, Winston. Let's kill who we have to kill, resurrect who we have to resurrect to get there, and make our stand against the vectors. And then, win or lose, we can finally rest."

THEY FOUND THE OWNER of an amphibian plane and although they had no money to speak of, they persuaded him to drop everything and fly them across the Aegean Sea. The only hazard Dillon and Winston could see was how clouded the man's eyes were with tears as he took off. It was a small plane, a four-seater. Just enough room for Dillon, Winston, the man and his wife. His wife was thoroughly confused—too confused, really, to question much of anything—and with good reason. Until about a half hour before takeoff she had been dead. Dead for about fifteen years. She still wore the dress she had been buried in; a teal gown the man had bought her for their tenth anniversary just weeks before she had died. He would have given his plane, his house, as many pounds of flesh as Dillon would have exacted, but all Dillon wanted was a ride.

Three hours later, Thira loomed in the distance, pushing up from the horizon's edge like Atlantis rising. Its jagged, striated cliffs, tinged in maroon and violet, gave the eerie impression of the Grand Canyon submerged. *So, I'm back in the Grand Canyon*, Dillon thought. Half a world away, but he was still waging the same battle—only this time he understood what he was expected to do. Perhaps not how to do it, but that, he had to believe, would come.

The sun hung low this late afternoon, beneath troubled clouds, turning the jagged burnt purple of old lava into red flames, as if the island reflected the sulfuric fires of Hades itself.

"Beauteous, no?" asked the pilot. Perhaps under other circumstances it would have been beautiful, but not today.

As they neared the island, the air became rough, and Dillon chose not to give them a capsule of order in which to fly. Letting the slightest bit of his power escape now would signal the vectors that he was here. And besides, the roughness of the flight was a healthy dose of reality in an existence that had turned so surreal. *Let me feel the reality of this place,* he thought, *Let me feel the harshness of what happened here before, and what is yet to come. Let it stir me into action; let it harden my resolve.*

The clouds directly above the island were high, and broiled with internal lightning. They bubbled and bled like a living thing, and the small amphibious plane pitched with the tempestuous wind.

Michael's wind, thought Dillon. He was somewhere nearby; this unsettled sky was his doing, and by the look of it, Michael wasn't doing well. What did a sky like this betray of Michael's feelings? Anger? Despondence?

"Soon," the pilot said. "Soon Thira. Down wet."

"He means we'll land in the water," Winston offered.

"I figured that one out, thanks."

The woman looked at them and smiled awkwardly, like a hostess with nothing to offer her guests, while up above them, the sky boiled.

As they approached the crescent-shaped island, Dillon could see that the center of this violent sky wasn't over the island—it was a few miles beyond it, to the south.

"Tell him to take us around the island to its south side," Dillon said. Winston translated, and the pilot turned to the right.

Beneath them now was the massive bay, almost closed into a circle by the curve of the land. Then without warning the plane took a violent, bolt-wrenching jolt. Anything loose in the cabin hit the ceiling, the woman cried out in Greek, and the plane dropped a few hundred feet before the pilot wrestled the plane under control.

"Air bad; boom boom," the pilot said. His best translation of turbulence. But that batch of turbulence had nothing to do with air conditions. Dillon had felt it even before the plane did. He felt it *within* him, not around him.

"Winston?"

"I felt it, too."

They will tear open an old scar, Okoya had said. Could this have been a vein of the scar they had passed through? A malformed thread of space that wove like a snake in and around Thira?

"Tell him to take us wide around the island," Dillon said, not wanting to experience another tendril of the ancient scar.

As they rounded the island, the ocean in the distance glowed white. At first it appeared to be a particularly violent patch of whitecaps, until they got close enough to see definition within the many specks filling this corner of the Aegean. These weren't waves, they were boats! Thousands of them, large and small, forging a wedge across the rough sea.

Forging a vector.

Dillon's teeth clenched at the thought.

This wedge of ships seemed endless. It stretched to the horizon. The pilot looked nervously to Winston and Dillon for an explanation.

"Lourdes?" asked Winston.

Dillon nodded.

"She can't be that powerful to control so many."

"She can, if she's in syntaxis with Michael and Tory."

Winston shuddered. "Then she's turned them."

"If she has, we've lost before we've started." But he knew Michael and Tory. They'd die before they were turned. So what was going on here?

"She's forcing them. That's why the sky is so rough—that's the reason for the winds. Michael's fighting it."

"And he's losing."

Dillon had the pilot turn around before she pulled them from the sky.

They headed back toward the bay, the pilot panicking as he tried to land on the surging waves. And although Dillon had the power to calm and order a strip of ocean for a smooth landing, he did not. He remained contained.

The plane survived the landing, and when they had taxied close enough to the shore, Dillon opened the door and hopped out. Dropping chest deep, he waded for shore with Winston close behind. The pilot shouted to them before he closed the door and powered for takeoff.

"What did he want?" Dillon asked.

"He wanted to know why we didn't just walk on water."

On a hill sloping up from the bay, they found a shack ineffectively guarded by two emaciated dogs that barked in perfect counterpoint. The grassy hillside around the shack was strewn with rusted objects. Bent bicycle wheels, washer tubs, a car engine on blocks—so many, in fact, that Dillon had to fight his natural urge to glint just the tiniest bit, repairing and restoring them all. The man who lived there was a tinker of sorts, salvaging parts from anything and everything, leaving the rest aesthetically abandoned in the tall grass. Winston bartered his watch for room and board for the night.

With the last rays of the settling sun, the first of Lourdes's fleet began to enter the bay. Dillon watched them from the tinker's window with uneasy vigilance. He was exhausted, and as he peered at the boats sailing into the bay, the watchful eye of the full moon gleaming off the water hypnotized him. He fell into a deep, anesthetic sleep.

35. GATE OF THE RISING MOON

THE THIRAN GATE STOOD AT THE HEAD OF A CLIFF, AT THE apex of the lagoon—a place where the crescent of the island stretched out on either side like a pair of arms engulfing the bay.

The gate was a simple rectangular stone arch, freestanding, thirty feet high, framing the sky. During the day, the gate stood like an empty picture frame, and at night, the gate was lit in dramatic green and red with spotlights strategically placed around the site. It was built thousands of years ago to frame the rising moon—and was originally meant to be just an entrance to a much larger structure—a temple of Apollo—but the temple itself was never built. Legend was that anyone who worked on it died of an unexplained malady; and thus the arch was believed to be cursed. Local tour guides still contended that tourists who stood beneath the arch for lengthy photo opportunities always came down with dysentery in the evening. For those who did dare to stand in the arch, even for a moment, they would never forget the eerie sensation it gave; a sense of disconnection—of muddled thought and disturbed equilibrium. Those who were particularly sensitive would even speak of a vision the place gave them; a knotty, gnarled tree with twisted branches spreading far into the sky, and roots worming deep into the earth.

As the tree image had deep significance to just about every deity that had inhabited the isle over the ages, the place had a long history of religious significance—most recently the Greek

Orthodox Church, which had added its own flourish to the sight, if only to dispel any pagan connection. The church had erected a small chapel nearby, and along the thousand steps that led from the gate down to the sea, they had constructed a dozen small shrines, each one dedicated to a different patron saint, of which there was no shortage in Greece. Religious significance had waned in recent years, except around holidays, but the tourist trade kept the offering tin full.

The novice priest who lived behind the chapel substituted for a night watchman, as it was less expensive, and frankly more effective. Local youth were far less likely to vandalize the gate with the prospect of a Man of God casting his eye, and an accusing finger, at them.

On this night, however, the gate's visitors were of a very different ilk.

At about nine in the evening, the young priest was disturbed by voices coming from the gate. When he went to investigate, he found a woman and a child exploring the structure. Tourists, no doubt. At night the splendor of the gate was to be observed from a distance, but tourists were drawn to its light like moths. He was always amazed by their audacity and tenacity, making pilgrimages to every spot in their Fodor's guide, regardless of weather or posted hours.

"We're closed until morning," he told them. "Please come back at nine."

The woman and the child stared at him with the blank expressions of foreigners, so he tried it again in German, and then in English. The third apparently worked.

"Please. It's late. Come back tomorrow."

"Forgive us our trespasses," the woman said. Then the boy smiled at him, but it didn't appear right. It wasn't the smile of youth, but of wizened, jaded age. Had he not been pondering that grin, he might have heard someone coming up behind him, but as it was, he didn't hear a thing—only felt the palm cup around his chin from behind, and then the snap of his own neck as a strong arm wrenched his head one hundred and eighty degrees around. His dying thought as he hit the ground was that the woman had something hideously wrong about her face.

They left him lying in the dirt, not caring to bother with his disposal. Memo turned to the man who had come out of the darkness to dispatch the priest. "We were worried that you wouldn't show up," he said, in Spanish.

"English, please," the man said. "This host does not speak Spanish."

Apparently his new host didn't speak English very well either, and spoke it with a strong accent that Memo did not recognize, for he too was limited by the memories and experience of his host body.

The woman stepped forward with a slinky gait. "Your new host," she offered, "is much more attractive than the old man."

"And yours is still as ugly."

She whipped her hair around indignantly. Memo felt deep within his host body a pang of human sorrow at the mention of the old man. *"Abuelo,"* the child mind said. *"I have killed Abuelo."* But he handily crushed the emotion. Such feelings were useful in manipulating Lourdes, but had no purpose now.

"I see that you failed," Memo said to the temporal vector.

"Not entirely," he answered. "I have now—how do you call it—an insurance policy." He explained how his last few days had unfolded, and Memo listened, weighing what he heard, pondering all the contingencies.

"Less than we wanted," Memo concluded, "but it will do."

Then he looked to the gate. While his human eyes could not see the scar, his inhuman spirit could. The central vein of the scar ran directly through the gate like a jagged bolt of lightning piercing a window. Human eyes couldn't see it but they had sensed enough of it to build this frame around it. Here is where the vectors would tear open the hole to their own dying world; a hole so massive that it would allow passage of the entire complement of their species in a matter of seconds. Then, once they were through, they would inhabit the hosts that Lourdes had collected for them.

"You see," Memo said, looking out over a bay so packed with vessels there was no room to maneuver. "Lourdes did the job."

Then he turned to the temporal vector, noting the muscular physique of his new host-body. "Kill Michael and Tory, but first kill Lourdes," Memo ordered. "This new host of yours is stronger than the old man, so you will not need our help."

The temporal vector pulled the lips of his host into a sinister smile and said, "This I will enjoy."

LOURDES SET UP CAMP on the shore of the bay, at one of the few places where the cliffs receded far enough to allow for a rocky beach.

The clearing she created for herself was a perfect circle, and at its edge a ring of people stood at rigid attention, shoulder to shoulder. Pressed against them from behind was another row, and another, and another; twenty concentric rings that provided Lourdes with a dense protective layer of human flesh. Things had come full circle for Lourdes—once again she was surrounded by flesh, only now the flesh was no longer beneath her skin. They stood there, her private army, jaws locked, bodies and wills under siege. She did not see or acknowledge their faces. She didn't care. To her these were no longer people and they hadn't been for quite some time. They were cattle. Meat to herd and manipulate.

In the center of these protective layers, Lourdes had built a fire, and now stared across it at Michael and Tory, who lay unconscious, still bound by handcuffs. This journey—this gathering of meat—had exhausted the two of them more than Lourdes, for they had resisted every mile across the sea. But even against their wills, their power had added to her own, sweeping across Crete, pulling together the army she had promised the vectors. Such power she had wielded! Such intensity! She had thought that having such power would fill her in some fundamental way, but like the food she ate, it only left her with a deeper void, craving more and more.

So she stared at Michael and Tory, hating them for fulfilling each other. Lourdes might have been thrust into this world as a broken fragment of a star, intricately intertwined with them, but she was not part of them anymore. She was part of no one. She looked around at the circle of standing bodies. *This is my universe*, she thought. *A circle of flesh, with me at the center. There is nothing outside the circle.*

But the vectors lie.

Michael had reminded her of that. It's what they were; lies transmuted into spirit. But still, their words had cut Lourdes too deeply to heal. Out there was emptiness, held together by threads of hatred and hostility. The universe at large. She could feel that emptiness in her bones like a hollow where her marrow should be. Hopelessness. Futility.

There came a shifting of bodies to her right, and she turned to see someone pushing through her meat-barrier. A man forced his way into the clearing; then her infantry closed the gap, shoulder to shoulder once more.

Lourdes stood to face him. No one should have been able to get through.

"Who the hell are you?"

"Do you not recognize me?"

She looked him over. He was tall, with closely trimmed, dark hair. A moustache. Early thirties, fairly attractive, and well built. His accent was markedly Mediterranean—maybe even Arabic, she wasn't sure. No, she had never seen him before, nevertheless she knew who he was. It was there in his eyes.

"The Old Man."

"I'm much better dressed now." He held up his arms and showed off the muscular curves of the new human body he wore. "You like?"

"I've done what you and the others wanted. Now leave me alone."

He took a step closer. "I was wrong about you, Lourdes. Memo was the smart one." Lourdes noticed that he wore a coat, even though the dead air was a sultry, salty balm. He glanced at Michael and Tory who lay inert beyond the fire. "It was wise to use these two as you did—adding their power to yours. Your cleverness surprises us."

"Enough to regret the way you beat me?"

He took another step closer. "A vector moves forward always," he told her. "No grudges, no regrets." And then he reached his hand forward to her. "Come. We celebrate your success." With his other hand he casually reached into the shadows of his coat.

What happened next came in a single fluid motion, like a step from a ballet. Something dark and shiny slid out of his coat, gripped in his right hand. Eight other hands reached from behind, taking him down to the ground. A bullet pierced the eye of one of Lourdes's minions, and although he fell limp, there was another behind to wrench the gun from the vector's hand. In an instant the vector was under a tackle of Lourdes's puppets, and with a single thought she had them rip off his coat, revealing a second gun and a knife. Further exploration revealed another knife strapped to his leg. Lourdes stood over him while he struggled beneath the hands and bodies of her minions. "Is this how we celebrate my success?"

"You misunderstand!" he shouted. "Please! It was for them!" He pointed across the fire to Michael and Tory, still unconscious on the dark pebbles of the beach. "I come to kill them—not you!"

"Come on, say it like you mean it." By now all of his weapons had been stripped from him, along with his jacket and shirt. Each weapon was trained on him now by her minions, poised at his head, his chest, his throat. "I suppose if I kill you, you'll just slip into another host."

"Believe me. Your friends are the enemy—not you." He let out a pained little laugh. "What purpose is killing you for? None. No, we let you live, and you keep to help us."

Keep helping them? Would they have her do that? Was that the true definition of hell?

"You rule all people." The handsome vector tempted. "Control them. We want this from you."

"The Queen of Cattle."

He looked up at her quizzically. "I do not know this expression."

"Never mind." She took a step back, and loosened the hands that held him. He pulled free, but his weapons were gone, passed back through the crowd. He made no move to attack her, but she knew better than to turn her back.

"Your two friends—they must die—you know this. Let me do it now."

"I'll kill them," she said. "They deserve to be put out of their misery by one of their own kind."

He considered this and finally nodded acceptance. Then he looked her over, showing some amount of admiration. "This host has desire for you," he said, puffing out his chest. "Now we celebrate. Just you and me. This I will enjoy."

"Get out of here." With a wave of her hand her crowd advanced, engulfing him, pushing him back, layer by layer, tighter together so that he could not squeeze between them again. Once she was sure he had been pushed completely out, she went around the fire to Michael. Dear, sweet Michael, who had once told her he loved her. Who had stroked her cheek, and looked into her eyes when no one else would as she lay on a stone floor, too fat to move. It was that lie that had destroyed her, even before the vectors snared her on their line.

She knew what she had to do.

She found a smooth stone about the size of a skull, so heavy she needed two hands to lift it. Then she knelt beside Michael, and raised the stone above his head.

I'll do this quickly.

Michael's eyes fluttered open then closed.

Quickly before I change my mind.

And she brought the heavy stone down with all the force in her soul.

36. SUDDEN DEATH

It was deep into the night when Dillon awoke. The tinker was nowhere to be found, and as Dillon looked out over the bay, he could see the moon had transversed the entire sky. There were voices—many voices coming from the shore below. He tried to see through the window what the commotion was about, but saw only the dim shapes of the tinker's mechanical graveyard.

Winston had fallen asleep as well, having crawled up onto the floor displacing the dogs from their mat—which was a better spot than Dillon's, which was nothing but a wobbly chair and a window sill for his head. It was a far cry from Hearst Castle or the plush trappings of Elon Tessic. So now they were lying with dogs. Dillon couldn't decide whether there was something wrong with this, or if such humility was a good thing; something to dilute their own innate arrogance that had always gotten them into such trouble. He woke Winston, and they left.

Outside, the sound of voices was a dense, white noise of people murmuring their excitement and confusion.

"Looks like we've got ourselves a Greek chorus," Winston said.

The shoreline was packed, and for each one who made it to shore, there were hundreds still stranded on boats in the middle of the bay—so many boats you could hardly see the water.

"Do we really want to go down there?" Winston asked.

"I can't see as we've got a choice."

They descended the steep slope toward the crowded shore, unnoticed, unquestioned as they moved through the crowds. It was clear to Dillon what was happening here. "Lourdes let them go. . . ."

"She must have broken off syntaxis with Tory and Michael."

Dillon nodded. When she broke off, her field would have gotten smaller. These were the ones who now fell outside of her influence. It would make sense—she only needed an expanded field long enough to get them here. And now, with the bay clotted with vessels, no matter how free these people were, they had nowhere to go. They went from being Lourdes's captives, to captives of the island itself, and they'd all be here at dawn, when the vectors tore open the sky.

Of those who had reached the shore, some had climbed up the hillside, toward homes, or the lights of towns around the bay, but most just lingered on the shoreline, sharing with each other the experience of a journey they did not understand.

"The poor bastards—they think they're waiting for something wonderful. A second coming. The opening of heaven." Dillon could see the way they trembled with wonder and anticipation. *No!* Dillon wanted to shout. *Get out of this place! It's more horrible than death—more terrible than the flames of hell. You will see a glow of heaven, you will think it's something glorious—but they will devour you, for they are the only beings in creation that can kill an immortal soul.* He wanted to tell them this, but what good would it do? If they knew, where would they run?

"I feel Lourdes," Winston said.

Dillon pointed. "Somewhere across the bay." But there was another feeling as well; a dark, visceral stirring. Intuitively, his eyes turned toward the source; a square arch atop a nearby cliff, lit an eerie green and red against the dark sky.

"The vectors are up there," Winston said. "That's where it will begin."

"If the vectors are there, then they're not with Lourdes." Dillon scoured the shoreline until spotting a small powerboat, and made his way toward it.

"What have you got in mind?"

"I won't believe Lourdes has turned completely to their side."

"Believe it," Winston said. "Even before they got here, she had rotted all the way through. Remember, she threw me overboard."

"She's got Michael and Tory—we've got no choice but to face her."

"And if she kills you?"

"If it comes to that," said Dillon, "I'll kill her first." He tried to sound decisive, but still his voice quivered with the thought. They didn't have Deanna—if Lourdes was too far gone to be brought back—if he was forced to kill her to save himself, and to save Tory and Michael, what would happen then? Would four shards be able to hold back the sky?

"You go," Winston said. "I want to get a better look at that arch. Maybe get a closer feel of the vectors."

"If they catch you—"

"They won't."

"We need to stay together!"

"We need to know what we're up against!" Winston said. "The vectors have got to have a weakness—I know I'll be able to sense it."

Dillon knew better than to argue with Winston once his mind was made up. "I'll meet you back here in an hour," Dillon told him. "Be careful." Then he started the small motor boat, and took to the water, taking a long look at Winston before he left. Like every parting glance he gave these days, it was laden with finality, as if he might never see Winston again.

DILLON WOVE THE SMALL motorboat in and out of the logjam of vessels filling the bay. The sea was calm now, the air hung still. Dead air. It was more troubling than a windy sky, because it meant Michael's emotional affect was completely flat. *Has he contained himself?* No, that was too much to hope for. More than likely he had fallen into a deep sleep the way Dillon had, too exhausted to emote at all.

As he made his way between the overloaded crafts, the sounds of the crowds began to soften until all the voices came from behind him. He looked to the nearby vessels to see that they were just as crowded, but no one moved. People just stood, or sat poised, as if waiting their turn in a halted conversation. He knew he had crossed into Lourdes's field of control. Bit by bit he crossed to the far side of the bay, where a huge mob pressed inward—an atmosphere of flesh around a hidden singularity. He left the motorboat, and tried to force his way through, but the crowd was defiantly dense. In the end, he had to hurl himself upon their shoulders and stumble over them, until finally tumbling headfirst into the circle at the center. When he looked up, he saw Lourdes standing there, holding a rock in her fist, ready to throw it at him.

The anger in her eyes almost made him look away, but he didn't. She was surprised, even shocked, to see him, but in the end she regained her composure, and put the rock down.

"I thought you were the vector," she said.

He looked around him. A fire burned at the center, casting shifting shadows on the stone faces of her army.

"Why couldn't I sense you?" she asked. "Did you lose your powers?"

To answer her, he took a glance at the fire, and it began to burn blue, pulling in warmth, rather than releasing it; unburning. "You knew I had to crash this party."

"The vectors knew you'd come. I hear they have something very special planned for you. Where's Winston?"

"Parking the car." There were two figures on the other side of the fire, but Dillon couldn't see them clearly.

"Go on," Lourdes said, deep bitterness in her voice. "They're waiting for you."

Dillon rounded the fire to find Michael and Tory. They sat up, groggy and weak. Drained. On their hands were handcuffs, but the chains had been broken.

"The rocks here are soft," Lourdes said. "I almost couldn't break the chains."

He thought for a moment that Lourdes might have taken a turn for the better, but the icy expression on her face said otherwise.

"It's good to see you alive," Dillon said.

Michael slowly looked up. "Are we?"

Dillon turned to Lourdes again. He had played this moment over in his head a hundred times, so sure he would know the words that would snap her spirit into place, but now, standing before her, he had no idea what to say. For all her posturing and poisoned barbs, her actions here spoke louder than her words. She could have killed Michael and Tory, but had not. If that meant there was some hope veiled within her, Dillon had to find a way to access it. He had to plant a seed; a single thought that could take root and attack the battlements she had built around herself. He had once shattered a mighty dam with the tiniest of blows. Surely he could find a way to break through to Lourdes.

"It's not too late," was all he could offer her at first, and of course she laughed.

"It was too late the moment I was born," she told him. "That is, if you believe in fate, and I know you do."

"Do you remember," asked Dillon, "when we first met? I mean *really* met? It was right after you had killed your parasite. You were still fat, but losing pounds by the minute."

"What's your point?"

"I had just helped my parasite of destruction kill thousands of people. In the end, it tricked me into killing Deanna. I thought I'd die from the weight—that there was no redemption for me—but I was wrong. I made it back. So can you."

She was silent for a moment, mulling the memory.

"These creatures are going to destroy everything human," Dillon said. "You know that, don't you?"

"Name me one thing human worth preserving."

"That's not you speaking, Lourdes. You think they've turned you into some kind of demon, but it's not true. It's just another lie."

The frown on her mouth twisted. "I've killed people for pleasure—not because I was tormented by a parasite, but because I chose to. I've even helped the vectors devour souls."

"Did you let them feed you?"

Lourdes faltered. "What?"

"Did you let them feed you on souls?"

Lourdes turned away, and hurled another log on the fire. "What difference does that make?"

"You didn't, did you? Because you're not like them. You'll never be. You're still one of us, and we want you back."

Lourdes looked to Michael and Tory. "I think they can tell you how likely that is."

Michael shook his head. "It's no use."

"Then why did you set them free?"

Lourdes shrugged, as if it were nothing. "I'd rather see you all die fighting. More interesting that way."

"When the vectors find out you released them, they'll kill you."

"They need me to help herd and process the world's masses." But Dillon could hear doubt in her voice; doubt that they would truly need her and perhaps a deeper doubt of her own capacity to stomach such a terrible mission. Dillon focused his thoughts on this minute crack in her facade, searching for a seed to sow in that fine fault of doubt. He took a step closer. "Will you watch?" he asked. "When we make our stand, will you at least be a witness to what we tried to do?"

"It's SRO," she said, "But I plan to have a front-row seat." She waved her hand, and her circle parted to the left and right, revealing two miles of empty shoreline. This part of the bay, all the way to the arch on the cliff, was under her stringent control. No one was coming ashore without the captain's leave.

Michael and Tory struggled to their feet, helping each other up, gaining strength from each other as they touched. Lourdes watched them, disgusted. "Go before I change my mind and have you torn to pieces instead."

Dillon concentrated for just an instant more, and finally he found the words he needed to plant.

"I'm not surprised this is what you've become," he told her in a precise, matter-of-fact tone that bordered on pity. "You always were the weakest of us."

It appeared to have no effect; she was as recalcitrant as when Dillon arrived.

"Don't slam the door on your way out."

Dillon turned from her and left with Michael and Tory. The mob closed the gap once they were outside of Lourdes's little world.

Dawn was already hinting on the horizon. Dillon had told Winston an hour, but how long had it been? It had taken at least that long to cross the bay. He looked at the uneven shoreline. It would be slow going, but the powerboat would be even slower, winding through the crowded bay. "There's an arch on a hillside a few miles away. That's where we have to go, and we have to move."

"And what do we do when we get there?" Tory asked. "Look for this 'infection'?"

"I don't think we'll need to look for it," Dillon told her, "It'll be about as easy to miss as a hydrogen bomb."

A cold and unforgiving breeze began to blow, pulled by Michael's fear. Michael gripped his arms. "I can already feel the nuclear winter."

But Dillon was shivering even before he felt the wind.

WINSTON KEPT LOW AS he made his way through the shrubs around the stone arch. This close, he could feel the scar slicing through it, filling him with a discordant energy that felt like ants crawling through the hollow of his spine. Feeling the vectors so close did not give him a sense of their weaknesses—only their imperviousness.

Something lay in the dust a dozen yards away and with no sign of the vectors he stepped out into the open to take a closer look. It was a twisted body in the dust, left in complete disregard.

He turned to leave, but then a voice spoke out.

"Winston Pell." It was a child's voice, with a slight Latin accent. "Lourdes has told us so much about you."

He turned to see two figures step out of a doorway of a small church. He turned to run, but a third one stepped out from behind the arch.

"You give people back their lost arms and legs," the boy said. "For you, things grow; people grow in any way you want. But not today. You see, nothing grows in this rocky soil."

The largest of the three vectors rushed him, tackled him, and effortlessly wrenched him into a choke hold as if he had been trained to do just that. Although Winston couldn't see his face, there was a smell—a stringent and musky cologne. He knew that smell. Why did he know that smell? Then it struck him that this same aroma had been aboard Tessic's plane that had first brought him to Poland. It had been aboard the helicopter that spirited them to Majdanek and Auschwitz. How could that be?

The vector pushed Winston through the door of the church, and as Winston finally made the connection, he discovered that the sickly sweet aroma wasn't the only thing that had been dragged here from Poland. The vectors had brought a prisoner.

It had taken many deaths to transport the temporal vector to Poland. The first had been the Old Man. Once freed from that host body, the vector had leapt from the boat to the Italian mainland, where he covered as much distance as he could before inhabiting a woman, who slept while he devoured her soul. He quickly realized that traveling within a physical body would not grant him the speed he needed, but neither could he travel discorporate for more than a few miles at a time. His solution, he felt, was most inventive. He forced this new body to drown itself, and it freed him for another leap. He found his range to be about twenty miles as a discorporate spirit, before having to take another host, which he immediately forced to take its own life. In this way he hopscotched across Europe, leaving a trail of death behind him, until reaching northern

Poland just as Dillon and Winston stepped into Birkenau.

In the body of Ari, Tessic's pilot, he tried to lure them, but was obstructed by Maddy Haas—a woman who, by the memory of the pilot, wielded some power over Dillon Cole's heart.

Before he could bypass her, Dillon was already skyborne for Greece—but he had an alternate plan. He already knew what it would take to render Dillon impotent. He had a secret weapon—an insurance policy now. He brought it with him all the way from Poland. Beating her into submission had been some heavy task, as she was well-trained in defensive arts—but then so was his host's body. She was almost his match. Almost. And for Maddy Haas, almost was the difference between freedom and being bound and gagged in the pulpit of a small Thiran chapel.

Winston couldn't look Maddy in the eye—couldn't bear to see the woman who had meant so much to Dillon so brutally subdued. Her face was bruised and her mouth gagged, but her eyes were alert and more furious than frightened.

"What did you do to Tessic?" Winston asked the vectors.

"He served us no purpose," answered the ugly woman. Did that mean they killed him or left him alone? Winston wondered. They were just as likely to have done either.

The chapel was in a state of disrepair, windows broken, weeds growing between the earthen tiles. Ari brought Winston down the aisle and forced him down on the altar. The child just stood by and watched, but Winston could see in this child's eyes that there was nothing childlike about him. He thought back to the days when he was growing backward—when he had "the stunt" on him, as his mother had called it. Fifteen, but trapped in a body of a seven-year-old, growing younger day by day. Did he look like this child looked now?

Winston now noticed that the woman held a steel pole in her hand.

"These bodies—they feel so many interesting things," the boy said. "Pain is something we are just starting to explore."

The woman brought the pole down across the middle of Winston's spine. He felt the pain shoot out from his solar plexus to his brain like his soul exploding within him. He screamed.

"Why do humans scream?" the boy asked. "Doesn't it just make the pain worse?"

The boy told Ari to let him go. Winston wasn't going anywhere now. "Take the girl to a place where Dillon can see her," the boy said. "I want to play with Winston some more." And so the pilot left, dragging Maddy struggling through the door.

Once they were gone, the woman brought the pole down again on Winston's back, a bit higher, and twice as hard. Winston heard it whistle through the air before making contact, and this time he not only felt the fracturing of bone, but felt his spinal column sever like a sheared cable. In an instant he could feel nothing beneath his waist. She swung again, his shoulder blades taking the blow, but the next blow came at his neck. The pain exploded in his neck, but went no lower. Now he felt nothing below the neck, and he opened and closed his mouth like a fish gasping for air, unable to work his lungs.

The woman stopped and watched.

"Does it hurt real bad?" the boy asked—not out of malice but curiosity, which was worse. Then the boy giggled. "Most things on earth have no backbone—I learned that in school. Now neither do you."

They were silent for a moment, waiting.

Then Winston felt the pain come back along his spine, first to his shoulder, then to his mid back, then exploding again through the small of his back, to his legs and feet which he could feel once more. He lost containment—his power spread forth from his soul. The weeds between the tiles grew denser.

The boy pressed his finger against Winston's spine, prodding the broken vertebrae. "You can regrow your nerves, but you can't fix the bones," he said. "You need Dillon for that, *verdad*?"

Winston's answer was another wail. His own body was the enemy now, forcing him to feel every ounce of pain, long after any other nervous system would have been rendered useless. He had never longed for death before through all he had experienced, but now he cared about nothing but ending the pain.

"We can't leave him like this," the boy said.

The woman agreed. "Dillon could still repair him. Even if he dies, Dillon could bring him back."

The boy got closer to Winston, looking into his eyes. "Cut off his head, and take it with us," the boy said. "Dillon can't do a thing if we take *that* away." And then the boy bounded out, playtime over.

The woman produced a stubby dagger that would make the job slow and sloppy.

As he watched her approach, Winston wanted the pain to end, and if death was the only way to end it he would accept that—but he would not let himself die at their hands. And so, as the woman approached with the blade, Winston reached out and gathered his power, narrowing it and focusing it on a single greening crack between the floor tiles.

MADDY HAAS, BEATEN AND bruised but still full of fight, struggled against Ari all the way to the Thiran Gate—her struggles were enough to pull her legs free from the ropes but not her hands.

It was maddening to not know why she was taken or what this was all about—only to know that she was some key variable in whatever equation these creatures were working. The first thing she saw as he brought her to the gate was the stunning mass of boats in the bay, and the crowds on the shore that kept their distance. She felt a strange force in the air pressing on her, trying to usurp her will, force her to be still. Perhaps she might have caved into it had she not felt so amped up, and had the source of that power not been so distant. Below, three people crested the rocks of the next cove. Even in the dim dawn, she recognized them right away. It was Dillon, Michael, and Tory.

Ari ripped the tape off her mouth. "Call to him," he demanded, but Maddy would not help him in any way, and so in the end, it was Ari who called out.

"Dillon!"

Dillon looked up, then stopped dead in his tracks. She could only imagine what he felt when he saw her there.

"We saved her soul for breakfast," Ari yelled. "Shall I eat it now?"

She struggled, but his grip only grew tighter. *Did he say soul?*

"She's not a part of this!" Dillon screamed. "Let her go!"

"You come to me now. You come to me and I leave her soul where it is. We make good trade. We trade you, for her soul."

Dillon hesitated, but only for a moment. He bounded toward the base of the stairs. Tory grabbed for him, but he shook her off, and pushed Michael out of his way.

"That's right, you come to me now."

"No, Dillon!" Maddy shouted. Dillon was filled with rage, and it blinded him. He would lose this fight. Ari would kill him.

Ari then put his lips against her ear. "You the lucky one,"

he said, planting a kiss on her neck. "He dies, you keep your soul. For an hour at least. Not bad."

She would not accept this. All her life was not going to come down to her being a bargaining chip. She would not be the reason that Dillon failed—she could not allow it!

All at once an explosion of glass and stone shook the Earth. Maddy caught a glimpse of it. The small chapel behind them had buckled outward and its stained glass windows had exploded from the pressure of a green mass which had swelled from within. Spiny limbs and mustard-yellow flowers still spread from the ruined structure like the tentacles of an octopus. It drew Ari's attention and he loosened his grip. Not much, but it was all Maddy needed. She jerked herself free, swung her tied arms like a broadsword, and knocked him down against the stone of the arch. When he tried to get up, she kicked him in the chin, shattering his jaw, and took off down the steps.

"Maddy!" Dillon had reached the base of the stairs more than a hundred yards below, and began racing up—but not fast enough, because Ari was already rising to his feet behind her, beginning his pursuit.

She picked up the pace, but with her hands still tied she couldn't balance herself and went tumbling down the stairs hitting the steps as she passed the altars of the patron saints. When she got control of her fall and wrestled herself back to her feet, there was someone standing beside her. Not Dillon; not Ari; someone else. Someone who grabbed her and pulled her close to him. It was a face she had seen once before and had never wanted to see again. Long black hair; a face both masculine and feminine at once. Okoya.

"No!" Dillon screamed from below. "Stay the hell away from her."

But Okoya ignored him. Holding her tightly he looked into her eyes. "It is your choice," Okoya said to her.

She didn't know what he meant until she looked up the hill to see Ari bounding down toward her. Dillon was much farther away and there was no question that Ari would reach her first. What then? Dillon would sacrifice himself to save her soul. His own virtue would destroy him.

And then it all fell into place. There *was* something she could do. She could remove herself as a variable and stack the equation in Dillon's favor again.

"You could save him," Okoya said. "It is your choice."

He was right. With Okoya's help, she had the power to turn everything, and what an awesome power it was!

Would you give your life for your country? Bussard had once asked her. *Would you give your soul?*

For her country, perhaps not—not anymore. But for Dillon? For the world? There was only one answer; *without pause.*

"Do it!" she ordered Okoya, pressing herself into his embrace. "Do it now."

There was no time for second thoughts. She steeled herself as a red light shot from Okoya's eyes and nostrils. She didn't wait for him to find her soul, she opened up her soul for him, practically hurling her essence out of her body and into those hungry, groping tendrils. She felt her spirit leaving her flesh and for the briefest of instants felt Ari pulling her body away from Okoya, but it was too late, for she was free from her body—and there was joy, immense joy in the knowledge that she had bested him! That she had won! But in an instant her thoughts and memories were tugged from her as her soul discorporated and disconnected from her mind. She was a spirit without a name, without memory and she was moving down a dark path. She was being swallowed. And although there should have been terror as Okoya devoured her, she had none, because there was one thought she was able to take with her, that silenced all fear. It was an unvanquishable sense of victory. She held on to that victory as long as she could, content in that singular knowledge until her soul met eternity and perished.

DILLON SAW EVERYTHING.

He saw Okoya grab her. He saw him hold her close. He saw the tendrils of light vomited up from the pit of Okoya's being, and he felt her soul pulled from her body and disappear into Okoya. He felt her die, and there was nothing he could do about it. How could he have let this happen? How could he have not seen the vector lurking inside of Ari back in Poland? Now Ari grabbed Maddy's empty shell, pulling her away from Okoya.

"Try bargaining now," he heard Maddy say to Ari, but it wasn't Maddy speaking, not anymore. It was just her empty shell that spoke; her dead, soulless shell, still mimicking life.

Another vector was descending the stairs; a boy, but his gaze wasn't on Dillon, it was fixed on Okoya. There was so much hate in that gaze that Dillon now knew everything Okoya had told them was true. Okoya was hated by his own kind. He truly had sided with the shards to save himself. But there was no salvation for Okoya. Not now; not ever, for he had devoured Maddy and no pit in hell was deep enough for him now.

With tears of fury blinding him, Dillon grabbed Okoya and hurled him down the steps. He lost his balance, and together they rolled down toward the bay.

"*I'll kill you! You son of a bitch! I'll kill you!*" Dillon began pounding Okoya's head against the stone, not wanting to stop; never wanting to stop.

Dillon couldn't help himself. He so much wanted to be the destroyer again and in that moment he longed for the spirit of destruction to return to him, allowing him to feed its hunger, creating waves and waves of destruction as he had done two years ago, so he could share his despair with the world.

It was Maddy's shell that pushed him off of Okoya, having pulled her hands from the bonds. He looked up to see her. It. Maddy undead.

"Don't be a fool," It said. "Get out of here."

He looked up at it, but didn't see Maddy's face—all he could see was the vacancy of her eyes.

"I chose this," It said. "Now make it mean something."

Okoya grabbed Dillon's hand. "They're coming for you," Okoya said, and spirited him away down the shoreline, toward Michael and Tory, leaving Maddy's undead husk behind.

"I'll kill you!" Dillon told Okoya, but it lacked conviction.

"Later," Okoya told him.

They ran to the rocks where Michael and Tory were waiting, and scrambled over them, to the next cove.

"What happened back there?" Tory asked, and threw a harsh gaze at Okoya. "What's *he* doing here?"

Dillon didn't want to answer—didn't want to think about it. Okoya urged them on, and they kept moving down the shore, until they were sure the vectors no longer pursued.

"Now that the vectors know I'm here, we have very little time," Okoya told them. "My presence makes the threat far more serious to them."

"What about Winston?" Michael asked. "Something happened to him—you felt it, didn't you? We all must have felt it."

"It's possible that the vectors had him—but I think he's gotten away." Okoya pointed to Tory. "You go look for him."

Tory scowled. "I don't take orders from you."

"Go, Tory," Dillon told her. "Michael, you go, too—there's no telling where he'll be."

Tory opened her mouth, as if to say something, but thought better of it and left. Michael lingered a moment more, taking in Dillon's distraught expression.

"Don't choke in sudden death, man," Michael said, clapping him on the shoulder. "We're counting on you to hold things together."

When they had gone, Okoya turned to Dillon. "Once they find Winston, you must all summon up your strength. Time is short, and all five of you must be ready."

"Four," Dillon spat at him. "Lourdes won't help us."

And Okoya said, "I wasn't talking about Lourdes."

WINSTON CRAWLED OUT OF the ruin of the shattered chapel, forcing his way through the thorny trunks of the weed he had cultivated. The ugly woman screamed her fury behind him, hacking the stalks of the monster weed with the knife that had been meant for his decapitation. Although the pain in Winston's broken spine was more than enough to tear him from consciousness, he forced himself lucid, for this, he knew, would be the most pivotal moment of his life. Dragging himself across the road, his legs and arms barely working, he brought himself to the cliff. There were no stairs at this ledge; it was a sheer drop all the way down to the rocks below, but the woman was running behind him now, swinging the knife angrily at her side as she ran, cutting her own legs in her fury to get to Winston.

It was his mother's voice that came to him then. He had barely thought of her for weeks, but now she rose to the forefront of his mind and sang to him a gentle song of faith; the gospel that had always comforted her. It used to comfort him as well in his childhood, before he had become this strange and wondrous changeling.

"I hear you," he whispered. Whatever darkness these vectors brought with them, whatever portents of despair, he had to have faith. No matter how unlikely, no matter how foolish, he had to believe that something larger than himself, larger than the vectors, would cradle him and catch him when he fell. With the woman only a few feet away now, he forced his body over the edge and let gravity take over.

37. SCAR AND SPIRIT

Less than a quarter mile from the steps where Maddy's spirit had died, Dillon waited with Okoya for Michael and Tory to return.

The vectors had not followed them here. They had completely dispensed with Okoya and the shards. Dillon could see the boy, and the man who had once been Tessic's pilot, standing in the stone arch at the head of the cliff, staring out over the bay, ignoring him.

"If we're such a threat to the vectors, then why haven't they come after us?"

"Because *they* ran out of time," Okoya said. "They can't pursue you anymore; they must begin working the scar, and that means we've won our first battle. You've all survived their attempts to destroy you. Now you will get to face them."

On the ridge, the third vector took her place beside the other two framed in the arch, and the moment she did something happened. They began to push out waves of energy; pulses of light that danced across the sky filled with color like a shimmering aurora—beautiful, but Dillon understood its dark purpose. The vectors were working the scar, caressing it, slowly tearing it open.

As the waves of energy passed, Dillon felt them resonate within him. He felt his own powers begin a new surge, rising like adrenaline. An automatic reaction to the vector's pulses. He held containment, but only barely. If he let loose now, he felt his power would cover the entire Mediterranean, and beyond.

"You are enabled," Okoya said.

It left him breathless, and yet he knew, even with all that power he held inside, he was powerless to bring back Maddy. A devoured soul was gone—irretrievable even to him.

Dillon turned on Okoya sharply, his hands balled into fists. Tears of anger flooded his eyes. "When this is over—if we survive—I will shatter you," he said. "I will find a way to make you feel the pain she felt when you devoured her."

He expected Okoya to lash out and vehemently defend his indefensible act, but he didn't. Instead he extended his hand and said, "I have a gift for you, Dillon."

Dillon felt a slight change in air pressure around him and his ears popped. The light of dawn changed.

He had felt this before. He knew what it meant.

He spun on his heels to look out over the bay, but he did not see the bay. Instead he saw a jagged hole in space, only a meter wide. A portal to the Unworld.

But even as he saw it, he knew this portal came with a heavy price—for Dillon knew Okoya was using the energy he had gleaned from Maddy's soul to open the portal.

There were no red sands and icy skies beyond this hole; Okoya had chosen his point of entry with much greater precision. Through the hole, Dillon saw a place that had been burned into his memory, revisited a thousand times in his nightmares. A vast throne room of an ancient stone palace, the cathedral roof held up by what few pillars had not fallen.

And there in the center was a throne.

But the throne was facing the wrong way—Dillon could only see the back of the carved stone chair. Hanging over the side was a corner of blue fabric—the royal robe that had become her shroud. And the edge of a white shoe. Her shoe. Deanna's.

His mind reeling, his eyes shot back to Okoya. Okoya strained to hold the portal. A vein bulged on his forehead, his face turned a virulent shade of crimson.

"Can't hold it—" he said through gritted teeth.

Dillon made a move to step through the portal, but Okoya grabbed him, his nails digging into Dillon's shoulder.

"No time—" Okoya spat. *"Seconds left."*

Seconds? Even if he pushed his spirit out before him, and revived Deanna from here, she was too far away, even if she ran, she would not make it to the portal in time. This was just another gift from Okoya's bottomless bag of cruelties. He offered a pained glimpse of Deanna, without enough time to bring her back.

"Not her flesh!" Okoya hissed. *"Draw her. Draw her now!"*

And Dillon finally understood.

With the portal collapsing, Dillon pushed forth a single impulse through the breach. He called to her. With every ounce of his soul, he called to her, and his call became an imperative that no spirit could resist. His call bypassed the corporal part of her that lay motionless on the throne, and reached to the far corners of the Unworld, until finding her soul.

As the portal collapsed to a pinhole, he felt her coalescing— moving toward him. And in the last instant before the portal sealed, he felt her—he actually felt her pass through him, like a bullet, in through his chest and out through his spine! But to where?

The portal was gone now, and Dillon searched around him as if expecting to see her there, like a ghost—an apparition before his eyes, but she was nowhere to be found.

"Where is she?" Dillon demanded. "What happened to her?"

Okoya had fallen to his knees, exhausted from his effort, barely able to catch his breath.

"How can you be so luminous, and yet still be so dim?" Okoya took a deep breath, and then another. The crimson left his face. "A discorporate spirit," Okoya said, "seeks a dispirited body."

DEANNA IGNITED INTO CONSCIOUSNESS.

She shot through the void, seeking something to grab on to, a body to join with her spirit, but there was nothing to give her purchase. Finally a vacuum drew her in, at last connecting her spirit with flesh. Now, out of the darkness and into light, only one thought filled her mind. It was a name. Her name—such a powerful thought she had to speak it aloud—but the name she heard was not the name she expected. An instant of fear. Uncertainty. But the instant passed and now the name she spoke—the person she was— no longer seemed foreign, it seemed right, and she forgot altogether why it shouldn't feel right. She was Maddy Haas. Why on earth would she think she was anyone else?

SITTING ALONE ON A boulder by the shore, Maddy turned to see Dillon running toward her, but as he neared, he slowed his pace. She could feel his trepidation as if the feelings sprang from inside her, and not him. She felt strangely radiant.

"Deanna?" he said.

"Don't be stupid, it's Maddy."

"M-Maddy," Dillon stuttered. "But . . ."

She slid down the boulder and slowly came toward him, feeling so calm, so in control, as if she had all the time in the world. *No . . . more as if the world was in perfect time with me.*

"I'm . . . different," she said. "Have you done something to me again, Dillon?"

"Your soul," Dillon said. "Okoya devoured your soul."

She looked at her hands as if that might betray something about her current nature.

"I don't feel like an empty shell," she said. "In fact, I feel . . ." She didn't finish the sentence. She looked up at the sky that radiated the pulses of the vectors. She was feeling it, the way Dillon must have felt it—the way a shard would feel it, deep within her. She spun to him, filled with intense excitement. "I'm beyond myself," she said, as Dillon had once said to her. "I don't know where I end and the rest of the world begins. I feel the sky. I feel the depth of the ocean."

"What do you remember?"

Maddy tried to put her thoughts together. She closed her eyes. She remembered everything from the life of Maddy Haas. The way she rescued Dillon and captured him again. The work she had done for Tessic. She remembered her childhood, her sister, her parents; but she knew these weren't the memories Dillon was asking about, she pushed harder, and suddenly gasped at an unexpected, unconnected thought.

"I remember a snake. It had no eyes. It was wrapped around me."

"Go on."

But as quickly as the thought had come to her, it was gone, like a dream she could no longer remember. But it had lingered long enough for her to know. She turned to Dillon in amazement. "I was Deanna Chang."

Although Dillon laughed with joy, Maddy forced down her own emotion.

"But that doesn't matter. I'm Maddy Haas now."

"Yes," said Dillon. "You are."

Dillon reached out his right hand toward her. "No shard takes this hand but you."

Maddy looked at the hand, hesitating—almost afraid that all this wasn't real, but in the end she touched him. She held his hand. The syntaxis that flooded both of them was so powerful, so perfect, she almost lost herself in it. His eyes were locked on hers, and hers filled with tears. For Maddy this was an answer to a prayer. All the times they had touched, shared each other's thoughts, shared each other's bodies—it paled compared to this.

Some things you can never share. Tessic had told her. *You can never be what he needs. You can never be his true companion.* Tessic had been right—and yet he had also been wrong.

"I didn't know," she said, filled with the joy of being one with Dillon; of being a part of each other; two shards of the same star. "I didn't know. . . ." Yet at the same time she cried in mourning, knowing that the true soul of Maddy Haas had to die to make this possible. She was a tenant in someone else's mind, in someone else's body, and in that moment she vowed she would no longer seek the memories of Deanna Chang. Out of respect for Maddy's sacrifice she would live this life of Maddy Haas and cherish it.

Let the flesh of Deanna Chang be dust.

Let her memories disappear with her.

It was a fair payment for the life she now claimed as her own. She gently let go of Dillon's hand, their connection flickering away, but only for now.

"Tell me what you feel?" Dillon asked.

"Peace," she answered. She felt the earth in balance with the sky, life in balance with death. Without her, life had been out of balance for so long, hadn't it? As she reached her spirit out she could feel it touching hundreds of thousands of souls, leaving a calming sense of peace, an indominable sense of trust, and an absolute conquest of fear. Dillon had told her that Deanna's gift had been faith, but she never understood it until now. How could she? So much of her life—so much of everyone's lives—was built on fear. It was the guiding principle of survival. To call what she felt now faith was an understatement. It was beyond that. It was a feeling of absolute acceptance and understanding that had no word to describe it. She looked up to the sky to see the waves of force flowing out from the three vectors who still stood in the gate.

"Those three creatures," she asked. "What are they, and what are we supposed to do to stop them?"

EVEN BEFORE THE VECTORS took their place in the Thiran Gate, Tory put all of her attention into finding Winston. Winston's sudden burst of energy somewhere on top of that cliff had taken Tory completely by surprise—because until that moment she hadn't even felt his presence there at all. Now as she searched for him, she realized how that could be. "Containment," Dillon had called it. An ability to cloak oneself from detection, and reserve one's energy until it was needed. It was a skill she would have liked to have learned, but there would be no time for lessons today.

The growth spurt Winston had incited had quickly tapered, fading even before they left Dillon to find him, and although she could now feel Winston's uncontained presence, it was faint—dangerously faint. Tory had thought she had seen a shadow drop through the corner of her vision, but she wasn't certain until she climbed an outcrop of rocks, and saw him wedged deep in a crevasse.

"Winston!" She tried to ease her way down into the crevasse, but lost her footing and slid to the narrowest point, where Winston was wedged. His body was mangled in an unnatural serpentine twist, and through his torn shirt, she could see terrible ridges poking from his back like a stegosaurus spine. His eyes were open, but only barely. A weak moan escaped him—the only hint that he was still conscious.

"Hurts . . ." he murmured.

"We've got to get you out of here," but there was no way she could see to do it.

"My Mama . . ." he said. "Damned if I don't hear my Mama's singing, you hear her?" He grinned faintly in his delirium.

"Yes, Winston," she said, doing everything she could to placate him, "I hear her."

"That witchy woman up there's got to be even uglier than you." Then his eyes opened from slits to half mast, and he looked at her. "Hey, swamp thing—you ain't ugly no more." He reached up to touch her face, but didn't have the strength.

Her affection blossomed into tears. "I haven't been that way for a long time, Winston." She thought back to the oozing mess she had once been in the days when the strange light from the supernova had filled the sky. Had that been her? "I'm not ugly, and you're not shrinking."

"Wish I was," he answered lazily. "Wish I was back home . . ."

"So do I, Winston. So do I." Being outcasts in rural Alabama had been horrible, but simple. Did she ever dream back then that she would have the fate of the world in her hands— back in the days when everyone in that same world was her enemy? When her only thought was surviving through the night without being eaten alive by the sores that covered her rancid, unclean body.

She saw Winston's eyes fluttering—fading, and she spoke to him to keep his thoughts focused, as she tried to shift her position enough to get a grip on him. "I wish we were back there, you with your Mama, and that silly little brother of yours."

Winston sighed. "Thaddy."

"Yes. Thaddy. Screaming bloody murder about some bogey-man coming to steal him through his window."

"Taily-bone," Winston mumbled, then rattled in a sing-

song voice. "*'Taily-bone Taily-bone all's I want's my Taily-bone.'*
I used to tell him Taily-bone was coming for him if he didn't
shut his mouth." Winston let out a wheezy laugh, then grimaced. "Damn fool Thaddy don't know enough to run from
a train." He grew solemn for a moment, tears filling his half-
shut eyes. "They gonna kill him, Tory. They gonna eat Thaddy
from the inside out. Taily-bone comin' for him after all." He
coughed a splatter of blood onto her shirt.

"We'll stop them, Winston."

"I'm gonna sleep first," he said. "You tell me if I dream."

And he closed his eyes.

"Winston, no." She tapped his face, and lost her footing,
wedging deeper in the crevice.

And then something happened.

A pulse of heat passed through her body. But it wasn't
heat—not exactly—it was something else. Then again, and
again. She looked up to see waves of color expanding across
the slit of the sky above the crevice. Whatever this was, it
touched her deep within, scraping against her, like the flint of
a lighter flicking, flicking, flicking, to ignite the flame.

And suddenly she did ignite!

She felt her power explode from her in a breathtaking rush,
cleansing, purifying. Not just the island, but the ocean beyond,
for miles and miles.

A sterile field, she thought. *I'm setting up a sterile field. My
part in this has already begun!*

And if these strange waves of light had affected her so, it
must have affected the others as well; she could feel that it
did, and Winston, as weak as he was, even in this unconscious
state, was pushing out his greening waves of growth. Ragweed
above them grew to maturity and broke open, sending loose a
mad flurry of airborne seeds, like a child blowing a dandelion,

and those seeds took root in the stone, their roots breaking the stone into bits. Something was moving down below. Something was alive in the darkness of the crevasse.

She heard them before she saw them—the awful clicking and scraping, then they rose into the light. Insects. A horde of insects—millions of them—spawning, reproducing like a plague beneath them. She screamed as they bubbled up from the depth of the chasm like living magma, but as the mass of insects grew closer, Tory realized that this was no plague, but their salvation. As the wellspring of insects reached their feet, she grabbed Winston in her arms. He moaned, but didn't open his eyes. That's all right, Winston. Keep dreaming.

She closed her eyes, trying to ignore the sensation of them crawling in her clothes, against her skin. They began to rise, carried by this living eruption, until they were lifted out, the insectoid eruption surging over the edge of the crevasse, running down the hillside to the shore.

"Tory? Winston? Jesus—what the hell is this?"

With Winston still in her arms, she stumbled against Michael, and he caught her.

"What happened to him?"

She opened her mouth to explain, but again her breath was taken away—not by the surges of light but by something entirely different. A feeling within as comforting as those waves of light were disturbing. It was the sense of something falling into place—something that they had gone so long without, they had grown accustomed to its absence.

Tory knew at once.

"Deanna?"

Michael pushed his hair back from his face with a shaky hand. Up above, the clouds shredded, not knowing which way to blow. "Son of a bitch, I think you're right!"

Farther down the shoreline, in the midst of all that was going on, Dillon was holding someone's hand.

"That's not Deanna! What is he doing?" Michael said.

With Winston's weight divided between the two of them, they hurried down to the shore toward them. Winston was still as broken as he had been back in the crevice, which meant Dillon still kept containment. Now, when they needed his power more than ever, he still held it back.

When they arrived, Dillon turned to them from Maddy, his eyes glazed in a sort of puppy affection totally inappropriate for this dire moment.

"Dillon, Deanna's back," Tory informed him. "I don't know how, but she's here somewhere. Somewhere close—can't you feel it?"

Dillon only smiled. "She's right here," he told them. "Only you've got the name wrong."

Their minds stumbled, trying to grasp what the hell he was talking about.

"Her name's not Deanna," he said. "It's Maddy. Maddy Haas."

As they grappled with the incongruous suggestion, Winston flinched in pain, and they lost their grip on him. He fell to the ground.

Maddy, who they could now sense was somehow the very essence of Deanna, glanced down at Winston. "What happened to him?"

"The vectors happened to him."

Dillon shook his head. "He went looking for trouble and found it." Dillon took a step closer. "C'mon, Winston. We don't have time for this." His eyes flashed like the shutter of a camera, opening for a fraction of an instant, then closing again, releasing a directed quantum of his peculiar radiance.

Winston's broken spine transformed, the jagged bulges receding, the serpentine curve straightening. He opened his eyes to see them all looking down on him.

"Aw, crap—did I get buried?" he asked. "What year is it?"

Tory helped him up. "You weren't even dead."

He took in his surroundings and deflated. "Damn—you mean I still gotta do this thing?"

The waves were pulsing out from the top of the cliff with greater intensity now. From this angle, Tory could see all three vectors standing side by side beneath the huge stone arch.

"The scar is weakening," said a voice behind them. "Can you feel it? In a few minutes it will tear wide." They turned to see Okoya. Tory still could not accept that he was on their side. She stepped aside, keeping distance between herself and him. There had been too many betrayals, so she watched him with distrustful vigilance, waiting for the next one.

Dillon looked down from the vectors, his eyes following the path of stairs leading down to the sea. "We'll make our stand there," he said. "At the base of the stairs."

There was a round platform there. A stone zodiac. A clock that measured superstition instead of time. Well, thought Tory, what better place for spirits conceived of the Scorpion Star to fight for humanity than a zodiac circle; that hopelessly human attempt to define an inconceivable cosmos—a task almost as impossible as the one they were charged with.

Yet now that they were in the presence of the long lost Spirit of Faith, this task before them no longer felt so impossible.

As the pulses from the vectors continued to intensify, the shards gathered on the zodiac circle with Okoya, the unlikely coach, standing off to the side.

"What now, Okoya?" Dillon asked.

"At any second the sky will tear open and when it does,

you'll have to stop the vectors from drawing the others through."

"Oh, is that all?" said Michael.

"You have a power that is beyond even my understanding," Okoya told them. "I can't guide you in its use."

"How the hell are we supposed to know what to do?" shouted Winston.

But Maddy put up her hand. "We'll know," she said, with such certainty it calmed everyone's fears.

MEANWHILE, STANDING AT THE Thiran gate, the vectors continued to emit their waves of sibilant, spatial discord. Space itself began warping, twisting, stretching the knotty scar until it could no longer hold. It tore apart with such force that the sky shattered.

38. FUSION

THE FORCE OF THE FRACTURING SKY SENT A POWERFUL earthquake rumbling across the island. It splintered the Thiran gate. The top of the rectangular arch fell, instantly crunching and killing the host bodies of the three vectors, and those deaths freed the vectors to fly to the edges of the hole and call to their kind. They were more than mere guiding beacons; they were impellers, pulling their dark species from the dying void of their universe along the axes of length, depth and time toward this new place of plenty. Now above the island was a gaping hole to the Unworld and a second hole beyond that; like smashed double panes of glass. Through the first hole were the red sands and ice sky of the Unworld. And through the second hole was darkness so absolute it dimmed the light of the rising sun.

To the masses that crowded the bay, which now rolled with a violently shaking earth, it appeared as if heaven itself had rended and they opened their minds and hearts, ready to receive whatever glory was about to be bestowed on them.

AT THE BASE OF the stairs, the five shards were barely able to stand. The granite zodiac circle beneath their feet cracked and heaved. Dillon stepped to the center. His whole life, all of their lives, had been meant for this moment. He looked to Maddy. "No fear," he said, and reached out his right hand. She took it and instantly the others were there as well. Michael took his left hand, Tory wrapped in Michael's arm; and pressed against

Dillon's chest. Winston moved in, finding his place, and a syntaxis of five exploded within them.

Dillon let loose everything, detonating his own containment. He felt his soul, his power stretching beyond the island to the shores of the mainland, to the coast of Africa, to the heights of heavens and the depths of the earth. He could feel life being pulled from death everywhere. The island greened, and the bay filled with kelp from Winston's powerful surge of growth. The clouds burned away to the edge of the horizon. All was scoured by Tory's purifying presence, and Deanna's peace, which now resided in Maddy, flooded every heart more powerfully than the shattering sky. They could feel all these things raging out of control but all these wonders still did not overwhelm the darkness of the breach, and all their efforts had no effect on the vectors.

"It's not working!" Dillon shouted. "We've done something wrong!"

Dillon could feel the full contingent of creatures—thousands upon thousands of dark spirits moving toward the breach from their world of living shadows—an infection that would poison this world, this universe, for all time to come. *What have we done wrong? Okoya, somebody, help us! What have we done wrong?*

LOURDES HAD MOVED TO the nearest cove, her controlled crowd now standing behind her. She had promised Dillon she'd have the best seat in the house, and now she watched in an ambivalence that was turning into a deep dread as the sky tore apart and the darkness beyond made itself known.

She had felt Deanna's return only moments before. There was no mistaking it. So connected were they still that a birth registered within the core of her soul just as a death would.

Lourdes could feel Deanna's conquest of fear whittling away at the stone of her own heart. It was almost enough to move Lourdes, but not quite. So she stood there and watched as the sky split open, revealing a demonic womb, hell crowning in the breach, ready to push through. And now the only thought she could find within her was this:

I have brought this about.

Not the vectors. Not Okoya. Me.

Because of her, Dillon was failing. They all were failing. Their mighty powers stretched beyond the horizons, but had no effect on the vectors and the darkness. She was responsible for the failure of the shards, and that was a weight she could not bear.

You were always the weakest of us.

Dillon had planted that thought into her, and she could not tear it free. The words echoed within her, fracturing her resolve. She was the weak link. This was not happening because she chose the vectors, but because she was not strong enough to resist them—and in this moment when she should have shared the triumph with the vectors, she could feel nothing but defeat, loss, and her own sense of inadequacy. With a single thought, Dillon had stolen her victory.

I hate him, she said to herself. *I hate them all for making me responsible. I hate them for needing me. I hate myself for needing them. For loving them still.*

She raced toward them across the pebbles of the beach. The earth shook and boulders fell from the mountainside. The stairs leading to the gate crumbled, but she avoided the falling stones until finally reaching the five of them, frozen in that perfect connection. She knew her place there. She felt it without having to be told. The vectors would kill her for her betrayal, but what would that matter now? They would kill her anyway. She pressed her way between them, cupped her hand gently around Dillon's neck, pressed up against Deanna, and reached out to put her hand on Tory's shoulder.

The moment she closed that final circuit, the world she knew, the life that she knew ended with an explosion of light and sound as her spirit fused with theirs, and she added to their powers the one thing they were lacking: absolute and perfect control.

THE WORLD HEAVED AGAINST the flow of entropy and eternity for a single sparkling moment, feeling the touch of the fused shards of the Scorpion Star like an embrace:

In Africa, a brown, barren plain grew green and fertile.

In India, the last vestige of smallpox bacteria quietly extinguished from the bloodstream of a carrier who had never known what he was on the verge of passing on to his friends and family.

In the halls of Oxford, a random number generator that for years had spat out chains of randomness, now put forth a growing series of sequential numbers in bold defiance of reason.

In a South American convalescent hospital, a paraplegic man stood from his wheelchair without even realizing he had done it, and crossed the room to turn down the heat.

In a fresh grave in Arlington, Virginia, Lt. Vincent Gerritson became aware. Not aware enough to know or understand his final disposition, but enough to acknowledge that he existed—enough to lend the force of his spirit to the wind of life flowing through him.

In Southern California, where the sun had just set, Drew Camden had a sudden jolt of connection as he sat in his bedroom. A satori filled with joy, and hope. As he looked out of his window to the clear, dark sky, a vine slithered across the pane like a garter snake, sprouting leaves, budding with red trumpets. It took his breath away, because in that instant he knew. Without a doubt he knew that the shards, whose lives had, for a short time, been so intertwined with his own, had finally received their destiny.

And in Poland, Elon Tessic, sequestered in his *dacha*, felt a blast of such enormous hope and light that he knew it could only be the finger of God.

DILLON WAS AT THE center.

The moment Lourdes touched him, he could feel himself the core of something infinitely powerful and intense. He—they—were no longer shards; his own power of completion had reversed the entropy let loose in the death of the Scorpion Star, and their souls forged into a single great soul, with six minds. He was no longer just Dillon—he was the sum of all of them—and he could hear their thoughts as clearly as his own.

As their spirits ignited, it burned away their bodies, incinerating the shore, the island, and miles of the Mediterranean, penetrating deep into the earth's mantle and beyond the ionosphere. They were as a star igniting on the surface of the earth, and yet even as he felt it all burn away, Dillon held the patterns in a mind now so powerful and vast, it could remember every molecule, every cell, every soul caught within the fusion flame. He held the memory of every pattern with the ease he could remember a name, a face, a feeling.

In that glorious moment, the soft swirl of clouds dissolved around the globe, leaving the earth a naked, unblinking eye in the cradle of the heavens, and a wave of spirit swept out across the globe, encompassing it, penetrating the dust and revitalizing the spark of every soul that had ever lived. Dillon held the history and essence of life together in this instant of resurrection, linking every spirit drawing on their energy, making them one with himself. It only lasted for an instant—but that instant had the essence of eternity.

A moment of enlightenment and ascension.

A moment of unmitigated faith;

of singular will;

of untarnished purity;

of unclouded joy;

pulled together and fused into a single force of life.

This was their weapon against the vectors; not six beacons, but a single spirit at the center of billions of points of light all focused on a wound in the flesh of space!

Dillon wanted to relish this grand expansion of their spirit—but—

"—*The vectors.*"

"*Yes, the vectors.*"

"*I see them.*"

"*I sense them.*"

"*At the breach.*"

Lourdes thought, *"Move toward them."* And their spirit impelled toward the breach at her command. As they moved, they now experienced the world no longer with senses of the flesh, but with a vision of sprit; a mind's eye that saw in all directions at once, altering their perceptions of everything around them. The space they moved through was not a sky—not an atmosphere, but a thick, gelatinous plasma; a living plasma that mere fleshly senses could not perceive. Now that plasma was violated by the breach, and at the edge of the breach they saw the true form of the vectors; not angels, nor beings of light, but beings of living darkness cloaked as light. Soullessness swallowing souls.

They approached the temporal vector, immobile now like an animal caught in their light.

"*I feel its fear,*" Maddy said. This creature had been encapsulated in flesh long enough to gain a rudimentary arsenal of human emotions. Terror, fury, and hatred enough to level a city. They enveloped the creature, cutting it off from the others.

Now it was up to Dillon.

He knew that his power of creation and life was only half of what he needed to do. Each of their lights cast a shadow and Dillon's shadow was destruction. With that in mind, Dillon pushed forth a single thought into the vector's tumultuous, furious mind:

Cease to exist.

It was the most horrible, most devastating act of destruction he had ever wished upon a living thing. The creature screamed, fighting the power of Dillon's terminal directive, straining against his will, but it had used too much of its power tearing open the hole. Michael injected it with fear; it panicked, and its spirit finally succumbed to Dillon's will. The temporal vector shattered, breaking into smaller and smaller fragments of anti-life until its consciousness was gone and its fragments imploded into nothingness.

The shards moved on to the lateral vector—the one who had abided within the woman. They surrounded it. Imploded it. Their light swallowed it.

"*Like antibodies.*"

"*An immune system.*"

"*Surrounding.*"

"*Isolating.*"

"*Devouring it the way it meant to devour us.*"

As their spirit crossed the breach to the leading vector, they caught a glimpse of the infection. Thousands of dark entities spilled into the Unworld, crossing the outer breach from their own dying universe, all ready to cross the chasm to the inner breach. The leading vector was calling to them, reeling them in. This had to be stopped—but this last, most powerful vector tried to elude them. There was nowhere it could run from their light; it was caught in their gravity, spiraling toward them until it reached the center of their spirit. It was the strongest, this creature that had hidden within a child. It lashed out now, probing its tendrils into their weakest points, trying to tear them apart, break them into pieces once again—and Dillon thought it might succeed, that their spirit would detonate from the pressure, separating into shards once more. If that happened, it would be over. The vectors would triumph and the shards' deaths would light the path for these infecting entities. The infection would take root and spread from this point to the rest of the earth and beyond. Dillon felt weak with the thought, and that weakness gave the leading vector the upper hand. He felt himself losing concentration, losing this battle of wills . . . but then Dillon felt Maddy in his heart.

"Trust," was all she said.

Not the voice of Maddy, not the voice of Deanna—but both at the same time soothing his panicked mind. Her touch stabilized him, strengthened him enough to bear down with the force of all the souls he held in his grasp, and the leading vector could not withstand it. It imploded and its final death wail was stifled, stolen before it could even begin.

"We've killed them! The vectors are gone!"

"But not the infection."

"I see them!"

"Hundreds of thousands!"

"Shadow spirits."

"*Thieves of Souls.*"

"*Crossing over.*"

"*Escaping.*"

"*Too many!*"

Now without the vectors, their orderly grid had dissolved, and they crowded the edge of the inner breach like ants, gripping onto the jagged edge of the sky, fighting to get through.

Then, beyond the Unworld, beyond the outer breach, the shards witnessed the death of a universe.

The living void Okoya had told them about was completely gone, consumed by two spirits—two parasites; one of destruction, the other of fear. They were Dillon's old friends—the spirits he himself had unleashed upon that dark place a year ago. Now those insatiable beasts had consumed the full volume of space itself. And finally, when the last of that universe was gone, with nothing left to consume, the parasites turned to one another. The blind snake of fear and the black-winged demon of destruction, now larger than constellations, wrapped around one another in an impassioned, but deadly embrace, and then began to devour each other. They grew smaller and smaller, their spirits disappearing into each other like a moebius strip, twisting fearfully, angrily, destructively, until they had devoured one another completely, and the universe that gave birth to Okoya and the vectors blinked out of existence forever.

And now the soul-devouring shadow-creatures lingered at the breach, lethal refugees of that lost place. Dillon felt the magnitude of their presence, and knew that the power of the shards was the only thing keeping them from crossing through. Dillon could hear the thoughts of his soul-mates as this infection loomed on the lip of the wound.

"*Kill them.*"

"Destroy them."

"Every last one of them."

"For what they have done."

"For what they could have done."

"For what they might still do someday."

But a voice of wisdom rose above them all.

"No."

Winston was the single voice of dissent. *"No,"* he told them. *"It's not our place. Our task is to stop the infection, not to wipe out a species."*

It was Winston's wisdom in the face of their own fury that they listened to, for if ever there was a time to trust Winston's judgment, it was now.

Hold them back. Keep them out. Let them live.

With their own power beginning to fade, Maddy held back their panic, giving them a final burst of courage. Lourdes moved them across the breach. Winston restored the gaps in space, Tory purified it, Michael cauterized it. Dillon repaired the damage, pulling back the edges of the wound until the sky was whole, and the creatures were sealed out, trapped forever in the Unworld, condemned to haunt the walls between worlds.

When it was done, Dillon finally let go. He let go of his grip of the world, he let go of the five who were a part of him, and as he did he pushed forth the patterns he held through the battle. Patterns of the sea, and of the island and of the thousands of boats in the bay and of every soul in every vessel in those boats. He pulled it all back from the smithereens, restoring it all, until he could feel his own body again. Tory pressing his chest, Winston on his waist, Lourdes holding the back of his neck, Michael at his left hand and Maddy at his right. He thought that beyond what they had just experienced, there could be nothing left to feel—but then came a final gift, the reward for what they had done, for what they had chosen.

It was as if an eye opened somewhere beyond the sky and projected forth for them from a perspective too vast to comprehend, a billion pinpoints of light that were not stars, but entire galaxies. This was their universe in its entirety, thirty billion light years across, alive, and pulsing with living light. It was a glorious vision of life, of majesty, and a sense of their own wonderful, terrible, insignificance in the vastness of creation. Then, within the soup of swirling stars there came a sudden series of explosions. Not just a few, but countless stars began to detonate, and with those blasts of light, billions of shards of life traversed the universe instantaneously towards them! Toward Earth!

The vision faded and they pulled apart, separating into six separate spirits, their powers spent, used up once and for all— but the power of their final vision remained.

"What was it?" Maddy asked. "What was that we just felt?"

"A billion stars," Winston said, his voice faint and wondrous. "A billion stars going supernova."

"Did we do that?" Tory asked.

Dillon shook his head. "Unless I'm mistaken," he said, "I believe that was God hearing the prayers of pigeons."

They said no more of it, but each held in their own heart the knowledge that, from this moment on, nothing on earth would ever be the same.

39. LUCK OF THE DRAW

SPRING CAME EARLY TO POLAND IN SLOW INCREMENTS after the winter thaw. For a brief time in December, grass had sprouted and trees had greened, but such an instant of growth could not last long. In a day, the leaves had fallen and the grass had withered under the numbing cold of northern winds. In April, when the snows had gone, the hills filled with green at a much slower pace, undetectable to the human eye, but steady enough to cover the countryside in a few short weeks. Ash mounds in and around Birkenau filled with wildflowers and rye, as if nature were somehow pining to ease the mind, without taking away the shape of the horror.

Ciechanow, which had once been a very small town, now had on its outskirts a pinwheel of 112 buildings. With each building thirty stories high and as long as a football field, the complex was twice as large as the rest of the town. Few of the brand-new buildings were occupied—in fact, most of them had been donated by Tessitech to the Polish government, and now an entire wing in the Ministry of Housing was filled with bureaucrats working to fill them.

However, one small corner of the complex was occupied. Six buildings and part of a seventh, a drop in the bucket really, but a community nonetheless; close knit and still a little bit wary of the outside world, but that was only to be expected.

It was a temperate day in April that Elon Tessic walked the paths of this towering apartment community with Dillon Cole.

"I did feel your joining," Tessic told Dillon. "Your 'fusion,' as you call it."

Dillon shrugged. "Everyone felt it."

"Yes," Tessic said. "But I understood what I was feeling."

Dillon grinned. "I suppose now you'll claim you were responsible for saving the world."

Tessic smirked. "Well, you said it yourself. I did help to develop the world's greatest defensive weapon, did I not?"

"That you did, Elon." And indeed Dillon knew that there was credit due. And who's to say that had Dillon not been put through Tessic's unusual boot camp, he would have had the fortitude to fill his role in the stand against the vectors?

"I even provided the means for imprisoning that creature you allowed to remain."

The reminder unnerved Dillon, but he didn't let it show. "How is Okoya taking to lockdown?"

"Far better than you did. He is content to stay in the cell— he actually seems to like it there."

Dillon was not surprised. The containment dome of the Hesperia plant wasn't exactly like being chained to a mountainside and left for the birds. This was a cushy exile, and in it, Okoya finally could find what he always wanted. He was the center of his own private universe with an entire facility devoted to his personal maintenance. He was out of sight, but never out of mind.

The path down which Tessic led Dillon came to a place where grass had not been sown, and the buildings before them were barren and bleak. Although Dillon slowed, Tessic seemed to know where he was going.

"There is a park around this next building. Another island in the ghost town. You will see."

"Do you still think of what might have been?" Dillon

asked, as he looked around at the vacant buildings.

"Of course," he answered. "But then I look around and see what is. There are almost eleven thousand there—a single one brought back from the death camps would have been a miracle—and we have eleven thousand! I look at these faces around me, and know that I will go to my grave a happy man," he said. "Although, I hope it's not in the too near future. I intend to enjoy my retirement."

"What could you possibly do that you haven't already done?"

"I have a goal, remember," Tessic answered. "I intend to die broke. Do you have any idea how hard it is to get rid of my kind of money?"

"It's not easy being the twelfth richest man in the world," Dillon scoffed.

"Twenty-third," Tessic corrected. "Building this place was quite a blow to my standing."

"Is that why you called for me, Elon, to see this place?"

Tessic hesitated. "My pilot—Ari—he was my nephew. You didn't know that, did you?"

Dillon looked away. "No."

"He was my only real family."

"I'm sorry," Dillon said. He wasn't certain if Tessic knew the circumstance of Ari's death. How he'd been taken as a host by the temporal vector. "I hope you're not considering making me an heir—that is, if you can't lose all your money."

"Certainly not, but I would like to see you from time to time, as neither of us has family."

The thought never hit him without a pang of regret, and loneliness. Far too few of the shards had anyone to go back to. With Tory's mother dead, she had gone with Michael and they were staying with Michael's father. Both were facing the ridiculous prospect of going back to high school—which might as well have been preschool, considering what they'd lived, died, and relived through. Still, their reintegration into the world had to start somewhere.

Winston, even with his gift exhausted, managed to retain quite a lot of his supernatural learning in his natural brain and blew the top off of entry exams into Harvard. No sooner did he return to his family, than he left them again.

And then there was Lourdes. Her family dead by her own hand, her deeds an anchor on her spirit—she had not landed with quite the same grace. Even there on Thira, when the six of them had broken off their syntaxis, and realized that their powers were spent forever, Dillon had known her path would be a hard one, for even then, she would not look any of them in the eye. Then when they had all parted company, she had slipped away without even so much as a good-bye.

"I had a dream about her," Winston had told him. "She was flipping burgers in some fast food place, in a town too small to be on the map."

"Hell on Earth?" Dillon had suggested, but Winston had said, "Maybe it's her new idea of heaven."

No, Dillon was not the worst off. After all, he had Maddy. She was waiting for him now, at her sister's in New York.

"Will you and Maddy marry?" Tessic asked.

Dillon laughed. "Come on, Elon, I'm just eighteen!"

"Forgive me," Tessic said. "You were robbed of your childhood—I only wish for happiness in your adult life. This is why I ask."

They rounded the empty building and came upon a park. As Tessic had promised, it was a crowded pocket of life. Old men played chess on built-in tables carved from only the finest Italian marble, and children played in a brightly colored jungle gym. Dillon found himself amused that, even though these children were speaking a language he didn't understand, their stylized gestures and battle postures gave away the nature of the game.

"They're playing Star Wars," Dillon said. Apparently, these children had already filled in their massive gap of time and culture, adapting to their own rebirths, as if they had done nothing more than oversleep the morning.

Dillon wondered how they—how everyone—would adapt to what was coming next. He had high, but reserved hopes, considering the progress made over the past four months. Since the shards made their stand, the world that was in such a steady state of decline found the capacity to heal itself. People who had lost their ambition returned to work. The unnamable sense of dread and dysfunction resolved into a fresh sense of direction. Hell, even the airports were starting to clean up. Pundits were already labeling the troubling time "the Cortical Recession," and called it "a collective psychosis of informational overload."

People were doing their best to forget about the Backwash, and all the documented feats of the shards, not realizing that those events were merely a taste of things to come. The age of science, the age of reason, was coming to an end after all, but not in a great collapse. Instead it would come in the form of a birth. Of many births.

"When I wrote to you, Elon, I told you about the vision that I had—that the six of us had—when it was all over; stars all exploding at once, thousands of light-years away."

"The way the Scorpion Star went supernova when you and your six friends were conceived?"

"But this time it was millions of stars. Maybe billions."

"That's still just a tiny drop in the bucket, when you consider how many stars are out there," Tessic mused. "A billion stars could go supernova, and God would barely blink."

"I was hoping you'd have an opinion."

"I always have an opinion."

"That's what I figured."

Tessic leaned against a light post and crossed his arms. "I believe there are three possibilities," Tessic said. "One: You and I are both entirely insane, your vision was a hallucination, and all these undocumented people around us are, as the Polish government claims, 'refugees from war-torn Lithuania' that I smuggled in over the border."

Dillon smiled. "I'd buy that."

"Or, two: The universe truly is a living thing, as you say, and the bursting of stars is an immune response. Therefore, by allowing those nasty *dybbuks* to survive, you triggered an even greater immune response to protect us against them in the future."

"And the third?"

"The third is simply this: By benefit of your mercy to creatures who deserved no mercy, the Almighty saw fit to gift humanity with a spiritual evolution."

"And which do you believe, Elon?"

Tessic grinned mischievously. "I keep my answer close to my heart," he said. "Between me and my creator."

Tessic looked around the many benches of the park, as if looking for someone or something. "If your vision was a true one, we'll know soon enough—the first premature ones will be born as early as next month—but I think people are beginning to have suspicions." Finally he spotted who he was looking for. "Ah, there she is. You see her?"

He pointed to a woman who sat throwing crumbs to a gathering of birds, with her husband beside her.

"They met shortly after they arrived here. A whirlwind romance," Tessic explained. "She is yet to show, but she expects a child. She is three months along now."

"Three months," Dillon said. "Lucky her."

"What caught my attention were the rumors. You see, there is an old custom; you hold your wedding ring on a string before your unborn child. If it swings side to side, it will be a girl. If it spins, it will be a boy. Do you want to know what the ring told her?"

"What did it tell her?"

"Absolutely nothing," Tessic said. "But it turned from brass to silver before her eyes."

"Silver, huh," said Dillon. "Not exactly the golden touch, is it?"

"The child is yet unborn—give it time."

"It won't be the same as it was with us," Dillon told him. "There were only a handful of us. But in a few years' time—"

"—in a few years' time," Tessic said, "we will all be obsolete. Cro Magnon men in a world of star-shards." And yet he didn't say it with downtrodden finality, but with a strange effervescence.

"It doesn't bother you?" Dillon asked.

"Why shouldn't it? Ascension is not extinction, my friend. I'm sure our knuckle-dragging ancestors would be thrilled to know what they have become, through us."

Dillon tried to imagine what the world would be like a hundred years—even ten years from now, with every child born a star-shard, but with his own powers of insight gone, he had a hard time envisioning it. Hundreds of thousands who could control weather and moods—just as many who could regenerate flesh, or bring life from death. And other powers as well—powers he had not even imagined.

"It's going to be a wild world," Dillon said. "At least until that first generation gets a handle on how to make it all work."

Tessic shrugged. "Every great change has its growing pains. I can't help but think that the ones gifted with wisdom will be able to see us through the change."

The pregnant woman stood and left, arm-in-arm with her husband. Others glanced at them and whispered. They didn't seem to mind.

"I have something for you," Tessic said. "A gift." Tessic reached into his coat pocket and pulled out a small gift-wrapped package, handing it to Dillon.

Dillon removed the bow, and peeled back the shiny paper to reveal a box of blue Bicycle playing cards. An odd gift to anyone else, but not to him. Tears began to fill Dillon's eyes in spite of himself. In his life there had been so many simple joys that were denied him. Tessic understood. Perhaps better than anyone.

"Thank you, Elon."

Tessic glanced at the sky, then at an unoccupied table. "It's a fine day for a game. Shall we?"

They sat across from each other, and Dillon pulled the cards from the deck, removing the jokers.

"Your shuffle," Tessic said.

Dillon's hands were shaking, but he forced them still enough to separate the deck in half, then glanced up at Tessic.

"Go on," he said.

Dillon flicked the left-hand cards into the right-hand cards, and wove them together again, and again and again, until the motion felt natural.

"What's the game?" Tessic asked.

"Five card draw," Dillon decided.

"And the stakes?"

Dillon shrugged. "If I win, I get to keep that jet of yours that brought me here—how's that?"

"Agreed. And what if I win?"

"If you win, I'll name my first kid after you."

Dillon dealt the cards face down. Tessic picked his up first, glanced at Dillon, but kept a fine poker face. Dillon could not read him at all.

Then Dillon reached for his own cards, hesitating. He had done this many times before, back when he still had his powers, and the burden of responsibility that came with them. He never needed to look at his hand then. A two-handed deal from a well-shuffled deck would always reveal for him the same cards: the deuce, four, six, eight, and a ten of spades; the direct consequence of dealing alternating cards from a deck in perfect order.

Now Dillon fanned out his cards to reveal: an ace, a five, a king, a nine, and a jack; two of them diamonds, two clubs and a heart. Although all his powers had been gone and he had been a "normal" human being for four months, this was the first time he truly felt it. His spirit was not only contained, but comfortable within his flesh. His sphere of influence was no longer defined by the gravity of his presence, but a function of his words and deeds.

"I'll take two cards," Tessic said.

Dillon dealt Tessic his cards, then looked to the randomness of his own hand once more. He had always been order in the face of chaos—but here chaos was looking him in the eye, and he had no weapon against it beyond the luck of the draw. Until this moment he never knew how beautiful not knowing could be. In his cards—in the world, there was an unmarked future out there. He would be a participant, but only a participant, like everyone else in the world. He would play, but would no longer bear the burden of redesigning the rules. Which meant that no matter what cards were dealt him, he had already won.

"What do the cards tell you?" Tessic asked.

"Everything I want to know."

Dillon kept only the ace of diamonds, and with all his soul threw caution to the wind.

John C. Hart Mem Lib (Shrub Oak)

3 1030 15489178 2

RECEIVED JUL 2 9 2019